AN EXPLOSION OF LIGHTS ...

Trapped in total darkness, I clutched my head as I toppled over. I lay there panting for a long time. At some point I caught my breath and held it—and heard breathing that was not my own.

I called out, "Aeslu?"

No response. Yet without a doubt I heard the clear, rhythmic sound of someone breathing. Slowly, carefully, I eased off my pack and reached for the ice-hatchet stashed there.

Something slammed into me just then, knocking me hard against the wall. A moment later I felt two hands claw at me in the darkness, grab my throat, and fumble for a grip around it. . . .

THE SUMMIT

Book Three of
The Mountain Made of Light

Edward Myers

A ROC BOOK

ROC
Published by the Penguin Group
Penguin Books USA Inc., 375 Hudson Street,
New York, New York 10014, U.S.A.
Penguin Books Ltd, 27 Wrights Lane,
London W8 5TZ, England
Penguin Books Australia Ltd, Ringwood,
Victoria, Australia
Penguin Books Canada Ltd, 10 Alcorn Avenue,
Toronto, Ontario, Canada M4V 3B2
Penguin Books (N.Z.) Ltd, 182–190 Wairau Road,
Auckland 10, New Zealand

Penguin Books Ltd, Registered Offices:
Harmondsworth, Middlesex, England

First published by Roc,
an imprint of Dutton Signet,
a division of Penguin Books USA Inc.

First Printing, November, 1994
10 9 8 7 6 5 4 3 2 1

 REGISTERED TRADEMARK—MARCA REGISTRADA

Printed in the United States of America

For E. P., *sine qua non*

Special thanks to Edwin Bernbaum,
Joanna Cole, Joanne Greenberg,
Faith Hamlin, Delia Marshall,
Susan Poor, Joe Reilly,
Chris Schelling, John Silbersack,
and Amy Stout.

Who could have helped me as I climbed the mountain?

—Dante Alighieri,
Purgatorio, iii.6.

The door to the invisible must be visible.

—René Daumal,
Mount Analogue

Deep into the snow mountains my search has led me. Now I have it fast. My dream has given it me, in utter clearness, that I may know it forever.

—Thomas Mann,
The Magic Mountain

Editor's Note

For years I had tried tracking him down, always without success. I had interviewed hundreds of people, both in the United States and overseas; I had contacted scores of anthropologists in hopes of hearing even the most general notion of his whereabouts; I had prowled about his hometown of Northampton, Massachusetts, in the off chance of finding someone aware of his fate. In each of these efforts I had come away empty-handed. In others, too, I had failed. All I had to go by was a rumor, now more than five decades old, that he had left Peru alive at some point in 1922, and that he had eventually returned to the United States. What had happened since then? I had no idea. Even the two books I'd edited and published—not just his own journal, but also other documents pertaining to the whole Mountain Made of Light episode—brought no response. His silence convinced me of what I most feared: he was dead. For surely the books (if nothing else) would have prompted him to contact me—though more likely in outrage than in gratitude.

Then, in 1975, I received a plain white postcard with the following words scrawled on the back:

Jesse O'Keefe
Anthropology Hall
University of Colorado
Boulder, Colorado

I was stunned. Not more than a year earlier I had spoken with members of the Anthropology Department there about Jesse O'Keefe. No one had known a thing about him. Now, suddenly, this anonymous card. Was it a mistake? A false lead? A trick, even? Or was it the breakthrough I'd been waiting for all these years? I didn't know what to think.

My first impulse was to call the Anthropology Department at Colorado and check things out. Then I held off. That card wasn't unsigned for nothing. I didn't know why its author was hiding from me; still, my tipping off the department, thus Jesse O'Keefe as well, wouldn't be the best way to proceed. Finding a man capable of giving everyone the slip for over fifty years would require a more thoughtful strategy.

For this reason I flew to Denver in June of 1975, drove the thirty miles to where Boulder nestles against the foothills of the Rocky Mountains, and arrived on campus unannounced.

"I'm here to see Jesse O'Keefe," I told the departmental secretary.

She stared at me in puzzlement. "Here to see *whom*?"

"Jesse O'Keefe."

"You must have the wrong department."

"I know he wants to maintain his privacy," I reassured her, "and I certainly understand the situation. But I need to speak with him. Please tell him he has nothing to fear from me."

This secretary—a prim, almost matronly woman who looked comically out of place among the T-shirted, bell-bottomed students drifting in and out of the office—now gazed with me with an expression far more intense than mere puzzlement. "I'd tell him," she said, "if there were anyone to tell."

"I know he's here."

"I'm afraid you're mistaken."

"Just tell me where to find him—I won't mention how I found out."

"There is no one here named Jesse O'Keefe."

I can't say precisely how I knew that this guardian at the gates, this palace sentry in the cotton print dress, was telling the truth. All I know is that I decided she wasn't lying. Against my inclination, I thanked her and left.

For fifteen minutes or so I wandered through Anthropology Hall. Summer school was in session; most of the lecture and seminar rooms were either empty or at best half-full. A few students strayed up and down the hall, their words and laughter echoing vaguely. I thought of stopping one or more of these people to ask my questions, but I felt too discouraged to bother.

Near the stairwell I stopped. Open windows let in the smell of early summer: newly mowed grass. Beyond the windows I could see some of the other campus buildings, the reddish hillsides beyond, then the Flatirons—vast, steep slabs of granite—rising beyond Boulder. Lingering indoors got more difficult by the minute. If I'd come to Colorado without achieving my goal, I could at least head for the hills and console myself with a hike.

Then something distracted me. A rhythmic sound: *whoosh, click. Whoosh, click. Whoosh, click.*

I looked up the stairs on my left. A janitor was working his way down with a big pushbroom. I watched him a moment, nodded hello, then turned to leave.

At once I turned back. "Excuse me—"

The janitor peered down the staircase.

"I wonder if you could help me find someone."

He stopped several steps above me, leaning on his broom. "I'd be willing to try."

"What do you know about someone here named Professor Jesse O'Keefe?"

The janitor guffawed. "*Professor* O'Keefe! Now that's a new one!"

I almost couldn't believe what I was hearing. "You've heard of him, though?"

"Jesse? Sure."

"Can you tell me where to find him?"

"I'll give you a start. Go out this door," he said,

"then swing around to the left till you see a little building. That's usually where he hangs out. If he's not there now, he'll be back in a while."

I was heading down the stairs two at a time even as I thanked him.

There must have been some sort of mistake. I followed the janitor's directions but couldn't find the building he'd directed me to. The only structure of any kind was a large brick shed of the sort that grounds keepers use for storing hoses, tools, and gardening supplies. I walked clear to the far end of Anthropology Hall, retraced my steps, then circled the entire building just in case the janitor had meant to direct me right instead of left. No such luck: the other side was just junipers and flower beds. Returning to where I'd started, now feeling uncertain, I looked around.

How long did I stand there? Not long. June mornings in Colorado start cool but warm up quickly. We were just a day shy of the summer solstice; the sun had been up for almost five hours; the day was already hot. I couldn't see much point in lingering.

Then, on impulse, I walked over to the garden shed.

The door stood open. A weathered plywood ramp slanted up to the concrete floor. I walked up the ramp, stepped inside the shed, glanced around. After having grown accustomed to the dazzle outside, my eyes took a few seconds adjusting to dimmer light.

No one was there.

Just in case, I looked the place over. Rakes, hoes, and spades in a rack. Other tools on a pegboard. Garden hoses in coils. Sprinklers on the wall. Two gas-powered lawnmowers in the corner. A low table and two chairs against the far wall. That was it. Altogether utilitarian: no sign of any individual presence, much less that of the man I sought.

Then something caught my attention. I crossed the room to the table. I saw some markings on the wall.

Scratched into a brick and darkened with ink or black paint were these lines:

"Yes?"

I looked up to find someone standing in the doorway. The light pouring in around him made his features hard to see at first. Embarrassed to be caught intruding, I stepped around the table and returned to the doorway. "Sorry."

I knew at once that I'd found him. He was old—a few years shy of eighty—but I knew it was Jesse O'Keefe. Time muddles some people's faces and clarifies others; his were now totally clear. He'd lost most of his hair, and what remained was white; his skin was now supple from scores of tiny wrinkles etched there. Yet his overall appearance somehow remained fundamentally like what I'd seen in the few photos dating from his youth. Long, straight nose. High forehead. Eyes brown and dark as agate. The only other changes were a pronounced stoop to his posture and an exaggeration of his hereditary leanness. Yet despite the man's years he looked spry, not frail, in his old age.

He walked into the shed without acknowledging me further. He set two large lawn sprinklers on the floor. "What can I do for you?"

"You're Jesse O'Keefe."

"True. And you?"

"Ed Myers."

Now he gazed at me with a new intensity. I'd read about that gaze, of course—how if often unnerved people—but I wasn't prepared for my own discomfort. It wasn't a stare in the usual sense; there was nothing aggressive about it, nothing hostile. But its *focus* . . . I couldn't shake the feeling that he'd caught me under a magnifying glass whose concentrated beam would make me smoulder till I burst into flames.

"I don't appreciate what you've done," he said at last.

"Are you aware of how hard I've tried to reach you?"

"Of course I am. That's not the point."

"I never would have published anything if you'd told me not to."

"That, too, isn't the point."

"People have a right to know what happened."

"And I have a right not to tell them." He walked over to his chair and sat. I noticed an obvious limp as he walked. He wore peculiar shoes: not exactly orthopedic but clearly modified in some way to compensate for a foot or leg injury. I noticed that he wore gloves, too, but then realized that they were just ordinary work gloves. Jesse tilted back in his chair till the back rested against the wall.

I tried a different tack. "You're in terrific shape, all considered."

"At my age one does whatever's needed to stay limber."

"You look after this whole part of the campus?"

He chuckled. "Just the lawn and gardens around the anthropology building. That's quite enough, thank you."

It occurred to me for the first time that the departmental secretary might not have been covering up for him. "Do the professors have any notion of your past?"

"They don't even know I'm here." Another chuckle. "I try to keep it that way. The university considers me some sort of a garden troll."

"What a waste."

"Look," he said, "my silence isn't accidental. I'd just as soon let bygones be bygones. You're not the first person who's managed to track me down, though you've certainly succeeded better than the rest in dragging my past into the light of day."

"You have nothing to fear."

"Can't you see it's not a question of fear?"

"Pride, then."

"Think whatever you wish."

"Don't you think you owe it to others—"

That gaze again. "I know what you're going to say now," he told me. "I should set the record straight. Put everything into a perspective that I alone can provide. And so forth. Sorry."

I grew more and more tense as this argument continued—not because I thought I might lose, but because I knew I could win but didn't want to at any cost. "What would convince you to explain what happened?"

"Nothing."

"Nothing at all?"

"I have nothing more to say."

"What if we swapped one tale for another?"

He shrugged. "I know what happened. Isn't that the point? You wouldn't be here otherwise."

"Maybe not," I said.

Now Jesse shifted his weight; the chair tilted forward. I didn't know quite why he did that just then, but I knew that somehow more than his chair had tipped. "What are you getting at?"

I could have teased or coaxed him for a long time, drawing him forth, but decided not to prolong the gambit. I pulled the photo from my satchel and set it before him.

He picked it up at once, not quickly but with immediate resolve, and he held it, staring, for a long time. His eyes welled up. He set down the photo abruptly.

"I'm sorry," I told him. "I haven't been fair."

"You could have picked a kinder method of extracting the truth—perhaps putting a pistol to my head."

I gestured awkwardly. "Please understand. I've been trying to locate you for years."

"All right, then, all right." He motioned once to the chair beside me.

"Now?" I asked, bewildered that my luck had changed so fast.

"If you're in such a rush to hear, then let me tell you."

I sat, scooting my chair close to the table. I opened my satchel again, took out my tape recorder, and got it ready.

Jesse O'Keefe stared at the machine intently—so intently that I assumed he'd object to my using it—yet soon enough his attention strayed. It wasn't the tape recorder that interested him; it was the photo.

Jesse O'Keefe gazed at the photograph so long I thought he'd never begin.

PART ONE

1

If you want to know what happened, I'll tell you. But I can't start at the beginning. This story's events had a beginning, of course, but I wasn't really there for them. Or at least I wasn't aware of them. I was too dazed, too damaged—lost in some sort of stupor that left me alive but little more than half-conscious of what I was doing.

The truth is, I came to my senses while climbing.

I was climbing a glacier. I became aware of the ice, of my boots, of my struggle to make the boots find their way over the ice. Even at the time I knew that I was moving like a sleepwalker. I staggered, stumbled, flailed. Even so I managed to gain some altitude without falling into any of the blue-gray crevasses gaping around me. My motions felt simultaneously awkward and resolute. Of course there's a contradiction in what I'm describing to you. Despite my somnambulistic gait, I was awake; yet despite my wakefulness, I was plagued by dreams. Nightmares, even. My mind was a jumble of grotesque images—images not just of many people, crushed to death under blocks of ice, but also images of my own blame in bringing about precisely these same deaths.

I plodded upward. Now and then I collapsed, falling facedown in the snow, where I then lay heaving for breath till at last, forcing myself up, I stood precariously and resumed my struggle. More than once I slipped and skidded feet-first, facedown, on an icy patch, then managed to catch myself with the ice-axe I almost lacked the strength to clutch in my mittened hands. On one occasion I tumbled down the slope, jolting so hard each time I rolled over my backpack that I scattered its contents in my path, and only by luck did I manage to halt my descent before accelerating out of control. No matter how often I fell, though, I always continued upward. No matter how long I took gathering my equipment, I always tried again. Why would anyone persist at such a hopeless task? I persisted because I saw no alternative. I saw only the Mountain. My vision had become spherical, and the Mountain lay at its center. All I could do was climb.

And so I climbed. I climbed all day, climbed until I fell two or three times for every step I took, climbed until I slumped, struggled to get up, and found my legs no longer capable of lifting me. Clawing a shallow pit in the snow, I passed out and slept. I awoke to find that night had fallen. The sky was overcast. To avoid a deadly chill, I rummaged through my pack and found a blanket, a leather flask of water, some bits of food. I drank and ate. I wrapped myself in the blanket. Again I slept.

When I awoke, I grasped my situation more clearly than I had till just that moment. I was alone on a peak that a day or two earlier had obliterated several thousand people. Despite my best efforts to find even a single survivor other than myself, I had every reason to believe that I was the only human being alive on the mountain. Now I was persisting in a solo climb that would soon leave me dead as well. What was the point?

I proceeded upward. Kicking my way up, hacking steps in the ice, crawling on hands and knees if necessary, I climbed in whatever way took me higher. All that mattered was the climb. All there *was* was the climb.

Soon the ice steepened, yet I kept climbing. With an ice-hatchet in one hand, a pick in the other, and cramponlike claws protruding from my boots, I climbed altogether indifferent to the dangers that increased with each step I took.

The Mountain loomed overhead.

The clouds streamed past.

Even so I just kept climbing.

It was only a matter of time before I slipped, so I wasn't surprised when it happened. Some ice cracked, he axe came loose, my weight exceeded what the pick and crampon points could bear. I toppled backward. Striking the slope threw me into a spin.

Everything happened so fast that I had no time to panic, much less to understand.

The last sound I heard was the thud of my own flesh and bone striking ice.

2

I awoke in some sort of hut. To tell you the truth, I don't remember much about it. My left eye was swollen shut; I could just barely open the right. I couldn't move enough to look around, and what little I saw lay right before me. Piled blocks of something grayish, whether rock or ice.... Harsh light entering through a gap big enough for a man to crawl through.... Snow drifting in through the same gap.... I lay there a long time trying to figure out where I was and how I'd gotten there. All I knew is that I was there, I couldn't move, and I hurt so much I didn't even want to try.

After a while I passed out again.

I have no idea how long I lay there. The light faded, intensified, faded again. For all I know, entire days came and went. Yet I can't imagine having survived that long without water, so it might have been a much briefer time, the passage of storm clouds creating an illusion of sunrise and sunset. I don't know.

At some point I managed to prop myself up and, despite the pain, I glanced about briefly. Two or three blankets covered me. Another blanket, this one extending overhead, provided all there was of a roof. A deerskin pack served as a makeshift door. Some climbing implements—Rixtir-style rope, hooks, and ice-hatchets—rested near me. None of these things were what I'd scrounged earlier and carried with me. I didn't even recognize them.

Of course the simple fact of my being there was the real mystery. I had no idea how I'd gotten where I was, much less who had improvised this little hut.

Even calling it a hut stretches things a bit. *Hovel* comes closer: a pit scraped into the glacier and shielded with chunks of rock and ice. It scarcely blocked the wind, much less the snow swirling in. Yet whenever I felt tempted to imagine it as something other than a human contrivance, I had only to reach out again to the gear around me to set myself straight.

Now and then I called out.

No answer. Beyond the hut I saw a desolate landscape: ice all around, snow-sky above.

I spent a long time alternately dozing and waking; sat bolt upright in feverish panic; collapsed from the pains wracking my legs, chest, and head. Whenever I slept, dreams plagued me at once. Great tides of ice and snow swept down on a host of men, women, children. . . . Countless bodies tumbled under its weight. . . . I myself fled what others had been helpless to escape.

Again I awoke. The light had shifted; the day had faded. Hungry and afraid, weaker even than before, I considered leaving but didn't know where to go or how to survive in my broken state. Within a few hours—a day at most—I'd surely freeze to death.

Then, as I felt my awareness fading again, I heard footsteps. Impossible: a trick of the wind. Yet I heard them—heard the crunch of boots growing louder on packed snow.

3

In the bad light I couldn't see who it was. The shape of someone crawling in, the sound of labored breathing, the smells of mud, wet wool, and something else—something rich and ferrous that could only have been blood—these were the only clues I had. I neither saw this person's face nor heard any words spoken. More than anything else I felt the presence of another body in that tight space: someone easing into the hut slowly enough to suggest an awareness of my injuries yet so awkwardly as to jolt me time after time.

Pain wasn't what I felt most intensely. It was fear. I'd lain for a long time in an unidentified hovel somewhere on a harsh mountain; I'd suffered injuries serious enough to immobilize me; I'd endured repeated bouts of fever, delirium, shock, panic, and exposure to the elements. Now someone was crawling clumsily into the hut right beside me. My rescuer—or my captor? One of the Umbrage who might have survived...? I didn't know what to think. Of course what I thought was almost irrelevant—I wasn't thinking so much as reacting. Whether my fears made sense or not was beside the point in a situation like that. Fear was the force behind doing whatever needed to be done.

Despite my pain I lay altogether still. I feigned sleep, stupor, coma—whatever might give me the advantage in sizing up this intruder. Such is the human will to live that despite everything I'd endured till that point, despite the hopelessness of my situation, despite my fatigue, pain, and fear, I still maintained a capacity to plot, calculate, and get ready for a frantic push out of that hovel onto the glacier itself.

I waited. I listened with every cell of my being.

For a long time I just lay there. The intruder made no motion. Was this a trick? A ruse to make me drop my guard? My suspicions increased by the second. Surely whoever this was had collapsed beside me on purpose and even now awaited my next move. No matter. I wouldn't succumb to temptation and respond. I'd wait till he succumbed first.

Nothing happened. All I saw was the dark shape before me. All I heard was a long series of labored breaths.

How long I stalled, I have no idea. At some point, however, I couldn't stall any longer. I reached out and nudged the reclining figure with my right hand.

No response.

Nudged again.

Still no response.

Far from reassuring me, however, this lack of response was precisely what alarmed me most. It suggested either the craftiest calculation—lying in wait till the last possible moment—or else a collapse before the same forces of fatigue and injury that had overwhelmed me as well. Either way I felt no cause for reassurance. Who was this person, and what danger did I risk in his presence?

"Tell me who you are," I said in Rixtir.

No answer—just the same rough breathing as before.

"Why have you brought me here?"

Again no answer.

At some point I realized what I should have known all along: that the advantage was mine, that whoever had entered the hut now lay even more debilitated, though perhaps not so badly injured, as I was myself. Mustering some sort of energy might give me a chance to regain control of the situation. At the very least I might figure out who had brought me here; I might even succeed in taking my captor captive.

The deed itself turned out even more difficult than I expected. Never mind that this other person lay just a few feet distant. My physical state at the time put a gulf between us almost as great as the widest crevasses I'd managed to jump before my fall. I wasn't even sure I could cross the distance between us, much less dominate my opponent if we came to blows. The only thing that prompted me to try was knowing that this would be my one chance.

First I rolled onto my left side. To this day I don't know what sort of damage I'd done to my ribs, but at least a couple of them must have been cracked. The act of rolling over was less difficult than the effort not to scream when I rolled. I bit my right sleeve to stifle myself. Then, bending my left leg and pushing with my left foot, I nudged myself toward the doorway. Lying on the glacier made this possible: ice didn't resist my efforts nearly as much as rock would have. Also, the floor slanted somewhat. I wasn't exactly sliding, but I moved more easily than I would have on the level. Ten or fifteen pushes got me more or less head to head with this intruder. A questionable victory: by the time I got there, I was gasping for breath, and almost every bone in my body was throbbing.

Then came the hard part. Working my way close was all well and good; now I needed some way to take control of the situation. What were this stranger's intentions toward me? If they were benign, then of course my strenuous efforts were beside the point. If they were hostile, though ... Let's just say I wasn't going to all this trouble simply to stop by for a chat. This is why no matter how much I wanted to pass out, I kept struggling to reach across this motionless figure, grasp one of the ice-hatchets wedged between him and the hut's other wall, and ease it loose. His weight kept them in place. I could have tugged hard, but that would have risked waking him. I attempted to pull the shaft free more gently: a more difficult motion, given my injuries. No matter how hard I tried, though, I failed.

All along the light inside that hovel had been dusky—a bluish gray. I didn't have the least notion what time it was. Dawn? Twilight? Middle of the day? The storm outside wasn't especially violent just then, simply dense enough to have dimmed even the noonday sun. What little light got past the rocks, ice, and cloth that made up this shelter didn't amount to much. I couldn't see which way this intruder was facing, much less the intruder's face. I wouldn't have been surprised to have ended up cheek by jowl with him. For that matter, it wouldn't have surprised me to discover not only that we were face to face, but that he'd been watching me the whole time.

Two events took place simultaneously just then that transformed the situation.

First, this person slumped toward me, releasing the ice-hatchets from where they had been stuck and allowing at least two of them to topple toward me. I grabbed one and pulled it free. Despite the pain of moving so hard and fast, I yanked it upward till the spike rested just short of my opponent's throat.

The other event was that the light changed. The snowfall eased somewhat, the clouds parted, or the storm relented—I don't know which, but one change or another made all the difference. All I can say is that for the first time since I'd ceased to be there alone, enough light entered the hut to reveal the figure before me.

We were face to face. The features before me were haggard, bruised, filthy, yet recognizable at once. High cheek bones, acquiline nose, and full, sculpted lips— a fine face caught up in tangles of jet black hair.

It was Aeslu.

I must have been mistaken. My injuries or fatigue must have been deluding me. Someone else lay here, some Rixtir woman I didn't know. Perhaps no one lay here at all: I was hallucinating.

Yet watching her, touching her brow, I knew this woman and knew she was Aeslu. In whatever way my

state of mind may have deluded me, I could not have
been mistaken about Aeslu.

I would like to say that I nudged her gently, that
she roused, we embraced, we reveled in each other's
company. Nothing of the sort took place. First of all,
I couldn't seem to wake her. I spoke her name and
caressed her face. No response. I stroked her arm.
Again no response. I shouted, shoved her, called out
in alarm—all without the least reaction of any sort.
More than once I worried that she might have died
of exposure and fatigue right before my eyes. In desperation I jolted her: shook her shoulder hard enough
that her head lolled about like a cadaver's. Yet she
was alive. I could hear Aeslu's breath; I could see the
vapor of her every exhalation. Whatever she'd been
doing out there beyond the hut, she was simply too
tired to surface from the depths of her fatigue.

After a while I reached the conclusion I should have
grasped from the start: this was all for the best. Not
just for her, but for me as well. We were both completely spent. I myself was so depleted by then that I
could scarcely move. What a joke to think that I might
have fended off an intruder! All I could manage was
to keep my eyes open.

And even that not for long.

The storm hadn't stopped but had eased somewhat.
Snow now blew into the hut less violently than before.
What had been a nearly nocturnal darkness all around
now lightened into mere gloom. The wind eased.

Despite our vulnerability there, I felt some sort of
warmth entering my flesh. That she had survived ...
That against all odds I'd found her ... Or rather—
just as good—that I'd been found ... It was wonderful
beyond imagining.

I recall my last thought before sinking away: this
seemed an odd way to spend what was only our second night together alone. Yet just then, regardless of
our wretched state, I couldn't have wanted to be anywhere else on earth.

4

I jolted awake.

Piled rocks and chunks of ice still surrounded me. Weak sunlight slanted into the hovel. Against the opposite wall I saw the same equipment I'd seen before. At the hut's far end, some packs and bundles.

I was alone.

For a few moments I lay there, head pounding and lungs heaving, as I tried to guess what had happened. Was Aeslu a figment of my delirium? Had I been alone from the start—or else keeping the company of someone far different from the person I'd imagined? Both possibilities terrified me.

I tried to force myself up but succumbed at once to the almost electrical shocks of pain coursing through me. No matter how hard I tried, my bones and muscles didn't seem willing to do what I commanded. I felt as helpless as a beached dolphin. After repeated efforts, I collapsed again and lay there gazing out the door.

Footsteps again. This time there was enough light for me to see their source: someone drawing near. Within a few moments Aeslu approaching the hut's entrance, crouched, and eased her way inside.

I could scarcely speak. "How did you—?"

She gripped two ceramic bowls in her hands as she entered. I caught the aroma at once. I didn't know what she had cooked, simply that it was food. That was enough. Even during the war I'd never been so hungry. When she set one of the bowls beside me, I groped for it, devoured everything there, then licked the bowl itself like an idiot or a madman. I must have stammered my thanks then—or else more questions about how she had found me and rescued me.

She did not reply. She had moved to the far end of the hut by then, where she ate her share of the food with her right hand while holding the bowl in her left. I watched as best I could in my weakened state. Her appearance was awful—clothes tattered, hair dishevelled, face caked with dirt and blood—yet nothing about her suggested serious injury.

"Are you all right?"

Again no reply. If anything, she acted as if I weren't even there.

"What's the matter? Speak to me."

Now she glanced up for an instant before returning to the meal at hand.

"Aeslu, please—can't you speak to me? I can't believe you're all right. God Almighty, you survived! *We* survived!" For a moment delight overwhelmed my bafflement.

"We alone," she said at last, once again more attentive to her food than to me.

I must have rattled on then, exclaiming with the full intensity of fear and revulsion that I felt about the avalanche and its consequences on the Rixtir legions gathered at the Mountain's base. I don't remember what I said. I remember that my emotions overtook me at some point, and I began to cry.

"You destroyed my people," said Aeslu just then.

She couldn't have caught me short more abruptly if she had splashed me with ice water. "What did you say?"

Even now she avoided my gaze. "You destroyed the Heirs' forthsetting."

I didn't know how to respond. Of course in one way—perhaps more than one—Aeslu was right. Her accusation hurt precisely because I had already grasped its truth. Yet hearing her state it outright, and state it before the slightest greeting of any sort, stung more than the truth itself. All I could say was, "Forster Beckwith—"

"He, too. But you as well. Both of you."

"Aeslu, don't you understand? I had to stop him. He was the Man of Ignorance. I'm the Man of Knowledge—"

"If only you could have spared us such knowledge."

What came over me then I can call nothing but despair. Not sadness, not depression, not any of the words we use these days to name dark emotions. It wasn't an emotion so much as a state that permeated every aspect of my being. By comparison, the broken bones I'd suffered did little more than tickle. To put matters bluntly, I grasped the nature of what I'd done. More than that: the nature of what I'd become. Intent on destroying Forster Beckwith for the risk he posed to the Mountain Land, I had transformed myself into what I most abhorred.

Yet I strove again to defend myself. "I wanted to save the Rixtirra," I told her.

"You failed."

"And *you*," I went on. "I wanted to save you as well."

"You two fought over me—fought like dogs hungry to gnaw the same bone."

"Aeslu—"

"Man of Knowledge indeed."

Helpless to fend her off, I asked, "Am I the Man of Ignorance, then? Perhaps you should have cast your lot with Forster Beckwith after all."

She gestured her indifference. "It is not that. He *was* the Man of Ignorance, and you were right to destroy him." Here she faltered, shaken, squeezing her eyes shut. "But did you have to—"

Despite her accusations, I would have comforted her if my damaged body would have allowed me to move closer, reach out, and hold her. As it was I could scarcely prop myself up well enough to keep watching her.

"Come to me," I told her. "Please come to me."

*   *   *

All that day Aeslu stayed clear. I felt like a leper, an outcast, an apostate so dangerous that she kept my company for no reason except mutual necessity. Aeslu responded to my questions now and then but never initiated any conversation. She avoided my gaze if at all possible. Not once did I see her smile.

At the same time, she attended to me as if anything but indifferent to my fate. She brought me food and water. She washed me, wrapped my chest and legs with strips of cloth, salved my wounds with some kind of Rixtir unguent. She stood guard outside our hut and, as the storms waxed and waned, either secured the cloth roof and door when the weather deteriorated or else opened them when it improved. Although she reviled me in words, she nurtured me in actions.

"What would you have me do?" I asked her that afternoon.

"What you will."

"Your own preferences aren't exactly irrelevant."

"Do what you will," she said, then added: "You always have."

I resisted the temptation to anger. "Shall I go back down? Leave the Mountain Land?"

"If that is what you want."

"And what would *you* do then?"

"I would have no choice. I would go down, too."

That night brought the first clear sky I'd seen in weeks. Like almost all changes of weather in the Andes, it happened fast. The snow eased, then stopped altogether. The clouds disengaged from one another, lifted, and dissipated. By sunset the transformation was complete. Blue faded to pink, yellow, blue again, indigo, black. And almost as we watched, the stars emerged—that great southern mass of light, that celestial avalanche.

5

And so she looked after me, stood guard over me, nursed me back to health. I wasn't always clear about what Aeslu was doing; I wasn't always even aware of her. She told me later that half the time I raved like a lunatic—called out to people whose names she didn't recognize, rattled on in English too fast for her to understand, babbled in Rixtir, pleaded for help, screamed, cried, shouted. Raving was just the start. More than once I went berserk and tried clawing my way out of our hut. Only my own injuries saved me from escaping into the storm. If I'd made it outside, she never would have succeeded in getting me back. In snowfall that heavy, she probably wouldn't even have found me. Yet somehow Aeslu stayed patient; she would administer some sort of Rixtir balm, herb, or poultice; the fever would break; I'd calm down. Gradually my flesh and bones started healing, and with it my state of mind.

Of course, even as my body recovered, another malady afflicted me. This was an awareness that thousands of the Mountain-Drawn—two thousand? three? even more?—lay entombed in the glacier below. Never mind that a natural calamity had resulted in their deaths; my own actions had triggered the calamity. Was this possible? Had my unrelenting pursuit of Forster Beckwith really caused the avalanche? More than once I tried dissuading myself from a conclusion that I was to blame. Surely the avalanche would have happened anyway. Or else if human actions had caused it, then Forster himself was culpable. After all, the dynamite had belonged to him. Some months earlier he had wilfully destroyed the City of Rope by unleashing a flame from his cigarette lighter; how much more likely, then, that his even more appalling fire had set off this new catastrophe. Yet I knew the truth. The dynamite may have been his alone, but I was the one who chose to use it. No effort to convince myself otherwise succeeded. Despite my dazed state, I could remember the sequence of events. I'd seen what came of them. Wandering half a day at the edges of the avalanche had made it impossible to deny either the cause or its effects.

You ask what I saw. Are you positive you want to hear? It wasn't quite as tidy as you might imagine.

Of course the main bulk of the avalanche was so massive that it covered everything in its path. How does one estimate the size of something like that? How does one calculate the mass of an object in which the component parts are blocks of ice the size of cars, houses, whole buildings? How does one gauge the force it created in its descent from the mountain? I'm not a physicist. I can't even guess. Even with the aftermath right before me, I couldn't truly grasp what had happened. Recalling it now, I can barely describe what I saw. All I can do is give you an impression.

The collision of those blocks of ice against one another had smashed some of them into smaller chunks; these in turn had collided so hard as to grind them into icy pebbles; and the whole mass had engulfed the Umbrage and the Heirs in its path. Almost the entirety of both expeditions had simply vanished. The avalanche had buried two or three thousand people alive. I can't even speculate how deep the rubble lay once it came to rest on top of them. Twenty, thirty, forty feet? I'm just guessing. Ice, snow, and fragments of rock embedded in the rest had spread out over the glacier and spilled into the valley. I can tell you that from the side it looked like some sort of gigantic organism—an incalculably huge amoeba, perhaps—that had devoured a host of smaller creatures with its pseudopods. Part of what made the situation so horrifying was precisely this organismic quality: the contrast between the inanimate nature of ice and rock on the one hand, the bestial nature of the whole avalanche on the other. In some sense all those people got eaten alive.

The edges, though, were another story.

I wish I could describe something merely pathetic—bodies strewn about, perhaps—the glacier transformed into a morgue. What I saw was far worse than that. Even the aftermath of the Web disaster seemed gentle by comparison. The edges of the avalanche weren't a morgue so much as a charnel house. Any Heirs and Umbrage who had avoided live burial but hadn't escaped altogether got torn to pieces. The great icy beast may have devoured everyone else, but those who avoided the misfortune of falling only partway into its jaws got chewed up all the same, then spat out. Mangled bodies lay jumbled with chunks of ice and stone. Severed body parts rested here and there. At one point, I found a single boot with an amputated foot still in it.

Was I the only one who had survived? Staggering over this expanse of desolation, I had assumed that I alone remained among the living. If I'd roamed more widely or looked more closely, perhaps I might have known otherwise. I might have seen hundreds of footprints leading down from the glacier and back toward the Middle Realm. I might have seen one other set of prints heading up toward the Mountain. But in fact I didn't. I didn't roam more widely; I didn't look more closely. I fumbled about neither dead nor fully alive, for some sort of trance had taken hold of me, something no less severe than the shell shock that so many of us suffered during the war, in fact even more mind-numbing and flesh-chilling.

You ask why I didn't flee. I don't really know. Perhaps the possibility occurred to me at some point, but I don't recall even considering it. Was this a consequence of injuries? Of some kind of dementia I'd suf-

fered? Even during the heat of battle I'd always
mustered enough presence of mind to flee when it
seemed necessary. If anything, I'd been all too adept
at turning tail. Yet nothing of the sort happened now.
I strayed about at the fringes of the avalanche, observed what had come of it, and grasped the nature
of my place in these events.

Thus the Heirs and the Umbrage alike came to
grief, and I found myself alone to witness the full extent of their ruin. Thus, too, I proceeded to do what
I did next. I'll admit outright that I didn't think things
through. I didn't really think at all. I simply chose
what seemed the only alternative before me: I headed
up. And thus in turn I crossed paths with Aeslu well
above the avalanche that had left us to do alone what
we had intended to do in the company of so many
others.

This leaves one question unanswered. If she held
me in such contempt, why didn't she just abandon me?
Why, for that matter, did she persist in nursing me
back to health?

The answer was evident to me even at the time.

Many months earlier, Norroi and Aeslu had told me
the founding tale of the Mountain Land: how, in the
years right after the Spanish conquest of Peru, a Lowlander named Ossonnal had fled to the mountains,
walked for weeks, and climbed beyond reach of the
people who threatened his safety and freedom. I
couldn't remember the whole story just then, but I
certainly recalled the gist of it. Ossonnal climbed because he had no choice but to climb. He climbed till
everything he did was the climb. It made no difference
to him if he died climbing. All he could do was climb.

Yet I remember, too, that he did not succeed in his
solitary quest. Climbing, he slipped on the ice and fell,
lay a long time near death, and woke to find a woman
guarding him and coaxing him back to health.

How does the story go? Perhaps the particular

words don't matter. What I recall is that he was no longer alone; he found himself in a rough hut; snow blew in through the doorway; and a young woman knelt beside him.

"My name is Lissallo," she said. "I found you and brought you here."

Ossonnal wanted to ask how and why but couldn't.

"You want to know how I found you," said the woman.

He could only nod.

"And how I came to this place?"

He nodded again.

Lissallo told him that she, too, had come from the Lowland, had fled the invaders below, had reached the Mountain but had failed to climb it. She told him that perhaps two people could succeed together where each of them had failed alone. She told him that they should join forces to seek the summit.

I recall as well that Lissallo nursed Ossonnal back to health, and that Ossonnal recovered, regained his strength, and soon wanted to climb even more intently than when he first left the Lowland. I recall from this story and from other Rixtir legends that Ossonnal and Lissallo then not only founded the Mountain Land but eventually set off together to find and climb the Mountain Made of Light, the mountain that Aeslu and I now clung to in hope and desperation.

Thinking over this tale now—sitting in a tool shed seven or eight thousand miles away and half a century distant from the events I'm relating—it's easy for me to see what was reality and what was myth. It wasn't quite so easy at the time. First of all, I was hurt. I don't know if I'd actually broken any bones, but at the very least I'd taken a bad beating. I was bruised all over. I'd lost some blood. I was suffering from dehydration, malnourishment, and what we'd now call hypothermia. It's amazing I was alive at all. Is it so surprising that my state of mind was at once muddled and pathologically focused?

More to the point, I had steeped in the Rixtir myths

for almost a full year. I was the Man of Knowledge—
the Sun's Stead. The Rixtirra themselves had followed
me all the way to the Mountain itself on that assump-
tion. Never mind that my choices along the way had
been a nearly unmitigated disaster—that my best intentions had led almost directly to the deaths of thousands. I knew I was to blame; even so, the stories still
held sway over me. How could I deny the truth of
what I saw taking shape? The details lined up convinc-
ingly. Aeslu herself had reached the same conclusion.
We were destined to make the climb.

Perhaps in this case—just as in so many others—
destiny was just a side effect of having no alternatives.
How could we have left the Mountain? How could we
have gone down without at least making an attempt
at a climb? It wasn't a matter of having to explain
ourselves right then and there. Everyone right below
the Mountain was dead. No doubt we would have encountered others soon enough—members of the
Mountain-Drawn who had swarmed into the Inner
Realm to seek their refuge or, if nothing else, to determine the significance of the great avalanche that had
surely been audible for fifty or a hundred miles. What
would we have told the Mountain-Drawn? That wasn't
the point. It wasn't our worst problem. The problem
was, What would we have told *ourselves*?

And so we did the one thing possible for us to do.
Not right away. Not without a sense of deep dread.
But certainly with great earnest. We had no alternative. Just as Ossonnal and Lissallo had set off together
long ago, so too did Aeslu and I now set off to climb
the Mountain Made of Light.

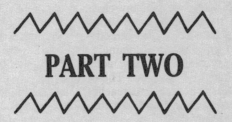

PART TWO

PART TWO

When Jesse O'Keefe fell silent, I thought nothing of it. He was given to long silences—though whether they served to let him collect his thoughts or to evade them, I couldn't say—and I took this one simply as another pause. Yet this time the silence lasted longer than usual. He stared at his gloved hands resting before him on the tabletop. His expression revealed the faintest tinge of a smile.

I felt an urge to interrupt his reverie. Now and then I'd asked questions or made comments, more out of genuine curiosity than from a need to prod him, but I'd spoken less and less as the story unfolded. He had spun his yarn. We'd been talking a couple of hours, though, and it didn't seem fair to keep coaxing him against his will. He looked tired. I also started feeling guilty about how I'd used the photo as bait to catch him in the first place. Yet after five or six minutes had passed, temptation got the best of me. I asked, "Did you understand what you were getting into?"

Jesse looked up at me. He didn't look startled so much as totally focused. Despite the white eyebrows above his eyes and the wrinkles surrounding them, this was not an old man's gaze. I waited, forcing myself to gaze back.

"Of course not," he said. "That's the whole point."

He stood, the chair stuttering as he pushed it back. Then he crossed the room, lifted a huge coil of garden hose from a rack, and hoisted it with the agility of a mountaineer shouldering a rope.

"I've taken too much of your time," I told him as I switched off the tape recorder.

"Maybe, maybe not."

"I'm sorry."

"Don't apologize. I assume you haven't been chasing me for years just to have a five-minute chat."

I thought he'd go on, but he didn't. Without another word, Jesse walked out of the garden shed and set off across the lawn.

I hesitated a moment, then followed.

"Should I wait?" I asked. "Should I come back later?"

"Perhaps you should go get some lunch."

"Just tell me when to return."

"When the time seems right," he said. He dropped the coil, then dragged one end toward the building opposite Anthropology Hall. Without warning he stopped, turned, and spoke. "By the way, you needn't dangle that photograph before me. I'll tell you the whole story, all right? You can show me the picture again when we're done."

1

You asked if we knew what we were doing [Jesse O'Keefe said later, once we'd settled back into his shed again]. I can only emphasize what I told you earlier: of course not. We had no idea at all. The clearest evidence for that is simply that we went ahead.

Let me put it to you more strongly. We must have been mad. We must have been suffering already from the altitude, from hunger, from shock and cold and dehydration. To tackle a mountain like that! Two exhausted, injured refugees—a man and a woman with only the most limited notion of where we were, much less of what the Mountain had in store for us! No one in command of his or her senses would have done what we set out to do. The Mountain was too big, too dangerous, too far beyond our skills, our understanding, even our most basic resources of strength and stamina. It seemed less a mountain we intended to climb than another world we were about to reach.

In the years since then, I've often tried to find an image that reveals how the Mountain appeared to me as Aeslu and I prepared for the climb. I mean *appeared* not just visually but viscerally. Not just how it looked, but how it felt. A wall, a tower, a parapet? Out of the question. That sort of metaphor suggests something too man-made, too architectural. A vast wave cresting just before it breaks on the beach? That's closer but still not right. Waves are transient, supple, protean. The Mountain gave the impression of having always been there and simultaneously of being destined to stay there for the rest of time. I could rattle off all sorts of potential metaphors. The truth is, the usual figures of speech don't do the trick. None captures the sense of mixed attraction and repulsion. How it inspired both delight and dread.... How it came and went, alternatively hiding in the clouds and revealing itself from behind them.... How, when it deigned to appear, it filled the sky and teetered over us.... How by turns it blinded us with its radiance and plunged us into deep shadow....

But a long time after those events, another image occurred to me. One that comes closer than all the rest.

Remember some years ago—it must have been 1968 or '69—one of the Apollo capsules first orbited the moon? I don't refer to the actual landings, but to one of the space shots a few months earlier. Astronauts voyaged to the moon, circled it a few times, and checked out all the various systems necessary for landing on the lunar surface the following year. At some point, just before the men went into lunar orbit, they took some pictures of the moon from their module's port. And what had been the same old moon, the radiant orb hung in the sky since time immemorial, started growing. And it grew. Grew. Grew. Grew till it loomed before them, towered over them, and seemed ready to absorb them altogether.

I followed the whole Apollo project closely at the time, but despite the later drama of the landings themselves, what impressed me most were the photos taken from that first voyage. Those images of the moon looming—that's how the Mountain looked. Not just the size, but the sense of otherness. The Mountain wasn't part of the world so much as a separate realm.

So: did we know what we were getting into?

No.

Don't get me wrong. It wasn't as if Aeslu and I didn't talk things over.

"Do you think we can do it?" I asked her.

"I do not know."

"Yet you feel willing to try."

"Not willing," she replied. "There is a Rixtir word—*asfahhi*. What one wants to do because one must."

"You feel a duty?"

She shook her head. "That is different. *Asfahhi* is more than duty, and better."

I still wasn't sure how she saw the situation. "And you feel this *asfahhi*—whatever it is—even though I'm the one who will go up with you?"

She nodded.

"Because I'm the Man of Knowledge."

Again she nodded.

"Even though my knowledge isn't worth a damn."

Once more she nodded.

"Aeslu—why?"

She shrugged. "It is what we must do. What we are destined to do."

It's hard for me to explain why the climb itself seemed so compelling. Not just compelling: inevitable. You suggest that we could have chosen otherwise than to proceed—or that, if nothing else, we could have proceeded at another time. We could have gone back down, rested, considered our options; we could have reached some sort of agreement with the various factions we'd left behind among the Rixtirra; we could have planned a communal expedition; in short, we could have gone about the whole business in a more reasonable manner. True. But we didn't. By then a reasonable manner wasn't even a possibility.

As I say, it's hard to explain. What I've said about steeping in the Rixtir myths goes only so far. Likewise regarding the consequences of what Aeslu and I had done despite our best intentions. None of that is irrelevant—I'm just coming at the main point from a different angle.

Try this instead.

The Apollo astronauts' voyage to the moon was the

consequence of enormous labor—their own, their mission team members', and in some respects their fellow citizens'. Obviously they were also on their way because of the rockets' thrust. But all those factors were just the start. By the time the moon started looming in their capsule's port, something else had taken over. The moon itself drew them forth. The pull of lunar gravity gave them no choice but to reach their destination. Having decided to go that far, they had no alternative but to conclude what they'd begun. No change of mind would have made the least difference. Once they reached a certain point in space, no one—not the astronauts themselves, not the engineers at Mission Control, not the physicists who had calculated their trajectory, not even President Nixon—could have brought them back.

At least not till the deed was done.

2

Of course we had no Mission Control, no physicists, no president cheering us on. We didn't even have what most climbers have—some sort of expedition. Team members. A base camp. A plan for accomplishing what we'd set out to do. All we had was each other. And—this was critical—we had some gear.

I can't overstate the importance of the gear. It's true what I said about the desire, the compulsion, the almost physiological drive we felt to climb the mountain. But no matter how intense that drive, no matter what role it played in the events that followed, it was the gear that made expressing our drive possible. The gear was what distinguished our decision to climb the Mountain from mere psychotic delusion.

I won't rattle off a whole laundry list of what we had with us. If you really want to hear the whole story, there will be time enough for me to mention one thing or another. Let me say simply this: we had enough in our possession to make an attempt plausible. Notice I said *attempt,* not *ascent.* Even at the time we knew the effort was just this side of suicidal. Yet on some level it seemed worth attempting. Why? Not just because we had some gear. It was the *kind* of gear.

Some months earlier, in a city called the Veil, the Heirs had unearthed a cache of ancient equipment. Actually, "defrosted" might be a better way of putting it: the entire stockpile had been packed away inside a huge icy pyramid. The rank-and-file Heirs—the ordinary men and women—had overruled the Masters at my urging and had lit bonfires to melt the pyramid to see what lay within. No one knew if there was anything there at all. I didn't, certainly. It was just a hunch. For all I knew, I'd simply fallen prey to my own wishful thinking. Thawing out that pyramid on the off chance of finding gear inside was the biggest gamble I took during my whole time in the Mountain Land. (The biggest gamble, at least, next to attempting the Mountain itself.) If I'd been mistaken, my whole quest would have come to an abrupt and not very pleasant end. But I wasn't mistaken. We found the gear—precisely the sort of gear I'd been hoping for but never quite believed I'd find.

It was what the Masters ended up calling the Founders' Gear. Had the Founders actually made this stuff? Were Ossonnal and Lissallo, progenitors of the Mountain-Drawn, in fact the artisans who personally created a remarkable variety and quantity of mountaineering equipment? Unlikely. The stockpile we had uncovered was so vast—thousands of items—that the vastness itself argued against what the Masters assumed. Likewise the variety. Likewise the sophistication of the craftsmanship. Ossonnal and Lissallo would have necessarily been artisans of prodigious capability in every possible way. No, I never really believed that they made everything themselves. Yet I suppose my disbelief didn't rule out this stash being the Founders' Gear in another sense. Perhaps Ossonnal and Lissallo had invented these tools, or else had inspired them. Perhaps they'd directed their followers to make them. Perhaps they'd hidden the whole stockpile before they left to find the Mountain Made of Light.

All I knew was that the so-called Founders' Gear was unlike any I'd seen before in the Mountain Land. It wasn't ceremonial climbing gear of the sorts that the Masters found so compelling—sacramental objects used to perform rituals in their Sun-Moon religion. Neither was it Western gear of any kind I could recognize. The unusual nature of the clothing was conspicuous enough: coats, leggings, boots, gloves, and headgear made of beautifully sewn wool, deerskin, and various materials I couldn't even identify. The hardware was even more striking. Hooks, nails, pegs, spikes. Hammers, axes, picks, and the adaptable climbing tools that the Rixtirra called ice-hatchets. I'd never set eyes on so many different kinds of ironmongery. In fact, I never again saw anything like the variety or sophistication till just recently, what with all the new-fangled alloys and designs. I call it ironmongery. A misnomer: it wasn't iron at all. For all intents and purposes, the Mountain-Drawn were a Bronze Age culture. This gear wasn't bronze. Neither was it copper, tin, or any of the other metals that ancient South American cultures developed. What, then? I have no idea. I didn't know at the time; even today I still don't know.

I'd give anything to have even a single item of that cache now. An ice-hatchet, perhaps. A piece of rope. A single glove. Something to examine, study, analyze. Something just to gaze at. Never mind that almost everything in our possession was beautifully made— not just well-crafted, but almost perfect in its harmony of form and function. My point is something else. Even the smallest artifact casts a shadow capable of revealing the entire culture.

But I'm straying from the wordpath, as Aeslu would have said.

What I mean is that we had an assemblage of gear. Not assemblage, really: a *scrounge.* Aeslu had scrounged odds and ends that the avalanche had either missed or scattered. It was more than I'd expected— more than we could use. Was it enough, though? Did we have what we needed of the proper items? We didn't know. *I* didn't, certainly. Yet there was a good bit of it. I promised not to rattle off the whole inventory, and I couldn't do it even if I tried. But the piles in our little hut somehow looked persuasive. Clothing. Hardware. Rope. Food. I can't explain precisely why, but the Founders' Gear was powerful. It made us feel we could do what needed to be done. The mere fact that we had it—the fact that this hodge-podge

of implements and supplies had survived the avalanche—fed into our belief that an attempt to climb
the Mountain was our fate. This gear asked to be
used.

More than asked: demanded.

3

Something else demanded our attention, too: the Mountain Stone. This was my chief contribution to the cause. Aeslu may have acquired all the rest—climbing gear, food, clothes—but if nothing else, I brought the Mountain Stone.

Actually, I wasn't even aware at first that I still possessed it. I'd been too sick, injured, and delirious to give it a thought, much less to remember that I had it on me. But I did. The Mountain-Drawn didn't use pockets in a Western sense; some of their clothes, however, had pouches sewed into the linings. These pouches weren't convenient or comfortable, but they were fairly secure. The robe that the Masters had given me—quite a regal affair, with weasel fur inside and cloth woven from vicuña wool and gold filament outside—had a couple of these pouches. Before I'd set out with the Heirs' expedition, I'd put the Mountain Stone in there to keep it safe. All along it had been nestled right against my torso. One of the reasons I got so banged up fleeing the avalanche was that the big lump of quartz rested right next to me. If someone had stuck me in a burlap bag, tossed in a brick, sewed the bag shut, and shoved me down a hillside, I couldn't have ended up much more badly bruised. Yet somehow I'd survived, and the Stone was safe. In the long run, the Stone was what mattered most.

One morning well before I'd recovered from the worst of my injuries, the weather eased. This must have been late March—near the end of the rainy season. Any change at our altitude was still fairly slight. We still suffered almost daily snowstorms. Yet day by day something had begun to shift—the density of the clouds, perhaps, or the height at which they drifted. It wasn't hard to believe that during the next few weeks, the overcast would diminish and ultimately lift altogether. That morning, after an early snow squall, the storm dispersed. What had been a continuous pall surrounding us soon congealed into individual clouds. They sailed by above us, below us, around us. We weren't in the clear by any means—yet we weren't hemmed in now, either. Then, without warning, as the clouds tightened further into distinct entities, the Mountain materialized as if out of nowhere.

I'd be mistaken to say that we gazed at it. We gazed *up* it. Our camp lay at some distance from it—half a mile, perhaps—yet the Mountain was so huge that it rose above rather than before us. And of course how could we gaze at something that we couldn't really take in? To see the Mountain we had to scan it, our eyes ranging from the lower reaches still steeped in shadow; up the cliffs hung with snowfields and, here and there, with massive icicles; then up the avalanche chutes that gave this peak its serrated appearance; and at last up toward the summit ridge only then catching a rim of dawn. No, we didn't gaze at it. Gazing implies something leisurely, relaxed. What we did was both more intense and more passive. It wasn't even volitional. Our vision got dragged up the Mountain both by force and by choice—we simply couldn't cast eyes on this sight and do anything else but stare.

This was only the third time I'd seen it and the first time I'd seen the whole peak by daylight. As before, I found myself transfixed. No—paralyzed. The Mountain, trailing the clouds that swept around it, seemed to topple toward us. Like a creature caught in a predator's stare, I felt torn between the helpless urge to stare and the equally helpless urge to flee. Only my sudden awareness of Aeslu beside me broke the spell that might otherwise have lasted forever.

When I turned, I found her right beside me. She had fallen to her knees. Both arms reached toward the Mountain as if to embrace it, yet her hands trembled. She stammered in one of the Rixtir languages while tears streamed down her face.

Her wonderment shouldn't have surprised me. Aeslu had waited her whole life long to see this peak. I knew her well enough—and knew the Mountain as well—to understand how she might now feel simultaneous exaltation and alarm. Yet as I watched her, I could tell at once that these tears showed more than just the complexities of awe. I saw something else there, too, something stark and ordinary.

After a while—after I'd regained my own composure—I asked, "What is it? What's the matter?"

She kept staring at the Mountain but now shook her head.

"Are you all right?"

"We can never do this," she blurted. "We can never climb the Mountain, never find the way up, never reach the Summit."

"You yourself said we must."

"It is hopeless," she said. "Hopeless."

"We have what we need. Rope, tools, food—"

"We can never do it."

I told her, "We can try."

"But how can we find the way? We will be lost at once."

With great effort I tore myself away from the Mountain's pull on my attention, staggered back to our hut, and started rummaging about. I'd been wearing clothes from the Founders' Gear for some days by then—Aeslu had helped me out of my robe into something warmer—and so the dirty, bloody old garment must have been lying somewhere in our hut. I found it at once, ransacked it, and pulled out the Mountain Stone. From there I worked my way back over the glacier to where Aeslu stood.

It's hard for me to explain the impact of that chunk of quartz on anyone looking at it. As you surely noticed in my journals, I've tried explaining. What shall I tell you now that you don't already know? That it was the tip of a large quartz crystal? That it looked substantial beyond its size and weight? That, at the same time, the Stone's clarity made it seem ethereal, as if ready to waft away? That it appeared both complex and simple? All true. Yet what I'm saying belies the power of the Mountain Stone. It was merely a stone. At the same time, it was a mountain. Even a single glance revealed its dual nature: both what it was and what it meant. The Stone, though silent, shouted its tidings about the Mountain it represented.

No wonder Ossonnal and Lissallo had bestowed this Stone on their people. No wonder that the Mountain-Drawn had always cherished it. That Saffiu and her lover had squabbled over it. That the Woman of the Wood had clung to it. That Forster Beckwith had coveted it, Soffosoiti had confiscated it, and the Heirs had then rejoiced to have it back. And that Aeslu, taking it from me now, grasped it eagerly, raised it up, and in one motion both performed her obeisance and revealed the precise similarities between the lesser Mountain in her hands and the greater one whose mysteries it would unlock.

4

And so we ransacked our supplies for whatever we could use; we filled our packs; we abandoned our hovel; we headed up.

I'll spare you a detailed account of those first few days. Neither Aeslu nor I knew what we were doing. We were in bad shape—exhausted, sick, hurt. We still felt dazed by the events that had brought us there. We didn't know where we were or where we were going. In more ways than one we just stumbled about. Perhaps what matters most about our departure is simply that we survived it.

Even at our starting point we were already at the upper reaches of the glacier; given its size, though, we still had some distance to go before we started climbing the Mountain itself. So our first task was to surmount the icefall jumbled against the peak. This proved both easier and more difficult than I'd expected. Easier, because some sort of beginner's luck led us through the maze of towering ice-blocks without our getting lost. Difficult, because the glacier's angle made our effort strenuous, unpredictable, and treacherous. Time after time great slabs of ice shifted around us in response to the forces at work inside the glacier. Most of the time Aeslu and I were well beyond reach of these slabs when they tipped, rolled, or came crashing down. Sometimes, though, we happened to be closer—close enough that we scarcely managed to get clear of them when they fell. The entire icefall was unstable. Only upon reaching its upper edge did we feel safe.

Of course what we felt was an illusion.

As it so happens, almost every glacier detaches slightly from the peak that has produced it; the weight of all that ice pulls it away from the cliff. The result is what the Germans and Swiss call a *bergschrund*. This is the gap between the glacier's upper edge and the mountain itself. "Gap" is too good a word. What faced us just then was a chasm extending right and left as far as we could see and gaping before us about twenty feet from one side to the other. I don't even know how deep it was. Aeslu got down on her hands and knees, crept over to the precipice, and peered in.

"What do you see?" I asked.

The answer came back at once: "Nothing."

"Nothing at all?"

"Ice on this side, rock on the other. No bottom." She picked up a shard of ice, tossed it in, and waited for the sound of its impact. I heard a clattering noise that took a long time to fade into silence.

We struggled for half that morning to find a way across. First we headed off to the left, for the *bergschrund* seemed to narrow in that direction. No luck. Besides, that way led toward the avalanche—we'd have been wasting our time and effort even to consider it. So we tried the right. No luck that way, either. The *schrund* narrowed, but not by much. We couldn't jump fifteen feet to the other side any better than twenty.

"There."

I didn't pay any attention at first. Aeslu had spoken quietly and without emotion; she might as well have been muttering to herself. When I noticed that she'd stopped, however, I turned to look at her.

"There." She pointed down the trench.

It took me a while to see what she meant. Then I made sense of her gestures. Still far ahead—scarcely visible, in fact—I could see some sort of variation in the textures of white and gray before us. I couldn't actually see what it was, but I could figure it out.

Something white extended over the chasm. A snow bridge.

It was just what we needed but wouldn't dare to have hoped for. Sometimes storms or avalanches pile enough snow on a glacier's upper slopes to close the *bergschrund* altogether. The accumulation doesn't usually stay there—it falls in or pulls away when the glacier shifts. But sometimes a tenuous arch of snow briefly links one side to the other. What we saw before us now was precisely such a link. It wasn't big—four feet wide in the middle and badly eroded along the entire span—but it was our one hope for getting across.

"The Sun and the Moon have guided us here," Aeslu said just then, sounding resolute.

"Maybe so—"

"—and will protect us."

"Aeslu—"

"The Mountain Stone has shown the way."

In fact the Mountain Stone couldn't possibly have included this snow bridge as part of its route. First of all, even the Stone's most detailed markings didn't reveal anything on such a small scale. Besides, this bridge probably hadn't been here two or three years ago, much less four hundred. Finding it was nothing more than a bit of good luck. I said nothing, though, unwilling to burst the bubble of Aeslu's confidence. We needed every bit we could muster.

Without much more discussion, we set to work preparing to cross. Obviously we could simply have walked over: the bridge was big enough. But neither of us—not even Aeslu—wanted to take any chances. The bridge's upper surface was slick and heavily worn by the wind and the sun. The slightest misstep would have sent us into the *schrund*. I wasn't even sure that it would hold our weight—especially not with the big packs we carried. So we took out some of our gear, laid it on the snow, and prepared to set up a belay that would provide a lifeline if one of us fell.

Aeslu looked unfamiliar with what I was doing but

grasped my intentions immediately. I, in turn, was unfamiliar with the specific items of Rixtir mountain gear
but quickly saw how to use them. Most of the equipment could be adapted to what I knew of Western
climbing technique. Some of the pieces, too, suggested
uses for which the Founders must have intended them.
Before long I had a whole belay setup ready: an ice-
hatchet stabbed into the snow five feet shy of the
chasm; another hatchet bracing the first transversely;
rope laid out properly and coiled around the vertical
hatchet for support.

"You go first," I told Aeslu while strapping on the
cramponlike devices that the Rixtirra called footclaws.
"I weigh more—I'm more likely to damage the bridge
while crossing. If I fall, you'll have far more trouble
pulling me out."

Hesitant for a few seconds, she strapped on her own
footclaws. Aeslu then tied herself to the rope. At once
she picked up a hatchet and stepped over to the
bridge.

Two steps. Three. After a few steps more Aeslu was
already to the halfway point. The bridge seemed as
solid as the Ponte Vecchio. Aeslu was so sure-footed
that even the iciest patches didn't faze her.

Once she had worked her way about two-thirds of
the way across, however, I heard a crunching noise.
A chunk of the bridge suddenly dropped away from
its underside and dropped into the depths. Aeslu,
hearing the noise, tightened up. I could see her struggle to keep her balance: how she crouched, how her
arms wavered.

"Go!" I shouted. "Just go!"

She almost slipped. Somehow she stayed upright,
then scampered gingerly to the other side.

Once she was safe, we surveyed the damage. I
couldn't tell how serious it was. The piece that had
fallen wasn't especially large, but it was literally central to the bridge. Its loss was equivalent to having
dropped the keystone from an arch. What were the
odds that this structure would hold my weight?

I couldn't contemplate what we were facing. Our situation was dicey enough already. Aeslu was on one side; I was on the other. Either she would have to cross back or I'd have to go over. The risks of falling were the same either way. Retreat would probably mean the end of our attempt on the Mountain. On the other hand, my proceeding might end the attempt just as easily—and my life as well. Neither of the alternatives appealed to me.

Ultimately Aeslu herself made the decision. Finished setting up her belay on the other side, she called out, "I am ready for the packs."

I responded as if my own actions had never been in doubt: I tossed over both packs, then the extra coils of rope that Aeslu might soon be needing.

Under normal circumstances I would have more or less skated across. I've always been light; my weight wouldn't have stressed the snow bridge much more than Aeslu's did. Ordinarily I would have been sure-footed, too. But the circumstances weren't normal. Both Aeslu and I had taken enough of a battering that our strength was already compromised. I have to admit, too, that my long fight with Forster Beckwith the day of the avalanche had used up my appetite for crossing crevasses. Just the thought of working my way over this chasm made me dizzy.

But there was no way around it. I tied the rope around my waist, then started over.

The first few steps weren't so bad. I managed to keep my feet placed well enough to spread my weight. Also, the footclaws held better on the surface of the bridge than I'd expected. Now and then I glanced up at Aeslu where she sat right ahead of me, and her presence calmed me every time. It wasn't just her belay stance, though she'd seated herself behind a low hummock of stone that would have held almost any weight brought to bear against it. It wasn't the sight of the rope stretched tight between us, either, or my belief that she'd hang onto it with all her might if I took a fall. The reassurance I felt was something more than physical security. It was Aeslu herself—her presence—that calmed me.

I took a few more steps. The ice stuttered under my weight. I didn't like that sound—the sound of a brittle substance starting to fracture—but it seemed not to change step by step.

Then, without warning, the bridge opened like a trap door. I plummeted at once. Even at the time I knew that only the center had dropped out, but the center was bad enough simply because that's what I'd been standing on. The brief warning I'd received made it possible to do little more than fling myself forward rather than fall straight down.

Aeslu must have tightened the rope at that instant, for I managed to hug the broken span tighter than I would have otherwise. Whatever tension she brought to bear on the rope prevented me from slipping into the *schrund*. My feet kicked at the air. My fingers clawed at the ice-encrusted snow I'd been walking on just a moment earlier. For a long time I struggled not to lose my grip and slide backward, which would have dragged the rope out of Aeslu's hands.

But I didn't lose my grip. I didn't slide backward. I just clung there hugging what remained of the snow bridge—a ludicrous posture. My predicament bewildered me. Why wasn't I falling? Little by little, I made sense of the situation. Aeslu wasn't able to pull me out by brute force, yet she was strong enough to hold my descent in check. As long as she could maintain her grip on the rope—and as long as the rope held, for that matter—I wouldn't drop any lower. Of course the snow I clung to might collapse into the *schrund*: that was another possibility. So the task before me was to inch my way up the damaged span, hoping that Aeslu's tug on the rope would maintain whatever distance I gained.

By the time I pulled myself off the snow bridge and found my first stone hand-hold, my hands were bloody and numb.

5

We didn't need anyone to tell us that we'd burned
our bridges, so to speak. Even the briefest glance at
the *bergschrund* made it clear. The middle third of
the span we'd just finished crossing now lay shattered
somewhere in the depths below; the rest was too badly
damaged to trust. We couldn't have gone back over
even if we'd wanted to.

Did we want to? I suppose in some sense we did.
It's hard to make such a bad start and not wish to
begin again—that, or else abandon the effort altogether. I can't say we weren't shaken by having a close
call so early. Aeslu and I both just sat there, propped
on a ledge, for a long time afterward. We were already
exhausted. Neither of us was in good shape. My hands
had gotten cut and abraded from clawing my way to
safety. If we could have packed up and left right then,
we certainly would have done so.

But of course we couldn't do anything of the kind.
We were stuck. Find another snow bridge? The
thought occurred to us. No doubt more than one
crossed the *bergschrund*. But during several hours of
looking earlier, this was the only one we'd spotted.
Besides, we were now on the lower reaches of the
Mountain itself. The cliff angled steeply from where
it met the ice. Both to our right and left, great angles
of stone rose out of the glacier and effectively blocked
our path in both directions. We couldn't just wander
along the cliff as we'd wandered along the glacier's
upper edge. In fact, the snow bridge had deposited us
in one of the few places that wasn't a nearly vertical

rock face. So there we were. All for the best? Maybe so. If nothing else, we were now committed to doing what we claimed we'd come there to do.

That night we camped on a ledge. It felt claustrophobically small at the time—a narrow place where the cliff leveled off for a yard or two, then rose steeply again. Little did I know what a palace it would have seemed later in the climb. At the time, though, it was a hardship to tolerate. We made our peace with it. We were just too tired to try finding anything else.

Snow had accumulated there and grown dense. The surface was crusty but not too hard underneath, which allowed us to use a tent Aeslu had brought along. Till then I hadn't even known what this tent was like— only that she'd salvaged it from the Founders' Gear. We pulled it out, wrestled with it a while, then examined it. Like all the rest of that ancient equipment, it was a remarkable piece of work. Nicely sewn, tightly woven—a low-slung tent perfectly suited for two people hiding from the elements. I couldn't identify the cloth. Alpaca? Vicuña? It was soft to the touch but lacked the stretchiness of the various camelids' wool. It was also closer in weave. I have to admit that in some senses I didn't really care who had made it; all I wanted was a warm place to sleep.

Without speaking, Aeslu and I set it up. We stamped out an area in the snow, buried some pegs, anchored the lines with chunks of ice, and raised the tent without much difficulty. Aeslu looked at the results of our handiwork, then set to work fixing dinner.

I was so tired that I just sat near the tent and watched. "Are you all right?" I asked.

"I suppose I am."

She stood near the front of the tent and stared at the cliff above us. From that shelf I couldn't see the mountain, since the cliff blocked our view. Another sight rose before us, though: the mountains to the west. The sun had set by then. The sky retained a little light. The sunset was the simplest imaginable. The sky turned yellow, then pink, then blue again, a deeper blue than before. Soon the stars erupted.

I watched Aeslu a while, hoping she'd say something. She just crouched there. The Founders' Gear included an odd little stove. It consisted of a ceramic pot filled with a waxy substance, a perforated bronze cylinder about eight inches tall and six inches across to shield the pot, and a copper kettle designed to sit on the cylinder. The waxy substance looked and smelled flammable—some sort of fat. It caught fire easily even from a bit of the dry grass we'd brought along and now lit with a flint. And so it appeared that Aeslu's forebears had even provided us with hot meals for the climb. Calling them meals isn't an overstatement. What appeared initially to be unappealing blocks of pemmican—sweet-scented brownish stuff— turned out to expand into porridge when mixed with snow and heated. I tasted it reluctantly at first, then gobbled the entire bowlful that Aeslu gave me. Delicious. Not bad, especially considering almost four hundred years' cold storage.

We ate in silence. A few minutes after we'd both finished, Aeslu walked over to her pack, pulled out the thick vicuña blanket that would serve as her bedroll, and carried it to the tent. She pulled open the flap and crawled inside.

I sat outside a while longer. Her silence bothered me. She was exhausted, of course, and for good reason. I couldn't have held that against her. But her silence revealed more than exhaustion. What, exactly, I couldn't say. There was no point in finding out now.

Before the sky darkened completely, I walked closer to the *bergschrund.* I kept my distance from the edge. I looked over the glacier dropping away before me, the valley below, the mountains opposite, the sky now just a single shade lighter than the land. There was a light wind. I hesitated there, watched the land steeping in dusk, felt the wind ease for a moment, and stood motionless and without breathing. In that stillness I noticed what I've noticed before: that precisely such a stillness makes it possible to hear the passage of blood within my own inner ear: a rich, hot hiss, though all else here was ice and shadow.

6

The next morning we started up. We ate a quick breakfast, packed our gear, and scaled the cliff we had camped below that night.

As it turned out, the snow bridge had accomplished more than simply getting us across the *bergschrund* to the Mountain. It had also placed us more or less at the base of a prominent ridge angling up the peak from left to right. Finding that ridge was better luck than I'd thought possible at this stage of the climb—I'd expected at least a couple of days' steep, precarious ascent up the cliff—and we soon found ourselves in a much more favorable situation than earlier. The ridge would be far easier to climb than the cliff. Both Aeslu and I were delighted by the sight before us.

This isn't to say that the situation lacked difficulties or risks. The ridge wasn't quite a red carpet rolled out before us. It was essentially a vast jagged edge. It was the juncture of the Mountain's two westernmost flanks. From a distance—I'd seen it earlier, following the avalanche—this ridge resembled some kind of serrated cutting tool. A knife, perhaps, except that the blade was so irregular. An axe, then: something massive but sharp. Mountaineers even speak of a certain type of ridge as a knife-edge. I couldn't use the word for this one, however, especially once Aeslu and I made our way onto it: not when the blade itself was a hundred feet thick. It was more of a stone chopper than an axe.

We didn't take long finding our own delight a little premature. Even this easier route upward took all the effort and concentration we could muster. What had first appeared a relatively unbroken expanse of stone turned out to be a succession of stone slabs, boulders, and pinnacles wedged one after another to form the ridge. Working our way up required finding a path among these adjacent bulks of rock. In itself that wasn't too difficult. When we were lucky, the uneven nature of the terrain worked to our advantage. Sometimes big blocks formed a V whose groove we could scramble up without much difficulty. Sometimes smaller rocks—not discrete chunks, but the exposed tips of what must have been huge pillars—created a kind of staircase for us to ascend. But often as not it wasn't so easy. For one thing, the slabs and boulders lay cluttered with lots of smaller rocks. Fragments of all sizes: everything from fist-sized pieces to gravel. All of this rubble made our task more difficult because it made the surface underfoot so slippery. At best it was messy; at worst it was treacherous. I slipped time after time. I never took any bad falls, but I kicked lots of stuff loose. When I went first, this stuff skittered down toward Aeslu. When she went first, the same thing happened to me. Whoever followed caught the worst of it.

Yet I suppose that what mattered was simply that we got going. We were on our way. Despite all the reasons for this climb not to happen, it was happening. Despite all the reasons for Aeslu and me to stop short, we had continued. That ridge was at least a start.

All day we fumbled our way upward, somehow surviving our own clumsiness, ignorance, and incompetence. By late afternoon it seemed hard to believe both that we'd gained so much altitude and that we could ever have doubted our ability to climb.

7

"Why did you join Forster Beckwith?" I asked her.

"*Join* him?" Aeslu asked in return.

I knew her well enough to know that she understood my question. At least she understood the words; they weren't what tripped her. Something else puzzled her, even baffled her: perhaps simply that I could ask this question at all. Yet I persisted. "You were with him for months. You went where he went and did what he did. You helped him ransack the Mountain Land."

"I did not—"

"Aeslu, there were witnesses. All kinds of people saw what happened."

"Please believe me—"

"It's been hard to believe what you've said when so many people contradicted you."

She fell silent. We were sitting on a slab of rock that jutted out from the cliff. The sun was blocked (as it would be for half the day yet) by the Mountain at our backs. We felt cold. Some sort of sour tea brewed from tangled roots helped take off the chill. I suppose we could have gotten up, moved around, stirred up some heat in our flesh and bones, but we didn't. We sat side by side staring out toward the splintery peaks opposite the Mountain.

Then at last she spoke. "Before the Sun and the Moon, and in the name of the Founders, Ossonnal and Lissallo, whose laws I serve, I swear to you that I never joined the Man of Darkness. I admit that I was with him for many Moon-spans, just as you claim.

It is true as well that I went where he went, and in that sense I did what he did. Yet never did I join him. Never did I serve him. Never did I act to advance his cause. Never! Quite the contrary: I sought to stop him. I did everything within my power to defeat him and the Umbrage who did his bidding. Doubt me if you will. Listen to whatever witnesses, as you call them. I can only tell you the truth. I did everything to oppose the Man of Ignorance—" Here she faltered, as if catching her breath. "—to protect the Mountain-Drawn—" Again Aeslu hesitated. "—and to join you, my Jassikki—"

I waited, fighting the temptation to prod her. Perhaps I would have succumbed if she had spoken more theatrically. Yet despite the intensity of Aeslu's words, she stated them in the most matter-of-fact, almost casual tone. She wasn't one to throw around a lot of emotion. I'd seen her cry three or four times, all but just one of those times a shedding of nearly subliminal tears. Only her inability to continue revealed her depth of feeling. Against my own expectations, I found it easier to believe her under these circumstances than if she'd clung to me and begged for understanding.

Of course since then—in fact, a long time after that conversation at the Mountain's base—I've read accounts substantiating what she claimed. Her own *Chronicle of the Last Days* is first and foremost among them. At the time, however, I didn't really know what to believe. But of course Aeslu didn't know, either; my own choices over the past months must have baffled her. So all we knew was what we heard from one another—and, too, the evidence we saw spread out over the glacier below.

"We are such fools," I said at last.

8

Where were we? That was a question we kept asking but couldn't answer.

The odd thing was this: although we stood right there on the Mountain, we knew almost nothing specific about our situation. The Mountain loomed right before us, yet we couldn't see it. We were too close to see something so big. We could look up the cliff but never quite make sense of what we saw, for at such a steep angle the distances foreshortened till we lost all sense of perspective. We could look down or sideways, too, but at once we ran into the same problem. Of course we could gaze off the precipice at other mountains and at the valleys between them. That provided some sort of context, I suppose. But as for getting a sense of where we were on the surface of the Mountain—we just didn't know. In the most practical terms this meant that even while groping our way upward, we were just guessing at the route. The climb was an exercise in ignorance. We knew no more about what we were doing than ants do as they scurry about on a boulder.

We checked the Mountain Stone, of course. We did everything possible to determine our whereabouts. What cliff had we scrambled up? What ridge had we reached? Were we on our way toward the summit? Or were we headed up a dead end of our own devising? The Stone was less help in answering these questions than I'd expected. I shouldn't have been surprised, though. We could have been almost anywhere on the Mountain. The cliff could have been almost any of its cliffs. The ridge could have been almost any of its ridges. The Stone wasn't an oracle—just a map. Like all maps, it needed some information before it gave any back. The Stone needed us to provide some sort of reference point before it could tell us where we were. But we had no reference points. All we had was the granite cliff before us, the hand-and foot holds that took us upward, and the undeniable sensation that we were leaving behind everything we understood.

One afternoon, though—this must have happened about three days after Aeslu and I had started up—we were taking a rest. The climbing had been good that day: a strenuous but fairly straightforward scramble up the ridge. Our effort consisted of scaling a seemingly endless series of stone slabs, some of them badly fractured, others monolithic and intact. I wouldn't call it easy work, but it felt less overwhelming than what we'd faced earlier. If nothing else, we could at least consider each slab a separate problem. Some were relatively small and well-channeled with cracks, thus easy. Some were relatively large and smooth, thus difficult. Either way, we could surmount the obstacle, rest briefly, and proceed. During one such interval of rest we reached an unexpected insight.

Aeslu and I sat side by side on a rock. Typical of such times, neither of us spoke. We had been climbing well—better than expected, even—but we were tired. It seemed best simply to sit there in silence. I pulled out the leather flask that served as my water bottle, I drank, and I handed the flask to Aeslu. She drank, too. At some point she turned to her pack and started rummaging about for something. I thought perhaps she was hungry. Instead of pulling out food, though, she pulled out the Mountain Stone. She set it before us on the rock.

Both of us stayed silent. We simply gazed at the Stone.

One of the remarkable things about the Mountain Stone was that the real Mountain, the Mountain Made of Light, never seemed to diminish it. The Mountain Stone was small enough that I could cover it with one hand. The Mountain itself was so vast that I'd never really seen it—not the whole thing, only certain faces or angles. Yet somehow they seemed to be one and the same. Both were baffling, bewildering, entrancing. The differences between them appeared to be more a matter of scale than of substance. So it was again. Aeslu and I stared at the Mountain Stone as it glinted in the light cast off by the greater self it represented.

Aeslu picked up the Stone and placed it in the palm of her left hand. She raised it slightly, held it between us. Then she said, "Look."

I did just that. Right away I sensed what she intended. The ridge we'd been climbing—a ridge that angled upwards at about a forty-five-degree angle till it intersected with a cliff to our right—bore a remarkable resemblance to one facet of the Mountain Stone. Held at the proper angle, the Stone seemed to line up so persuasively with the Mountain that some other features soon made sense. If we had possessed a map of the Mountain Made of Light, we would have needed to orient the map at some point—to line it up properly in relation to geological features. We didn't have a map in any ordinary sense. To the degree that we had one, though, the Mountain Stone was our map. What Aeslu had just accomplished was orienting the map.

And by this means we could see where we were, where we wanted to go, and—or so we hoped—how to get there.

9

I won't say that what followed came easily or fast. On the contrary, Aeslu and I struggled day after day to surmount the obstacles before us. We labored to climb each of the slabs and boulders making up that ridge. Now and then we suffered small accidents. At least once a day we miscalculated and found ourselves up a cul-de-sac that required immediate retreat. All too often we made foolish mistakes. Yet somehow we prevailed, we avoided committing any fatal errors, we made more and more efficient progress. In short, we worked our way higher.

Neither of us was an accomplished climber. Despite Aeslu's having lived her life in the High Realm, she was little more than a novice. Her membership among the Heirs had limited her to a more theoretical than practical sort of mountaineering. She knew much about Rixtir history and mythic lore, little about the actual task of climbing a peak. At the same time, she couldn't have grown up in the Mountain Land without developing certain skills and—perhaps this was even more important—having a gut sense about what climbing demands. Just getting from one valley to the next required agility and stamina. She was also accustomed to the harsh Andean environment. Not just accustomed: Aeslu was literally built for that climate and terrain. The Mountain-Drawn people had adapted physiologically over the millennia to high altitude and cold weather. Although she wasn't nearly as short as most of the Rixtir women, she wasn't tall, either—at least not by Western standards—maybe five three or four. Yet otherwise Aeslu's features were typical of her ethnic group. Wide torso. Strong legs and arms. Broad, powerful hands. Huge lung capacity. I can't imagine a body type better suited to climbing. Despite her relative newness to the task before us, Aeslu wasn't what I call limited. She was simply inexperienced.

And I? I wasn't inexperienced, yet what experience I'd gained over the years hadn't really prepared me for the Mountain Made of Light. Not climbing in the Berkshires, certainly, where I'd scrambled up crags as a boy. Not on the Shawangunk cliffs that taught me most of what I knew about rock climbing. Not in the Rockies—though I'd learned a lot there about getting about in the wilderness, finding routes, pacing myself, and so forth. Not in the Alps, either, which provided the challenges most nearly comparable to this one. Not even on the other climbs I'd attempted earlier in the Andes. The Mountain was simply a peak of an altogether different order of magnitude. Perhaps nothing could have prepared me for what it demanded. That's not to say that I'd wasted my time doing what I'd done in the past—just that what prepared me to climb the Mountain was climbing the Mountain.

Our effort on the ridge was a time of breakthroughs, but not breakthroughs in a dramatic sense. Nothing we did gave us any reason to believe that our quest would succeed. The Mountain still loomed above us so high that we couldn't even hope to see the summit; so wide that we couldn't take it in without turning almost the full span from left to right; so steep that as the clouds swept by it, the Mountain seemed ready to tip over at any moment and crush us. No, I don't mean breakthroughs in any way that made either Aeslu or me optimistic, much less confident, about what we were doing. I mean breakthroughs simply in that against all expectation, we managed to proceed. At a time when we thought we'd falter, we kept going.

The Mountain Stone was one reason why. We'd found out where we were. We had a sense of where to go. If nothing else, the discovery that the Stone and the Mountain itself truly matched one another—and especially that the route etched in quartz matched our ridge—at least freed us from wondering if our exertions were altogether pointless. The Mountain Stone gave us at least a flicker of hope that we might reach our goal.

But the climb itself was what gave us hope. This probably sounds self-evident. We climbed. We gained altitude. It was more than just the progress we made, however. The climb did more than simply taking us higher and higher; the climb also strengthened us. If each day had left us progressively weaker, then Aeslu and I would have felt no cause for delight. What happened was just the opposite, though: we grew stronger, more agile, more supple, more resilient to the weather and the demands of our quest. The climb itself made us climb better, faster, more confidently.

I suppose to some degree we simply acclimated and grew accustomed to the ordeal at hand. To put it in contemporary parlance, we got in shape. Yet even at the time I suspected that something else was at work, something other than the healthful side effects of our own efforts. The stock of provisions that Aeslu had selected may deserve some of the credit. The Founders' Gear included an array of peculiar but salutary foods. Most of them were what I'd call pemmican— various sorts of fruit, grain, and dried meat pounded together into dense blocks. They were almost indigestible if eaten straight, but when boiled in water they reconstituted into a delicious stew. What their ingredients might have been, exactly, I can't say. Millet of some sort? Dessicated potatoes from any of several dozen native species? Venison? Sugar cane? I couldn't even identify most of these substances. All I know is that Andean peoples have excelled in preserving food for millennia—some of the pre-Incan cultures even invented the process we now call freeze-drying—and I suppose these provisions were yet another instance in a long tradition. What mattered to us at the time was simply that we had a compact source of nutrition with us. The food was often tasty, which boosted our spirits at a time of great physical hardship. It sustained us, nurtured us, even healed us. Best of all, the Founders' provisions were so dense that they kept us well-fed without requiring periodic descents to haul up more food from stockpiles we might have cached below. What we carried on our backs was by all appearances sufficient to get us to our goal.

Yet the climbing was hard. None of it would require extraordinary skill by today's standards, but back then what we did was unusual. The angle of the rock was less a problem than the relative scarcity of fissures in it. We simply didn't have much to take hold of. Other climbers of that era would have found it difficult, almost impossible, to find places for anchoring themselves with their pitons. We would have, too.

This is where something worked to our advantage. The Founders' Gear was different from Western mountaineering equipment of those times. What Ossonnal and Lissallo had used as hardware didn't bear much resemblance to ironmongery made during the twenties. Apparently they hadn't gone around pounding pitons into the cracks when they climbed; they secured themselves to the rock with devices much more like what contemporary climbers call their "protection"—all sorts of hooks, nuts, and gadgets of irregular shapes that prevented serious falls if they slipped. Of course Aeslu and I didn't know exactly how the Founders employed all of these devices; that cache of gear didn't include an instruction manual. But little by little we discovered what to do. That was the beauty of this equipment: in many ways we could simply figure out what was what, and how to use it.

Even while using the Founders' Gear, though, we proceeded by means of techniques already well-established in the West for fifty years. One of us led. I led more often at first; later, we took turns about equally. With a rope securely tied about my waist, I headed up. Aeslu, having passed a length of the same rope around her own waist, sat in a secure place and played the coil out as I climbed. I climbed without direct use of any tools—that is, I didn't work my way up by any means except my own hands and feet. Now and then I'd note a crack or hole in the rock I was climbing, however; if it seemed well-located and secure, I'd insert one of the devices into it. These were mostly hooklike things of various shapes and sizes. Some resembled what climbers today would call chockstones—metal plugs to jam into the cracks. Whether hooks, plugs, or something else, these devices had short loops of rope attached to them, loops that I'd then secure to my own rope by means of a carabiner—essentially a big metal clip that can open and close. Using these several devices wouldn't stop me from slipping off a hand- or foothold; if I were to fall, however, Aeslu would pull her end of the rope tight around her waist until friction stopped the rope. This is what was called, and is still called, a belay. Then as now, one climber belaying another wouldn't eliminate the possibilty of a fall. Better a short fall than a long one, though, and thus the belay techniques and equipment add a margin of safety over climbing unbelayed.

The Founders' Gear widened that margin still further. I felt far safer using the Founders' Gear than the twenties-era implements—Western-style ice-axes, crampons, rope, and so forth—that Forster and I had brought with us to the Mountain Land. In fact, I hadn't seen anything like the Founders' Gear before, and since then I never saw anything of comparable effectiveness until just recently.

As for what it was—what metals and fibers made up the Founders' Gear, and what techniques of craftsmanship made it possible—I have no idea. It seemed clear, however, that Ossonnal and Lissallo had known more than even their descendants among the Rixtirra had assumed.

10

We saw an odd sight from the ridge.

The weather remained overcast; the rainy season wasn't quite over yet. Even so, the overcast had started to ease. Clouds were now abundant rather than inescapable. Most days dawned relatively clear, then clouded up fast. Sleet and snow flurries struck without warning, but they were by no means continuous, as before. Now and then each day—most often before noon—Aeslu and I could actually gaze out from the Mountain Made of Light and see the High Realm spread before us.

After a few days' climbing we'd gained enough altitude to see over the lower peaks surrounding the Mountain. These were the peaks that both the Heirs and the Umbrage had circled in an effort to find their goal. I don't know how tall they were. Sixteen, seventeen, eighteen thousand feet? All I know is that before long Aeslu and I could look right over them. What we saw on the other side was, of course, the Mountain Land.

But not the view we expected. Not the velvety gray-green tundra I'd seen so often while gazing into these Andean valleys; instead, great palls of billowing smoke.

"What's all this?" I asked Aeslu.

"The harvest," she told me. "The harvest is almost over. The farmers are burning their sheaves."

Yet the smoke was so dense—at times spiraling up in tornado-shaped cones—that I couldn't feel convinced by Aeslu's words.

"Are you sure?"

"It is the harvest festival."

"You don't think there's some sort of—"

"No, it is only the harvest," she insisted. "The harvest. The harvest."

Yet as Aeslu gazed out over the gulf and the billowing valleys beyond, her expression belied her own reassurances: a look of sadness beyond the possibility of tears.

11

More than once it struck me, and struck me hard, that I knew nothing about this woman. I'd met her maybe ten months earlier; I'd endured a sequence of extreme events with her; I'd made love with her once. Yet I had no idea who she was. Almost everything I *did* know derived from what you might call the Rixtir mythic assumptions: that she was the Moon's Stead, and so forth. But as for knowing her as a person, as a human being—as opposed to knowing her as the focal point of tribal assumptions—I knew nothing at all.

And so I watched her, listened to her, tried to make sense of her. I watched the care she took in climbing. The precision of her movements in using each tool. The strength with which she wielded them. The delight she took in getting them to do what needed to be done. I watched her observing the landscape around us. Not just the devastation below, but also the expanse of the Mountain above. How she examined each cliff and ridge from our limited perspective. How she noted any features revealed under the changing conditions of light and weather. How she waited, waited, waited, as if the Mountain would suddenly explain itself and justify her lifelong patience. Most of all I watched her watching back. What did she expect from me? What did she want? What would she accept? What would she allow me to be?

I listened, too. Listened to her speech, to her precision both in her own languages and in mine. Listened to the words themselves. Listened to the silence between them. Aeslu spoke English so well—not just grammatically, but with great control and nuance—I sometimes had to remind myself that I was almost certainly the first native speaker she'd ever met. When she said, "You climbed well today," I tended to take the words at face value. Then at once I'd remind myself that however well-pronounced the words, what lay within them were Rixtir ideas and Rixtir emotions I couldn't altogether grasp, much less understand. It's as though words were the exoskeletons of thoughts—thoughts almost certain to perish, shrivel, and disappear if I picked too hard at what protected them.

Small wonder, then, that I tried to make sense of her, tried to the point of preoccupation, but never quite succeeded. Yet how could I have done anything else but try?

12

Something else preoccupied me at the time.

To put it bluntly, what grounds did I have for making this climb? By what right should I have been working my way up the Mountain while the Realm below erupted into flames?

I ask the question as I do—what right did *I* have—because Aeslu certainly had her own agenda. Whatever else she believed, Aeslu was convinced of her right and responsibility to be there. She saw herself as fated to make the climb. I don't think she ever so much as entertained the notion of any alternative. The climb was simply what Aeslu had been born to do.

As for me, though—that's another question. At some point during the previous months, I might well have considered myself fated to climb the Mountain. Not right then, however. I felt like little more than a Johnny-come-lately. An interloper. A poseur who had bungled everything else among the Mountain-Drawn yet now presumed to tackle the grandest task these people could have granted me. What right did I have to be there? The easy answer would have been: precious little!

But the real question should have been what alternative I had. Nothing I'd done to save the Mountain Land had saved it. On the contrary, my efforts had been little more than a disaster for the place and its people. Having done so much damage, what could justify indulging myself in the lofty task of the climb? Yet ultimately the troubles I'd unleashed were precisely what prompted me to proceed. There was simply nothing else to be done at that point. The suffering and destruction I'd unleashed made it all the more important to do the one thing capable of justifying precisely that suffering and destruction.

What I'm saying is this: the climb wasn't necessarily a privilege. It was a task I felt obliged to complete. It was my last-ditch effort to salvage something from the wreckage of the Mountain Land.

13

Soon we had nearly reached the culmination of the ridge we'd been climbing. The ridge angled up to the cliff; the cliff rose almost straight up from there. Simple as that. And in seeing the terrain change before us in such stark terms, neither Aeslu nor I felt any doubt that one phase of the climb would soon end while another—one of an altogether different sort—would soon begin.

We approached this transition with a mix of delight and fear. On the one hand, we had already ascended far higher than we'd thought possible when we first set out; we had mastered a particular sort of climb; we were now drawing near to a genuine milestone. It's no wonder we felt pleased with ourselves. At the same time, we could see what we were in for. The ridge had been difficult enough—every day was a series of close calls and small accidents—but the cliff would unquestionably prove far more difficult. It wasn't just that the cliff rose at a much more acute angle. What alarmed us wasn't so much what we saw as what we couldn't see, for the cliff vanished into the clouds that customarily hovered over the Mountain. We didn't really know what we were getting into. We couldn't fool ourselves, however, into believing that the task would be anything but more strenuous and far more dangerous than what we'd endured already.

How long had we been climbing? Sometimes I tried to figure it out alone, and sometimes I asked Aeslu's help, yet whatever we decided never quite made sense.

For one thing, neither of us could agree with the other.

"It has been five days," Aeslu said, "not counting today." She then proceeded to enumerate the days and to note what had taken place on each of them.

I felt sure she was mistaken. "You left one out. There was that day near the beginning when you slipped on the first pitch."

"Ah, yes. I remember now." But then she went on to argue that we hadn't forgotten one day but two. "There was another—the day when you dropped a coil of rope and had to climb down and fetch it."

We discussed the possibilities for a long time. How did this all add up? Six days? Seven? Six seemed most likely. Almost a week! All that just to fumble our way up a ridge which, if the Stone were accurate, was a mere ramp onto the main bulk of the Mountain itself.

In fact, I never felt altogether confident of our calculations no matter how meticulously we made them. The estimates always seemed too low. It baffled me to think that we might have been climbing just six days. Surely our struggle had lasted at least a week—maybe nine or ten days. Then I wondered how it could have been only ten. The climb seemed to have lasted much longer than that. Aeslu could name days and recount events, but what about all the other days and other events that somehow slipped by, quick as the rocks we sometimes dislodged?

I tried to remember what had preceded this climb. To my astonishment, I couldn't. Not in detail. Not with any vividness. I could recall the war, of course, and before it my youth in Massachusetts. Yet both phases of the past seemed to have happened so long before that I questioned whether I'd lived through them or merely imagined them. They seemed far too distant to be possible. Remote. Intangible. Insubstantial. Even the preceding months—all the jumbled events that had ultimately led through the Mountain Land to my presence on this peak—now appeared vague and uncertain. It was almost as if the avalanche had swept away so much of the past that only the present remained.

All I felt sure of was the climb. The textures of stone against my skin. The hiss of the rope playing out. The sharp odor of the wind. The sight of Aeslu working her way up the ridge ahead of me. The solidity of stone against my side and the softness of her hand when one of us reached out to assist the other. Nothing but the climb had much substance. At times I wondered if I'd ever done anything but climb.

The cliff loomed. Within another day at most we'd reach it; then we'd face a decision about whether we could risk continuing.

Aeslu was convinced that our success up to that point guaranteed our ability to proceed. "Ossonnal and Lissallo have marked the path," she told me. "The Mountain Stone will show us the way."

I wasn't nearly so confident.

First of all, I wasn't sure what our success to date really meant; I knew still less what, if anything, it guaranteed about the future. The Mountain Stone did indeed seem to help us on our way. But was it really proof that Ossonnal and Lissallo had preceded us? That they had reached the Summit? That they had established a refuge there? The truth was that the Stone might have been less a map of the Founders' route than of their descendents' wishful thinking. The Stone didn't necessarily provide us with a route to the Summit any more than Dante's *Divine Comedy* showed the way from Hell up Mount Purgatory to Heaven.

Second, even if the Stone showed us the way, our climbing skills would have to rise to the occasion. We had barely managed to get this far. What were the odds that we could succeed in surmounting obstacles many times more difficult?

But of course I couldn't express my doubts so bluntly. Aeslu's confidence had provided a momentum capable of carrying us far higher than we would have gone by relying on my doubts alone. No matter how unrealistic, her confidence offered a lifeline as crucial to our ascent as the ropes we trusted to break a fall.

14

That afternoon, within a few hours' climb of where the cliff began, Aeslu called out to me. I'd been leading at the time; I was about eight or ten yards ahead of her. The slope wasn't especially steep—steep enough, though, that we were heading up in our usual way. One of us led while the other belayed. On that particular pitch, I happened to be leading. Yet somehow—perhaps on account of the bulging slab I clung to just then—Aeslu had caught sight of something even though I was far closer to it than she.

"What is that?" she asked.

I looked down and saw her pointing up toward me. "What is what?"

"That thing up there."

Gazing upward to find what her finger pointed to, I saw the stone slab curving off to the left, where it met another slab of about the same size and shape. Ice had accumulated in the juncture between the two slabs. Rock and ice. Otherwise I saw nothing. "I don't see what you mean."

At once Aeslu abandoned her belay stance and started up after me. I would have objected under other circumstances—she was leaving me essentially unprotected from a fall. But the slab wasn't very steep. We had maintained the procedure of alternate belays just for good measure. Besides, Aeslu never deviated from whatever we'd agreed to do without good reason; she wouldn't have come after me like that just for fun. So without objection I watched her approach. Within a few minutes we were together right where I'd stopped.

"Something is up there," she said when she reached me.

"I don't know what you mean."

Her only response was to head up again.

For several moments I watched her climbing. Bits of gravel and grit sprinkled down on me. Then I set off, too, catching up with her just as she slowed and stopped.

"Look."

Aeslu had found something on the slab. Or rather, something bolted into the juncture of that slab with the one above. I stared at it for a long time. My eyes told me right away what it was, but my mind took a while to accept what I saw.

It was a piece of rope. A piece of rope similar—in fact, almost identical—to the sort that Aeslu and I had scrounged from the Founders' Gear. Yet it was different in one obvious and striking way. It was old. How old, I couldn't say. All I knew was that wind, snow, and perhaps rockfall had torn off most of whatever had hung here at some point; the elements and the passage of time had left only this mere snippet. Just a shred. I doubt it exceeded a few feet in length. The free end had unravelled. Yet no matter how flimsy and damaged, that rope strengthened our grasp on the Mountain as firmly as if it had been woven of steel.

15

"This is what I have always believed," Aeslu told me, more and more excited—no, exhilarated—with each word she spoke. "The Founders came this way. Ossonnal and Lissallo climbed the Mountain, reached the Summit, and built a refuge for their people." She grasped that shred of rope in one hand while caressing it with the other. "What I have always hoped for is true."

"Aeslu—"

"It is *true,* can't you see? *True!*" She held out the rope: the simplest, most convincing refutation of my doubts.

In some ways I found it hard to argue with her. The rope itself—its presence on the Mountain—was undeniable. Its age was pretty obvious, too. Not just age: the type as well. I'd seen a lot of rope in the High Realm, and this piece resembled only what came from the so-called Founders' Gear. It wasn't any of the Heirs' innumerable kinds of ritual rope; it wasn't the human-hair rope from the Web; it wasn't any kind of Western rope. Its appearance both in age and type made a strong case that it had been dangling there for a long, long time.

Did this mean that everything Aeslu claimed about it was true? That this rope proved that Ossonnal and Lissallo themselves had put it there? That they had made it all the way to the Summit? That they had established the refuge Aeslu felt sure we'd find there?

Hardly. This bit of rope didn't guarantee that all her other assumptions—or any of them—were valid.

Someone other than the Founders might have come this way. Even if Ossonnal and Lissallo had once used a rope now reduced to this vestige, they might not have proceeded to the Summit. At this point we couldn't say one way or the other.

This didn't stop Aeslu from believing what she believed. Should I have been surprised? Since childhood, she had known with all her heart that Ossonnal and Lissallo, the Founders of her race, had set off long ago to climb the Mountain Made of Light. Here, now, was the first concrete evidence that Aeslu had ever seen to support her beliefs. And not just Aeslu: the first evidence *anyone* had seen. Rope. Real rope. Rope from the Founders' time. Rope of the sort that the Founders themselves had used. Any arguments I could have made were, in Aeslu's eyes, the merest quibbles.

But in saying what I've said, I sound more distant from this incident than I felt at the time. I wasn't really standing back from the situation and examining it, analyzing it, judging it. In fact, what we discovered that afternoon affected me almost as much as it affected Aeslu. Not in the same way, of course. I hadn't subscribed to those beliefs my whole life long. I hadn't soaked for years in the Rixtir mythology. Yet I wasn't immune to it, either. For nine months I'd waded deeper and deeper into what the Mountain-Drawn believed—how they saw the world. I'd floundered in the depths of their beliefs; I'd nearly drowned; I'd ended up tossed on the shore half-dead. But there I was. It wasn't by accident that I was climbing the Mountain.

This much we knew, however: we'd found a piece of rope. Whose rope? I didn't know. Put there en route to what ultimate success or failure? I knew that still less. Whatever else, though, this relic renewed not only Aeslu's confidence, but mine as well, that our exertions would prove worthwhile.

Within a half-hour of having made our discovery, we headed up again, climbing quickly, eagerly, and without the encumbrance of belays.

16

We climbed all that afternoon, reached the cliff we'd been approaching, and, after a chilly night huddled together, awoke to the clearest day we'd seen during the whole climb thus far. From our little roost we could gaze out over the ridge we'd finished climbing, over the glacier below, over the peaks beyond, over the valleys of Lorssa and Leqsiffaltho. The Mountain Land lay steeped in its own shadows. Only the tips of the highest summits before us had started to catch the sun's first rays. Yet within a few hours we felt ready to head up again.

It almost didn't matter to us that the climb would probably confront us with a far more difficult task now than what we'd faced so far. In our minds, the very fact of its difficulty proved that we were that much farther along. And the Mountain Stone, when we checked it, revealed that the cliff before us was unquestionably the next step on our path toward the Summit. Knowing that we were on track would have been enough to spur us on. Having discovered that bit of rope one day before, though, made us almost uncontrollably eager to proceed. We couldn't wait to pack our camp and head up again.

I won't go into detail about the start of our climb that day. The task before us was certainly harder and more dangerous than what we'd undertaken earlier. The cliff wasn't as nearly vertical as it looked from below, but it was steeper than anything Aeslu and I had attempted so far; and though it wasn't as smooth a surface, either—we found abundant cracks for hand-

and footholds—it was demanding all the same. We made much more laborious progress than before. We tired faster and rested more often. We advanced more slowly and more carefully, too, since the least slip here would be fatal. Yet somehow we managed. Within the first hour we had already gained several hundred feet.

Then everything changed.

The only warning was so incongruous that it wasn't any warning at all: a spattering sound. Hearing it, I thought of hot fat—doughnuts in a vat. But Aeslu had already screamed her warning.

I was too startled to be afraid. Clinging to the cliff, I just pulled myself closer, hands in a fissure, my whole body tense. Aeslu was somewhere above me. Nothing happened for a moment except for the rope tugging at my waist. Keeping a grip got more and more difficult. I glanced upward.

Rocks were all around—above me, around me, to the right and left—chunks, fragments, little pieces, all at once, bouncing and scattering. I turned away, averting my gaze, only to see a football-sized rock strike a granite outcropping fifteen or twenty feet in front of me and smash into a hundred pieces. Fragments sprayed in every direction. A few little bits struck me, but everything happened so fast that my fear came only afterward. Then some small chunks came down, clattering. Then big ones: blocks tumbling end over end. One passed so close that I felt its wake of air nudge me as it passed.

I hugged the cliff so hard that I wanted to merge with it, seep into the fissures, disappear.

Silence.

Then shouts from above. The rope tightened again, almost pulling me off the cliff.

After waiting a long time, I tilted back as carefully as possible. I looked around.

Above me I saw the cliff, the rope quivering, a brown shape. Below, the cliff also. That was all. The rocks had vanished. I kept expecting a crash, some kind of finality, but there was none.

Then more shouts.

I tried answering, but neither of us seemed able to hear the other. I could see her trying to twist around and look toward me without falling.

She called out again. I still couldn't grasp the words. She seemed unhurt, though, and I took comfort at least in that. But how long could we stay out in the open before one of us ended up getting hit?

Gravel started pattering down: first a little off to my right, then lots everywhere, a dry rainstorm. Wincing to keep out the grit, I couldn't see for a moment or two; I almost lost my grip again. Something else: a smell. The rockfall left a smell in passing. I turned this way and that, sniffing. Stone against stone. It was *sweet*. I couldn't explain that smell, but I knew it at once. Bread, egg bread, muffins—something so incongruous I had to stifle a laugh. I found myself transported abruptly to my mother's kitchen in Northampton, Massachusetts, where the great cast-iron, wood-burning stove almost constantly emanated the aromas of her baking. . . .

When I came back to reality—clinging to the cliff—the jolt nearly knocked me loose. To be here, not there. To want much and have little. That smell was hopeless: a taunt, a tease, a promise without any possibility of fulfillment.

We managed to reach safety. I mean in a relative sense, of course: "safety" was an ice-coated ledge with a slab overhanging it. Both Aeslu and I got struck a few times by small stones before we got out of harm's way. Yet the overhang made even a cramped ledge seem like paradise.

"Are you all right?" I asked her.

"I think so."

"No injuries?"

"Little ones."

Even as we spoke, two big chunks plummeted past. They huffed as they fell: the sound a rowboat makes in parting the water. A few moments later we heard a vast roar as they struck the ridge below, the same ridge where Aeslu and I had camped the previous night.

We set to work securing ourselves to the ledge. First we pulled up our packs, since they were connected to ropes but waiting for us below. Luckily, no rocks hit them—the impact would have split them apart and might even have yanked Aeslu or me down, too. Then we inserted five or six anchors into various cracks in the rock, ran ropes through the anchors, and tied ourselves to the ropes. If nothing else, this arrangement served as a kind of safety belt in that precarious place. We fastened our gear as well: anchored both packs to the ledge.

"This is insane!" I muttered, settling in.

"Why is this happening?" Aeslu asked. Even without her explaining further, I understood what she meant: not a naive question about how the rockfall could be so impudent as to come down on *us,* but rather a puzzlement over why now rather than earlier. We had spent hours at the base of that cliff before heading up. There had been no rockfall. Then, in good weather—

Maybe that was it. The weather had warmed, cooled, and warmed again. The previous night's chill had frozen the cliff tight; then it thawed. It's a notorious hazard. The action of ice expanding is one of the great forces wearing down the mountains—even the Mountain Made of Light. Aeslu and I should have known better. We should have anticipated the consequences of venturing up this cliff at such a time. The worst rockfall generally occurs each day when the sun has a chance to shine on the cliff and thaw the ice that bound the rocks together overnight. This is why climbers usually try to climb in the early morning hours—or even at night—before all hell breaks loose. But Aeslu and I hadn't thought ahead far enough. Now we were in no-man's-land, trapped by an artillery barrage as severe as any I'd survived in France.

I explained the situation to Aeslu as best I could.

She grasped what I said at once. No, more than grasped—she accepted the situation as if this, too, were simply one of the hardships she had to face in undertaking our quest.

"How long will we have to stay here?" she asked.

"I don't know. At least till the rockfall lets up. It's often a question of temperature. This warm weather has loosened the cliff. Once it cools again, the face will stabilize."

"And if it does not—*stabilize*?"

"Don't worry."

"But what if?"

Three boulders shot passed just then, hurtling down without a sound. A long time later—they must have fallen all the way to the glacier—we heard the explosion of their impact.

"We'll have to face that later," I said.

17

The day passed slowly. All we could do was wait on our ledge. Once the sun cleared the overhang we felt some of its warmth, which boosted our spirits. Yet the same rays that warmed us also warmed the cliff. We ended up under siege for hours.

Most of what came down wasn't very substantial—bits and pieces, egg-sized chunks—but even a small stone can be lethal. Sometimes bigger rocks came down, too: blocks and slabs. When the rockfall eased, gravel rained down. I doubt that more than a half-hour elapsed without some sort of barrage.

Luckily, our ledge was an adequate bunker. It was about a yard deep and maybe nine feet wide: almost opulent under the circumstances. The overhang provided an upwardly slanting roof that could have spared us from anything but its own collapse. Apparently a block about the size of a pickup truck had simply cracked off at some point and dropped away. To secure us there, Aeslu placed more anchors and clipped each of us into a safety belt she devised. I felt like a dog on a tether, but captivity had its own consolations. I couldn't move more than a foot to my right or left; I couldn't move more than six inches forward. Good enough. It allowed a little freedom of movement without the constant risk of falling.

Odd: though we had nothing else to do, we didn't talk much. Perhaps we were just too scared. Not that we were in immediate danger—the rocks couldn't reach us there. But the magnitude of our dilemma wasn't easy to forget. How long could we hide out in our little bunker? One week, maybe two? I wasn't sure how long our supplies would last—the food was so dense I couldn't calculate how many meals it would provide—but I knew our water wouldn't hold up. Whatever we drank came from the ice and snow accumulated on the far ends of our ledge. Scraping it and melting it would keep us going a while. Once we used up that supply, though, we'd have to venture out. Thus the solution to our dilemma was obvious but difficult to contemplate. Even the quickest rappel down the cliff to the ridge below would have placed us in immediate and mortal danger. Small wonder, then, that neither of us wanted to talk about the situation.

But even at the time I felt that something else accounted for Aeslu's silence. She avoided my gaze. She kept her distance. Whatever we might have talked about earlier, something weighed us down—something as heavy as the stone slab overhead.

Afternoon faded to evening, evening to dusk. Typical for the late rainy season, clouds had materialized earlier, drifting west, obscuring most of our view. All we could see with any clarity were the rocks hurtling past. It wasn't a view we enjoyed. We had already laid out our bedrolls by nightfall; if nothing else, sleep gave us our one escape from confinement on the ledge. Small wonder, then, that darkness soothed more than alarmed us.

I lay there a long time, convinced that Aeslu was asleep, before the desire to speak overwhelmed the desire to let her rest. I whispered her name.

After a brief pause, I heard Aeslu sit up abruptly.

"Are you all right?"

"I think so. Are you?"

I wanted to reassure her—to say, Yes, I'm fine, everything will be all right—but I didn't reply.

"Jassikki?" Her shadow-form leaned forward slightly as if searching for me.

"I'm right here."

"It seems hard to believe this is happening."

"I know."

Now Aeslu fell silent. Although not distinctly, I could see her watching me.

"I didn't mean to upset you."

"It is not your fault. I was just thinking."

"About whether we can continue?"

"That—and whether we can get out alive."

"I'm thinking about that, too."

After another pause she asked, "Do you think we will?"

"I don't know."

I watched Aeslu watching me for a few seconds. I wanted to say something further—to reassure and comfort her—but I held off. I settled deeper into my blankets. Aeslu rustled around briefly, too. Then she lay back and eased over, nestling against me.

18

I couldn't shake a hunch that the Mountain was trying to kill us. Never mind that it was inanimate. The Mountain seemed capable of willfulness, even malice, all the same. It blocked our path with obstacles and treacherous conditions of every possible kind. It blasted us with wind, snow, and sleet. For days now it had bombarded us with rockfall. Given what we'd already faced, was it any surprise that I considered the Mountain intent on our destruction?

Of course I could have argued that the various difficulties we encountered and the hardships we endured were no evidence, much less proof, of any attitude the Mountain held toward us. We had chosen to enter a harsh realm; now we took the consequences. The Mountain was rock, ice, dirt, snow. Nothing more, nothing less. Any willfulness or malice we perceived there was nothing but our own delusions.

Or was it? Much had already happened to test even my habitual skepticism.

Earlier, climbing a gulley, I had noticed that the snow there was unusually white. I saw none of the stone fragments that studded the snow in so many other places. In short, I saw no signs of rockfall. The cliff overhanging this particular passageway was no doubt capable of unleashing rocks from time to time, but some quirk of geology—perhaps a diagonal stone ridge at the cliff's base—must have been ducting rockfall to the side. There was no sign that this way up would be dangerous to climb.

And so we climbed. Halfway up, though, a rock

came down. More accurately, a boulder. From the moment I caught sight of it bounding down, I knew it was big, probably at least half a yard in diameter. It came straight toward us. The boulder descended in great leaps, striking the snow in the gulley so hard each time that it gashed a trench there several feet deep, then took another leap till gravity brought it down again. All this happened so fast that neither Aeslu nor I had any chance even to warn each other. Luckily, we both saw it coming at the same time. Yet we reacted differently. Aeslu, taking the lead just then, dashed forward. At the same instant, I leaped backward. Under other circumstances, our contrary reflexes wouldn't have caused us any trouble; unfortunately, though, we happened to be roped together at the time. Aeslu's advance yanked me so hard that I stumbled, falling face-forward in the snow. My fall in turn threw Aeslu off balance, so she fell, too. The boulder shot straight toward us.

We wouldn't have needed a direct hit to kill us. If that boulder had merely snagged our rope, it would have yanked both of us to our doom.

But it didn't. The rock missed. It crashed into the gulley right where Aeslu would have been standing if she hadn't fallen; it gouged another trench in the snow; it bounded off again; and it alternately gouged and bounded its way down the snowfield until at last it disappeared over the edge. A long time after that—easily a full minute—we heard a noise like that of distant thunder.

Yet if the Mountain sometimes appeared intent on our destruction, it treated us at other times in an altogether different way. On more than one occasion Aeslu and I seemed on the verge of succumbing to the elements. The temperature dropped so far that we couldn't keep warm, or else great winds battered us so severely that we almost lost our hold on the Mountain; then, without warning, we found some sort of refuge, just as we had on the stone shelf we now clung to. At other times, having lost our way, we suddenly found an unexpected route opening up right ahead: a ramplike ledge on a cliff or a notch in a seemingly insurmountable buttress.

Two days before the rockfall pinned us down, the temperature had dropped and the wind whipped up so fast that we were chilled within minutes. We proceeded anyway. There wasn't much choice. We worked our way up the ridge to the base of a stone abutment. That outcropping at least gave us some shelter from the wind. We found somewhere to set up our bivouac.

There a new problem plagued us, though: the wind kept snuffing out Aeslu's fire-pots. Our concern wasn't even fixing a meal; it was more rudimentary than that. We were desperately thirsty. We obtained most of our water by melting snow. Eating snow or ice wouldn't have served the same purpose—it would have drained our body heat and, besides, wouldn't even have provided sufficient liquid. What we needed was simply water.

We hunkered down in all our cold-weather garb and waited for the wind to ease. No such luck.

Yet at one point, while gazing off to our right, Aeslu caught sight of something, disengaged from the cocoon of layers protecting her, and eased her way around a corner in the cliff for a closer look.

I was too exhausted to protest what she was doing. Though increasingly concerned about the pointlessness of her actions, I just watched her go.

Aeslu returned not long afterward. "Water!" she shouted. "Water is coming out of the cliff!"

To my surprise, she had discovered some sort of spring that gushed straight out of a cleft in the rock. Ice had formed below the spring itself—in fact, a great frozen cataract hanging more than a hundred feet down the cliff—yet the water itself was warm. Not tepid: warm. Warm enough to drink. Warm enough to mix with some of the food we'd brought along. Warm enough to quench our thirst, warm our flesh, lift our spirits. Warm enough to baffle us about the spring's own origins and, for that matter, about the Mountain's nature.

Was the Mountain trying to destroy us or sustain us? Both, perhaps? Or neither?

As with so much else about the Mountain, I didn't know. Sometimes the situation seemed clear-cut in one direction, sometimes in another, sometimes in yet another. Sometimes I felt foolish ascribing either malice or benevolence to the Mountain. Yet if those attributes were inappropriate, then surely indifference was, too.

Ultimately I didn't know what I was dealing with.

19

For hours I stared at the stone slab like a kid in a meadow gazing up at the clouds. I found things there: animals, faces, landscapes. I saw a boat and boarded the boat and traveled down a river to a town. I wandered through the town staring at the streets and stores. I ate dinner at a restaurant where the food was hot and the lights warm and yellow and the waitress friendly. I went home with the waitress and made love with her, and afterward the bedsheets had the same rumpled look as the slab before me. I stared at the rock till it became a map of Italy, streaks of dark minerals for the rail lines, flecks of something shiny for the cities. Then the rock became the window in a train compartment, the Tuscan hills going by, poplars, villages, olive trees in the mist; and I left the train, walked along a road, spoke in passing to stocky black-garbed peasants. An old man carrying a hoe greeted me, and he looked so old that his wrinkles reminded me of the stone and returned me to it. I kept watching the stone till it became a canvas, the picture on it a mere sketch—contours, textures, shades of gray on white—which I then painted every color I could imagine, jungle greens, fire yellows and reds, eggplant purple, water blue, dirt brown.

This rock wasn't what I'd expected to find on the Mountain. It wasn't granite—wasn't the sparkly gray-white rock I'd encountered throughout the Mountain Land, but was something much darker instead—often charcoal gray, at times almost black. It crumbled far more easily than granite, too, so that the expanses of snow right below a cliff often ended up dark from fallen fragments. If I'd been a better geologist than I was, I might have made sense of what I saw at the time. But I wasn't, so I didn't. I could only guess at what I was dealing with. Basalt? Gneiss? Shale? I knew the names but little or nothing of what they meant. Oddly, I knew more about these rocks from the Rixtir standpoint. *Newmoon-stone, which looms and glows, puffed up with borrowed fire. Frost star-stone, which sparkles like the sky on a chilly night. Smoke rain-stone, the darkest stone of all.* For our purposes at the time, however, I didn't know enough about either the Lowland or the Rixtir schemes to grasp what I saw surrounding me. I wasn't thinking about geology at all.

What accounted for my state of mind? The altitude, perhaps? We must have reached a level of about 18,000 or 19,000 feet. That was probably the highest I'd ever been, though not by much. After almost ten months in the Mountain Land, I was nothing if not acclimated. I won't deny that some sort of altitude sickness might have been affecting me. Enough to derange me somehow? I don't know.

Was it hunger, then? We weren't starving by any means. We had lots of food with us—most of it the rich, concentrated fare that had come from the Founders' Gear. Living off it, I can't say I ever felt undernourished. The density itself took some getting used to, but if anything I found it overly rich. No, I don't think I was suffering from malnutrition.

So what was it that affected my thoughts so intensely? Hunger and the altitude combined? Something else altogether? I'd say it was probably several elements affecting me at once—elements that may in fact have been partly but not altogether physiological.

Years ago, back before the invention of scuba gear, deep-sea divers used to get in trouble when an imbalance of the gases in their blood distorted their thinking. They'd lose interest in the task at hand—sponge-collecting, scientific research, whatever—and gaze in ecstasy at the sights and sounds of the ocean swirling all around them. Sometimes they lost track of time, lost track of their location, lost track of everything. Sometimes they got so disoriented they even died. That was rapture of the deep.

Maybe there's rapture of the heights, too: some kind of similar combination of physiological and psychological effects. Not just symptoms—the imbalance of oxygen and carbon dioxide in the blood, and so forth. Something else as well. Something I didn't understand at the time and even now find difficult and frustrating to explain. Something that left me dazed, at times nearly anesthetized to our plight, no matter how desperate it might have been.

20

The rockfall continued. Its persistence baffled me. I'd never seen such heavy rockfall so early in the morning. Chunks came down even when the cliff should have been frozen solid. Most remarkably, some of the heaviest rockfall occurred at the worst possible times—that is, when Aeslu or I ventured off our ledge to have a look up the cliff. It was enough to make me paranoid about our situation. Once again I couldn't shake the feeling that the Mountain was a force, even a being, intent on rebuffing our approach. I worked hard to resist this notion but without much luck.

Stuck on that ledge, I soon stopped believing that Aeslu and I would get out of there alive. We could have made a run for it, I suppose, but soon enough we'd cross paths with a rock coming down at two hundred miles per hour. At the same time, staying put for too long would have had its own fatal consequences. What was the solution to our dilemma? I couldn't even guess. All I knew was that we'd been too impulsive. We'd overestimated our own skill; we'd simultaneously underestimated the difficulties we'd confront. How long would it take before we weakened, lost our will to struggle, succumbed to the elements, and died?

The views from the Mountain didn't do much to boost our spirits. Beyond the peaks surrounding the Mountain, we saw the Mountain Land in turmoil—or rather, we saw the billowing smoke that revealed the turmoil at its sources.

Aeslu said little about how these sights affected her,

but I saw her gaze out over the valley, at the peaks beyond the valley, at the Mountain Land spreading out beyond the peaks; and I saw that the vistas before us struck her hard. I mentioned earlier that for all Aeslu's habitual delight in talking and in hearing others talk, she had said little during the days of our climb. If anything, she said less and less as we climbed higher and higher.

Yet now, sitting on our ledge, she began to speak.

"This is my fault, too."

I saw no point in pretending that I didn't understand. There was no point, either, in pretending that I ought to draw her out. I sat there, waiting and listening.

"I, too, am a fool," she said. "By trying to prevent what happened, I made it happen. By trying to trick everyone, I tricked only myself."

"You did what made sense at the time," I reassured her. "You didn't know what else to do."

"I tried—" The words dried up in her throat. I thought she might have begun to cry, but she hadn't. Aeslu simply stared out over the void.

For a long time we just sat there. I didn't want to interrupt Aeslu if she wanted to say more, yet after a while my own silence started to bother me. What did I expect from her? A more detailed apology? Some sort of explanation of how things had gone wrong? More questions about my own role in bringing the Mountain-Drawn to grief? I meant no harm, but simply sitting there soon felt increasingly cruel.

I eased to my left, forced myself onto my knees, and reached over to her. I put my arms around her. I pulled her head against my chest, I kissed the top of her head, I caressed her neck through the hair lying against it.

Aeslu held back from me for longer than I'd expected. She didn't resist; she simply didn't respond.

I held her tight.

Then, turning toward me, pressing her face hard into my chest, she reached up with both hands and grasped my arms. Her tugging felt so gentle that I took a long time realizing how earnestly she was pulling me toward her.

I eased myself down just as she leaned back. Rixtir climbing garments open easily; it took us just a short while to pull them this way and that till they enclosed us together rather than kept us apart. She wanted me almost at once. I hesitated at first, not wanting to rush her, but hesitance wasn't what either of us desired.

The preposterousness of it, yet the rightness, too—that our merged flesh could matter; that the urgency and delight of our passion could offer us more than the flicker of warmth on an icy ledge. Yet that was precisely the point, precisely what made it necessary and good: that this was all we had—each other's warmth and the consolation it provided—and that was enough. No, not enough. In a few days, maybe less than that, we would be dead, cold and frozen like everything else there. That's what made it so foolish. Pathetic, even. Yet that's also what made it good. When Aeslu cried out—a sudden cry more like a frightened child's than a grown woman's—I felt the warmth even of the cry. Then I held her even tighter, warming myself not just by the heat of her flesh but by her longing for me as well.

21

Yet whatever the warmth we shared, it didn't solve our fundamental problem. We were still stuck on a ledge. Tons of rocks still rained down just a few feet from where we sat.

"Here's how I see it," I told Aeslu. "Either we can stay right here, under the overhang, where we'll be relatively safe till our food and water give out. Or else we can venture onto the cliff again and hope to escape before the rocks catch up with us."

"There is one other possibility," she responded. "We could stay here a while longer, then try escaping. Maybe the rockfall will stop at some point."

"So far it hasn't." If anything, the volume of rubble coming down had increased. I couldn't explain why. In fact, I felt more and more baffled by what was happening. The rockfall appeared almost continuous. I told her, "The question in my mind is how long to wait. The longer we stay here, the less food we'll have left over."

"We have a lot."

"*How* much, though?"

Aeslu checked over our supplies and, after thinking a while, said, "Enough for half a Moon-span."

"Fourteen days' worth."

"Maybe more."

"What about water? All we have is what we can make from this little patch of ice. That won't last long—three days, maybe four."

She didn't seem convinced. "Perhaps we should wait three days, then go."

"Here's what worries me," I told her. "You're right—staying here a while might be best. Certainly it's the cautious thing to do. But I'm not convinced the rockfall will diminish. It may well increase. And every day we wait is a day we've used our supplies just sitting around. The sitting worries me, too—I've gotten sore and weak simply crouched here. If we wait here much longer, the only choice left will be to go down. To abandon the climb. I don't think that's really an option."

My words seemed to surprise her. "You want to continue upward?"

What I'd said surprised me as well. I wasn't really intending one thing over another. I didn't know what I was intending. Surely my main thought just then was survival—getting off that increasingly cryptlike ledge while somehow evading the rocks as well—yet I hadn't really thought through the next step. Heading up? Heading down? Surely retreat was the most sensible option, but was it the proper choice? Given the commitment that Aeslu and I had made, was retreat even a possibility? What alarmed me more than the prospect of getting picked off the cliff by a stray rock was languishing, dying, and rotting in the middle of nowhere.

After a long pause I said, "We should keep going."

I never intended to sway Aeslu against her own preferences, but she found my unexpected confidence persuasive. Within just a few hours we had all our equipment sorted, apportioned, packed, and ready to go. We melted some ice to fill our water bags. We melted a little more to fix a meal, we ate the food, we rested briefly. Then we set to work.

The first task involved lowering our packs to a smaller and much more exposed ledge below the one we'd been using. That was a gamble: rocks might knock the packs off and dash them on the ridge below. Yet we couldn't climb with them on—they were too heavy in the first place, and they jutted off our backs far enough to make us easy targets. We intended to park them temporarily, then hoist them up at an opportune time.

So far so good. We lowered both packs without a hitch.

Then the hard part. Aeslu set up a belay just to the right of our protective overhang; when she finished, I headed up the cliff.

Aeslu and I had decided that I should lead for one simple reason. Under the circumstances, we were roughly equal in our ability as climbers. I was probably more powerful in terms of sheer strength; Aeslu's stamina, though—she'd lived her whole life at high altitudes—far exceeded mine. I was more experienced in techniques of the sort we were employing; Aeslu had better natural balance. So in many respects we might have done just as well with either of us going first. Yet in one way, if no other, I had the clear advantage: I was taller. She stood maybe five feet three inches tall. I was about five eleven. That eight-inch difference might well determine the speed of our ascent, hence the odds of our getting up the cliff alive.

But of course I knew all too well that eight inches of height offered only a meager advantage in the task ahead. It might hasten the climb, but it wouldn't protect me in the least. Even a rock the size of a child's marble could, if it struck my head at terminal velocity, kill me in an instant.

To describe what happened next, I must compare it to another experience in my life—the Meuse-Argonne offensive against the Germans in 1918. What I witnessed was a bombardment so intense that I couldn't believe I'd stay alive from one moment to the next. In both instances the air was thick with missiles—whether artillery shells or chunks of stone, it made no difference. My emotional response was the same.

But it's precisely that emotional response I find hard to describe. Fear, of course. Fear so intense I felt as if I'd taken hold of a live wire. Yet fear that not only jolted the flesh but intoxicated the mind and left me drunk enough that I saw everything from a distance. Gazing up the cliff, I looked at it as if across a horizontal rather than vertical surface. Boulders shot toward me, exploding to the right, the left, straight ahead. Smaller rocks clattered all around. Tiny bits of stone sprayed through the air. There was no place to hide. At any instant a chunk could have dashed my head off, broken my back, fractured every bone in my left foot, or simply snagged the rope and yanked me off the Mountain. Once or twice I felt the sting of pebbles striking my back and thighs. Under siege like that, I found it hard to climb. Not that I didn't want to: I mean simply that controlling my muscles in the most ordinary ways—reaching out, finding a handhold, pulling myself up, taking the next step—nearly exceeded my abilities. Yet somehow I climbed.

I looked down toward Aeslu. Although she turned away now and then to avoid the rockfall, she gazed up toward me more often than not. I could see her playing out the rope as I climbed higher. I could see her trying to gauge my progress and guess how close I was coming to the top.

She could probably tell better than I. From my angle, all I could do was concentrate on the next move, the next, and the next after that.

Then, suddenly, a cry.

I wrenched away from the cliff to look downward. Nearly lost my grip. Pulled myself to safety. Then looked down again.

Aeslu had toppled sideways; she half-sat, half-hung from the ledge supporting her. I couldn't see her well, but her contorted posture terrified me.

I shouted to her.

No response.

Again I shouted.

Still no response. Just then a chunk of rock struck the cliff precisely where I would have been if I hadn't twisted to gaze downward—struck with a grunt and bounced off into space. The impact sprayed me with chips. I scarcely noticed. I was already fumbling with the rope—a rope that had gone limp—and was preparing to set up an anchor that would let me rappel back to where Aeslu lay wounded.

22

I couldn't tell how badly she'd been hurt. Even before I reached her, I could see the blood: her right shoulder and the right side of her face were soaked. But once I'd stepped onto her ledge—I managed to descend without mishap—I still couldn't see the source of her bleeding. My big worry was a head wound. So much blood dripped down her face that I found it hard to believe her skull hadn't been bashed. Yet I couldn't see a scalp laceration. And despite her slumped posture just after she first called out, she didn't seem to have been knocked unconscious. In fact, she greeted me with a wild shout.

"Someone's coming down!"

I ignored her. "Let's get under cover."

Aeslu pointed up the cliff. Even during the span of that brief gesture, five or six more rocks shot past. "Someone's coming!"

These words alarmed me as much as all the blood. She was disoriented, dazed, crazed. Damage done to her brain? "Aeslu, please—"

"Can't you see?"

For good measure, if nothing else, I shot a glance up the cliff. All I saw there was yet another scattering of rocks heading our way. I untied her from the belay rope that had been anchoring her to the ledge. She resisted me—did nothing to help, and rattled on the whole time about someone she'd seen heading toward us from above.

It took all my strength to pull her sideways onto the ledge we had abandoned just a half-hour earlier.

*　　*　　*

"Do you believe me?" Aeslu asked once we'd settled in again. "Or do you think me a liar—or a fool?"

I tried cleaning her wounds with a cloth and some water from my water bag. She cooperated better than before; still, she was so agitated that I couldn't get her to hold still. "You're upset," I told her. "Just let me take care of you."

"Not upset—*excited*."

"All right, then. Excited."

"Someone is coming down."

"Please hold still."

"We must go back and watch."

"Too dangerous."

"We *must*."

"Aeslu, you're badly hurt."

She shoved my cloth away. "The wound is nothing. What matters—"

"That's what Norroi said."

"—is to wait for whomever is descending—"

"Aeslu—"

"—and greet this person."

"Listen to me—"

"It must be the Founders—"

"Aeslu, *listen* to me!"

"—or someone the Founders have sent to help us."

Now I took her by the shoulders and jolted her once, hard. At once I recoiled from my own harshness. Having longed so intensely for Aeslu just a short while earlier, here I was roughing her up. I would have apologized but felt too scared. Speaking as calmly as possible, I managed to ask her, "What, exactly, did you see?"

Aeslu stared at me from within a sudden calm. "Someone. A man, a woman—I am not sure which. Someone coming down the cliff."

"Alone?"

"That, too, I do not know."

"Was this before or after you got hit?"

"Before. No—just as it happened. I saw what I saw, then the rock hit me."

I felt a great sense of relief. Even this brief exchange clarified what had taken place. When I eased over to embrace Aeslu, she did not pull away or push me back. She let me hold her. "I understand what you're saying," I said. "You looked up and thought you saw someone descending. But you didn't. You saw the rock coming down. Or else the rock hit you just then, and your brain played a trick on you—made you see something. Sometimes that happens."

She moved slightly. I thought she'd disengage now or start arguing again. She remained silent, though, her face turned toward me but her eyes gazing slightly to one side. I nuzzled my face against her scalp and smelled the smoky, oily scent of her hair. Another scent clung there, too: meaty and warm.

"You think I saw nothing?"

"I think you saw a rock coming down."

After a long time she said, "Maybe so."

As nearly as I could tell, most of the damage was to her right ear. The rock must have just grazed the side of her head, scraping the ear itself and the flesh of her right temple. An ugly wound: the skin had been torn away as though by a metal rasp. Yet Aeslu had been almost bewilderingly lucky not to have come away from this accident far worse than she had. If the rock had struck another half-inch closer, it would have ripped the side of her head off.

Still, our situation was now much worse than it had been before we'd started out. Even the brief effort to climb the cliff had exhausted me. Aeslu was worn out, too, and not just because of the injury she'd suffered. I wasn't worried about Aeslu's wound in the long run—the cold, dry air would help it heal—but in the short run she almost certainly needed a chance to rest. Neither of us seemed likely candidates just yet for a new push up the cliff.

And so we passed another long afternoon. Another

cold evening. Another cold night. All we could do was cling to each other, seeking solace in each other's arms like two children in a thunderstorm.

23

"Did you hear that?" she asked just as the sky lightened.

"Hear what?"

"Someone called out to me."

"I didn't say a thing," I told her.

"I mean someone else."

My first reaction was annoyance—not *this* again!—but I caught myself fast. She must have been delirious. I reached up in the half-light and felt Aeslu's forehead. No sign of fever. Demented from her injury, then? Perhaps I'd underestimated the extent of damage done. As calmly as possible I asked, "What are you talking about?"

She hushed me instead of answering. "Listen!"

We both fell silent. All I heard was the crackle of small stones on their way down the cliff. "It's your imagination."

"It is *not*!" she exclaimed, and at just that moment forced herself up. "I heard a voice. Someone calling out. Whether you believe me or not, I heard a voice."

"Aeslu, listen to me. You've been hurt—"

"The Founders are calling out to me."

"The Founders have been dead for centuries."

"The Founders' people, then. The people who live at the Summit." She took hold of my sleeve and pulled it hard. "Can't you understand? The people who live on the Mountain have come partway down to help us up."

I didn't know what to think. What she said sounded like delusions—if not the derangements of someone suffering from a head injury, then at least the wishful thinking of someone near exhaustion.

Before I could argue with her, though, Aeslu said, "You saw the rope yourself, that piece we found on the ridge. You yourself believed that the Founders put it there."

"I never said that. I said *someone* put it there— probably someone long ago."

"The Founders."

"Maybe so—"

"And now they are sending someone to meet us. To help us. To lead us to the Summit."

I was too tired to argue. I spent the whole morning at work on our equipment, melting ice into water, doing anything I could to keep busy. Anything to avoid facing the mess we were in. Anything, frankly, to avoid Aeslu.

24

As the day wore on, she fell silent, too. She called out early on: stood at the far end of our ledge and yelled as loudly as possible up the cliff. Once or twice she nearly got hit by rubble coming down, so she retreated. Aeslu went back briefly, however, and called out for a while longer.

Nothing came of it.

I fixed our lunch. She must have been feeling chastened by then, for she sat with me—right next to me. We ate in silence.

At last I said, "I'm sorry."

"So am I," said Aeslu.

25

Yet that afternoon, not long after we'd eaten, we both heard something that even I thought sounded like a human voice. It was so faint I didn't even know what I'd heard. A shout? A scream? The note of a yodel-like cry? All I knew was that it bore no resemblance to the sounds I'd been hearing throughout the climb thus far: the warble of the wind, the crackle of rock-fall, the thunderclaps of the glaciers shifting far below.

Aeslu and I turned at once toward the source of what we'd heard. The noise seemed to have come down the cliff—down precisely the stretch we'd attempted to climb the day before. We stared in that direction for a long moment. Then we turned to face each other. Aeslu's expression was tense—totally alert. Neither of us spoke.

I stood carefully, ducking to avoid the overhang, and eased my way across the ledge to its far end. Near the packs I stooped to take up my ice-hatchet. I grasped it carefully in both hands, the pick jutting outward from my right, then continued over to where the overhang slanted upward and exposed our ledge to the cliff above.

Just then half a dozen rocks smashed into the ledge. They weren't much bigger than grenades but landed so hard that they might as well have been, detonating almost simultaneously and showering us with stone shrapnel. I staggered back, shielding my face.

Silence. Even the wind was still.

By this time Aeslu had forced herself up and half-stood, half-crouched at the mid-point of the ledge. We exchanged a long glance but neither of us spoke.

I eased forward again. Before I could work my way far enough to look up the cliff, more stuff came down: this time a sprinkle of grit and gravel. What struck me as odd even at the time, however, was that the noise of their descent seemed wildly disproportionate to the size of the rocks themselves. I heard a lot of crunching, clattering sounds somewhere above us on the cliff that dwarfed the pebbles coming down. And in fact the noise continued even when the rocks themselves ceased falling altogether.

I could hear Aeslu easing forward even as I moved back. When we met, she rested her hands against my shoulders and nestled close.

At just that moment a human figure descended from the cliff on a doubled rope and landed on the ledge with a massive jolt. This sudden arrival so startled both Aeslu and me that we staggered backwards, nearly tripping, and scarcely managed to catch each other before toppling off the ledge altogether. Yet it wasn't just the suddenness that took us aback. The appearance did, too: tweed coat, corduroy knickers, hobnailed climbing boots, and big canvas rucksack.

It was Forster Beckwith.

PART THREE

"Forster ex machina," *I told Jesse O'Keefe.*

"If only that were so," he replied. "More like Forster cum machinae."

"Cum machinae?"

"With gadgets. He was always rather well-equipped." *But instead of continuing, Jesse O'Keefe stood, stretched, crossed the garden shed to its far wall, and took down a nylon shell jacket hanging there. He gazed back at me a couple of times as if hesitating to end our conversation so abruptly; then, as he looked over the whole shed, I realized that he was just trying to find something. He spotted it on the floor behind me: his black metal lunchbox. He crossed back and picked it up.*

I wasn't about to plead with him. I'd been crass in how I'd lured Jesse; using the photograph as bait still nagged at my conscience; it seemed best not to push my luck. "I've taken up too much of your time," I told him. In fact, we'd been talking almost all day. It must have been well after five by then.

"Not too much," said Jesse O'Keefe. "Just enough."

"I haven't let you get much work done."

"I don't work much, really. I just putter about."

"I haven't gotten you in trouble?"

He dismissed the question with a wave. Slinging his jacket over one shoulder, he stepped toward the door.

I stopped the tape recorder, packed my satchel, got up, and followed him out. "No one expects more of me than what little I do," he said. "But I'm an old man now, and I need to rest."

We walked across campus toward a busy street. Across this thoroughfare I could see some sort of shopping district: a scattering of restaurants and shops. When I sensed that Jesse O'Keefe no longer wanted company at all, I muttered an excuse about needing to find some dinner.

"This is what Boulder people refer to as The Hill," he told me, gesturing across the traffic. "You shouldn't have trouble finding what you need to tide you over."

I thanked him, preparing to break away. But I wanted to know if he meant anything specific by "tide you over." Tide me over to what? To the rest of the story? I couldn't believe he'd leave me hanging.

"Tomorrow, then?" he said abruptly.

With great relief I told him, "Whenever suits you."

"Any time after eight-thirty. My time is my own."

1

Both of us simply stared at Forster [said Jesse when we met at his shed the next morning]. I could only guess what Aeslu was thinking; as for me, I wouldn't have felt much more surprised if the Abominable Snowman himself had landed there right before me. Not just surprised: shocked, appalled, disgusted. Forster Beckwith, of all people! I can't think of anyone I'd have felt less eager to have pop in like that.

"What a pleasant spot for a picnic," Forster said, glancing our way as he disengaged himself from the rope. Then he stepped closer to us on the ledge, unhitched his pack, and dumped it at his feet. "A bit cramped, I suppose, but at least it's out of the rain. Nice view, too."

When neither Aeslu nor I responded, Forster spoke again, now in the tone of a genteel lady suffering a lapse in her host's hospitality. "Would you mind terribly if I join you?"

My words burst forth as if of their own accord: "God damn you, Forster—"

"Now, now," he said, seating himself on his pack. "That's no way to greet a guest." He then opened a side-pouch and extracted a tin of food. I saw the label: kippered herring. Once he'd snapped off the key and unrolled the lid, he pulled out a fork and began to eat.

Throughout the time since Forster's sudden reappearance, Aeslu had been silent. This in itself was unusual. She wasn't by nature a chatty person—the Rixtirra didn't talk much without good reason—but a forthright personality and abundant verbal gifts tended to make her expressive. Yet now she said nothing. Nothing at all. She watched Forster with a wariness so intense that it virtually warmed the air between us. Standing to my right, she didn't exactly hide behind me but stood close enough that I felt like a barrier of sorts between her and Forster on my left. Not an altogether unpleasant feeling: I myself would have felt even more uncomfortable with the situation if Aeslu had felt less so. Yet her silence complicated things in some respects. It certainly raised the tension among us, a tension not unlike what I've felt on mountain ridges when a thunderstorm approaches: the air begins to crackle, every metal object starts bristling with tiny sparks, and it seems only a matter of moments before lightning strikes.

Surely you understand the effects of what had happened.

First, both Aeslu and I had long assumed that Forster was dead. We'd seen no sign of other survivors after the avalanche. Of course our own survival proved that someone could squeak through, but nothing we'd seen or heard suggested that we had any company on the Mountain. Forster had been so much higher up when the ice and rocks came down that both Aeslu and I figured his chances for escape had been even slimmer than our own.

Second, we'd both assumed that we were alone in making our ascent. Over the past week, we'd seen no one ahead of us, behind us, or anywhere else in the area. The only indication of any other human presence on the Mountain was the bit of rope we'd found—and that was hundreds of years old. So we took for granted that even if others had survived, no one else had headed up the Mountain. Yet here was Forster popping in out of nowhere.

But it wasn't really the shock of the man's reappearing *ex nihilo* that got the best of us. It was Forster himself. After all he'd done. After all I—Aeslu and I—had done to stop him. His very presence stunned us. It almost literally took our breath away.

So I'm not surprised now to realize how little we responded to him. Aeslu seemed stricken—all she could do was stare at him as if at a horrible apparition. As for me, I wasn't stricken so much as bewildered. From the time of my first encounter with him, Forster Beckwith had seemed to appear unexpectedly, and he did so time after time, each time in ways that seemed both opportune for him and intrusive for everyone else. Here he was once more. Yet no matter how often he had showed up before, his appearance was startling and offensive all over again. It was also undeniable. We couldn't wish him away. He was right there in front of us.

How these developments affected Aeslu, exactly, I couldn't say. Of course we could have discussed the situation in Rixtir, a language Forster probably didn't understand, but at the moment of his arrival, we didn't talk at all. I suppose Aeslu and I both worried about aggravating him. He might not have understood us, but he would have known we were conspiring against him. Then again, perhaps he understood more Rixtir than we thought. Thus for whatever reason, neither Aeslu nor I spoke to each other. Everything was unstated. I could only guess at Aeslu's reactions.

She was clearly upset. Not that she carried on in any way, but I could tell. As long as I'd known her, Aeslu had always been one of the most self-possessed human beings I've ever met. A sense of calm pervaded her being, a calm I'd compare to that of a glacial lake. She was cool, serene. I never quite knew what was going on beneath the surface. Precisely because of her calm, however, I could detect signs of exterior events playing on her, much as every shift of the wind manifests itself on the water. As for the depths—I had no idea.

What I could at least imagine, however, was her reaction to Forster. Aeslu's old nemesis was back. The man she claimed to have spent the past eight months trying to thwart now stood right before us. The man she wanted most to keep from the Mountain Made of

Light was on his way toward the Summit. But something else seemed to disturb her, something beyond Forster Beckwith's reappearance. This was simply that he had shown up precisely when she had been expecting someone else. Aeslu had been convinced that someone from among the Founders' descendants was coming down to meet us. Instead, here was Forster. Expecting help, Aeslu had ended up with trouble instead.

Forster himself was anything but dumbstruck. The man was downright gabby. "What's been taking you so long, anyway?" he asked, poking about in his tin of kippers. "I've been waiting for you two or three days now. I spotted you and decided to wait till you caught up. Little did I know you'd squander so much time covering so little distance. If only I'd known, I could have attended to other matters."

"Forster, what do you want?" I demanded.

"Now, now—you're sounding altogether too accusatory. I'm trying to do you a favor. The least you can do is hear me out."

"What do you want?"

He held a forkful of herring suspended halfway between the tin and his mouth. Sounding astonished by my inability to perceive the obvious, he said, "Look, I thought I should see if you'd gotten yourself in a fix. When you didn't show up, I decided to come down and make sure you were both all right."

"I'm touched by your altruism."

"You shouldn't be. Let's just say I didn't feel sufficiently confident of your abilities to get by without help."

"That still doesn't answer my question."

"And which question is that?" he asked with a quizzical expression as he took the bite of fish from his fork.

"What you want from us."

"Ah, yes. Well—that's certainly something we should discuss. But we can do so in a more relaxing atmosphere than this, don't you think? If nothing else, I'd like a spot of tea."

And with those words he set down his lunch, stood, pulled open his pack, removed a brass Primus stove, and set to work firing it up.

2

Aeslu and I had little choice but to go along with Forster's invitation to himself. This wasn't a matter of spinelessness on our part, simply one of facing reality. The three of us were sharing a ledge that ran about nine or ten feet long, narrowing from a width of maybe three feet at one end till it merged with the cliff at the other. Above us was the overhang. Below, a sheer drop of five or six hundred feet. The wide end provided the way on and off the cliff. Forster, having landed on that end, essentially blocked our way out. Not that he forcibly restrained us—he merely went about his business melting ice and brewing tea. Yet even if Aeslu and I had tried to leave without his resisting us, we would have struggled simply to get around such a big man and his equipment. Would he have resisted us? I don't know. More to the point, we would have been hard put to leave anyway for the same reasons we were marooned there in the first place. Surely the rockfall wouldn't cease simply because Forster had shown up.

So we waited. We watched him fix his tea. For the first time since his arrival, we talked.

Or rather, Aeslu talked. More than talked: ranted. "He is the Man of Ignorance!" she told me, speaking fast in her own language. The words came forth in a torrent now that the dam of her preceding silence had broken. She was whispering, but so harshly that Forster wouldn't have needed to know Rixtir to understand what she meant. "He is the Man of Darkness! The Cutter—"

"Aeslu—"

"—of Wounds!"

"All right, so what should we do about him?"

She went on at some length, almost out of control. At one point I had to physically restrain her from pushing past me toward the object of her wrath. None of this commotion escaped Forster's eye, of course; he gazed her way now and then, never for very long and without any sign of discomfiture, as if Aeslu neither posed any threat nor even deserved much notice. If anything, I felt more taken aback than he was. Aeslu had always seemed so entirely self-contained—even, or especially, at times of adversity—that her wildness shocked and alarmed me. It wasn't as though she didn't have good cause for rage. I felt it, too. But I knew this man well enough to know that rage wouldn't prevail against him, and whatever rage I'd expressed in the past had left him unscathed. No, it seemed better to proceed in other ways, to stop him by other means.

I have to admit, however, that Aeslu's reaction pleased me in at least one way. For months I'd doubted her allegiance. Even during the climb so far— and despite the confessions we'd made to each other— I couldn't quite shake some kind of uncertainty over what she'd done, and why. Now here she was hissing and spitting, ready to tackle Forster on a ledge so narrow that the least altercation between us and him might have sent us all tumbling onto the ridge below. The uncertainty I felt now turned to satisfaction—an odd satisfaction, I'll admit, but satisfaction all the same.

By this time Forster had melted enough snow to boil water. Infusing tea leaves through a metal strainer, he set to work brewing himself a cup of Earl Grey. "Care for some?" he asked just then, raising the cup—bone china, no less—as if in a toast.

Neither Aeslu nor I responded.

"Look," he said, looking rather peeved with us, "I

could beat around the bush, but I won't. I assume you'd rather I go straight to the point."

"To the point, then," I replied.

"I want to climb this peak. So do you. But let's be realistic. You're unlikely to manage without my help, aren't you? In fact, it's amazing you've made it this far without getting yourselves killed."

"I wouldn't worry too much," I told him, "about who's got whom killed."

He smiled as I spoke, then said, "You wouldn't? Well, if I were you, I'd worry quite a bit."

"Don't try blaming me for what you yourself—"

"Let's forget the past," Forster said abruptly, taking a sip from his teacup. "We've all acted in a beastly fashion—myself included. None of us comes away from the past few months smelling like a rose. Perhaps it's to everyone's best interests now to kiss and make up." Before I could react to these words, he continued: "Hence the matter at hand. Don't take offense at what I'm suggesting—it's nothing personal. Not many people could tackle a peak like this and survive. So why not accept my offer of help and thus increase your own chances for success?"

At this point Aeslu broke in, shouting, "Never! Never!" She leaned past me, latching onto my shoulder and throwing her weight so hard against me that she almost knocked me down. She relented only when she lost her balance and nearly fell.

Forster watched us without comment, nodding once, as though our fumbles proved his point irrefutably. "Don't be so categorical," he said. "It pays to keep an open mind, don't you think?"

"We will never accept your help," Aeslu told him, now more calmly. "Never!"

"Never? Then you'll never reach the summit."

"We *will*."

"Not without assistance."

Before Aeslu could lash out at him again, I said, "Suppose we consider what you're suggesting. To what can we attribute this great act of benevolence?

Your devotion to Aeslu? Your deep concern for the well-being of her people?"

Forster smiled. "Here, too, we could assume all sorts of poses. Under the circumstances, though, I think you'll admit that's a luxury we can't afford. Let me be blunt. I could climb this peak easily enough if I knew the route. I've made some progress already—considerably more, I might add, than you have. But it's fair to say that this peak is a tough nut to crack." He had spoken these words as if to me; at least, he looked at me almost the entire time. Then he shifted his gaze to Aeslu. Raising his cup again, he said, "Your ancestors didn't indulge in all this Diadem business just because they like costume jewelry."

Did she grasp what he was telling her? Did she catch the implications of his word choice? I don't mean to imply that Aeslu wasn't alert to nuance, simply that the rage she felt toward him may have deafened her to almost everything but the rage itself. In any case, she didn't respond. At least not quickly enough, since Forster wasn't in a mood to be interrupted.

"Unfortunately, I've had less luck recently than I did at the start. I've hit some unexpected wrinkles. Not encouraging. Far be it from me to give up, though. There must be a way up. There always is."

Both Aeslu and I waited, watching him closely.

Forster set down his teacup. "I assume, however, that the much-touted Mountain Stone would iron out precisely those same wrinkles," he said. "And I assume you have the Stone in your possession."

"So you'd like to make a deal," I told him.

"That's it. A deal. Even-steven. You let me share the Stone and what it shows about the way up; I'll share what I know about getting there."

"You son of a bitch."

"I think you'd agree the benefits are mutual."

"What fucking *benefits*—"

"Of course if you want to play dog-in-the-manger," he said, "there's not much I can do to stop you. Pro-

ceed if you wish. You'll get nowhere, but never mind.
You'll slip at some point, but never mind. You'll dash
yourselves to bits, but never mind. Meanwhile, I'll
take my chances and just proceed on my own."

I forced a laugh. "You yourself said you'd hit an
impasse."

"I have. But I can follow you up, can't I? Who's to
say I can't? You'd be hard put to stop me."

"Don't count on it."

"Perhaps I won't. You've become rather adept at
doing whatever suits your purposes, haven't you?"

"Forster—"

"Let's not squabble," he said. "It's a waste of time.
And I think you'll agree that all considered, time is
already short." Then he started dismantling his stove
and putting away his supplies. "Just tell me yes or no.
Shall we join forces to our mutual benefit? Or shall
we proceed separately to our mutual detriment?"

I can't say how much of this interchange Aeslu understood. She was fluent in English—remarkably fluent, all considered—but Forster talked so fast, and
with such an unfamiliar accent, that she might well
have found him confusing. What I can say, though, is
that whatever she understood now enraged her. In fact
she grew so angry that she dispensed with English
altogether and let loose in her own language. I have
no idea what she said. If the Rixtirra use profanity,
I'm sure she let go with every possible insult and re-
vilement. What's more likely is that she cursed him—
I mean cursed in the most literally damning sense—
and here, too, she can't possibly have spared him any
threats of punishment or pain that the Mountain-
Drawn could imagine.

None of this was lost on Forster Beckwith. You
can't get blasted point-blank and pretend your attacker has missed. Yet even as she railed at him, leaning against me in a way that made me both a barricade
and a means for pulling herself closer, his response
showed only the slightest acknowledgment. He looked
over once or twice while packing his gear; he went

about his work with a concertedness far exceeding what the tasks required; he simply ignored Aeslu in a way that belied his real attention.

When she quieted down, though—not finished but simply out of breath—he turned our way again. "Well? Yes or no?"

"You can't be serious," I told him.

"*Serious*," he said, standing to his full height. Even at the high end of the ledge, Forster's head bumped the overhang. "Oh, I can be quite serious. Maybe not as serious as you are, but serious enough."

Then, moving as calmly as he spoke, Forster stepped closer to where Aeslu and I stood, reached down to our packs, and pulled open Aeslu's. Without hesitation he began rummaging around, jabbing his hands into the pouch, and pulling things out.

Aeslu and I understood at the same instant what he intended, and we moved simultaneously to stop him. I crouched and, in a single motion, yanked the pack away from him. Aeslu flung herself around me and struck Forster as hard as she could. Yet our efforts came to nothing. He'd already found what he wanted. Just a few frantic gropes within Aeslu's pack let him locate the Mountain Stone, get a grip on it, and pull it out.

Even so we tried to stop him. Aeslu, stumbling forward, ended up belly-down on the now-plundered pack. Her sprawl blocked me enough that I couldn't reach Forster. Of course I could have pushed past her. I could have forced my way over Aeslu—could have clawed at him despite her lying there—but I didn't. She was in a precarious enough position already; any nudge I gave Aeslu would have knocked her off the ledge altogether.

Forster now held the Mountain Stone in his right hand, the tip pointing straight up, his fingers reaching up and curling around the base. "So," he said. "I guess this simplifies the situation."

"It's no good!" I shouted at him. "You can't make sense of it on your own!"

He huffed at me as if I'd cracked a tedious joke. "Who said anything about making sense of it *myself*?"

"You need Aeslu's help."

He gestured quizzically, hefting the Stone once or twice, as someone might test a melon for ripeness. "Fine."

At once Aeslu set him straight. "Never will I help you! Never!"

Now he tossed it gently into the air, caught it, tossed it again, and caught it once more. Watching that brazen gesture, I could tell that Aeslu felt a temptation to rush Forster and grab at the Stone rather than let him risk it further. But she knew as well as I did that precisely the effort to save it might prove its doom, so she made no further move.

"Then I suppose you know you have three choices," he said. "You can persist in all this nonsense and try to get the Stone away. You can let me go ahead without any further fuss. Or you can come to your senses and join forces with me. The first two choices will get you nowhere. The third, though—that has real possibilities."

3

Real possibilities. I can't imagine a phrase less appropriate to what I felt just then—or to what Aeslu herself must have been feeling, too. Forster Beckwith's arrival in our midst seemed an almost unimaginable calamity. It may not have been a calamity like some of those preceding it; still, it was a calamity all the same. In some respects, Aeslu may even have considered it far worse. I have no doubt that she grieved for the hundreds of Mountain-Drawn—thousands, really—who had perished during the course of our quest; yet even all those deaths didn't rule out reaching the goal she felt duty-bound to seek. On the contrary, the Rixtirra had always believed that the very act of seeking and climbing the Mountain Made of Light would result in casualties. But joining forces with the Man of Ignorance? This was a disaster of a magnitude that Aeslu seemed incapable of articulating.

It wasn't just that Forster had started to climb the Mountain Made of Light. Rather, it was that Aeslu now found herself in a position of having to collaborate with him in making the climb. But collaborate we did. Within just an hour of his commandeering the Mountain Stone, we were preparing to head up the cliff again.

"I was watching you earlier," said Forster while repacking his equipment, "and I could tell your efforts would come to nought. It's amazing you've survived at all. You set yourselves up like bowling pins, then just waited for something to roll down the alley and knock you down."

I tried to defend what Aeslu and I had attempted. "We weren't prepared for the sheer steepness—"

"Of course you weren't. That's the whole point."

"—and the rockfall."

Forster smiled at my words. "The *rockfall*. Cliffs are by nature steep. Rocks tend to fall. You can either waste your time complaining or else deal with the situation." Then he moved out beyond the overhang's protection. The rope dangled before him. Forster took hold of it, brought his weight to bear against it and, satisfied with its soundness, started attaching prussik knots to the rope. Prussiks, in case you're wondering, are a kind of slipknot that climbers use to ascend fixed ropes. These knots are small coils wound several times around the rope you intend to climb, and they make it possible to slide a sling upward without having it slip downward again. Prussiks allow a much safer means of ascent than what climbers would have otherwise, given the circumstances. When I saw him tying these knots to the fixed rope, Forster's intentions were obvious at once.

Aeslu and I exchanged glances. Forster had hidden the Mountain Stone somewhere in his pack—a huge Western-style canvas pack now lying on the ledge between him and us. By all appearances he intended to leave it behind; no doubt he expected us to attach a rope and let him hoist his equipment up to wherever he planned to rest. Our brief glance let us signal our intentions to one another.

But inadvertently we signaled Forster, too. Without a word he stepped back to the ledge, removed the Stone from his pack, and inserted it into the small knapsack he wore slung over his shoulders. His only acknowledgment of the conspiracy was a single gaze he shot my way, a gaze more of annoyance than anger, the scolding gaze of a father who has caught a five-year-old with one hand in a cookie jar.

He said, "Here's the plan. I'll go up first. Once I'm up, I'll tug the rope twice. That means get the packs ready. Tie them on, tug twice, and I'll hoist them. I'll throw down the rope when everything is safe and sound. Aeslu comes up first. Then Jesse."

"No—I'll follow you," I told Forster abruptly, not about to have him with Aeslu unattended.

At just that instant, she herself said, "Jesse goes first."

Forster listened to us without comment. I thought he'd object, but he didn't. "All right, do as you wish. I don't suppose it makes much difference."

He started up.

The man's climbing prowess once again took me by surprise. Never mind that he was climbing a fixed rope, which unquestionably simplified his task. It would have simplified anyone's, mine included, yet I could never have made such rapid progress. Forster pulled himself upward so easily that from below his ascent seemed more a sprint than a struggle. By the time I would have made five or six clumsy moves, Forster was already well past the point where Aeslu and I had gotten ourselves marooned. Shortly after that he worked his way over a bulge in the cliff and disappeared altogether.

Aeslu and I were now alone together for the first time since Forster's abrupt arrival on our ledge. What we had just witnessed so thoroughly bewildered us, however, that neither of us could speak. Such was Forster's power that we felt constrained even in his absence. No matter how repellent we found him, no matter how appalling we considered the quandary this man presented, we could somehow perceive no alternative to accepting his plan.

Yet I suppose our situation wasn't as passive as what I'm suggesting. At the time, almost all the gear lay at our feet. Forster had the Mountain Stone and whatever personal equipment—food, canteen, clothes, climbing hardware—fit into his knapsack. Everything else was in our possession. Why, then, couldn't we have countermanded his orders, lowered the packs rather than raising them, and thus left Forster somewhere high above us without the least hope of his proceeding? In fact we could have. We could have left him stranded like a kitten in a tree. Yet we didn't. We went ahead and did what he'd told us to do. We waited for his signal. We secured the rope to the first pack, signaled back, and waited as he hauled it up. Then we waited for the rope to come down; we tied on the next pack; we saw it off. We then repeated the process for the third pack as well. In short, we cooperated as fully as if Forster's goals had been identical to our own.

Reflecting on those actions from a distance of almost fifty years, it's hard for me to explain why we proceeded so willingly, even energetically. All I can do is say that no matter what force Forster Beckwith exerted over us—a force residing chiefly in his possession of the Mountain Stone—that force coincided with something far greater. The Mountain itself pulled us upward. This is why Aeslu and I, though pressured to go along, also went by choice.

I watched my pack bump and scrape its way up as Forster reeled it in. Now Aeslu and I were the ones without equipment. A wave of panic struck me just then: so this was what he had in mind! I couldn't believe we'd been so stupid. We'd let him plunder all our supplies and leave us stranded. Aeslu and I were now even more desperately stuck on the ledge than before, altogether without food, clothes, or equipment. How long would we last there before freezing to death? One night? Two?

But before I could speculate further about our choices and their consequences, the rope came thrashing down near my feet. I took hold of it at once. Manila hemp: Western rope, Lowland rope. I didn't trust it as much as I trusted rope from the Founders' Gear, but it would have to do. I took hold of it and tugged twice.

"Ready?" I asked Aeslu.

"Ready."

"We'll find a way to deal with him."

"I hope so."

Impulsively, I embraced her. The warmth and solidity of the embrace she gave in return pleased me, reassured me.

"Upward to the Summit."

"Upward to the Summit."

I started up.

4

It was bewildering how much better we climbed with Forster guiding us, but from the start I could see two reasons why we did.

First, we now encountered only the slightest rockfall. The absence of falling slabs, boulders, chunks—everything but the most ordinary bits and pieces—was obvious at once. More than obvious: startling. What had been an ongoing barrage diminished to the most occasional event. It almost seemed as if the Mountain deferred to Forster Beckwith in a way that it hadn't to Aeslu and me. The nearly malicious timing of the earlier rockfall now became the routine hazard familiar to all climbers.

Of course I didn't take long to imagine an alternate explanation for the cliff's sudden benevolence. Perhaps the Mountain had never been to blame for the barrage at all. Perhaps the Mountain didn't deserve credit, either, for the present calm. Perhaps the dangers Aeslu and I had faced—dangers that had trapped us on our ledge for almost three whole days—could be traced to a less impersonal, more easily identifiable source.

But what should I have done about my suspicions? I couldn't have proved any accusations I might have made. Forster would have denied everything. More to the point, my suspicions added nothing to my knowledge of the man. This was hardly the first time he'd tried to kill me. If anything, our collaboration might serve to insure against whatever new mischief he might attempt. I took solace, too, in believing that if my suspicions were correct, we would at least suffer less risk from rockfall now, a risk I believed to be greater than what Forster presented.

The second reason for our proceeding so well was—I'll admit it outright—Forster himself. With him in the lead, we made it all the way up that cliff in less time than Aeslu and I had required several days earlier to climb just a few hundred feet. The first stretch—what climbers call a pitch—was, of course, a fixed rope, so our rapid progress came as no surprise. But every pitch after that was *terra incognita.* Forster led; Aeslu and I followed. Our pace was steady, almost unrelenting. The cliff apparently presented no major obstacles to him—just a series of minor problems to solve.

Yet Aeslu and I often struggled to follow Forster even on the pitches that seemed to challenge him least. More than once Forster ended up virtually dragging each of us up when our own technique proved inadequate to accomplish the task by more dignified means.

I recall watching him during an especially difficult pitch. At the outset he wasn't more than five feet above me and about that distance to my right. He stood there a while just staring at the rock. I thought he might have forgotten something; he had the look about him of someone sifting his mind for recollections. Then he reached up, took hold of an imperceptible ridge or ripple in the rock, and at the same time brought his right foot up, caught it somewhere, hesitated another instant, and immediately boosted himself off the ledge. Almost at once his left foot extended to another ridge—nothing I could see, but it must have been there—and the left hand moved to a more obvious hold. Forster rose another foot or so. Then the right hand again. The right foot. He proceeded like this, move and countermove, for at least a minute. There was no sense of exertion, no noise except for the rasp of his boots on the rock. Soon he had climbed high enough that my angle of vision made it difficult to see what he was doing. Legs and arms reaching out. Torso shifting. Head leaning back. I couldn't follow much more than that. An odd sensation. I felt as helpless as a fat, ungainly beetle watching a water strider zoom across the water.

I'd have expected Forster to rub our faces in the situation, but he didn't have to. No one could have missed the nature of what was happening. We made quick progress and were safely bivouacked on a new ledge by noon. Thus we settled into our new camp, we fixed a meal, and, gazing out from an altitude now nearly a thousand feet higher than the spot we had left just that morning, we took in the view.

"What says the Mountain Stone today?" Forster asked when he opened his pack, removed the quartz pyramid, and thrust it toward Aeslu and me. Resting point upward on Forster's palm, his fingers hooked tightly around it, the Stone lay right before us yet far beyond our grasp.

Aeslu stared briefly, then said, "The Stone speaks only to those worthy of listening."

At once Forster pulled back what he had offered. "Let's cut the mystical crap, all right? No more riddles. No more secret meanings. Let's just climb the peak."

"But to do so—"

"Just explain what the markings—"

"—you must—"

"—tell us to do."

"What Aeslu is saying," I interjected, "is that you're acting like such a son of a bitch, you wouldn't even notice if the Mountain Stone spelled things out in black and white."

He feigned indifference to my words. "Just tell me where we are, where we're going, and how to get there."

I could see that Aeslu understood him and that his demand troubled her deeply. She gazed at the Stone for a long time, glancing my way only once or twice, always returning to the Stone. It's not that she needed my permission to capitulate—just that she wanted to avoid capitulating alone.

I told her, "Go ahead."

Her eyes welled up, but she suppressed the tears.

"There's no other way," I said.

What the Mountain Stone showed us was the route we had followed thus far and, where the cliff met the slope above, some odd little marks etched near the juncture:

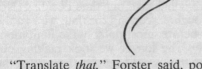

"Translate *that*," Forster said, pointing toward the mark.

"It is not a word," Aeslu told him.

"Another symbol, then? An ideogram?"

"Perhaps so."

"Like the needle and the eye?"

I wasn't sure what he meant, so I asked him to clarify. Aeslu cut him short, explaining about some markings on the Diadem that had baffled everyone— herself included—when the Umbrage had been searching for the Mountain. That is, they had baffled everyone till Forster guessed what they represented. His guess had been correct: the route had led the Umbrage through a cliff to the ring of valleys surrounding the Mountain Made of Light.

"So you're assuming these etched marks show us the next step," I said.

"What other purpose *could* they serve?" asked Forster.

Aeslu stared at the Stone where it rested in Forster's hand. I couldn't tell if the Stone itself or simply the task of interpreting it was what mystified her. After a long silence she said, "I do not know what these marks mean."

This is what we knew, and what we didn't know:

If the Stone accurately represented the Mountain itself, then we had nearly arrived at a vast snowfield; once safely ascended, this snowfield would take us nearly halfway to the Summit. Yet we hadn't reached the snowfield itself. The cliff we had climbed that day bulged outward at its upper reaches; the bulge blocked us from exiting the rock face onto the less steeply angled snow above. How could we get up there? That was the problem. Luckily, we'd ended up on a ledge so spacious that we could take our time deciding. Not too much time, though. Excepting rockfall, we had the same problems as before, most notably the limitations of our food supply. The longer we took making our next move, the less time we'd have for the rest of the climb. Yet the more we examined the ledge for some sort of way up, the more difficult the task appeared.

Even Forster Beckwith wouldn't have been able to climb a concave cliff. Not in those days. Not without all sorts of gear that didn't even get invented for another fifty years.

5

At certain points during the events preceding this climb, I'd had dreams that broke an impasse or solved a problem I was confronting. Locating the Founders' Gear was the result of one such dream; using dynamite against the Umbrage was another. I suppose one could call this phenomenon creative in some sense, though the consequences of the dynamite would argue against using the word too loosely. But the dreams unquestionably turned the tide in more ways than one. They were a powerful influence on what I'd done at the time. I hadn't experienced anything quite like them before then or since.

I mention the dreams because we could have used their help just then. Stuck on a ledge, we knew we had to climb the cliff's last few dozen feet onto the snowfield, yet we had no idea how to surmount the obstacle above us. All efforts to find the route got us nowhere. Forster's impulsive attempt to scale the cliff by force of will accomplished nothing and nearly led to a fatal slip. (Aeslu and I would have welcomed his death if Forster hadn't made sure he'd have taken the Stone down with him.) In short, our waking minds failed to solve the quandary. Would we do better asleep?

If my own dreams proved any measure, the answer was negative. No images floated upward to me from the depths of my being; no words called out to me unbidden. I tried to make sense of the glyphs we'd seen on the Mountain Stone, but my efforts proved pointless. What did those squiggles mean? I couldn't even guess. Sliding toward sleep, my mind didn't even linger on the Stone. Instead, I found myself barraged with recollections of the Umbrage and the Heirs: the sound of clubs and maces thudding into flesh and bone; the sight of the dead and dying sprawled about afterward on the ice; the sensation of the avalanche shaking the entire Mountain as it descended. Against the weight of these memories, the image of a few lines etched in natural glass didn't stand a chance.

6

Something else troubled me at the time, something more prosaic but baffling all the same. I refer to Forster's pack.

I'd been rather in awe of this pack ever since I'd first met Forster eight or nine months earlier. His pack was bigger than any I'd ever seen. In those days most climbers used the traditional German-style rucksacks, knapsacks, or haversacks—various sorts of packs whose common elements were inconvenience and discomfort. They were generally made of canvas, though sometimes of leather. They didn't carry much but nonetheless rode hard on the shoulders. Certainly they bore little resemblance to all the fancy internal- and external-frame packs, many of them made from lightweight alloys and synthetic cloth, that mountaineers use nowadays. The one I'd used during my first weeks in the Mountain Land was little more than a big canvas bag with straps. The Rixtir equivalent I acquired while on the run wasn't much different—simply indigenous in origin. What Forster used, however, was something else altogether.

In size it looked at least three times bigger than anything the rest of us had at our disposal. It was two feet wide and at least three feet tall. The fabric comprising it appeared to be canvas, though of an unfamiliar kind, for an odd sheen suggested some kind of treatment to make it waterproof. Mind you, this was decades before the invention of nylon. Leather trim made it look even stronger than it was already, and big loops of rope attached right and left allowed

Forster to dangle things—ironmongery, boots, even tin cookpots—till the great bulk of it jangled and clattered like a tinker's cart on a bumpy road. On anyone else, such a huge pack would have dwarfed the man who carried it. On someone of Forster's physique, strength, and stamina, the pack's size somehow augmented him.

But of course it wasn't the pack itself that drew my attention. Rather, I couldn't help wondering about its contents. The usual stuff, no doubt. Food, clothing, cold-weather stuff. Climbing gear—all of Western origin. Stove. Fuel. Maybe personal effects, too, of whatever sort someone like Forster might carry with him. Obviously that would all accumulate into a substantial load. Yet looking at his pack, I couldn't believe that even these items fully accounted for everything inside. Forster must have had something else hidden there as well. More food? Maybe some hoarded survival rations? A stash of chocolate he wouldn't allow anyone to see? Secret gear, perhaps, such as an extra rope? Or possibly something elicit, something plundered from the Mountain Land?

I couldn't guess. This, despite days of waiting for the least slip to reveal what lay within. Perhaps he'd leave the flap open and things might fall out. Perhaps he'd pull on a garment, thus dragging out precisely what he wished to hide. Perhaps the pack would simply burst from the uncontainable bulk of too much stuff inside, so that jewels, plundered artifacts, and clandestine items of astonishing nature would reveal themselves at once, thus illuminating Forster's true purposes.

Of course nothing of the sort took place. Nothing fell out. Nothing burst forth. Nothing revealed itself. The pack remained either safely on Forster's back or just as safely beside him.

Forster was nothing if not careful.

7

I awoke to a scream.

For a few seconds I couldn't move. I just lay there, my whole body tensing as the noise went on and on.

Then I heard a voice say, "What is it? *What is it?*" A light shined on me. When I forced myself around, I saw Forster leaning toward Aeslu, who lay between us, and I saw Aeslu looking first at him, then at me, wide-eyed, grasping at her throat with both hands.

"Sit up!" Forster shouted. He lurched out of his bedroll, crawled closer, almost dropped the light—shadows skittering everywhere—and crouched beside Aeslu.

She managed to gasp something, but I couldn't understand the words.

Forster said, "Here," and forced her to sit upright.

Aeslu pulled herself forward, groping almost randomly for whatever might support her—the bedroll, the ground, my leg. Once upright, she started breathing easier, though she still nodded and swayed with each breath. Forster braced her back while I held the flashlight.

"You're okay," he said.

She shook her head.

"Just relax."

"I—can't—breathe!"

"You're all right," he said. "Just take it easy." Then he told me, "Untie her collar."

I did so at once. Aeslu's struggle to breathe shocked me less than her expression just then: she looked so fearful and alone. Within a short while, though, Aeslu started breathing easier. The noise she made still alarmed me: those raspy inhalations. Even now she kept rocking forward each time she breathed. Then she lay back carefully.

I could see Forster better by then: watching, always watching. His face, lit from below by the flashlight in his lap, looked bizarre, distorted, not quite human, with a triangle of shadow cast by his nose up his forehead. He asked Aeslu, "Better?"

"Better," came the reply. After a long silence—she was glancing around—she said, "Much better."

"You'll be all right," Forster said. "It's just a touch of altitude sickness."

"I hope so."

"I promise. It's no fun but nothing serious. We won't worry unless you start gurgling from the lungs."

None of this reassured me. Aeslu did indeed look better now, yet the incident frightened me enough that I couldn't relax. I didn't fully trust Forster's assessment of the situation. "Is she really all right?" I asked.

"She'll be fine. Our bodies are adjusting. She has mild hypoxia—not enough oxygen in the blood. It's not a big deal unless it affects your strength and judgment. Which, of course, it sometimes does. You can get disoriented, suffer hallucinations, that sort of thing. Once, in the Karakoram, I was descending from a peak—rappelling after we'd reached the summit—and suddenly I looked up and saw animals coming down the rope after me. A bear, a goose, a sloth, a monkey. Life-sized. Rather disconcerting. Better company than I was keeping at the time, however."

Aeslu glanced at each of us in turn.

"You're all right," he told her. "Go back to sleep." Without further ado he switched off the flashlight. In the dark he said, "This is the least of our worries."

8

For the whole next day, we clung to that ledge without any clear sense of how to proceed. We didn't want to retreat but didn't know how to advance. How long would our food last? A week, maybe ten days. And how long would the weather hold? It could turn against us at any moment. So we knew we needed to make a move soon, whether upward or downward, but couldn't decide what that move should be.

Our overall situation didn't make matters easier. Forster paced like a caged animal, glowering at the curved wall overhead as if to scold it for the audacity of blocking his path. He didn't seem capable of tolerating the notion of obstacles. Or perhaps he couldn't grasp the notion that anything might actually obstruct *him*. I'd seen him manifest this attitude before—in Makbofissorih, for instance, when the Masters in that city held us captive in a cliffside prison—and despite his anger it seemed as much bafflement as rage. "There's got to be a way up," he said, repeating the words off and on all day like a mantra. "There always is." Of course his restlessness soon got on our nerves.

But the tension created by Forster's mood wasn't all that afflicted us. Aeslu and I grew restless as well. Not *about* each other—it was Forster himself we both resented—but *toward* each other. I suppose we ended up mutually irritable for lack of any way to strike out at the real source of our frustrations. Why had we allowed this man into our midst again? True, we'd gained some altitude, but at what cost? Now we were stuck again. To make matters worse, we lacked even the solace of unimpeded companionship. We had allowed Forster Beckwith, of all people, to crash our little party. No, we didn't lash out at each other. The problem was that we didn't do much of anything at all. We scarcely talked.

Something else weighed on us at the time, especially on Aeslu. This was simply the panorama before us. The Mountain Land seemed impossibly far below, its farmlands vague, its lesser peaks partially blocked by masses of clouds and palls of smoke, its villages almost indistinguishable from the land surrounding them. What I saw seemed more the possibility of towns and farms than the real thing. When the clouds relented, however, we saw Rixtir towns in flames almost everywhere we looked. Gazing at the valleys of her realm and at the palls spiraling up from them, Aeslu's expression was that of a widow keeping vigil beside her husband's body at a wake.

Forster and I could have ignored Aeslu as she stared out over the High Realm. She was so quiet and still, we could almost have forgotten that she sat there among us. How could we have ignored the object of her grief, though? And how could we have pretended that we weren't implicated in what had happened?

"It seems the Rixtirs are making rather a hash of things, doesn't it?" Forster asked abruptly at some point.

I couldn't believe he'd put it that way—as if the holocaust unfolding even as we watched were an expression of nothing more than aboriginal incompetence. I told him, "No thanks to you."

"Look, I didn't *make* them fight each other," he responded curtly. "It makes no difference to me whether they fight or don't. No difference at all whether they obliterate each other or live in tribal bliss. Either way it's none of my business."

"You certainly sparked the fire, though."

At these words he laughed, throwing his head back.

"Oh, did I? I daresay you sparked a thing or two yourself!"

I couldn't really argue with him. "Maybe so," I told him. "Maybe so. But in that case we're both guilty, aren't we?"

Forster raised one shoulder briefly, then let it drop, too indifferent even to muster a full shrug. "Suit yourself. My conscience is clean."

I couldn't stand his blasé attitude any longer. "That's the whole problem, goddamn it!" I shouted. "Your conscience is *always* clean—"

"It's these people who should face the music—"

"—no matter what you've done—"

"—and take a little responsibility for their own actions."

"—while you just sit there pontificating!"

We shouted like this for a while, both at the same time, neither of us listening to what the other said. It's a wonder we didn't come to blows. I suppose what restrained us was knowing that even a small conflict would have sent us both toppling off the ledge. After a minute or so we fell silent, glared at each other for a while, then forcibly averted our gazes.

I felt surprised at the time that Aeslu never leaped in, whether to calm us down or to berate us. More than once she had halted these arguments in the past before they escalated further; now and then she had joined in herself. It's not as though she lacked strong opinions on the subject, or a vested interest. Yet this time she said nothing. She didn't even acknowledge us. Aeslu sat gazing out toward the Mountain Land as if Forster and I didn't even exist. Ultimately her indifference, her obliviousness to Forster and me, was what silenced us.

I doubt her behavior revealed a concerted effort to constrain forces that might get out of control. I think she had simply withdrawn from us. She was too preoccupied with her vigil to care what either of us thought, said, or did.

* * *

Ultimately, though, Aeslu's vigil over the Mountain Land was what solved our dilemma.

"Smoke," she said abruptly, late on the second afternoon.

Forster, seated beside me at the time, made no response. I said nothing, either, though I roused from a daze and turned to her just then.

"Smoke."

"Indeed it is," Forster said at last, his tone full of the weariness a parent's voice might express toward a two-year-old who persists in practicing the same words ad infinitum.

"Curls of smoke."

"Curls?"

By now I was fully awake—well aware that Aeslu's words must have been something other than idle chatter. What, though? I didn't know.

Aeslu made an odd gesture: with the palms facing each other about two inches part, she raised her hands to eye level, then made a swirling motion with all her fingers.

Forster and I both stared at her.

"This is what the Mountain Stone is telling us," she said.

I asked, "What are you talking about?"

"Those lines."

At once Forster reached over to his pack, rummaged around, and pulled out the Stone. We all drew as close to it as he'd allow. The motions that Aeslu had been making did, in fact, bear some resemblance to what I saw there.

"Smoke," she said yet again. "Curls of smoke—like what rises in a hearth."

I said, "A hearth. A chimney. A narrow passage."

"That is what the Stone is telling us."

Still clutching the Stone, Forster stood, leaned back, and peered up the cliff. "What fucking *chimney* ... ?" Yet even the contempt in his voice didn't stop him from looking around with great care. First straight up. Then off to the left. Then to the right. Then—slowly now—very far to the right. A bulge of granite blocked our view of what must have been fifteen or twenty feet of nearly vertical granite before the cliff curved outward again to reveal itself. "So what you're telling us," he said without looking our way, "is that you think the Stone indicates a chimney here? We're supposed to climb a chimney?"

Aeslu made no reply. She glanced at me once, as if to question whether providing Forster with this information were such a good idea after all.

Forster went on, speaking mostly to himself: "Where, though? There's no chimney anywhere above us. Are we on the wrong ledge? Perhaps. Or did this ledge extend farther in the past? Perhaps a piece of it broke off." He took several steps toward the far end of the ledge. "Perhaps what we're standing on once extended all the way around the bend."

But of course he couldn't see any farther because that bulge in the cliff obstructed our view.

He stood there gazing outward for a long time. Then, placing the Mountain Stone in his knapsack—the one he used mostly just to keep the Stone out of our grasp—he put on his pack, slung on his rack of climbing hardware, and started coiling a rope. "I guess there's just one way to find out."

9

Months earlier I'd seen Forster solve a climbing problem similar to what faced us now. That had taken place the previous summer, when he'd joined forces with me briefly in the company of Aeslu and Norroi the Tirno. We were trying to locate the so-called Hermit of the Stones—the crazy old man rumored to be hoarding the Diadem in his mountain aerie—but we'd gotten stuck halfway up a cliff on our way to finding him. We couldn't get off a dead-end route up the cliff to a route that looked more promising. The second route started about twenty feet to the left of where the first route ended. Of course we considered simply traversing—working our way sideways using whatever hand- and footholds we could find—but there weren't enough holds to make it possible, much less safe. As nearly as we could tell, we were stuck.

Forster had solved that problem with a technique I'd never seen in action before: anchoring a rope at the upper reaches of the dead-end route, then using the rope as a pendulum to swing over to the other route. It was a dangerous stunt, but brilliant and effective. Since then—in fact, just during the 1960s and '70s—this technique has become one that climbers use routinely. Back then I'd never even heard of it. Norroi, Aeslu, and I were all stunned by what Forster had pulled off. I suspect that his audacity contributed to Aeslu's fascination with him at the time. Nothing I could have done or said just then might have altered her opinion of him for the worse. I hadn't even tried. What seemed most important then was simply that

Forster had gotten us out of our cul-de-sac and on our way upward again.

Now we faced a similar situation. We were stuck. The route we'd been climbing had reached a dead end; if the Mountain Stone were accurate, another route started nearby. But there was a lateral gap between them. How could we cross it? Forster's pendulum trick seemed the best bet.

This time, however, the difficulties facing us proved more complex than during the earlier instance. Even Forster couldn't find a place suitable for anchoring the pendulum. The cliff between us and the bulge we wanted to circumvent looked almost entirely smooth. There really seemed no way to get across at our level. Yet just as I'd begun considering the situation hopeless, I noticed that Forster had turned his attention to a much lower section of the cliff. He was scanning the rock face far below where we rested at the time.

"What good will *that* do?" I asked out loud. "We're trying to get up, not down."

Aeslu answered me before Forster could: "He will descend on a rope, then use it to swing over. From there he can climb upward till he finds the chimney."

Even as we discussed the situation, Forster was preparing to do precisely what Aeslu had anticipated. He pounded an iron piton in the ledge, clipped a carabiner through the piton's eye, ran a rope through the carabiner, coiled the rope's twin ends, and flung them over the edge. He then slung the now-doubled rope under his right thigh, across his back and over his shoulder in preparation for rappelling over the edge.

"Don't touch the anchor till I tell you to," he said at last, tugging the rope to test the piton's strength. "Once I've worked my way sideways, I'll want Jesse to set up a good solid belay. I'll explain what to do as we proceed." Then, without even wishing us good luck, Forster eased off the ledge and, boosting himself backward to clear the cliff, disappeared.

We couldn't see him for a while; the ledge blocked our view. Aeslu and I then got down on our hands and knees to peer over the precipice. Forster was already fifty or sixty feet below us. Every ten feet or so he'd kick away from the cliff, bound outward, and drop once more. Soon he was so far below—at least ninety feet—that the sight of his figure diminishing with each passing instant filled me with dread.

Aeslu and I glanced at each other.

A thought raced into my mind just then: *cut the rope.* I'd take my knife, cut Forster's lifeline, and watch him plummet to his death on the ridge five or six hundred feet below. Then we'd be done with him and his designs on the Mountain.

I didn't do it. I'll admit I reached for the knife—I went as far as grasping the handle—but I didn't draw the blade from its scabbard. Why, exactly, I can't tell you. I wish I could say it was some deep moral hesitance. . . . I'm not so sure it was. Not that the notion of cutting Forster loose didn't shake me up; I felt revolted by the impulse. Yet revulsion wasn't what made me falter. It was something far more practical. Cutting the rope would have been suicide as well as murder. Forster would have been dashed on the rocks, but Aeslu and I—relieved of Forster's company but trapped without the benefits of his knowledge—would have starved and frozen to death on our claustrophobic ledge. In some respects cutting the rope would have left the parties on both ends of it plummeting.

And so, as Forster descended, all Aeslu and I did was watch.

Forster then proceeded to do what he'd done on the Hermit's mountain: he secured the rope around his waist and—dangling at right angles to the cliff, so that its vertical surface became the ground he stood upon—he then raced in one direction, twisted about at the last moment, raced in the other direction, twisted again, and by this means swung farther and farther outward from the plumb line. After just a half dozen swings, he managed to clear the bulge of stone that had obstructed us before. In fact, he caught hold of it, pulled himself around it, and disappeared from our view again.

A long moment passed. Forster's plan had been to signal us, to wait for me to set up a belay, and to ascend in the relative security that these climbing procedures would allow. When no signal came, however, I wondered if he'd somehow got himself in trouble— perhaps snagged an outcropping or grabbed a handhold that gave him no way to advance or retreat.

Nothing happened. The rope curved gently toward where the cliff blocked our view.

Aeslu stared for a long time, then shot me a glance.

"I don't like this," I told her.

But no sooner had I spoken than the rope began to move. Not outward, stretching itself tighter, but upward, growing more and more slack with each passing second.

I couldn't believe what I saw. "He's climbing unbelayed."

Aeslu muttered something in Rixtir.

The rope sagged more and more as the far end rose closer to our own level.

At no point did I see Forster or what he was doing. Aeslu stepped back several paces on the ledge in the off chance that she might catch a glance of him. Nothing. Forster went about his business entirely beyond our view. Was he pounding in pitons to catch his fall in case he slipped? I had no idea. For all I knew, he'd gotten so intoxicated by his own prowess that he'd decided to climb free, unencumbered by the task of anchoring himself but unprotected from any but the slightest missteps.

Then, without warning, the rope began to tighten abruptly. The deep sag between the ledge and the granite bulge grew shallower; the rope itself skittered around the corner with a loud hiss. At this sight, Aeslu cried out, and I dropped to my knees near the rope's anchor point as though in an effort to restrain it myself. A foolish impulse: if I'd gotten hold of the rope just as it pulled loose, it would have yanked me down with it. But maybe the impulse wasn't so surprising. Forster's death would have meant ours as well.

Aeslu and I stared for a long time as the rope quivered against the cliff. It hadn't run out so fast that a bad fall seemed certain; perhaps Forster had lost his grip and slipped partway down a less than vertical surface. We just didn't know. All we could do was wait.

The rope fell still.

A long time passed before it started to move again.

Slowly at first, then faster, the rope began to sag once more. Soon it dangled far into the gap between the ledge and the granite bulge that blocked our view of Forster.

I saw his left hand first. Then his head. Then half his torso easing around the bulge.

He gestured, beckoning, as if we might just stroll across the void between us. "It's not bad," he called out. "Easier even than I'd expected."

What followed wasn't quite what he so breezily described. It was, in fact, much harder: Aeslu's efforts to duplicate what Forster had done, followed by my own. Forster coaxed us through the motions, however, and even provided a secure belay from the ledge he'd sought and found on the other side. Yet both Aeslu and I made it up there without more than a few minor slips.

The payoff wasn't finding the ledge, though; it was the chimney itself. Visible from the ledge was a steep shaftlike passage angling up from the ledge.

But simply making it to the chimney didn't solve everything. This wasn't a chimney in the usual way that mountaineers use the term: a narrow vertical passage between two slabs of rock. In fact, I could scarcely see any rock at all. Thick layers of snow had accumulated in the cleft that split the cliff's upper edge. This snow was nearly but not quite as hard as ice and formed a chute that we would now attempt to scale. Fortunately, the angle wasn't too steep—maybe thirty-five degrees—but it was steep enough. One slip on packed snow like that would send us sliding down the chimney, thus ending our climb.

Forster seemed oblivious to the risks and unconcerned about the close call he'd suffered a short while before. When Aeslu asked him what had taken place to pull the rope tight so fast, he rebuffed the question: "Nothing worth the effort to explain." His badly scraped hands suggested otherwise; still, no one pressed the issue. I suppose Aeslu and I wanted to keep moving just as badly as Forster himself.

So we did. We set up a new belay; Forster used his ice-axe to hack a little staircase up the chute; he worked his way up without a slip; he set up yet another belay; Aeslu followed him up; then I followed her in turn. Nothing went wrong. After two days' tedium on the ledge and two hours' terror crossing over to this chimney, our escape was almost amusing in its simplicity.

Then we were out: out of a world that intermingled rock and snow, into a world made of just one thing.

Ice.

10

Up to that point we had been scaling cliffs and ridges made of rock. The medium before us had been stone. What we employed to climb it was first and foremost our own hands and feet. True, we brought tools to bear as well: boots and gloves to protect our limbs, pitons, carabiners, and ropes to secure us against the risk of a fall; now and then other devices, too—the occasional use of a pick or an ice-axe, perhaps. But for the most part we climbed simply by working our way upward on whatever cracks, bumps, knobs, edges, or dips the surface of the rock presented. The surface we clung to was stark and hard, but it bore a fundamental similarity to much of the horizontal world. Only the angle of steepness made it different.

I should mention that ever since the time of Forster's reappearance on the scene, the three of us had been using Lowland techniques to climb. Forster wouldn't have it any other way. He wouldn't really acknowledge even that there *was* a Rixtir technique—that is, something other than what he called "Indian folderol"—and he derided us for keeping the Founders' Gear that Aeslu had collected and that she and I still carried in our packs. "You may as well jettison that stuff," he'd told us early on. "If you insist on lugging heavy packs, why don't you fill them with an equal weight of stones? They'll serve more purpose." Forster wouldn't even consider the notion of using any of those Rixtir tools. He used only his own. Since Aeslu and I had, in fact, chosen to rely on Forster to solve our impasse, we didn't have much choice but to follow his whims. That's precisely what we did. Lowland tools granted us the altitude we gained; Lowland spikes anchored us to the rock; Lowland rope linked us to the spikes. Aeslu and I weren't pleased with the situation. Aeslu, especially, saw our reliance on Lowland gear not just as ill-considered but as something akin to blasphemy. Still, as Forster himself frequently reminded us, we weren't in a good position to complain.

Now everything changed. What had been a rough, complex surface—stone overlaid with patches of ice and snow—was now a simpler but potentially more treacherous medium. A vast snowfield sloped upward from where we clung to its lower edge. How big was it? We couldn't tell, for the lack of reference points and the foreshortening of distances on such a steep surface combined to distort all sense of perspective. It could have been a few hundred, five hundred, or a thousand feet tall. As for the angle, I found that only a little easier to determine. I'd say it slanted at an angle of about fifty degrees. On rock, that angle wouldn't have seemed at all threatening; on ice, I couldn't contemplate it without a sense of deep, tingling fear.

Climbing ice was entirely different from climbing stone, and Forster's Lowland techniques weren't really up to the task. I don't mean to suggest that he was unskilled. Quite the contrary. Forster was nothing if not a superb climber, and his skill in using contemporary Western technique on ice exceeded any I'd ever witnessed. But the technique itself was deficient.

In those days, climbing ice relied heavily on step-cutting. This was true whether the slope in question was truly ice or, as with what we faced now, very dense snow. Forster himself was a master of this technique. Leaning slightly into the slope, he'd brace himself against it with his left hand while wielding his ice-axe in the right. Axes had long handles in those days— a stave more than a yard in length wasn't uncommon. He'd hack a little step in the ice just ahead of where he stood; then, while hacking a step another foot or so beyond, he'd take one pace forward, settling the points of his iron crampons securely into place. Then he'd hack another step and take another pace. The axe swung into the ice just ahead, then his boot kicked home, showering chips like sparks. On and on he went up without any sense of a struggle. Forster advanced so methodically that he might as well have been some kind of climbing machine.

After advancing a half-dozen yards or so, he'd stop, plunge the shaft of his axe into the ice-encrusted slope, secure the rope around it, and take his belay stance so that Aeslu and I could follow him with at least an illusion of security. The truth was, this procedure offered only minimal help in the event of a fall. That expanse of the Mountain was both steep and slick. Even a minor slip would have quickly gotten out of control. If I'd lost my balance, I could have done little but claw at the surface in hopes of digging my fingers in. I could have jabbed in the point of my ice-hatchet to arrest my fall. I could have leaned on the point while kicking the toes of my boots in hard. Those were standard techniques even then—techniques that often worked. But what chance would I have had, really, unless both my companions hadn't been caught off guard and, tensing up at the same moment, they'd braced themselves against the tug on the rope that my fall would have exerted?

In fact, this was precisely what happened. Except that I wasn't the one who fell.

Forster had taken the lead right off, as usual; he never even broached the notion of either Aeslu or me going first. We hadn't objected, either, since we acknowledged him as our superior in this regard no matter how much we reviled him otherwise. So there he was again, five yards ahead of us while I played out the belay rope and hoped with all my might that he didn't slip. In theory, Forster could have dug into the ice with his axe if he fell, and my sudden effort to pull the belay rope around my torso could have created enough friction to slow his descent. What happened in practice, though, might well be something else. Forster might not manage to dig in. He might lose control of his axe, or might even let go of it. He might slide so fast he'd yank both of us off the slope. There was no telling.

Of course nowadays there are various devices that make ice climbing safer than it was then. There are ice screws, pickets, dead-men—all sorts of gadgets to pound or bury in the snow and use to anchor the rope. The situation was far different in the twenties. About all you could do was set up the belay, climb skillfully, and hope for the best.

I didn't doubt that we'd set up a good belay. I didn't question Forster's skill. I certainly hoped for the best. What worried me was simply the unpredictability of ice and, for that matter, the fact that Forster outweighed me by fifty or sixty pounds.

The face was uneven, coated with layers of ice over a sheath of snow that in turn coated still more ice. Forster hacked through the top layer to expose the more solid one below. He looked as amused with himself as a little boy breaking old windows in an abandoned warehouse. The ice came down like glass, too, sometimes with the sound of shattering panes, sometimes with that of bursting light bulbs, sometimes with a tinkle so delicate that he might as well have been throwing wineglasses over the edge. At one point, Forster reached the mouth of a small ice cave. It wasn't much bigger than a laundry chute, and the opening was overhung with icicles. He twisted around to us and called out: "Listen to this!" Wielding his longer axe, he then swept the icicles away, sounding a rough chromatic scale as the pieces broke off.

He slipped at precisely that moment. Or rather the snow beneath him slipped—slipped so fast that he toppled over as if someone had yanked a carpet out from under his feet. In fact, that's just about what happened. A whole flat carpet of snow had disengaged from the surface underneath and slid away, carrying Forster with it. He was some yards off to my right just then, so he plummeted past Aeslu and me without coming near us.

Seeing him on the way down, I leaned on the head of my ice-hatchet. My hope was that shoving the embedded shaft deeper into the snow would hold the rope. Aeslu, meanwhile, tightened the rope where it passed around her body. The rope played out at first, then slowed. The ice-hatchet grunted in its effort to escape from me, but somehow it held. Forster rode the rope down till it tightened, swinging till he came to rest about fifty feet below us. The mass of loose snow he'd been riding broke up around him, skittered down the snowfield, and bounded off the cliff into oblivion.

For a long time, Forster lay facedown. I was sure he'd been hurt—he didn't budge.

Aeslu called out: "Forssa!"

No response.

I considered easing my way down there to check on him but held back: too dangerous to abandon the one anchor that restrained him from falling further.

Then, slowly, Forster raised his head and gazed upward at us. He raised one hand. He waved. Then he forced himself up and worked his way gingerly to where Aeslu and I awaited him.

11

He wasn't injured—at least not physically. But something other than Forster's body had taken a beating when he fell.

"I keep breaking through," he complained later that morning. "The ice isn't strong enough to support my weight."

He was right. Whatever his skill, Forster was too big to lead at this stage of the climb. His superior size had become a disadvantage. Aeslu and I, being lighter, could proceed more safely. Never mind that we weren't as strong. This was a fragile place, one where a light step went farther than a powerful stride.

We should have realized this earlier; or, realizing it, we should have acknowledged it. In fact I'd worried about Forster's massiveness from the time we first set foot on the ice. He was one of the biggest men I'd ever met—six three, six four, something like that. He must have weighed at least two hundred pounds. I couldn't imagine how someone of his size would avoid breaking through the crust at some point, perhaps even triggering a slide and dragging half the snowfield down with him. I said nothing at the time because my objections would have done nothing but enrage him. Forster had commandeered the climb to suit his own purposes, to be sure, but he was skillful enough that Aeslu and I had capitulated. Better to humor him while reaping the benefits of his skill than to anger him, thus jeopardizing the whole situation. Besides, he never would have consented to any alternative till faced with the irrefutable evidence of nearly going over the edge. This is why both Aeslu and I had kept quiet.

Having persuaded him to relinquish his position as the advance guard, however, we now won yet another victory. I brought up the issue myself, but Aeslu was the one who pressed it till Forster consented.

"Half the problem is your size," I said shortly after the three of us switched our positions on the rope. "But the other half is how we're climbing."

Predictably, Forster took offense at my words. "You have any better ideas?"

"Maybe, maybe not. All I know is that hacking away at the ice will bring us nothing but grief."

"That's the standard technique," he said with a huff.

"The standard Lowland technique."

His expression shifted from annoyance to amusement. "Are you suggesting that the Rixtirs have something better?"

Aeslu picked up the argument: "We must now switch to the Founders' Gear." She sounded as if everything had been decided.

"Founders' Gear," Forster said, his voice more than tinged with contempt. "And what, precisely, is the Founders' Gear?"

She gestured calmly toward the two Rixtir packs beside us.

"*That* stuff?"

She nodded without the slightest hesitation. "We must do what the gear itself tells us to do."

I could see Forster smile to himself at this notion, but he said nothing, so I stayed silent as well. There was no point in making him any more defensive than he felt already. Besides, I myself wasn't altogether confident in what Aeslu had asserted, though I thought I knew what she had in mind. Here, too, I stayed silent. I was too busy watching Aeslu pull pieces of equipment out of our packs.

Hooks, ice-hatchets, cramponlike devices: some items were easily recognizable. Others looked more unusual, yet I could guess the purpose of each item even when I'd never seen anything quite like it. For instance, there were some gloves—heavy gauntlets, really—with long, curved metal fingernails. They looked bizarre, almost sinister. Yet at a glance I could see what they were: the manual equivalent of foot-claws, the cramponlike devices that Rixtirra strapped on their boots to hold them steady on ice. How they worked, and how effectively, I didn't know. But at the very least Aeslu was right that in some senses, the gear would tell us what to do.

I can't understate the oddness of the situation—nor the mixture of excitement and apprehension this odd-ness created. Looking at the array of gear now spread out before us, I felt an almost uncontrollable eager-ness to put these things to use. Now we would get down to work! Now we'd show Forster a thing or two! At the same time, I couldn't feel entirely confident of what we were about to do. The Founders' Gear looked impressive, persuasive, powerful. But trusting it to take us to the Summit felt much like trusting a home-made flying machine that the Founders might have left us—a contraption, say, built from bamboo, feath-ers, osiers, pottery, and leaves. Would it fly? Maybe so. Would the Founders' Gear take us upward safely? Again, maybe so. I didn't have much choice but to hope it would. But I didn't *know*.

As I mentioned earlier, we had no idea where these things came from. No idea who made them. As for *what* they were made of—I didn't know then, and still don't. Even Aeslu didn't know. On some level, I sup-pose we weren't in a good position to care. The crux of the matter was this: we had the tools—enough tools for all three of us to use—and we needed them. How they'd come to be, and who had made them, were matters that puzzled us but concerned us far less than simply not falling off the Mountain.

And so we headed up, Aeslu and I taking turns in the lead position, Forster following; the Founders' Gear in full use, the Lowland gear now packed up and dragged up after us; the long-forgotten Rixtir techniques emerging as if from the old tools themselves, the Lowland methods soon discarded.

Aeslu was the one who figured things out. Should this have surprised me? Despite her ignorance of practical mountaineering, she learned fast—not just learned, but invented the techniques themselves even as she mastered them. Perhaps an element of tribal memory contributed to her nascent skill. Long ago, Aeslu's ancestors had apparently devised what now seemed a subtle means for climbing mountains. The Founders' descendants had lost this means, had let it distort into ritual and sectarian squabbles. Now, possessing the implements that the first generations of Mountain-Drawn had invented to pursue their goals, this young woman could see them and understand what they showed her; could grasp them and feel what they wanted her to do. This sounds superstitious, even animistic, but that's not what I have in mind. What she did with those climbing tools was no more remarkable, and no less so, than what a gifted young violinist might have accomplished while exploring the possibilities inherent in a Stradivarius. She found what was there. She helped these tools do what they were made to do.

Here's what I saw. I don't mean the preliminaries: how Aeslu sorted through the Founders' Gear, picked out what she wanted, and examined the various implements. I don't even mean how she tested them—trying out the ice-hatchets on the snowfield, kicking at the slope with the cramponlike devices that fit over her boots. Likewise regarding how Forster and I interacted with her throughout the process—he offering a derisive commentary on each tool and each attempt to use it; I trying to fend him off without aggravating him to the point of insurrection. Rather, I mean what she did once she got the hang of these things. How she started up the slope armed with an ice-hatchet in each hand, a set of footclaws on each foot. How she anchored herself first with the right hatchet, then with the left; next with the right claw, then with the left. How she repeated the sequence, each anchor in turn. How she advanced so smoothly and securely that even Forster's earlier step-cutting, for all its finesse, seemed sloppy, crude, precarious. How she climbed so far up the slope—unbelayed, since none of us, not even Aeslu herself, had expected her to go so far so fast— that when she turned to look back, her expression turned from exhilaration to alarm at the expanse now between us.

Using the Founders' Gear, was she as fully at risk as she would have been using Forster's Lowland equipment? Her stance was solid, anchored not just at the feet but at the hands as well. With the heads of both hatchets planted securely in dense snow and the footclaws hooked in as well, Aeslu seemed to be in little danger of slipping. She wasn't on the slope so much as partway in it. By comparison, Forster's step-cutting had always left him more or less tiptoeing up an icy staircase. Small wonder, then, that following her initial panicky glance, Aeslu gazed down at us with a smile that revealed Forster and me as the more precarious party.

"Well?" I asked Forster.

He stared upward at her for a long time. "Interesting."

We did not speak further as Forster and I selected our own share of the Founders' Gear and prepared to join Aeslu.

12

For two days we climbed rapidly and uneventfully. The effort was demanding but exhilarating. There was something congenial to me about ice. Despite its inconsistencies and instabilities, ice appealed to me more than rock. The hatchets seemed the perfect tools, ice the perfect medium. I didn't have to find my way up the ice—I *made* the way. I was a sculptor. I'd carve my way up the peak.

Sometimes Aeslu insisted that I go first. I was almost as light as she, and this allowed me to climb with scant danger of fracturing the face we climbed, thus pulling down chunks of ice, perhaps even the whole snowfield, on everyone else. Going ahead put my life in more immediate danger than going second or third, but not by much.

Once, when I was about twenty feet above the others on a slope glazed so hard and shiny that I saw my reflection there, Forster called up to me: "How is it?"

I was winded just then, exhausted in a peculiar way that made the air seem light, almost dustlike, a substance in suspension. I clung to my hatchets without moving—unless the quiver of my calf muscles counts as motion. I looked down. Somehow I'd managed to reach an almost perfectly smooth panel of ice, clear as a pond frozen overnight. Forster and Aeslu waited far below, slightly to my left, looking very small and precarious. I looked at the ice again.

A face gazed back at me.

I was so startled that the sight nearly jolted me off the cliff.

Forster again: "Well?"

I couldn't answer. There was a man inside the Mountain!

"Anything wrong?"

I turned away from my reflection, then back. I eased closer to the cliff. The expression was shadowy, wistful.

Aeslu called out, "What is it?"

"Nothing."

"Are you all right?"

"There's someone—"

"Do you want me to come up?" she asked.

These people below me, these real people, surely had their own reflections here, too, the ice-Forster and the ice-Aeslu looking out when they looked in. I returned to my reflection before me, watched for a few seconds, then went on.

13

Since the start of our effort, we had climbed in fair weather. Remarkably fair, given the time of year: this was still the rainy season. The weather wasn't perfect, but we'd suffered far fewer consequences so far than I would have expected. Not exactly what I'd call balmy—thirty degrees by day, zero by night—yet all in all it wasn't as harsh as it could have been. So far we'd been spared any storms. If the air wasn't altogether still, neither was it windy. We felt cold all night and all morning till the sun worked its way over the Mountain; all afternoon, though, we caught the full force of the sun's rays and soaked up its warmth. One of the delights of mountain climbing in that part of the world is one's proximity to the Equator: even in mid-April we found the sun powerful, consoling, sustaining.

Then, late one afternoon, the weather changed. There was no storm as such, just a sudden drop in temperature. Clouds moved in, streaming around the Mountain from the east and surrounding us. The wind picked up. Within half an hour, we were under siege.

I should have counted us lucky: most of the snow swirling around was probably spindrift—snow blown off the mountain itself, into the air, then down again. If we'd been caught in a blizzard, I don't think we could have survived. What truly threatened us was the wind. But *wind* is putting it mildly: this was more of a blast. The wind drove so hard against us that any exposed flesh seared as if from an open flame. Once the attack started, we were chilled almost at once. It was as if our gear—the Founders' Gear, even—counted for nothing. We couldn't have felt more exposed if we'd crouched there naked.

"Shit!" Forster exclaimed. He hunched down against the slope, burying his head in the crook of his right arm.

Aeslu and I, crouched to his left, huddled together. The wind pounded us so hard that I worried about being blown off the Mountain.

"What are we going to do?" she asked me, the words themselves swept away.

I tried to answer but couldn't: turning toward her, I felt the wind hit me hard enough that I could scarcely breathe, much less speak. I glanced over at Forster. He'd started digging a hollow in the snow. A snow cave? The slope we clung to was so dense—old snow collapsed into a material as hard as packed dirt—that I couldn't imagine we'd be able to dig very far. Yet even a relatively shallow depression would have helped. Anything to get out of the wind.

Working our way up to Forster, Aeslu and I joined him at his task.

We managed to dig a better snow cave than I'd thought feasible. After a depth of a foot or so, the outer crust relented, exposing a firm but less compacted substance below. This underlayer made it possible for us to scoop out a true cave—not exactly a suite at the Ritz, but better than being out there unprotected. It was dark inside, only a dull gray-blue light working its way in through the entrance tunnel, and the thick walls muffled the sounds both from inside and out. In this crowded space we sought refuge from the wind.

That night was one of the longest I've ever spent. Huddling next to one another, we crouched close to conserve warmth. Our cave wasn't deep, but at least it offered us a little protection from the blast. We nestled our packs on the windward side, then burrowed into our blankets and bedrolls. It was the best we could manage.

Early on I managed to fall asleep, but not for long. The cold woke me. Ordinarily I start out chilly, then warm up; this time I wakened so much colder than before that I actually sat upright in surprise. Maybe it was the wind. I could hear it everywhere—shrieks and moans. Needles of cold poked at me. Worse than needles: knives, daggers, bayonets of cold. I curled up to evade them. This helped at first, but not for long. I managed to fall asleep again but woke almost at once, startled by my own trembling.

"Are you awake?" I whispered to Aeslu.

Almost at once she whispered back: "I am."

"Are you all right?"

"Just cold."

I pulled her close, tried to shield her body with my own. "What are you thinking about?" I asked.

"Ice," she answered. "Lying in ice."

Before I could respond to these words, Forster's voice intervened: "Would you people hush up? How am I supposed to sleep with all this racket?"

We ignored him. Neither Aeslu nor I said anything for a while. Then, intrigued by her previous utterance, I asked what she meant.

She didn't speak for a long time. All I heard was the muffled storm noises outside the cave. "Something the Umbrage did once."

Right away Forster started in again, now nearly shouting: "Goddamn it—is this a mountaineering expedition or a slumber party?"

I said, "Let her speak."

Forster began jostling across from us—shifting his position so abruptly that he jolted Aeslu time after time and kicked me twice in the shins.

Aeslu called out in surprise or pain.

"Stop it, would you?" I shouted.

After a while we settled down. The space was absurdly tight. None of us could move without bumping into at least one of the others. An odd image came to mind just then: triplets, jockeying for position in the womb.

I asked Aeslu, "What was it that the Umbrage—?"

"Ah yes, the old Heir-Umbrage tiff," Forster said at once. "I never did understand why you people hate one another so much."

I couldn't believe what I was hearing. "I suppose the next thing you'll be saying is that you can't tell them apart," I told him.

"But isn't that the point? What real differnce—?"

"When I was twelve Sun-spans in age," Aeslu began, now in a clear, calm voice that immediately silenced both Forster and me, "I had been living with my adoptive parents for a long time. How long, exactly, I did not know, and I knew nothing at all about the circumstances of my birth. My parents told me that I was an orphan. So it seemed. But an orphan of whom? I suspect that even they were unaware of my origins. Only much later did I learn how I had been settled in their midst to hide and protect me from those who wanted me dead. If only they could have protected themselves as well.

"Umbrage came into town early one morning. Or perhaps the Umbrage were already among us. One never knew with the Umbrage; like shadows, they prided themselves on being everywhere and nowhere. All I know is that whether from within or without, a band of Umbrage raided our town.

"My adoptive parents were high-ranking Heirs, thus heavily guarded at all times. Yet the Umbrage moved with such stealth that even the presence of guards made no difference. Or perhaps the guards themselves were Umbrage. Either way, the Umbrage ransacked the town, rounded up all the Heirs, and prepared to kill them."

She fell silent a while. To my surprise, Forster made no effort to intrude himself into her narration.

"Do you know how the Umbrage kill their victims?" she asked us. "They use no ordinary weapons. No slings, no ice-hatchets, no knives, maces, or clubs.

They use ice. Ordinary ice. They do so—or at least say they do—in revenge for a massacre of Umbrage long ago. At that time, Heirs trapped a rebellious group of Umbrage near a glacier and, lacking sufficient weapons to use against so many people, pelted their number with chunks of ice until everyone had died. Whether the Heirs did what the Umbrage claim, I have no idea. My belief is that they did, but with better reason than the Umbrage will admit. What I know is that ever since, the Umbrage have struck out at the Heirs with ice. This is precisely what they did in my city: rounded up their victims, gathered chunks, blocks, and slabs from the nearby glacier, and brought ice against flesh till the deed was done.

"They made me watch. I saw my people—my adoptive parents, my aunts and uncles, my cousins, in fact all my kin—dashed and battered till the snow ran red. I alone escaped the rain of ice.

"Why did they spare me? I wish I knew, for I would rather have fallen beneath the Umbrage blows than watch everyone I loved go first, leaving me the sole survivor. Yet I do not mean to say that I escaped. The Umbrage held me captive the whole time. Perhaps they knew more about me than they would admit—more, at any rate, than I knew myself. Perhaps the Umbrage so detested me that they wanted me to suffer the deaths of all these people, not my death alone. Perhaps they chose to leave one witness because their revenge would thus seem all the greater. You would have to ask the Umbrage to explain themselves; I have never understood how they think.

"But as I say, I did not escape. Not altogether. The Umbrage had other plans for me."

She said nothing for a long time.

I gambled on prodding her. "What did they do?"

"When they had finished killing everyone else—" Again she faltered.

At first I thought something might have caught Aeslu's attention, so I listened closely for what she might have heard. In our icy womb, however, there was no noise but that of our own breathing and, sounding far away, the muffled shriek of the wind.

"When they had killed everyone else," she went on, "some of the Umbrage forced me down on the snow and—what is the Lowland word?—*violated* me."

Once more she fell silent. Except for that silence, I heard nothing that belied any emotion in her words. No cracking of the voice. No sobs. No thwarted rage. Simply the words, then silence.

Then, abruptly, she continued: "I did not conceive a child. Perhaps I was too young. Perhaps I was just lucky. But their violation conceived something else— my hatred of the Umbrage and of everything they believe."

I held Aeslu tight for a long time. Our position in that snow cave allowed me to embrace her, in fact let me do nothing else, with my own back against the curved wall and Aeslu's back nestled against the curve that my chest, belly, and thighs provided for her.

Hearing her tale, I couldn't think of anything I might do that would have soothed her, nor any words that would have consoled her. Not just words that would have consoled her for the pain she had suffered as a girl. I mean something else, too—words of consolation for the pain she had felt ever since, caught in the ongoing collision between the Heirs and the Umbrage. In some respects she'd never had a chance to live her own life; Aeslu had always lived the life the Masters and their foes had assigned to her. Which was the worse violation? The rape of her body? Or the rape of her entire life?

Unable to comfort Aeslu for either, I just held her tight in my arms.

Forster lay somewhere in front of her, though in the darkness I couldn't see him. Was he facing us now or facing away? I couldn't tell. If I'd reached out I might well have found him within reach, but I didn't. I felt his presence weighing on us too much already.

What did he think, though? What did he make of

Aeslu's tale? Did he understand her any better now, or understand her people?

I kept wanting to find out, to ask him for his reaction to all this, but I didn't.

I didn't have to.

After several minutes of my holding Aeslu in the snow cave's silence and dark, I heard Forster's commentary: beyond the woman I held came the low rasp of his snore.

14

I awoke the next morning almost paralyzed by the cold. At first I wasn't sure if I could move at all. Then I realized that I *could* move—I just couldn't feel what did the moving. My feet, especially, felt numb. Had I frozen? It took me a long time to realize that I hadn't. But whatever I'd suffered was too close to frostbite for me not to be alarmed.

Aeslu lay next to me, having eased onto her left side sufficiently to face in my direction. I gazed at her a while in the snow cave's blue-gray light. Her expression looked so peaceful—remarkably so, given our situation—that I hesitated to disturb her. Then I panicked. During several minutes of watching her, I hadn't seen her move even once. Had she died during the night? Or had she suffered such severe exposure that she was on the verge of death? I reached over abruptly, grabbed her clumsily by the shoulder, gave her a shake. She started, pulled back, and struggled as if with an attacker. When she gazed toward me, though, she relented. She stared at me for a long moment, then eased back. Her face revealed what little of a smile its chilled flesh could manage.

At this point I heard a rustling sound before me. I forced myself up high enough to see Forster struggling out of the cave. His efforts were ungainly, almost precarious, less controlled than any I'd ever seen him make. Just the sight of him struggling stunned me. To think that Forster—even Forster—might suffer the ills inflicted by a cold night! Did this thought please me? I can't say it didn't. In some ways I felt reassured to see him brought low by what had struck down Aeslu and me. Yet his struggle frightened me as well. It was bad enough that Aeslu and I might freeze half to death on a cold night; how much worse was the situation if Forster froze, too?

Without turning all the way around, I could tell he was intent on setting up his stove right there in the cave's mouth. All to the good: we couldn't take much more of this; the sun wouldn't come over the Mountain for another five or six hours; we had to warm ourselves by any means possible. But would his brass kerosene stove hold up against the elements? I had my doubts.

Forster flicked his lighter. His face flared briefly in the half-light as he cupped a hand to keep the flame from blowing out. It went out anyway. Leaning forward, he flicked his lighter once more. It went out again. He flicked it again. Again. Again. At last, he managed to get the lighter going and start the stove. When the blue flame started pulsing from the burner, he leaned to one side and flipped the lighter shut with a precise little click.

"What a shame you missed Aeslu's story," I told him once the tea was ready.

Forster and I crouched near the snow cave's entrance, where we clutched our cups close, desperate for whatever warmth we could absorb from the metal and ceramic. Aeslu, exhausted, still lay deep inside the cave.

He gazed at me through a pall of steam. "I didn't miss it."

"Your snores suggested otherwise."

Now he huffed in amusement. "Well—perhaps I missed the punchline."

"I resent the implications—"

"Don't even bother," said Forster, waving his hand as if to disperse me like steam. "Even if *she* won't spare me a sermon, I don't need one from you as well."

"Forster—"

"I'm up to here with all this Heir-Umbrage non-sense. Can't you grasp that? It's none of my business."

I could have struck him. I could have shoved him out of the snow cave and down the slope. I could have grabbed an ice-hatchet and lashed out at him. I didn't. Instead I said, "You certainly made it your business."

"Look," said Forster, setting his china cup down, "let me save you some trouble. Have you ever watched a pond freeze?"

"What do you mean?" I asked. "What pond?"

"Any pond."

"I've seen lots of frozen ponds—"

"That's not what I mean. Have you ever watched *how* they freeze?"

I just watched him, uncertain of what he intended.

"I've always been fascinated by the whole process, the strangeness of it. Just a few degrees difference and the water turns to ice. How ordinary, how unremarkable. But it has always seemed nearly miraculous. What is supple grows rigid. What is soft turns hard. What is shapeless gains shape. It might as well be magic."

"Get to the point."

"The point, Jesse, is that pure water is hard to freeze. It needs something external—something to crystalize *around*. Add a speck of dust to frigid water and the process begins almost at once. The needles of ice form and criss-cross the whole surface. A sheet of ice forms on top. Then it thickens—thickens fast, too—till the whole thing is ice."

"I don't know what you're talking about."

He looked at me with a quizzical grin. "No? I thought that's just what you were going to lecture me about. What we've done to the Mountain Land. But you see, what has happened here hasn't really required me to attack these people—or for you to, either. It's been enough simply for us to show up. The conditions are ripe. These people have been killing and raping one another for millennia. Once we came here, events only intensified. People thought of us in a certain way. Our presence made things crystalize—to take on form and substance—but the potential for disaster was already here. The shapeless took shape. Fears. Hatreds. Longings. Beliefs. And everything changed all at once."

He gestured beyond the cave to the snowfield beyond.

"Like ice," said Forster. "Just like water turning to ice."

15

How long did we hide in that cave? Several hours, at least. Of course I can't speak for the others, but the incessant wind left my whole body in such acute discomfort that I lost what little time sense I still possessed. We kept track with Forster's Rolex, yet the dial and the hands told us a story that made no sense in relation to our suffering. Time itself slowed as if on the verge of freezing. All we could do under the circumstances was hunker down and wait for a lull.

I wanted warmth, heat, fire, anything radiant. I wanted them with such intensity that simply wanting them so much should have warmed me. It didn't. Nothing but the real thing would have made a difference. If anything, the intensity of my desire chilled me further—slowed my body, addled my brain, muddled my thinking.

At one point I caught the scent of coffee in the air. Forster drank tea, not coffee, yet it was coffee I smelled. This brought forth all sorts of memories: waking up during my boyhood to smell the aromas of breakfast wafting in from the kitchen; camping trips; my residential house at college. Soon the scent was so persuasive that I couldn't restrain myself any longer. "Smell that?" I said.

Forster looked at me, expressionless. "Smell what?"

"Coffee."

"What coffee?" He turned away.

Aeslu glanced in my direction without seeming to notice me.

When I sniffed at the air again, all I could smell was the sharp, empty odor of the cold.

I decided not to press the issue. The sun already hung low before us, sinking into haze over the cordilleras. The whole sky filled with bright orange light. This should have brought some kind of warmth along with it but didn't. If anything, it left me colder than before.

Then, abruptly, I saw something that made me tingle all over. I had tilted back a moment to gaze upward at the Mountain. Something rose from the slope in a plume and dissipated into the air above us. "Look!" I shouted. "Steam!"

Only Aeslu budged, and then just to glance upward briefly.

"The Mountain is a volcano—a dormant volcano!"

"Ease off, damn it," Forster said.

"Once we get up there we'll be warm."

He stayed motionless, his head tilted back against the rock wall. "Just stop it—it's not a volcano."

Aeslu looked at me but didn't speak.

I said, "Tell me what accounts for the steam."

"Nothing. There's no steam," Forster said. "It's snow."

"I saw it dissipating into the air."

"It's snow blowing off the summit."

Maybe he was right. The weather didn't ease. On the contrary, the clouds thickened just after nightfall, churned all around the Mountain, swept past. The only change I detected was for the worse: what had been empty wind before now brought snow. Sharp, icy snow. Snow that stung as it struck, hissing, more like sand than snow, as if we were imperfections on a stone facade that sandblasters would now wipe clean from the surface.

16

I won't claim that we slept that night, but we hunkered down, we hid in our cave, we sank into a kind of cold-induced stupor that gave at least the illusion of rest. And I won't claim that we awakened, for you don't really awaken from that sort of daze—you surface bit by bit, like someone after almost drowning. Surface we did, though. We stirred and groaned and struggled to move. We pushed the snow from the cave's entrance. Well after noon we forced ourselves out.

What lay all around now dazzled me. I couldn't even see at first, I just looked this way and that trying to make my eyes open. Mountain Made of Light indeed! As if the whole peak had transmuted itself from matter into energy, the Mountain quivered with the most intense glare I'd ever seen. Only with great effort could I pull back my hands from my face to squint at the spectacle before me.

The whole Mountain was caked with new snow. The sun, just now breaking through the cloud cover, shone down on us and left everything so bright—painfully radiant—that I feared for the safety of my vision even as I tried to see what lay around us. Yet I rejoiced in my bedazzlement. Light meant warmth, and all I wanted was to be warm.

"Well, now what?" Forster asked as we dug ourselves out and established something more like a real camp.

We'd been lucky. The temperature had risen as the snow started falling; the new layer was dense. If it had been made of light, fluffy snow, we would have found ourselves in grave danger of an avalanche. To our delight, the new snow stuck to the old like wet plaster. What lay around us now didn't improve the odds of our getting out alive, but it didn't worsen the odds much, either.

Aeslu gestured upward with one hand as if no other comment were necessary.

Forster smiled at the sight of this gesture. "Fine. Now the question is how. Not to mention where."

"We must consult the Stone," said Aeslu.

"Indeed," he said. "The Stone."

I should mention that from the time of our first setting off together, I'd sometimes caught Forster staring at the Mountain Stone, huddling in a position that both allowed him to examine it while simultaneously protecting it from our intrusive gaze. The effect wasn't unlike that of a teenage boy poring over some dirty pictures. Forster was at once thrilled by what he saw and ashamed of the thrill. He tried to keep us from seeing what he had and from seeing his response to it. Yet in our close quarters, those efforts at secrecy revealed precisely what he wanted to hide. What did he make of the markings on the Stone? What were his intentions in contemplating them at such great length? I could only surmise that Forster hoped to figure out the glyphs etched there and, if possible, to undertake the rest of the climb alone. He'd made no bones about having Aeslu and me along just to tap her knowledge of the Stone. If he could have proceeded successfully without her, would he have done so? I never doubted that the answer was yes. If he couldn't, though? That's where things stood. And so in the dazzle following the storm, Forster took out the Stone yet again but kept it to himself and examined it alone.

Aeslu and I watched him for a while, pretending not to, well aware that we shouldn't interrupt or distract him.

Then, abruptly, grasping it by the base, Forster thrust it toward us and asked, "What's the next step?"

Aeslu pondered what he held out to her. She said, "If I could only examine it more carefully—"

"Out of the question," he said at once. "Just look it over, do what you can, and tell me what you think."

From what we could tell by examining the Stone, it appeared that we had angled most of the way up the snowfield and were now approaching another ridge. Where we were, exactly, none of us knew. But our overall position seemed clear enough. The question now—a question that puzzled not just Aeslu and me, but also Forster—was what happened to the route. The etched line indicating our path proceeded diagonally on that particular facet of the Stone; instead of reaching the ridge that it formed with the adjoining facet, however, the line simply ended. It did not extend all the way to the edge. Neither did it head in a more nearly vertical path toward the Stone's point— the tip that represented the actual Mountain's Summit. The Stone seemed to be telling us we were about to arrive at a dead end.

Yet that couldn't be. Around the corner, so to speak—on the adjoining facet—another etched line started up just short of the edge and resumed its upward course. There was a gap between the end of one line and the start of the other.

Forster, still grasping the Stone in his left hand, now raised it to eye level. He rotated that big chunk of quartz slowly, first clockwise, then counter-clockwise. "Odd," he said quietly. "It sort of ends in the middle of nowhere, then picks up again on the other side."

Aeslu asked, "May I see?"

Once again he showed her the Stone.

When she tried to examine the object in Forster's hands, though, he pulled it away. "I think you can see it well enough," he said.

"Forster, damn it," I grumbled, "give us a chance."

He smiled faintly without bothering to glance my way. "I rather thought that's what I'm doing."

"How can we see what we're dealing with—?"

"There is a hole," said Aeslu just then.

Both Forster and I fell silent.

"There is a hole in the Mountain Stone," she went on. "Right there." She reached out and pointed to where the route line seemed to disappear.

On hearing these words, Forster pulled the Stone closer and tilted it this way and that, trying to catch the light in a way that revealed whatever Aeslu had seen. For a while he seemed unable to detect anything like what she had described.

Aeslu reached out again to note the spot.

Forster shoved her hand away. "Ah-ah-*ah*!" he exclaimed. At once he resumed his examination of the Stone. Then he said, "You're right. I see what you mean."

I leaned forward to look.

He withdrew the Stone at once from my intruding gaze. "It goes precisely from where one line leaves off to where the other begins." Forster held the Stone close to his face, blew abruptly on it, then held it close again. "Seems to be plugged up, though," he said. Without so much as setting it down, Forster rummaged around in his coat pocket till he pulled out some sort of leather kit. He flipped it open with his thumb. Inside were an assortment of jewelers' tools: tiny screw drivers, wrenches, awls, and others I couldn't even recognize. Forster picked out the narrowest of the lot—not much more than a needle—and carefully prodded at the Stone with it. Almost at once the needle poked through whatever had been obstructing that tiny hole and went straight through to the other side. "There we are."

Aeslu and I stared at what rested in his hands.

"The question remains," Forster went on, "what does this hole indicate about the route?"

Aeslu spoke without hesitation: "Is it possible that we should not be going up the Mountain but *through* it?"

"Through it!" Forster huffed. "What an absurd idea."

Aeslu asked me, "What is this 'absurd'?"

I told her, "Ridiculous. Foolish."

At once she replied, "It is not absurd."

"Damn right it is," said Forster emphatically. "At least on this kind of mountain. Maybe not on a volcano—but this isn't a volcano. There's no way this kind of peak would have a tunnel running through it."

"And what if someone put it there?" she asked.

"Put it there! Now *that's* certainly a big 'if'!"

"She has a point," I told him. "There's plenty of evidence that someone has already climbed the Mountain."

He leaned back and smiled as he did when feeling most thoroughly contemptuous. "You're jumping to conclusions. There's evidence that someone has *attempted* it. Not much evidence, to be sure—just a little. But there's certainly none at all that anyone has succeeded or even come close to succeeding."

"What if they did, though?"

"Then they did. But that doesn't mean there's a tunnel."

"The Mountain Stone has showed us the way every time," Aeslu said abruptly. "It will show us yet again."

Forster smiled once more. "Fine." He gestured as if inviting us to proceed straight into the icy wall. "After you."

Aeslu could have taken this as a rebuff—mockery intended to stop her right then and there. Instead, she raised her ice-hatchet, stabbed it into the snow slanting toward the face, and started up again.

17

The new snow coating the Mountain added little to our difficulties. Though almost five inches thick, it was claylike in consistency and secure in its hold on the old layers beneath. We faced no new risk of dislodging masses of it—masses that would have dislodged us in turn—and thus we made good headway up the snow-field. If anything, our pace was faster than usual. The prospects of nearing another ridge drew us forth with great haste.

Something else made a difference, though: the Founders' Gear. I've mentioned some of the items there already. These and others now helped us climb in ways that would have been impossible otherwise.

There was a picklike tool with a point so sharp that it penetrated even the hardest ice as if heated first in a forge. I don't know what material it was made of—metal, stone, ceramic?—or what let it slide so easily into anything it struck. I don't know what made it hold so tenaciously once I'd anchored it. All I know is that this particular tool allowed me to work my way up icy surfaces that I never would have managed by other means.

There was a narrow spike—roughly the size and shape of a knitting needle, but with an eye at one end—that was the first ice-screw I'd ever seen. And not just the first: the most reliable, too. More than once during that climb I twisted one of those shafts into the ice, clipped the rope onto its exposed head, and proceeded to climb, all the while wondering how such a narrow bit of metal could hold my weight if I fell; and more than once I fell soon afterward, only to find that the spike held fast.

There was a pair of gloves with fingertips ending in claws that would have done justice to a mountain lion. Some sort of ceremonial accessory, like all the Heirs' animistic garb? That's what I thought at first. Yet everything else among the Founders' Gear was practical in nature, and these gloves were no exception. Those claws turned out to be just what they seemed. Worn properly—not just put on, but strapped tight to the wrists—they functioned as a kind of manual crampon. The tips provided a remarkably firm hold on all but the slickest ice. One didn't dig with them but rather *eased* them in. With a little practice, I found it possible to climb the most treacherous slopes.

I could go on and on. There were all sorts of gadgets. Climbing gadgets, camping gadgets, survival gadgets. Not just gadgets: clothing, medicine, food. An unguent to counteract the effects of frostbite. Goggles, woven of osiers and covered with a dark, porous tissue, that saved our eyes from snow blindness. Powder that, when mixed with snow, made a tasty pudding. Any one of these items might have made our struggle less arduous or the dangers we faced less overwhelming; together, they let us feel that we might even succeed in reaching our goal.

What we reached by means of this equipment, however, was one of the most complex barriers we had encountered so far. We arrived at a ledge of accumulated ice and snow about ten or twelve feet deep and perhaps a hundred feet long. It was irregular in surface—a series of icy humps that were relatively high or low depending on how heavily the last ten or twenty years of snowfall had built them up. The far end of this ledge met the low end of a huge glacial slope that slanted above us from left to right. The overall effect resembled that of our facing a huge roof. The icy wall before us was the house. The slope above was the roof itself. Our temptation, of course, was to walk along the ledge, reach its juncture with the roof, and proceed upward on its mostly gentle angle. That certainly would have been the obvious route. Yet that wasn't the route that the Mountain Stone indicated— hence our dilemma.

Something else about the wall: it was clearly the result of many decades of snowfall. A quirk of the winds in that particular place had prevented the formation of a cornice—one of those snowdrifts on slopes and summits that accumulate, forming a kind of pompadour that either builds up higher and higher or else sags over the edge. Nothing blocked our side view of the mountainside. The mountainside right there was essentially a huge pile of strata, each stratum about three feet thick, each the result of a full year's snowfall. The sight reminded me of what one sees driving along certain modern highways in mountainous terrain—layers of rock exposed for the road to pass through—except that here the layers were densely packed snow instead of rock. Some of the layers had been eroded by years of seasonal freezes and thaws. Other layers looked almost pristine. To extend the metaphor of the huge house, it appeared as if the layers of ice were shingles—shingles a yard thick— piled one atop another as deep as we could see.

What made the sight even more impressive were the icicles. Thousands of icicles hung off the roof above us. Some of these looked like ordinary icicles, though longer than usual: four, five, six, seven feet long. Others were icicles of an altogether different order of magnitude: ten, fifteen, twenty feet long. It's hard to imagine icicles that big but not hard to find them on a glaciated peak. That rooflike slope was covered with them. They dangled overhead in vast parallel rows—thin, white, dense—the baleen of a massive whale.

What Aeslu did just now was to work her way up to the wall itself and, wielding her ice-hatchet, hack through some of the icicles to expose more fully the strata beyond. Initially her actions struck me as foolish. She was knocking down the icicles at their lower reaches—chopping them off at the tip—yet the impact of her hatchet on their shafts sometimes fractured them far higher. Pieces of ice showered us. Not just pieces: teeth, fangs, whole tusks of ice. At times entire icicles came loose and skittered around us.

"What are you doing!" exclaimed Forster as he dodged some of these fragments.

I was too busy avoiding what fell to shout my own disapproval. As icicles shot past all around, I could easily imagine that Aeslu's impulsive attacks would end up getting us killed.

Yet within a few minutes she had penetrated the first barrier of icicles—the whale's baleen—and now stood as if in the mouth itself.

"Here," she said.

Forster had ceased his objections when the barrage let up. Now, without further hesitance, he followed Aeslu's path, entered the place she had reached, and stood there with her. I followed, too.

It wasn't really a snow cave. It was more of a conical depression, a concavity resulting from unidentifiable forces—the wild winds that had eroded all this accumulated ice and snow, perhaps. To my eyes, nothing about it looked promising.

Nor to Forster's. He gazed on Aeslu's discovery without any sign of enthusiasm. "So?" he muttered.

Aeslu paid him no attention. Without even stopping to rest, she started hacking at the ice with her hatchet's blade. Chips flew in every direction. Forster and I had to back off just to avoid getting hit.

"This is pointless," he said. "You can dig if you want, but you'll dig for months before you get anywhere. And all you'll reach will be the rock underneath the ice."

I didn't feel much more optimistic than Forster. I felt badly about Aeslu's effort, though; after watching a while, I pulled out my own hatchet and set to work beside her.

Forster put down his pack nearby, took out his stove

and cookpot, and prepared to melt some ice. It was Forster's teatime. He had trouble starting the stove, however: his lighter seemed to be malfunctioning. Out of fluid? Time after time it wouldn't light. He persisted, though, coaxed forth a flame, and soon had his pot hissing nicely.

Meanwhile, Aeslu and I managed to hack our way past some inner layers of icicles into a passageway beyond, and we did so quickly enough that Forster's tea strainer never even made it into his Wedgwood cup.

18

"It's just an ice cave," said Forster, not sounding altogether persuaded, but his actions seemed less skeptical than his words: he set down his kettle, stood, and stepped closer to where Aeslu and I had been at work with our hatchets. He all but pushed past me for a closer look.

Even a quick glance revealed this to be something far different from an ice cave. Enough light entered the mouth to illuminate not just the ice-choked throat but also the passageway beyond. It wasn't a cave at all; it was a shaft. What kind, exactly, we couldn't tell. Whether natural or man-made was uncertain, too. But this much we knew: it was far too long, narrow, and rocky to be an ice cave.

As if to disarm the rebuffs that he knew would follow, Forster took the offense. "All right, it's not an ice cave. Maybe it's not even a cave. But either way we're not about to plunge in headlong."

"The Stone tells us to enter the Mountain," said Aeslu.

"Once again you're jumping to conclusions. There's a hole in the Stone—"

"Which means we should enter the Mountain."

"Not necessarily."

"The Stone is always right," she said, resolute.

Forster picked up a piece of ice and threw it into the shaft. We listened to it clatter and fall silent. "Look," he said, "I've never heard of climbing a mountain by crawling inside. This is crazy."

As he spoke, Aeslu eased backward down the heap

of broken icicles we'd accumulated under foot; she stepped over to where all our equipment lay; she rummaged around for something in her pack; she returned to where I waited with Forster. I saw at once what she'd brought: a small clay bowl. It resembled the fat-filled pots that Aeslu had scavenged from the Founders' Gear—pots that provided a heat source for our cooking. This was smaller, though, and narrower at the top. A thick string dangled from the opening.

Aeslu told Forster, "I need your fire-tube."

"My *what*?" he asked, glancing my way.

"Your cigarette lighter," I told him.

He hesitated a moment, then complied reluctantly. Aeslu took the lighter and fumbled with it for a while. She couldn't get it going. Forster then took it back, tried his luck, and failed as well. The sparking wheel and flint seemed to work well enough, but the wick just wouldn't catch. Then, almost ready to give up, he managed to produce a flame. He held it close to the pot's string. It didn't catch immediately but burned well once the fire took hold.

Handing the lamp to me without a word, Aeslu then retraced her steps to our pile of equipment, hoisted her pack, strapped it on, and returned once more to the shaft. She took the lamp from me in silence and, ducking her head, took the first few steps inward.

Forster railed against her—she was nuts, this was total madness, we'd get ourselves stuck!—yet in the end he followed. Perhaps he just planned on humoring her: going along till she realized her folly and backed out. Perhaps his doubts wavered: she'd been right all too often. Perhaps he just feared being left behind. One way or another, he followed.

The task turned out easier than I'd expected. After we got past the initial icy constriction, the passage widened. It resembled an artificial shaft—a mine or a tunnel—more than a natural formation. It was sinuous, with irregularities in both its vertical and horizontal shape, yet it was also tall enough to allow

Aeslu's walking through it without stooping. (Even I, and certainly Forster, had to hunch over to avoid blows to the head.) At times the walls were heavily obstructed by chunks of rock jutting into the passageway. I found it hard to balance the evidence one way or the other to explain how this structure had come about. Overall it seemed far more predictable than what was likely as a consequence of geology alone. The Mountain was made out of rock I never found easy to identify, but in any case I couldn't imagine any natural origins for such a long passageway. I wasn't sure which explanation disturbed me more: that this shaft resulted from human efforts, or that it didn't.

One reason for the difficulty in deciding was, of course, Aeslu's lamp. Although it allowed us to proceed, it literally didn't shed much light on our surroundings. Its flame was feeble and erratic and gave off little more than a warm, buttery glow. Aeslu certainly benefited from it most. Holding it in the palm of her hand, she seemed able to advance confidently by whatever light it cast. Her body blocked most of its rays, though, so that I walked almost entirely in her shadow. Forster in turn walked in mine. The best he and I could do was to follow her shape and trust that she stepped carefully.

Under these circumstances, it didn't surprise me that Forster cursed the lamp almost nonstop. It scarcely deserved the name! Even a candle would have been dazzling by comparison! It cast more shadows than light! He went on and on. I ignored him, intent simply on not stumbling.

Just then the lamp went out. Darkness hit so hard, fast, and totally that I recoiled as if from a blow.

We stood there motionless for a long moment. Just ahead of me, Aeslu muttered to herself in Rixtir; behind me, Forster shouted curses and demands. I called out, too, pointlessly, as if the force of my denial could ignite the lamp again.

"Give it to me!" Forster yelled.

Just then he jolted into me. The impact didn't hurt,

but it threw me off balance hard enough that I fell
against Aeslu. A moment later I heard a thump and
a clatter just ahead, the noise precisely that of breaking crockery.

Aeslu cried out at the sound.

Forster shouted: "God damn you, Jesse! What the
fuck did you do *that* for?"

"What the fuck did you bump me for?"

"I didn't fucking bump you—I just tried to get the
lamp away before you did something really stupid."

"Well, you *did* bump me—"

"Look, God damn it—"

"Stop!"—Aeslu's voice now. "Just stop!"

Everyone fell silent.

It's hard for me to explain what I was feeling right
then. It's hard enough to explain what I saw and
heard. First of all, the darkness. It was absolute. Imagine the darkest night and you're not even close, for at
night you could detect a glint of illumination somewhere. Imagine yourself in a windowless room that
same night and you've come closer but still not close
enough—at least a glimmer of light would somehow
make its way in. Here there was nothing. Not a glimmer, not a glint, not the merest hint. Nothing. The
darkness surrounded us, engulfed us, flooded us,
drowned us. Yet when I say nothing, that's not quite
true. It was nothing and everything. Or rather, nothing
and anything. The human eye can't really tolerate
darkness that deep. For lack of anything to see, the
eye conjures something anyway. Not things, exactly,
but shapes, colors, contours. I could have sworn I saw
Aeslu off to my left at one point: a rim of light deline-
ating her left arm, shoulder, and the side of her face.
Yet when she spoke a moment later, the words came
from somewhere else altogether.

Which brings me to what I heard. I heard what
Forster and Aeslu said, of course—we stood within a
few feet of one another. But I heard something else,
too. Not silence, really. It was a staticky sound, a kind
of hiss. I've learned since then that in the absence of

anything else to hear, the human ear detects the sound of blood pulsing through capillaries deep within its own flesh. A reassuring thought? Not really. I didn't know the source at the time. Besides, this phenomenon is unsettling in its own right: as if the ear can't tolerate the notion of real silence and resorts to its own burble and swish for consolation.

At this point I heard a real noise, though—a scraping noise—somewhere behind me. I turned to see something as well. Sparks. Tiny golden sparks. The sight baffled me till I realized that Forster was trying to restart his lighter.

"Damn!" he said under his breath.

Aeslu bumped into me then; she, too, must have been turning to look. "What is it?" she asked.

"Damn lighter won't light."

We waited, almost too anxious to breathe, while Forster sparked his gadget time after time.

"If you weren't so obsessed with your goddamn tea," I told him, "you'd at least have had some fuel left for emergencies."

The answer came at once: "Don't push your luck, Jesse."

"We cannot waste time arguing," Aeslu stated just then. "We must proceed."

Forster struggled with his lighter for what seemed a long time. Nothing came of the struggle, though. If anything, those sparks taunted us, mocked us, made the darkness even darker than it was already.

"We must proceed," Aeslu said again.

Never mind that what she said made sense; the words themselves—I mean simply the sound of human speech—brought me to my senses quicker than a splash of cold water.

Forster interrupted at once. *"Proceed?"*

"Into the mountain."

"This is insane!" he blurted. "We'll be lucky to find our way back to where we entered."

"All the more reason to proceed."

I felt uneasy to find myself agreeing with Forster, but I did. "He's right, Aeslu. Let's not push our luck."

A long silence. Then her voice again: "The Stone says we enter the Mountain—"

"Not without a light, though."

"—to reach the other cliff—"

"Not groping blind."

"—and then continue to the Summit."

"Out of the question," said Forster. "We'd have no idea what we're getting into."

She went on no matter what we said. "The Stone has showed us the way. Now we must proceed."

Before anyone spoke again, I heard something else: not a word but a slow, dull scraping sound. Nothing loud—simply unmistakable. A footfall.

"Aeslu?"

Another footfall.

"Aeslu?"

"Here," she replied. The tone was calm but shocked me anyway: I could detect the distance she had already walked.

Forster spoke next: "All right, then."

I heard his own footsteps almost at once—louder, more pronounced—as he passed from my right toward the left.

I had no alternative but to follow.

19

We adapted to the circumstances as well as possible. Unable to see the tunnel, we groped our way through it by touch alone. Unable to see one another, we linked hands. Aeslu led; she reached back to Forster; Forster in turn reached back to me. I have no idea how Aeslu managed—whether she patted the rock floor ahead of her, followed the walls, or did something else—but she managed. She went ahead with surprising speed. Not that we went fast: simply not as slowly as I'd have expected. There were fewer stops, too. Now and then one of us—usually Forster, given his height—bumped into a rock jutting from the walls or ceiling. Otherwise we moved forward without mishap. If not exactly level, the path before us was nonetheless almost bewilderingly free of major obstructions.

For this reason I found it hard not to wonder again about the origins of this passageway. Was it simply a fissure in the mountainside? A kind of lateral chimney? In all my years of mountaineering, I'd seen nothing like it. Was it a true tunnel, then—something of human origin? This seemed unlikely. How long would it have taken the Founders to burrow a shaft through solid stone? At this altitude, yet? Even with hundreds of workers they would have been tackling an almost impossible task. Yet here it was—whatever it was—a passageway wide and tall enough for adult human beings to pass through at a crouch.

The grade increased. Within a short while we weren't walking but scrambling. It wasn't steep: fif-

teen, perhaps twenty degrees. Any normal illumination would have let us use our hands only for balance
and occasional assistance. But in the dark, it was steep
enough that we had to go up on all fours. Handholds
were all over the place—no problem in that regard.
The problem was that we had no idea where we were
going. I know *I* didn't. I suspect that Aeslu didn't. I
could hear her muttering to herself in Rixtir as she
grappled her way upward. Forster fared better: he
could follow Aeslu's noise. And I could follow hers
and Forster's both, an odd duet of words, grunts, and
heavings for breath as they struggled.

Suddenly something bashed against the side of my
head. The blow hit so hard, I lost my grip on the
rocks. Luckily it wasn't steep enough just then that I
fell; I just toppled forward. The motion sent me face-
first into the slope I'd been climbing. I took another
blow then, this time right to the forehead, but at least
I regained my grip. And precisely at that moment,
something scraped across my right hand, nearly dislodging it yet again. Forster's boot!

"Watch out, would you?"

"Watch out yourself."

"You keep stomping me."

"Then don't climb so close." He didn't sound apolo-
getic: I'd inconvenienced him by obstructing his boot
with my face.

I held back briefly, allowing Forster to get farther
ahead. But not too far.

A troubling thought kept nagging at me—a thought
that had struck me almost as hard as Forster's boot
but which, unlike the boot itself, kept pounding away
despite my effort to ignore it. The kick wasn't
accidental.

We proceeded uneventfully for a while, however, so
I made no further objections. Our progress must have
surprised all of us to the point that it seemed best
simply to keep going. That's certainly how I felt. I
tried to ignore my own uneasiness; the main thing was

just getting out of there. And somehow that's exactly what we were doing.

Despite these preoccupations, something else preyed on my thoughts: Forster's pack. I couldn't stop wondering what left it nearly bursting at the seams. Granted, Forster carried a lot of supplies. He had more cold-weather clothes than Aeslu and I combined. He had his own stash of food. He had his Lowland climbing tools and a share of the Founders' Gear. No doubt the sum total of all this stuff accounted for most of his pack's sheer massiveness. Even so, I couldn't suppress a hunch that something else, something hidden, added to the size and weight of what Forster carried on the climb.

I'd toyed with this hunch ever since he first arrived in our midst. As I mentioned earlier, I waited and watched, hoping that Forster might inadvertently reveal his secret. I even contemplated the possibility of probing for an answer to my question. No such luck: he never let down his guard. And in our tight quarters—we were always stuck together on the same tiny ledges and outcroppings—no opportunity arose in which Forster might have wandered off even for a few minutes. My question remained unanswered.

Then, to my surprise, precisely such an opportunity presented itself. The tunnel that confined us also freed me to explore. The darkness that hemmed us in also gave me a veil with which to obscure my actions.

What happened took place during one of our frequent rests. Working our way through the tunnel was strenuous, exhausting work. In addition to the physical effort of crawling in a constricted space, we felt the strain of uncertainty and claustrophobia. The air, too, oppressed us—it was close, fetid air, yet so thin from the altitude that it gave no sustenance to our lungs. We stopped often. We rested, heaving for breath. It

was during one of these rests that I grabbed my
chance.

Sitting perhaps three feet from Forster, I knew his
pack lay between us: I'd heard it thump down beside
me when he took it off. It may even have lain closer
to me than to him. I reached out. Surely enough, there
it was. I touched the canvas gently. I ran my fingertips
over its surface without making a sound. *The flap was
open.* Slowly, carefully, I eased my left hand into the
pack itself. Moving blind, I forced my way in among
the supplies packed there.

Just then something clutched my wrist, yanked my
hand out of the pack, and shoved my arm away with
such force that I toppled over.

At once I heard Forster's voice in the dark: "Try
that again, Jesse, and I'll break every bone in your
body."

So much for resting. So much for solving mysteries.
I felt no dismay when we headed off again.

Soon the angle of the slope diminished till we
were crawling almost on the level. Oddly, this
proved as difficult as working our way uphill. Each
of us was carrying a heavy pack. These packs—two
of Rixtir design, one of Western—were all intended
for someone walking upright. Despite the effort of
climbing, I'm sure all of us found them least obtru-
sive when scrambling up relatively steep terrain. I
did, certainly. And they weighed most heavily when
we fumbled along on all fours. The weight burdened
the shoulders and the back. The mass of my pack,
at least, flopped from one side to the other as I
crawled. Sometimes folds of the leather caught on
rocks jutting from the passageway. This wasn't just
inconvenient but scary: while struggling to disengage
and keep moving, I'd hear Aeslu and Forster heading off right ahead, oblivious to my plight. It wasn't
hard to imagine getting stuck in a narrow spot and
left behind altogether. Luckily, they got stuck, too—

Forster especially, given his size—so I wasn't the only one slowed from time to time.

I bumped into Forster, this time my fault, head to rump. He muttered but otherwise ignored me. He'd stopped right in front of me; I could tell where he was not just by bumping into him but by sensing his body's warmth in such a chilly place. Aeslu had stopped, too: I could hear her breathing, loud and fast, just beyond where Forster crouched.

"What's the matter?" I asked.

"—catch my breath—"

She was clearly winded but didn't sound any worse than the rest of us. Ordinarily the sound of her wheezy exhalations wouldn't have worried me. However, the high altitude and the tunnel's stagnant air combined to leave us all gasping—even Aeslu, born and raised in the Mountain Land, was breathing hard—and our distress concerned me more and more.

"I don't like this," said Forster abruptly. "How much longer can we—"

"We must go on," she told him.

"—put up with this?"

"We *must* go on," Aeslu repeated.

"But we don't have the least idea where we're going."

Again I found myself agreeing with Forster. I asked Aeslu, "How do you know this tunnel goes anywhere at all? Maybe it's just a crack that runs deeper and deeper and never opens out again."

By now she had caught her breath. "The Stone tells us to enter the Mountain."

"Maybe the rock has shifted over time—maybe it used to go somewhere, but now it's blocking our way out."

"I trust the Mountain Stone."

Before anyone could respond, Aeslu headed off again: the *scrape-thud-scrape-thud* of her motions against the rock were unmistakable.

"This is nuts!" Forster exclaimed.

We fell silent for a few moments. Already Aeslu's noises were diminishing.

"She's deranged," he went on. "The thin air. Hypoxia."

"So what do we do?"

"I don't know," he said. "I don't know."

Then, before I could say anything, he, too, headed off.

20

How long did we go on like that? I have no idea. I didn't have a watch. Forster did, but we couldn't read it for lack of light. The only unit of time we could discern accurately was the second, since Forster's watch ticked with disconcerting loudness in such a quiet place, yet that served no useful purpose. (Quite the contrary, it rubbed salt into the wound.) All I know is that hours passed—many more than I cared to contemplate. Deep inside the Mountain, we couldn't even judge the passage of time by the most fundamental means: the sun's transit, the alternation of darkness and light, the air temperature's rise and fall. It was always dark. Always cold. Nothing tipped us off about how long we'd been working our way through the Mountain. Or perhaps just deeper and deeper into it.

Now and then we stopped. We rested, ate, and drank as much water as we dared to drink from our dwindling supplies. We talked about the situation and argued over what to do. We tried to sleep but couldn't—not in a place like that, not in a place where the silence pounded in our ears and the darkness left our minds to conjure up any sight they pleased and the cold stone all around felt like nothing so much as the inside of a tomb. No, better to stay awake. Better to keep talking even if we couldn't say a word without bickering. Better to keep moving even if we didn't know where to go.

"Now what?" Forster asked, his voice at a near-shout in such a tight space. "Now what do we do?"

Aeslu said little but the few words she kept repeating: "We must go on."

"Great. We must go on. We'll go on till we drop dead from exhaustion and thirst."

"What's the choice?" I interjected before he could browbeat her. "What's the alternative?"

"That's just the problem. We've gambled on this one loony plan. Now it's clear we've gambled and lost. We don't even have the energy, much less the water, to cut our losses and make our way back."

"Then we have to do what Aeslu suggests."

"Maybe *you* do."

"You figure on going back alone?"

"I'll do anything I damn well please," said Forster, twisting away from me with a motion that shoved his shoulder against my jaw. "If I'd followed my own hunches, I wouldn't be groping toward a fucking dead end like a fucking mole. I'd be sitting atop this mountain, not stuck inside it."

Once again he shifted; once again he jolted into me.

"Stop shoving, God damn you."

One of Forster's huge hands reached out just then, grabbed the front of my coat, and shoved me backward. "Then stop getting in my fucking way."

Aeslu's voice then: "If you want to fight, then fight. But I will go on."

Forster and I argued briefly, then stopped short. Once again we could hear Aeslu heading off.

21

Not long after that, as I worked my way along an especially wide stretch, I realized I could no longer hear my companions. I froze, staying altogether still. I'd lost track of their noises from time to time, then regained them. Now I couldn't hear them at all. Only that deep, awful silence.

"Aeslu?"

No answer.

"Aeslu? Forster?"

Still no answer.

"Aeslu!" I shouted. "Forster!"

There were no gradations to my fear. I went from puzzlement to panic in a flash. To be alone down there—

I swung around to backtrack. In haste and desperation that motion hurled my head straight into the stone wall. The pain was instantaneous. Not just pain—light. More light than I'd seen in a long time. What people say about seeing stars is true: I was positively dazzled. But not just by stars. Light. My head exploded with light. I fell over from the force of it and lay there panting as wave after wave of brilliant light rolled over me. The pain was there but overwhelmed by the light. I was in pain yet indifferent to the pain. Then, as the light diminished in force and intensity, the pain revealed itself again, rocks jutting out of the sand as the tide receded. My head pounded so hard I couldn't believe I hadn't cracked it wide open.

I lay there a long time. I couldn't move—couldn't

imagine moving or wanting to move. Then, little by little, I brought a hand up to feel my head. The right side was damp. I smelled the hand: the warm odor of blood. Yet I found far less blood there than I'd expected, no gash, no discernible cut whatever, just a broad lump and the blood-damp hair. The lump stung. Beneath it my head hurt even worse—a headache worse than any I'd ever felt. I should have counted myself lucky; I could easily have bashed my skull in. By all appearances I'd come off easy. Then I recalled my real predicament, and at once my whole body shook with the fear that had gotten me into trouble from the start.

How could I have lost track of them? Forcing myself to stay calm, I probed the air around me with my right hand. I felt rock to my right, nothing straight ahead, more rock to my left. I crawled forward a few paces, patting the uneven rock floor as I went.

Still nothing. No sound at all.

Then, without warning, more rock. I could feel the wall right before me. A dead end. I felt it narrowing as I proceeded. Within a few more paces the floor, ceiling, and walls converged to a seam.

Somehow I'd gotten off the path. A side-tunnel? Maybe so. Apparently I'd strayed to one side as Aeslu and Forster had gone ahead. The notion of having wandered off terrified me, yet it offered at least an explanation for what had happened. And having gone astray, perhaps I could retrace my steps and find the main tunnel.

I backtracked. Forcing myself around, I headed off down the passageway I thought I'd come up. "Headed off" makes it sound faster and less awkward than it was. I'd been following Aeslu and Forster up to that point; I hadn't really grasped how hard it was to take the lead. Now I was fumbling about on my own. There was no way of knowing what came next. Batting my head into solid stone seemed as likely as taking another step. To protect myself, I crawled with one hand wavering ahead like the antenna of an ungainly insect.

Time after time I scraped against the stone walls or banged my knees on the stone floor beneath me. Even calling it a floor misstates the situation: it was anything but flat. Sometimes I had to climb over obstructions in the path. Sometimes the walls narrowed to a V. My whole body ached from the countless times I misjudged how to go the next few feet. Time after time I ended up with still another cut, another scrape, another bruise.

Yet I wanted nothing more than to keep going as fast as possible. It's not that I felt no pain. Rather, my fear left me indifferent to the pain.

Every few paces I stopped, fell silent, and listened. Surely at any moment I'd hear Forster's and Aeslu's voices—muffled, perhaps, but still audible. Or else I'd hear the thump and scrape of their boots. I'd hear something.

Nothing.

Soon after that I began calling out to them. First I shouted only Aeslu's name—I couldn't imagine calling to Forster for help. Then I started shouting his name, too. Not that it made much difference. All that mattered was making them hear me.

I'd shout, then wait, fall silent, and listen.

No answer. No sound at all—just that same eternal hiss.

By this point I was close to panic. I grappled my way down that passageway so fast that I collided with something almost every time I moved. My right hand clawed at the air ahead of me. When I found open space there, I shoved my way toward it, into it, through it, even if doing so left me stuck, a piglet trying to squeeze through a fence. More than once I managed to get my body through only to end up caught by the pack still strapped to my back. I'd flail a while. Then I'd have to back up, slip off the pack, go through the stricture unencumbered, and reach back to pull the pack after me. Of course I could have junked the pack altogether. It's not that I wasn't tempted. But despite my increasingly frantic state of mind, I clung to the pack like a drowning man to a life preserver. It contained my water, my food, my clothes, my climbing tools. More to the point, it was my only link to the outside world I wanted so desperately to reach. It was the only thing here that wasn't stone. The only thing of human origin. I couldn't imagine leaving it behind.

Maybe I should have. Maybe I should have shed it, a bug's molted skin, and fled for my life. Lord knows it slowed me down. But somehow I couldn't leave it. If nothing else, it spared my back the blows that the rest of my body was suffering.

An explosion of lights. I reeled, clutching my forehead as I toppled over. I lay there panting for a long time.

At some point I caught my breath and held it. I listened as hard as I could to the silence all around.

The exhalations I heard were not my own.

I called out, "Aeslu?"

No response.

Surely my ears must have been tricking me. Or if not my ears, then my whole head, which pounded as if ready to explode. Yet without a doubt I heard the clear, rhythmic sound of someone breathing.

"Forster?"

No answer.

At this point my whole body, no matter how bruised and weary, became totally alert. My back tingled, my arms tightened, my legs coiled like springs. Slowly, carefully, I eased off my pack and reached back for the ice-hatchet stashed there.

Something slammed into me just then, knocking me hard against the wall. A moment later I felt two hands claw at me, find my throat, and fumble to get a grip around it. I toppled to one side, though, and accidentally slipped free. But then my attacker's full weight collapsed against me with such force that I felt altogether pinioned. I grunted as the burden coming down on me knocked the wind out of my lungs. Reflexively I brought my right arm down against my assailant. I found I'd succeeded in clutching the ice-hatchet I'd located only instants before the first blow; I brought it down as hard as I could time after time.

Hands clawed at me, at once grabbing and shoving.

I swung wildly with the hatchet. I felt it struck home once, twice, three times. I heard the grunts of the person I struck.

"Forster—"

He took hold of my shoulders, grabbed them hard, and slammed my whole torso hard against the rock. Great jolts of pain coursed through me.

I swung again, hit hard.

His hands grappled again for my throat.

Twisting aside, I managed to get free. Now I took the hatchet in both hands and swung it like a baseball bat. To my astonishment I struck my target on the first try. It made a sound that horrified and exhilarated me at the same time: something halfway between a crunch and a thump. I'd heard that sound before, almost four years earlier, east of the Meuse River, near the border between France and Germany, and I hope I never hear it again. Yet I was thrilled by the sound just then, so thrilled I actually laughed out loud before I caught myself.

Then at once I tensed up again.

Fell silent.

Listened.

What followed was something I heard without the least delight: a deep, throaty gurgle.

I waited a long time, paralyzed by fear and revulsion. Against my better judgment I then reached forward, probed the air, and found my prey. A body lay right before me on its right side. The ice-hatchet lay beside it. I touched the wooden handle, then took it up and nudged the body with the blade.

No response.

Then, groping about for my pack till I found it, I shoved past my victim and scrambled as fast as possible down the passageway.

22

I can't account for everything that happened right after the fight. I can't even guess how long I blundered about down there trying to escape. Half an hour? An hour? Two hours? Three? It's not just that I lost a clear sense of time—it's that I kicked free of time altogether. For a while I ceased to be conscious, even ceased to be human. I didn't think, reflect, perceive, or make choices. I simply *acted*. I did whatever had to be done. I was nothing but a beast fighting for survival.

I clawed my way through the tunnel. I groped for the passageway, probed the air, grappled past whatever rocks obstructed me. I shoved my way around anything protruding into the tunnel and squeezed through the narrow places. I moved so fast that I slammed into the stone walls time after time, yet blows that would have stopped me earlier didn't even slow me now. Not that I wasn't in pain—I hurt everywhere. My whole body throbbed. Yet I ignored the pain. No injury or discomfort made any difference. All I wanted was to get out of there. My desire to escape the depths of the Mountain was that strong.

Then, without the least warning, I touched something that wasn't rock. I knew at once that it was flesh. Human flesh. A hand.

I recoiled at once—all but flung myself backward.

At that same instant I heard the scraping noise of whomever I'd touched pulling back as well.

Once again I felt the great jolt of fear: somehow I'd

doubled back on the place I was fleeing, and here now was Forster yet again! I hadn't killed him after all.

Then a voice—barely a whisper—said: "Jassi?"

My fear turned to exhilaration. *"Aeslu."*

"Where are you?" The voice was unmistakable.

"Here."

I reached out with my right hand, eased ahead, probed the air till I touched something soft. Hair. I could feel the silkiness of the hair itself and the warmth of the scalp beneath it. Then, reaching out with my left hand, too, and leaning forward to take her in my arms, I felt Aeslu reach back. She embraced me, nuzzled against me, kissed me, caressed me. She asked, "What happened? Where have you been?"

I felt as if I'd break down, but I was too upset to cry. "I got lost—took a wrong turn," I blurted. "Back there. Somewhere."

"Are you all right?" She must have felt me flinch from the pressure of her kisses, for Aeslu's hands came up and started delicately examining my face. "What has happened to you? Jassi—"

"Forster followed me and lay in wait. He found me and attacked me. I fought back. God, it was terrible. I think I killed him."

"Killed him—?"

"I didn't want to. Believe me, I didn't want to. All I wanted was to find you and get out of here, but he ambushed me and hit me and threw me against the wall. I didn't want to kill him—"

She hushed me then, holding me tight while I shook and raged. She kissed me, too, gently, as if to soothe my wounds.

"Aeslu, we have to get out of here."

"I know the way."

The words caught me short. "What? The way out?"

"I'm sure of it."

"How do you know?"

"I think I smell it."

"Smell the way out?"

"The air," she said. "Something in the air has

changed. It's not as heavy, not as stale. As if some fresh air is pushing its way in."

What she said thrilled me. "Let's go, then."

Yet she kept kissing me. Her lips made my face tingle and sting. The sensation left me wanting both to pull away and to draw closer. The same when Aeslu pulled herself closer, reached out to me with both hands, and began stroking my shoulders and back. I wasn't sure if I felt more pain or pleasure.

When I reached back to her, the back of my hand touched something that startled me. I reached out again, now with both hands, this time palms up, and, to my astonishment, found myself touching her breasts. Aeslu must have eased open her tunic; her chest was exposed. After such long contact with nothing but cold, rough stone, I found this unanticipated sensation bringing tears to my eyes. That there could be such softness and warmth in the world! Yet even the least contact stung my hands, and her embrace made my whole body ache.

"Now?"

"I need you," she said without the least hesitation.

Desire got the best of me. The delight of touching her both eclipsed the pain I felt and intensified it. Yet I could no more hold back from caressing Aeslu than I could have held back earlier from striking Forster. I pulled back the rest of her tunic. I opened my own clothes. I took her in my arms, eased her back, nestled down into a pool of our garments. When I thrust into her, the crescendo of pleasure and pain was so intense that I could no longer tell one from the other. My head pounded, my flesh burned, my bones pulsed, ready to explode.

I lay there a long time before I was aware of being awake. Total darkness. Silence. Aeslu must have fallen asleep, too.

Forcing myself up, I spoke her name.

No response.

"Aeslu?"

I reached out, patting the space around me. Right, left. At my feet, above my head. Nothing there.

"Aeslu?"

Now the darkness seemed to close in all around. The silence intensified to a roar.

I passed both hands over my body: fully clothed.

Once again I shouted her name, then stifled the impulse to continue. Fear overwhelmed me. Fear and anger. That after all we'd been through she could have abandoned me— That despite everything—

Then my fear deepened. Deepened to the point that fear became a liquid filling this passageway, a subterranean river streaming through the rock and sweeping me along with it. Riding the current of my fear, I clawed my way out, grappled with whatever blocked my path, struggled in whatever way escaping required.

Aeslu was right. No matter what else, she had been right. Something in the air: a scent, a hint of something different, something other than stone. How long did it take for me to understand what it was? I have no idea. All I know is that by the time I worked my way through the tunnel to the point where it opened out abruptly onto a sunlit cliff, even the ice all around me smelled as lush as paradise.

23

I couldn't see. It's not that I was blind—the light simply overwhelmed me. After spending God knows how long in pure darkness, I literally couldn't face the glare beyond the tunnel. Mountain Made of Light! The dazzle jabbed at me, battered me, almost drove me back inside again.

Yet all I wanted was *out*. I cupped my hands over my eyes and braced myself as if resisting a harsh wind. I'd weather this blast of light as I'd already weathered snow, wind, sleet, and cold. For a long time I just stood there. Then, as I felt my eyes start to adjust, I eased my way forward again.

The tunnel opened onto a porchlike promontory. I couldn't tell much about it—simply that it was the largest level surface I'd seen by light of day in a long, long time, and that it jutted out toward open space beyond. Something else caught my attention at once: a lone figure sitting near the edge of that promontory.

It was Aeslu.

I would have watched her a while before making any other move. I would have eased back into the tunnel, lurked there in the shadows, waited for an opportunity to size up the situation. Before I could do anything of the sort, however, she turned and stared right at me.

She couldn't have looked more astonished if I'd risen from the dead.

I staggered forth, took three steps, and collapsed.

I regained consciousness staring at an expanse of

black stone above me. I forced myself up and fell backward at once.

"Go to sleep," said a gentle voice nearby. "Go back to sleep.

Turning abruptly, I found Aeslu at my side.

I tried to get up again. She put her right hand against my shoulder as if to force me down, but her touch was gentle. My head pounded so violently that it did all the work of restraining me.

I said, "Forster tried to kill me."

"Shhh ... You are so tired."

"No, listen—he tried to kill me."

Now she gazed at me less in surprise than in bafflement.

"Inside the tunnel," I went on. "While you were off by yourself."

"That is impossible," she stated emphatically.

"It's true."

"You imagined it. Jassi, you have suffered great injuries."

Her rebuke stung more than all my wounds. Gesturing at my swollen face, I asked her, "Then how did I get *these*?"

"I do not know. But neither do I know how Forssa could have tried to kill you—"

"What makes you so sure?"

"Because he was with me the whole time."

"What do you mean, 'the whole time'?"

"While you were lost."

"He never went off by himself?"

"Never."

"Not even for a while?"

"I heard him beside me the whole time."

"Aeslu, he's back there in the tunnel—dead."

At this point I fell silent. It wasn't that Aeslu had won the argument; rather, I just didn't know what to think. What explanation did I find more frightening— that Forster had indeed ambushed me deep inside the Mountain, or that he hadn't?

Then, too, I had another event to struggle with:

what had happened with Aeslu. "What about you?" I asked her. "Were you alone with me while we were down there?"

"Alone?"

"With me alone."

"No—never."

"You really were with Forster the whole time?"

She gazed at me for a while. Then she said, "I would have done anything to be with you, but I was with him. We did not know where you were." She reached out, leaning toward me, and gently touched my battered face. "I was frightened. I was—terrified. I thought you were gone."

I didn't respond to what she said. I didn't know how. At some point, though, turning to one side, I saw someone else seated several yards to my right. A man sat in precisely the place where I'd first seen Aeslu—right at the edge of that promontory. This isn't possible, I told myself. This isn't even remotely possible. Yet even then I could see who it was: Forster.

24

What should I have done? Should I have confronted him? Should I have blurted accusations about what had taken place deep inside the Mountain? What would that have accomplished?

A few weeks earlier, Forster had spent the better part of an afternoon trying to kill me; I had done everything in my power to return the favor. Our enmity wasn't a closely guarded secret. As for the tunnel, though: what good would come of confronting him? If Forster had in fact nearly choked me to death, he wasn't unaware of his intentions. If he hadn't, though, then pressing the point would do little but raise questions about my sanity.

No, it seemed better to stay quiet. Better to keep my own counsel. Better to watch and listen and wait to see what Forster himself would do next.

"Seems you took rather a beating down there, old man," he said, nodding toward me and, I assume, toward the cuts and bruises disfiguring my face.

I looked him over cautiously. No one I'd ever met was so nearly opaque as Forster Beckwith; I couldn't interpret his facial expressions even under the best of circumstances. The task could only have been harder now, for his features had suffered the distortions of his own scrapes and bruises. I said, "Seems you haven't escaped altogether untouched yourself."

"Bit of a squeeze, wasn't it?"

"Rather."

Despite the man's share of contusions—the whole

right side of his face had turned purple-black—I saw no sign of a serious wound. Nothing, certainly, that suggested going head-to-head with an ice-hatchet. No gash. No blood beyond that released from a few superficial scrapes. As always, Forster had somehow gotten through almost unscathed.

"At least we all made it out alive, though, didn't we?" I added.

"So we did," said Forster. "So we did." After a moment he gave a nod toward the cliff on our left. "Let's just hope it wasn't a Pyrrhic victory."

As for questions about my own sanity, I raised them only with Aeslu.

"If it wasn't Forster who tried to kill me," I asked her, speaking in Rixtir, "then who was it?"

She sat staring at her hands for a long time. Her knuckles had become a mass of bruises and welts. Her fingers had suffered so many cuts and scrapes that some of them were black with scabs and dried blood. I could scarely hear Aeslu when she said, "I do not know."

"Some descendent of the Founders?"

She blinked at the sound of these words but did not reply.

I prodded her. "Assuming we're not alone here, could it have been one of them?"

"No—never."

"Are you sure?"

"No descendent of the Founders would do such a thing."

"But that's assuming they want us here. Perhaps whoever's living on the Mountain thinks of us as intruders."

Aeslu looked up, observing me carefully. Her face had sustained almost as many injuries as her hands: welts, bruises, abrasions, cuts. Her nose and cheeks had suffered enough sunburn for patches of skin to peel. Her hair was matted and tangled. What had once been a beautiful face—one of the most beautiful I'd ever seen—was now ravaged and worn. Yet the eyes there were still untouched and lovely. Her gaze was calm despite Aeslu's obvious concern.

"We are not intruders," she told me. "You are the Sun's Stead. I am the Moon's. We are here because we ought to be."

"What if the people up there don't know that?"

"Surely they do."

"Then why would someone try to kill me?"

"None of them would."

I looked past Aeslu at Forster sitting to one side. Leaning back against the rock wall that gave us refuge, he looked oblivious to Aeslu and me, altogether engrossed in gnawing at a piece of the Rixtir pemmican he claimed to detest.

Did I want to find Aeslu's argument persuasive? Did I prefer the possibility that Forster, not someone else, was the person who had come close to strangling me? Or did I prefer the company of an unknown assailant to one I knew?

As if reading my mind, Aeslu responded, "There is another possibility."

"And what is that?" I asked with some caution.

"Perhaps no one tried to kill you."

"What do you mean, no one?"

She gestured uneasily. "Not Forster but not anyone else."

The words stunned me. "Are you suggesting that I imagined the whole thing? The blows to my head? The hands around my throat?"

"I do not know."

"That's the implication, isn't it?"

"Jassi—"

"How did I get these wounds?" I asked her. I gestured at my face and the welts there—welts I couldn't see but whose presence I could feel even without touching.

"You could suffer such wounds," she said, "without anyone inflicting them. You could strike your head against the wall. You could trip—"

"So you think no one put them there?"

"I think—"

"You think I'm losing my mind?"

She raised both hands in a posture that seemed half embrace, half self-protection. "All I mean is that I no longer know what is happening and what is not."

25

The next morning, after scant sleep, we headed upward again.

PART FOUR

Then for a few days Jesse vanished, convincing me that I'd overstayed my welcome, annoyed him in some way, or simply tired him out. I stopped off at his gardening shed on Thursday and Friday and found it locked both days. Pounding on the door brought no answer. Peering in through the window at least showed me that he really wasn't there. But asking around didn't get me any farther: the buildings and grounds people said simply that Jesse had taken a few days off. I wandered through the campus for a while after that, frustrated and angry.

It wasn't just that he'd given me the slip. But to tell me half the story and then *disappear!*

Well, I assured myself, I can leave, too. I can leave the campus, leave Boulder, leave Colorado, leave Jesse O'Keefe to whatever mysteries he wants to keep unrevealed. On Friday afternoon I went back to the motel room I'd taken. I packed my bag. I loaded the rental car in preparation for the trip back to Denver.

Yet on the way out, succumbing to an impulse, I stopped off at the shed one last time. Stuck to the door with a thumbtack was this note:

Mr. Myers:
Monday a.m., here, if that suits you.
J.O.

I should have been furious to be yanked around like this, and I was. Yet I told myself to ignore his disappearing act; all that really mattered was hearing him

*out. And so I calmed down, retraced my steps, settled
back into the motel, and killed enough time to reach
Monday morning.*

"Nice of you to join me," said Jesse when I entered
the shed at our appointed time. He was sitting in his
chair at the table. A mug of steaming coffee and his
black loaf-shaped lunchbox rested before him.

"Nice of you to invite me."

He made no apologies; in fact, he said nothing at all.
He merely motioned for me to sit in the chair opposite.

After a while I said, "You could have just told me
to back off a while. I certainly understand if you've
needed a break."

"And what if even I didn't know?"

"You could have told me that as well."

We watched each other for a while. I sensed no anger
in his expression, only a calm uncertainty. "I needed
to decide how much I really wished to continue."

"Because of fear?" I asked. "Or shame?"

"Neither."

"Because you don't want to explain?"

He glanced at me briefly, then gazed out the window.
"It's not that I don't want to explain. It's that I'm still
figuring out how."

"You were managing rather well till the other day."

"Was I?"

"For my purposes, at least."

He fell silent for a long time.

I took advantage of the disruption. "The tunnel," I
said. "You'd just made it through the tunnel."

"The tunnel, then," said Jesse O'Keefe.

1

The tunnel had opened out onto a cliff that provided the biggest expanse of stone we'd seen since well before working our way up to the tunnel's entrance. Yet the cliff itself wasn't really a surprise. The surprise was finding a second cliff opposite the first. Almost exactly parallel, these cliffs ran straight up the Mountain to form a steep, narrow gully, a snow-padded ramp between two shadowy stone walls.

I should have noted that geological formation with greater alarm than I did. It wasn't that the task of climbing a ramp would be any more difficult than the other tasks we'd faced. On the contrary, it might prove far easier. Getting down from the tunnel to the ramp's lower end would require only a brief rappel; from there we could zigzag up the packed snow to wherever it led. Without any possibility of going astray on such a straightforward route, we could devote all our efforts simply to the climb itself. The route, though—was it really so straightforward? And was this ramp truly what we sought?

The Mountain Stone seemed to answer these questions in the affirmative. When we examined it, nothing the three of us saw there suggested anything to the contrary. A single line—vertical and clearly etched—started from the hole representing the tunnel we'd just emerged from, and, angling steeply up that facet of the Stone, it led (or at least appeared to lead) straight toward the summit ridge. A cheery sight, I assure you. For the first time, our goal seemed well within reach.

Yet I say "at least appeared to lead" because we

couldn't feel sure of precisely what led where. Small flaws in the quartz disrupted what must have once been a continuous line on the Stone's surface. For this reason, we couldn't feel altogether confident that the ramp would prove to be the straight and narrow path we so desperately craved. These flaws were puzzling in their own right: tiny fractures. At some point, whether recently or long ago, something had struck or scraped the Stone in such a way that bits of the quartz had flaked off, damaging that particular facet—damaging it just minimally, yet still sufficiently that none of us could detect the middle portion of the lines once etched there. Thus we could only hope that the lower portion of the ramp extended to the upper reaches without further obstructions.

On the other hand, what if our hopes were unfounded? What if the Stone's flaws left us facing new obstacles unprepared?

We couldn't answer these questions. All we could do was head up and take our chances.

2

Perhaps we shouldn't have worried. We started up; we made good headway. Scaling the ramp seemed easier than we had any right to expect. Fair weather, good firm snow underfoot, and only a moderate degree of steepness combined to make the task straightforward.

So straightforward, in fact, that we climbed without bothering to belay one another. All three of us advanced at the same time, fifteen or twenty feet apart: Aeslu first and farthest to the right, myself right up the middle of the ramp, and Forster last and farthest to the left. The rope linking us alternatively sagged and tautened. If one of us had slipped, no doubt the others would have dug in—ice-hatchets and footclaws jabbed into the snow—and would thus have caught the fall. In this sense, I suppose we didn't lack for a safety net. But this arrangement allowed us so much more flexibility and speed that we felt freer, less encumbered, than if we had relied on the complex leap-frog involved in belays.

My right hatchet plunged into the snow. Properly anchored, it then allowed me to plunge the left one a foot or so beside it. Then I'd kick my right footclaws into place. Then the left. In this way I proceeded, secure despite the steepness of the slope. I could scarcely believe what steady progress we made.

The Mountain seemed helpless before us.

THE SUMMIT

from his pack. Once again he examined the Stone,
the face representing the slope we strove for, and the

3

Then, little more than a day after we started up the
ramp, the path forked.

Of course even phrasing it in this way sounds foolish. *Was* there a path? We didn't really know. All we
knew was this: a gully or gulch angled up the Mountain; its straight-and-narrow course tempted us to perceive it as a path; and we climbed upward until, with
little warning, we arrived at a rock formation that essentially sliced the gully lengthwise from one path into
two. This formation was what geologists call a
cleaver—a big narrow blade of rock thrusting up from
a mountainside. This one was fifty or seventy-five feet
wide where it emerged from the ice and even wider
along its higher reaches. I can't even guess how long
the whole thing was. Hundreds of feet, easily. From
our vantage at the time, though, it could have been
anything from a hundred feet to a thousand. What we
could determine, though, was simply that to continue
climbing, we had to pass this stone slab either on the
right or the left. And we could also see that since the
slab widened at its upper reaches, the right branch
diverged from the left. By all appearances we couldn't
simply pick one side or the other, work our way past
the cleaver, and end up the same place we'd have
reached by the other means. We would probably end
up on an altogether different part of the Mountain.

So the question was, Which side of the cleaver was
the real path?

Before Aeslu and I could nudge Forster about con-
sulting the Mountain Stone, he had already pulled it

from his pack. Once again he examined the Stone, the facet representing the slope we clung to, and the imperfections there. "I don't get it," said Forster, sounding annoyed. "What does this mean?" He scratched the surface of the Stone with a fingernail.

"It means nothing at all," Aeslu told him.

"Come on—it must mean *something.*"

I understood Aeslu's intentions at once. "What she's getting at is that these marks aren't writing. They're damage to the Stone."

She said, "Something must have chipped it."

Forster pulled the Stone closer, tilted it this way and that, peered intently at its surface, then cursed under his breath. "Just what we need."

For a while we simply stood there, each of us gazing up one fork in the path, then up the other. The left fork looked wider than the right and somehow safer. Its relatively safe appearance may have been a trick of the light, however: the left wall of the gully rose to a lower altitude than the cleaver itself, which let in more sunlight, thus making it seem less ominous than the right fork, which lay almost entirely steeped in shadow. On the other hand, the snowfield filling the left fork lay studded with chunks of stone fallen from the cliffs on either side—not an appealing sight. Was the right side subject to the same kind of rockfall? Probably, but in the dimmer light there we couldn't tell how badly that cliff had been crumbling. We certainly couldn't see clearly where these two forks led, nor which would suit our purposes.

Aeslu and I started discussing which of the two alternatives to choose. Even as we spoke, though, Forster headed off to the left: simply untied himself from his end of the rope and started up the snowfield.

"Wait a minute!" I shouted after him.

He stopped, turned, stared. "Excuse me?"

"We haven't even decided which way to go."

"Maybe *you* haven't," he said, then set off again.

"Forster, damn it—what makes you think you're right?"

Again he stopped. "Let's just say I've established a pattern."

Now Aeslu joined in. "You are mistaken," she told him. "The right side will lead us upward."

"Oh?" He smiled, raising his brow in mock astonishment. "What makes you so sure?"

"I can tell."

Wearily, Forster descended to where Aeslu and I stood waiting. "You can tell. Wonderful. But how, may I ask, can you tell when the Mountain Stone is so badly scratched that none of us can discern the route?"

Aeslu stared at him briefly, then shrugged. "It makes sense. It seems—*right*." She gestured vaguely.

"Is that so? I'd say it seems rather left, instead." He then turned and took another few paces up the slope.

Aeslu and I conferred briefly: Aeslu explaining why she believed the right fork offered the most promising route; I in turn asking questions to clarify what seemed to be more intuition than rationale. Her argument hinged mostly on a hunch. Our route up the Mountain so far had always angled to the right—except, of course, when we had gone straight up—and thus she reasoned that this pattern would continue. Why would the Founders have climbed in a direction deviating from what they had established from the start? I couldn't answer that question. On some level, though, the answer was obvious: they would have climbed in the direction that circumstances required. If a geologic formation blocked their path in such a way that they needed to circumvent it on the left, I assumed they'd have done so. But Aeslu found my objection altogether unpersuasive. No, she said, the Founders would have headed off to the right.

By this time Forster had advanced to about fifty or sixty feet ahead of us. Each passing moment left him higher up. He proceeded as if now oblivious to Aeslu and me. Oblivious—or perhaps indifferent.

Then Forster turned to gaze down at us. "You're wasting your time," he said. "It's late. It'll be getting dark soon. Even under the best of circumstances you'd be going out on a limb, so maybe you should think twice about what you're doing."

"I have," said Aeslu, and she started up to the right.

What surprised me wasn't that I followed her, since for whatever reason—not a rational reason, but something else—I'd become convinced that Aeslu knew what she was doing. What surprised me was that after a predictable amount of grousing, Forster himself came down from the left fork, too. He descended to where the paths converged. He scrambled up after us. He brought up the rear until, two or three minutes later, he'd passed both Aeslu and me and had regained the lead.

Our easy start didn't last. When Aeslu and I had split away from Forster, we too had disengaged from the rope; we had stashed it in our packs and simply worked our way upward, kicking steps into the dense snow with our footclaws and anchoring our holds with the ice-hatchets. This risky method was partly a response to the relatively gentle conditions we faced just then but mostly a consequence of parting company with Forster. Soon enough, though, the conditions grew more treacherous. The slope tilted steeper and steeper. The surface turned crusty—a thin layer of ice glazed the snow. Now and then rocks tumbled down the gully. Half an hour of intense effort brought us to a point where even a quick glance down the chute was unnerving. A glance up wasn't much better: the chute grew even steeper, narrowing at last to a fractured stone abutment that seemed to be releasing the bits of rubble that now and then headed our way.

"So much for the proper path," said Forster.

Aeslu made no effort to argue with him. She simply uncoiled a rope, tied one end around her waist, and threw the rest at Forster. Then, more slowly now because of the angle, she resumed the climb.

Forster watched her a moment before stooping to

find the other end of the rope and tying it around his body.

While the rope played out, I tied onto the rope's mid-point, assumed the belay position, and took my stance during the last few dozen feet of her ascent.

The next several pitches grew more and more difficult. The problem wasn't just the angle, though that was steep enough; it was the condition of the snow. The slope faced almost due west. Although flanked on both sides by granite ridges forming the chute itself, the snowfield between them apparently caught enough sunlight each afternoon to soften its surface. The daily cycle of freeze and thaw had formed a layer of brittle ice over the much softer snow beneath it. On the chute's lower reaches, this layer had been little more than a glaze. Higher up it thickened sufficiently to become a crust—half an inch thick or so, maybe more. It wasn't hard to crack through. A single blow with a pick-head would smash it. And that was precisely the problem. We could easily have shattered the whole sheet and brought it crashing down on our heads. Shards of broken glass wouldn't have been much more dangerous.

Forster had been leading for a while. Yet when the precariousness of our situation hit home—a realization that struck everyone at the same time—he stopped and kept so still that I wondered if he, too, had frozen. Then he motioned to Aeslu. "I want you to take the lead," he told her. "You weigh the least and have the best chance of getting us through."

He was right. The truth of his words didn't surprise me, however, so much as his willingness to admit it.

Aeslu, gazing up from ten or twelve yards below, showed no resistance to his request. She paused briefly, then worked her way past me, then in turn past Forster.

She continued slowly and methodically for a long time. Her ice-hatchets plunged into the icy crust with a sudden *whump;* fractures radiated through the ice surrounding each anchor point; the metal points on each foot then kicked one after the other into the crust. Chips and fragments broke loose now and then, skittering toward Forster and me. Sometimes sheets the size of saucers, dinner plates, even serving dishes slid free. Most of them missed us, but a few—fortunately small ones—struck us, shattering, and showered the air below with tiny chips.

"This can't posssibly be the way up," Forster grumbled, mostly to himself. "Even if it is, she'll get us killed."

"She's doing a better job than you were."

"What's the difference if it's the wrong route?"

We watched a while longer. From that vantage point I couldn't see very well what she was doing—partly because of the angle, partly because of glare on the ice. My unease grew more intense as she proceeded. Now and then Aeslu dislodged great panes of ice that, like guillotine blades freed from the constraints of tracks to guide them, picked up speed quickly and shot down toward us. Only by chance did Forster and I escape getting hit.

Soon he couldn't tolerate the situation any longer. He muttered, "God damn it—" Then, abruptly, shouted, "Enough!"

Aeslu glanced down at him, then proceeded upward.

Another shout from Forster: "This isn't getting us *anywhere*!" Yet he started up after her.

"Forster—"

I didn't get the merest glance in return. After watching a few moments, I headed up, too.

He reached her first. By the time I did, Forster had launched into a loud diatribe against Aeslu and her insistence on taking this route. "—and I've never had much patience with hopeless causes."

"Right there," was her only response. She pointed to something far above us.

"Right *where*?" His voice sagged with derision.

She didn't bother answering him. Aeslu untied herself from the rope, took up her ice-hatchet, and started up alone.

Forster called out once, twice, three times but made no effort to follow. "What's the point? She's committing suicide."

But she wasn't. She moved quickly, first on ice, then on ice-encrusted stone, at last on pure rock. Aeslu's curiosity made her agile rather than clumsy; she made her way alongside the cleaver's base without the slightest mishap. Then, reaching what she sought, Aeslu stopped and knelt. For a long time she peered at something ahead of her. She pulled her ice-hatchet close and, grasping the shaft near the head, wielded it like a pick. Prying rather than striking, though, she managed to dislodge something from the rock. Then, turning toward us once again, she worked her way down the slope till she arrived at where Forster and I awaited her.

She didn't even speak—she simply reached out to us with something in her hands.

Four inches long and perhaps three inches wide, it resembled a miniature rake of the sort gardeners use: fingerlike claws splaying outward from a central shaft. Yet it wasn't a rake—that much I could see. The fingers spread too far apart, some of them opposing others, almost like a crab's legs. And close to where all six fingers met dangled a length of rope. I could see at once that the rope resembled what Aeslu and I had found earlier on the Mountain. Old rope. Tattered rope. Rope reduced to mere shreds. Yet rope all the same.

"You did not believe me," she said, addressing Forster. "You thought we were trying to deceive you. Yet here—"

"I see it," he told her. "I don't need a lecture." He reached out and took what she held. He turned it slowly, examining it with great care. He scraped at the metal tines with a fingernail; he ran his hands over the shreds of rope.

"The Founders—"

"Just let me examine it, would you?"

I interrupted him in turn. "Forster, there's no use denying it. They were up here a long time ago."

He glanced my way. "*They* were? Maybe so. Maybe not."

"Why resist the obvious?"

"Nothing's obvious except some metal stuck in the cliff."

"The Founders passed this way," Aeslu stated.

"Look, let's stop all this Founder nonsense, all right? You're jumping to every conclusion in sight. All we know is that *someone* passed this way. We don't know who or when."

I took the hook, held it, hefted it. "This is old, Forster. Hundreds of years old."

"I'm not disputing that."

"The higher we find these things, the more likely that Aeslu's claims are true."

"More likely but not certain."

Now Aeslu reached out to me and took back the artifact. "The Founders passed this way," she said again. "Surely they await us at the Summit."

4

All that afternoon Aeslu was nearly speechless with
joy. She didn't look happy in a superficial sense so
much as inwardly serene: calm despite the extremity
of our situation. The fatigue that had long burdened
her features now lifted. The hunger that had left her
hollow-eyed and sunken-cheeked loosed its grip on
her flesh. Something invisible to Forster and me gave
her rest, solace, and nurturance. For a long time that
afternoon, she sat staring at the ancient hook with an
expression of such wistfulness and longing that it
might have been a sweetheart's bouquet rather than
a corroded piece of metal.

Forster's reaction was altogether different. Nothing
in his appearance or comments suggested delight, excitement, fascination, or even curiosity toward what
Aeslu had discovered. On the contrary, his face
showed only a veiled unease. I heard nothing in his
voice but ill-hidden discomfort. Discomfort over what,
though? I'm not suggesting that we didn't have cause
for concern or bewilderment—simply that I didn't
know precisely what concerned or bewildered *him*. As
always, I found it difficult to make sense of what he
felt.

Was he fearful that the other people on the Mountain might prove hostile? Maybe so, but I doubted it.
Forster was pugnacious by nature—always ready for
a good scrap.

Was he disturbed by what the Founders' descendents might imply about his view of the world, even of

the universe? Not likely, given his disdain for speculation of that sort.

What, then?

I didn't know.

Watching him put away the Mountain Stone, however, I saw him pause, gaze at it, then glance up the
slope. And in that moment a shadow came over his
face, a shadow I recognized at once. He wasn't afraid
of other people on the Mountain, whether now or long
ago; he was simply disappointed. Never mind that the
Founders' descendents might help us upward. Never
mind that they might lead us to our goal. Never mind
that they might even spare us from blundering headlong into catastrophe. He resented their presence
more than he dreaded the possibility of failure and
death. Nothing mattered to him more than being first
at the Summit.

As for me, I felt a mix of emotions far more complex than what either of my companions revealed.
Aeslu's discovery of that hook boosted my spirits in
some respects. It certainly suggested that we were on
track. The hook also provided further evidence supporting Aeslu's belief that someone among the Rixtirra had climbed the Mountain long ago. Did this
mean that Ossonnal and Lissallo themselves had made
the climb? As Forster had insisted earlier, not necessarily. Just that *someone* had. Yet that in itself was
significant. Only a fool—or Forster—wouldn't have
found this discovery encouraging.

And I myself felt encouraged. But not merely that.
Far be it from me to feel just one thing at a time.

I also felt a sense of foreboding, even dread, that
hadn't cropped up when Aeslu had found the first relic
during the early days of our climb. Dread of what? I
can't entirely explain. Even though these bits of ancient gear encouraged us to believe that we might
reach our goal—and might even descend safely afterward—they hinted at other consequences as well. If
people awaited us at the Summit, how would they
respond to our arrival? Aeslu assumed that we would

be greeted with open arms. I no longer felt quite so confident. Deep inside the Mountain, someone had tried to kill me. I still tended to believe that my assailant was Forster, yet I had no real evidence. In fact, Forster's very presence before me now argued to the contrary. Who, then, had attacked me? Was it possible that we weren't so alone up there as we imagined?

We had only one way to find out.

5

Upward, then. Upward to the Summit.

I spoke those words over and over, chanted them out loud, strung them together like the fibers in a filament, the filaments in a thread, the threads in a strand, till the words made a rope I clung to, depended on, and used to pull myself still higher. Upward to the Summit! Out of breath, gasping more than speaking, I couldn't spare the effort that these words required, yet I dreaded what might happen if I failed to utter them. Stopping—letting silence cut the rope of words—I'd surely fall as quickly and as far as if the real rope broke.

Upward to the Summit!

6

"If we can make it up this next stretch," said Forster, "I think we can just about waltz to the top."

What he called "this next stretch" was the cliff rising above us. We had avoided triggering any snow- or ice-slides big enough to yank the snowfield out from under us; we had successfully scaled the last and steepest portion of the ramp; we had arrived at the cliff's base. In itself this feat filled me with delight. Some of that delight was a side effect of plain old adrenalin—the deep-in-the-flesh pleasure of survival. Some of it, though, was the equally visceral yet more complex delight of reaching a major milestone. The cliff rose almost straight up before us. According to the Mountain Stone, it was the last substantial barrier between us and the Summit. All we had to do was surmount it; then we could scramble up what the Stone suggested was a final, unobstructed snowfield. The summit ridge? So it seemed. Of course we might find something between us and the top—an icefall, a crevasse, an outcropping of rock, a deadly cornice, or any of the other obstacles that have so often thwarted climbers close to victory—but if so, then it seemed that we would find an obstacle that had formed only in the centuries since Ossonnal and Lissallo first climbed the Mountain Made of Light. If the Stone were accurate, however, then Forster was right. We were almost there.

Yet scaling the cliff looked harder up close than it had from a distance. It was steeper than all the other cliffs we'd dealt with so far—in fact, it was almost vertical. It consisted of a single expanse of ice-caked stone. And it lay overhung by cornices—those mounds of drifted snow that rise from ridges, summits, and the edges of high snowfields—mounds that from our vantage point looked fanciful, even enticing, like great drooping swirls of whipped cream on a cake, but that threatened us even more than the cliff itself.

7

First the right hatchet: raising it backward, bringing it forth again, slamming it into the cliff just hard enough to embed the point but not hard enough to shatter the crusty ice. Then the left: the same motions but more ungainly, the hatchet heavy in my weaker hand, the aim less steady. A quick check—a gentle tug at each stave—reassures me that both tools are solid.

I turn my attention to my feet. The right once again goes first: a single good, firm kick jams the footclaw into place. From the start I can tell I'm secure. I may as well have found a footstool to raise me up. The left is something else, though: not quite strong enough to kick the claws in firmly. I try again. Again. Again. By this time I've done so much damage to the ice that fragments are coming loose. I can hear them crackle as they break; I can see them sparkle as they plummet below me. Soon I'm sweating—no longer confident that I can find a proper foothold. Then, just as I start to worry about falling, my left foot hits hard enough to stay put.

A voice comes up to me: "Damn you, Jesse!"

I arch my back somewhat and gaze downward. Between my feet and three yards below is Forster, peering up at me with one arm brought up to protect his face, which from my vantage is upside-down.

"What the hell are you doing?"

"What do you think?" I answer, unwilling to grovel.

"You call this climbing?"

"Call it whatever you like, Forster."

"All right then, we'll call it climbing. Just try to climb without pulling down the whole goddamn mountain!"

8

That evening, while the sun sank into the clouds far below us, we huddled on a shelf we'd hacked in the snow. We had a kind of cold, oily pudding to eat and some slushy water to drink. Forster indulged himself in some of his Belgian chocolate—a private reserve he declined to share. (What else did he have stashed in that pack? I couldn't stop wondering, yet neither could I find opportunities to investigate.) Somehow we managed to avoid bickering over these scant rations, though, and I maintained a faint hope that we could settle down for the night without an argument.

Then Aeslu pulled out the ancient hook again. Forster watched in silence as she examined it, and I in turn watched him watching. None of us spoke.

Perhaps I should have warned her—told her not to risk baiting him—but I didn't. Even warning Aeslu in Rixtir would have baited him. Still, I should have taken the chance.

She said, "The Founders left this—"

"Let's stop all this silly talk about the Founders, all right?" he interrupted at once. "There were no Founders—"

"They climbed the Mountain," Aeslu told him.

"Maybe some people tried getting up it," he went on, "but they failed."

"No, they succeeded."

"They got nowhere."

"They climbed the Mountain."

"They failed as totally as anyone can fail."

"They built the refuge—"

"Impossible," said Forster, taking a bite of chocolate. "Totally impossible. They didn't know how to get there, so they never made it. They lacked the knowledge. They lacked the gear. They lacked all the necessary skills."

At this point I had to interrupt. "Look, I don't think this argument helps any of us, does it?"

Forster laughed as he always did at such times, tossing his head back. "On the contrary. What could help us more than dispelling this sort of illusion?"

"The Founders are no illusion," said Aeslu firmly.

"No? Everything you believe is an illusion. Everything you do is based on illusion. Everything you are—" and here he paused a moment, smiling his smile of mixed pity and contempt "—is in the service of illusion."

Momentarily stunned, Aeslu fell silent.

Then, before she could defend herself, Forster continued full force. "Let me tell you a tale. Not long ago, in another part of the world, I spent my time attempting to climb mountains almost but not quite the equal of what we're climbing now."

"There are no mountains like the Mountain," Aeslu stated.

Forster raised one hand to eye level and, holding it before us palm outward in magisterial dismay, he silenced her. "Your objections serve only to prove my point," he told her. "The world is rife with mountains. This one is admittedly rather grand—grand enough to justify the present efforts. Is it unique, though? That's hard to say. In fact, I've stumbled into more than a few people caught up in a similar pursuit."

Now I took a turn at interrupting. "I don't understand what you mean."

Another smile. "If you listen, maybe you will."

Aeslu and I glanced at each other but said nothing more.

"Let me phrase it this way," said Forster. "Influenced by the local culture—and, I suppose, by my relative youth at the time—I once saw my task in less straightforward terms than I do now." Again that smile. "You look puzzled. Both of you. Allow me to clarify. What I mean is that I saw the climb not just as the climb, but as something beyond the climb. Something at once subtler and more substantial."

"Something—"

The raised hand once again cut me short.

"Something not unlike what certain yogis, seated in the dust far below the peaks I sought, practiced even as I climbed. A discipline. A discipline capable of leaving the world's banality and squalor behind. Let's be blunt: a discipline whose elements included some remarkably similar to what have brought both acclaim and ridicule to the yogis for millennia. Techniques for physical mastery. Breath control. Mind over matter. I could elaborate, but I won't. Just take my word."

As we listened, Aeslu stirred, though whether in curiosity or discomfort I couldn't tell.

At this point I succumbed to temptation. "What does this have to do with us? With Aeslu and the Founders?"

Now his smile showed both contempt and amusement. "Jesse, I'm shocked. What a question from you, of all people! From the Man of Knowledge—the selfsame man who sought to lead his people upward to the summit!"

"Forget the Man of Knowledge."

"I don't need to forget him—I never paid him much attention in the first place. The question is, have *you* forgotten?"

"Never mind what I've forgotten."

"Surely it's dawned on you that climbing offers the perfect medium for what you seek. Why else would you have allied yourself with the Heirs in the first place?"

"I've had my reasons."

"Indeed."

"Something to do with you and the Umbrage."

"True—but not that alone. There was something else. Something to do with transcendence."

"I never said anything about transcendence."

He huffed at me: a single exhalation. "True. Not a single word. But have you *wanted* it? Of course. Why else would you be here, Jesse? Why else would you knock yourself out day after day, scrape your hands raw, freeze all night and blister all day in the sun? Why else would you risk your life with every step you take? Tell me."

To my dismay, all I could do was gesture in bafflement. "There, too, I have my reasons."

"Of course you do."

"And I feel no obligation to specify them."

"Especially when they're so vague in the first place. Never mind. They'll clarify soon enough. And yours will, too," he added, gesturing at Aeslu. "There's no avoiding it. You know that even if you won't admit it. The pot knows when it's inside the kiln. The knife knows when it's up against the grinding stone."

"Fancy talk."

"True nonetheless."

Then, abruptly, Aeslu said, "Just tell us the story."

"The story. All right, the story." Forster finished his chocolate, wadded up the wrapper, and tossed it off the edge.

9

"What happened was that, having worked my way into this state of mind, I came to believe that climbing mountains would induce some sort of insight well beyond the obvious. An insight into the heart of the matter, if you will. The mountain," he said, just then turning to the cliff and rapping it once with his fist, "beyond the mountain."

He paused a moment, gazing first at Aeslu, then at me. "I should mention that I was climbing at the time with a fellow named Sanderson. There were others with us then—mostly Brits, a few Swiss, and two Americans—and together we joined forces to form what, lacking a better word, we called our expedition. But Sanderson and I were the heart of the team. We were unquestionably the ones who ended up most often at the summit of whatever we happened to be climbing. No surprise there. He was a fine climber, the best I'd ever seen. British. Most of the good ones are. Spent his early years in Kabul, where his father was with the embassy. Learned to climb in the English Lake District, though, when he returned to England for boarding school, and did plenty of time on crags in Wales and Scotland as well. Then returned to Afghanistan as a youth and bagged his first big peaks there. Caught the climbing bacillus in a big way, it seems. By the time I met the man—that was in Zermatt—he was bored with the Alps and itching to get back to Central Asia. He made a good case for it, too. I joined forces with him quite rabid about the whole thing.

"So it was Sanderson who got me going on this whole notion of the climb beyond the climb," Forster went on. "The meta-climb, if you like that sort of language. Something he picked up in the Hindu Kush, I suppose—another, even deadlier bacillus. Highly contagious, believe me. I caught rather a bad case myself.

"You look impatient. Well, let me get to the point.

"In the Kush, not long before the war, we set our sights on an unclimbing peak of remarkable proportions. The name is inconsequential. Likewise the altitude. All that matters is that nothing either of us had previously climbed bore any resemblance to this mountain. We were intent on reaching its summit. More than that, though: we were intent on something far more important, something far more remarkable, than the mere highest point of the rock and ice making up the peak itself. How? It's no accident that the Himalaya is cheek-by-jowl with hermits, mendicant monks, and naked fakirs who cast about for whatever odd visions they seek. Or that en route to Samadhiville they habitually isolate themselves, undertake long fasts, contort their bodies, mortify their flesh, sit immobile in the snow, fiddle with their pulse and breath rates, and generally do whatever they regard as necessary to transport them to their destination. Is that what we did? No. But I suspect that even you two, no matter how dubious you feel about what I'm saying, can see the similarity between those age-old disciplines and what Sanderson and I were pursuing on the peak. At least that's what my high-born British pal had in mind. It's what I expected, too, despite a long history of skepticism in that regard.

"The general idea—not altogether implausible, I'll admit—was that climbing a mountain forces the climber out of his habitual states of mind into something less routine. From half-stupor into full alertness, if you will. We're all sleepwalkers. Climbing wakes us up. No doubt you've heard the adage: nothing concentrates a man's mind like the knowledge that he'll be hanged at dawn. Climbing serves that purpose. If nothing else, dangling by your fingertips from an icy cliff wakes you up. Sanderson's theory was that climbing a mountain of the sort we'd approached in the Hindu Kush—a mountain far bigger, grander, and more dangerous than any we'd ever seen before— would take the process yet another step beyond.

"Alas, things didn't work out quite as we'd hoped. It was a difficult climb. A lot went wrong. Never mind the details. What matters is simply this: Sanderson took a bad fall. Perhaps he was a better yogi than a climber. Perhaps he merely slipped. At any rate, he lost his footing, skidded down the snowfield, and went over a cliff. So much for transcendence."

Aeslu and I both stared at Forster, waiting.

He said nothing—just stared back at us.

After a while I said, "You don't seem very upset."

"That's rather presumptuous of you, don't you think? I was quite upset, thank you. I still am."

Again we waited.

"The story's not over yet. You see, Sanderson and I had been tied together when he fell. The poor fellow was leading at the time but shot right past me. Fortunately—or so it appeared—I had a firm belay stance on the snowfield, saw the accident coming, watched him slip, braced myself, and managed to keep my grip on the rope despite his velocity on the way down. That didn't keep Sanderson from going over the edge, but I'd at least slowed his descent, and ultimately I stopped it. The rope held. He was dangling over the precipice but he wasn't falling."

"How did you pull him up?" asked Aeslu.

"That was obviously the big question. There were just two of us at that altitude—the rest were several thousand feet below, some at our high camp, some at another camp even farther down. Sanderson and I were on our own. He was at one end of the rope; I was at the other. Neither of us could see the other. I shouted at him—in fact, shouted time after time— but got no answer. Did Sanderson shout back at me?

I'm sure he did. I never heard him, though. I didn't know the first thing about his state just then. Was he injured? Dead, even? Altogether fine, perhaps—except for the predicament of dangling two or three thousand feet above a Himalayan glacier? All I knew was that his weight had pulled the rope so taut that Sanderson must have been entirely unsupported. Thus the dilemma.

"There are standard alpine techniques for rescuing someone after a fall. I assume the Rixtirs have something comparable. What these technique take for granted, however, is more than one person to make the rescue. If someone is occupied in restraining the rope, he won't be able to do all the other things that need doing at such times. Anchoring ice-axes in the snow. Tying off the rope. Determining the fallen man's ability, if any, to get himself up without help. Rappelling down to assist him. Or, at the very least, throwing down another rope to winch him back up. Under the circumstances, I was incapable of performing these tasks. Any of them. Just keeping a grip on the rope was almost more than I could manage.

"I mentioned that we had been climbing a snowfield. That's what put us in the bind, really. On a rock slope I might have improvised. On snow—out of the question. I'd managed to dig in during the first moments of Sanderson's fall; I'd shoved my ice-axe deep into the snow. Lying on its iron head, though, I could feel the rope tugging at it all the time. The rope would probably have yanked the axe out altogether if I'd budged more than a few inches. How long could I have stayed like that? I don't know. Two hours, three.... The temperature was somewhere around five or ten degrees above zero. It doesn't take long to succumb when you're lying flat on the slope without shelter. To complicate the situation, my body warmth started to soften the snow I was lying on. I could feel the axe's stave gradually shifting beneath me. It seemed just a matter of time before the axe lost its grip on the snow. Once it pulled free, my body would be counterbalancing Sanderson's weight unassisted. I was by far the bigger man. Still, I would have been no match for someone dangling free. I would have lasted about two or three seconds before Sanderson pulled me down after him.

"What I said about the prospect of being hanged at dawn wasn't entirely inapropos," he went on. "Not entirely adequate, either. Something got lost in the shuffle. True, the situation prompted a certain fixity of mind. I certainly thought hard about what to do, how to do it, and what consequences might ensue. There was a degree of—what shall I call it?—*focus*. But transcendence?"

Once again Forster paused. I have no idea whether Aeslu understood every word he'd spoken. I don't doubt, however, that she grasped everything that mattered about his tale.

"I cut the rope," said Forster.

10

Forster's tale about the Hindu Kush surprised me only
in its frankness. I'd never trusted him; he'd amply
proved himself dangerous when he wasn't downright
lethal. My ten-month effort to survive his presence in
the Mountain Land had given me every reason to believe what he claimed to have done *in extremis.* To
hear him confess it, though—that's what left me
stunned.

Please understand what I'm saying. What appalled
me wasn't primarily that Forster had cut his partner's
rope. The ethics of mountaineering have always per-
mitted certain acts of self-preservation. If a companion
is dragging you to your death, you have the right to
sever the line that would doom you as well. Some
mountain climbers have suffered fatal consequences
rather than forsake their fellows; others have chosen
to save their own lives instead. Forster may well have
done the only sensible thing. It wasn't the physical
motions of cutting the rope, nor the instinct behind
the motions, that troubled me. It wasn't even the
man's matter-of-fact tone as he told the tale—though
he sounded like a sailor relating how, during a storm
at sea, it had been necessary to jettison part of the
ship's cargo. No, it was something else altogether.

Forster was in many ways the most isolated man I'd
ever met. He attended to his own business and nothing
else. That business was Forster himself. In doing so
he kept his own counsel; I rarely knew what he was
thinking beyond what I could divine roundabout. I
had no trouble believing his tale about a climbers'

accident in the Kush—what had taken place there seemed pure Forster. But to hear him tell the tale . . . ? It was altogether out of keeping with what I knew of him.

Why this sudden rush of words? Why the need to reveal himself—and in an unfavorable light? Was he trying to scare Aeslu and me? To brandish the incident as a cautionary tale? "Stay in line," he seemed to be telling us, "or you'll regret the consequences." But why warn us *now*? I had no illusions about my safety in his presence. This was hardly the first time I'd seen my acquaintanceship with Forster as potentially deadly; he could dispatch both Aeslu and me as easily as he'd dispatched his friend Sanderson. He knew as well as I that we relied on each other not out of trust but out of mutual necessity. His story thus served no purpose as a warning.

What purpose *did* it serve, then? I didn't know. Perhaps none at all. Perhaps the altitude and the cold had just loosened him up, intoxicated him, left him garrulous. Perhaps the story, like everything else Forster did, was a means of keeping hold on the situation, of keeping Aeslu and me at bay.

11

Aeslu clearly felt disquieted, too, by what Forster had told us, though her reasons differed from my own. She said nothing that night. She showed no visible reaction. Yet her silence was precisely what told me that something troubled her; she rarely withdrew like that. The next morning, though, was another matter.

"If the Mountain has no meaning for you," asked Aeslu during a long rest—we had just made an especially difficult traverse on icy rock—"then why do you persist in climbing it?"

The question clearly annoyed Forster. "I never said it has no meaning."

"You deny that the Founders climbed it."

"True."

"You refuse to acknowledge that they built a refuge at the Summit."

"True as well."

"You doubt everything that the Mountain-Drawn believe."

"That's not too far off the mark."

"So then why—"

"Look," said Forster. "This mountain is big enough as it is without all the stuff you people pile on top of it. I'm not interested in the stuff. Just the mountain. That's quite enough, thanks."

I couldn't hold back any longer. "What she's getting at is this," I told him. "In your eyes, the Mountain is just a lot of rock and ice. For the Mountain-Drawn, it's far more than that. It's something that your presence violates. So if all you see is a pile of rock and ice, then why not tackle some other pile? Why not leave this one—"

"This mountain is mine, God damn it!" he shouted just then, sweeping at the air between us with the back of his hand. "It's mine!"

"You don't own it, Forster."

"I don't own it—I *claim* it."

"Forster—"

"Get off my back, both of you! If you want to help and get me to the top, that's just great. Otherwise I'll give you a rope and you can try getting down by yourselves, all right?"

"Forster—"

"Just don't try stopping me from doing what I'm going to do."

12

We didn't stop him. To the degree that made sense, we helped him. Too much so? Not enough? By then we were too tired, hungry, and cold to know one way or the other.

Aeslu and I figured that we'd been climbing somewhat over two weeks. Fifteen days was her estimate. Mine was somewhere around sixteen or eighteen. How long, exactly, eluded us for two reasons: first, because we'd lost count early on; second, because we didn't know how long we'd spent inside the tunnel. Did a precise count really matter? Maybe not. What we knew without question was that all of us had nearly reached the limits of our strength and stamina. We had depleted our supplies of fuel—both Forster's kerosene and the waxy fire-pots salvaged from the Founders' gear. Little food remained: several chunks of pemmican, three small bags of pudding dust, some root tea, a few handfuls of spicy sugar. What little warmth and energy these rations provided, the Mountain drained from us within each day's first few hours. I felt surprised in some respects that we kept going at all. Perhaps having no alternative made it possible. Yet on arising each day, I felt amazed to find we were even alive. The night's chill hadn't overcome us altogether. The previous day's effort hadn't done us in. How long, though, could we keep up the pace?

Aeslu and I made no effort to disguise our fatigue from each other. "I feel so tired," she told me time after time. "So very, very tired. Sometimes I want to fall asleep and never wake up." I reassured Aeslu at such times; I said the things that people say to cheer one another on. Don't give up now! Just keep going a little longer! Only a few more days and we're there! In fact, I felt the same weariness that Aeslu did, or perhaps something even more intense. Not just weariness: a craving for rest I can't even describe. Even the longest journey would have seemed easier if it had taken place on the level. Here, though, in a vertical world, even sitting was a precarious act. We couldn't so much as sleep without lashing ourselves to the wall. Thus my effort to reassure Aeslu was at best an act of dishonesty, at worst of self-delusion. Did it serve a purpose, though? Did it offer some kind of sustenance for lack of any other? Maybe so. If nothing else, reassuring each other allowed Aeslu and me all the more reason to nestle close, oblivious or indifferent to Forster's envy, while we shared the scant warmth that otherwise would have frittered off into oblivion.

Forster. What surprised me was Forster. Strong as he was—and Forster was nothing if not strong—he, too, weakened from the demands of our climb. His prowess seemed no match for the task before us. I mean the task not just of climbing, of finding a path up the cliff, of slamming the ice-hatchets into place, of kicking the footclaws till they held, of pulling himself higher, higher, higher. I also mean the task of surviving. The task of keeping warm when there was so little heat, of staying strong when there was so little food, of keeping clearheaded when we had so little sense of where we were or when we might reach our destination. Like Aeslu and me, Forster weakened. I took a certain pleasure in his weakness, too, in seeing him find the limits of his strength and seeing the shadow of his power. Yet I shouldn't have. No matter how much I loathed the man, I depended on him and his superior abilty even in a depleted state. Whatever weakness he suffered lay heavily on my own shoulders.

13

One morning—what was it, day 19 or 20?—Forster had started a particularly dangerous traverse. This involved climbing diagonally across a snow- and ice-caked bulge in the cliff toward a snowfield that we believed might serve us well. If we could reach it, we might work our way higher in relative safety for a while. Getting up there, however, was a problem. The bulge between where we stood and where we wanted to be had acquired a coating of the slickest ice any of us had encountered so far. The cliff right over the bulge faced due west, hence caught the sun's rays all afternoon; the resulting warmth had alternated with each night's chill to glaze the rocks and their coatings of snow. We could barely tolerate looking at the bulge, it was so shiny. Why, then, should we risk crossing so formidable a barrier? Because the cliff above us was even more perilous. If we didn't proceed to the left, we would have to retreat altogether and try some other route. We were all too weary to contemplate that course of action. Besides, Forster was convinced he could get across. Aeslu and I agreed to his plan for lack of any better ideas.

We weren't oblivious to the risk, though. We could see what he was getting into. Or *onto:* for we couldn't imagine how any of our tools could penetrate ice that hard. Even the ice-hatchets from the Founders' Gear looked inadequate to the task. Thus uneasy about the situation but too dazed to offer an alternative, Aeslu and I at least mustered enough presence of mind to set up a good belay. A double belay, even—two of us anchored to the cliff and braced to protect Forster from a fall.

He did well for about ten or fifteen minutes. Though far heavier than Aeslu and I, hence less agile on ice, he managed better than we would have in our condition at the time. He picked his way across the bulge. He found occasional areas of exposed rock that gave him places to bolt in hooks and clip them to the rope. Forster even screwed in some of the Rixtir ice-screws—the only hardware we possessed capable of boring straight into the ice. In many ways his rapid progress encouraged us. He'd be across in no time.

His choice of equipment troubled me, however. During most of the climb, Forster had refused to use the Founders' Gear. He looked down on it; he thought it worse than useless. Yet here he was using a piece of the much-loathed hardware. Aeslu found this sight encouraging—not just a sign that Forster would get to the other side, but also a sign that Aeslu's people had somehow triumphed over his ignorance. I wasn't so sure. It smacked of deep concern, even alarm. He didn't manifest it in other ways, but I could detect it all the same.

Then, without the least warning, he slipped. Forster shot down the cliff at least fifteen or twenty feet. I tightened my grip on the rope the same instant he started down; he picked up so much speed on the ice, however, that several yards played out before I could pull the free end around my torso and, exerting as much force as possible, slow it to a stop. The rope's friction left my back feeling as if I'd burst into flames. Still, what mattered was simply halting Forster's descent.

Which I did. Kicking against the cliff about ten yards away and another ten lower, he struggled to find something to grasp. Rock, ice, anything. . . . At least the anchors he'd put in earlier kept holding. I could barely keep my hold on the rope; if the anchors popped free, though . . .

Almost at once they did just that: one after another,

chunks of metal came loose from the ice and stone, each with a remarkably delicate *ping!* as it did so. And as each piece came out, Forster dropped another five or six feet, not straight down but diagonally, for the rope's anchor-point moved closer and closer to just below where Aeslu and I were sitting, so that he tumbled and jolted over the convex surface of the cliff on the way down. All the while I heard a terrible noise: the thud and scrape of Forster's body on alternate patches of ice and stone.

I could barely hold the rope. Grunting, I struggled with it, tilting backward, as if I'd be tugged over the edge at any moment. Perhaps I knew I wouldn't: I was secured to the cliff by a separate rope, a loop around my waist that Aeslu and I had bolted into solid rock with one of the best Rixtir hooks. Forster's rope passed around my waist beneath the anchor-loop; it couldn't pull free unless it snapped. I didn't consider that likely—this was one of the Founders' ropes. But how long could I keep my grip on the rope? Forster weighed more than two hundred pounds. The tug of his body dangling free was more than I could tolerate for long. For a moment a ghastly fear shot through my mind: that the force of his rope around my waist would tear right through me. It didn't. My back ached but my flesh and bones held steady.

Something else crossed my mind just then. If I couldn't keep hold of the rope, what would happen? The rope would play out, whether all at once or slowly, till it tightened. Then the loops of rope tied around my waist would be all that supported Forster Beckwith. After that I couldn't even guess what would happen. The anchors holding me to the cliff might give out. Or the rope might break. The first of these two events would yank me over the edge; the second would leave me clinging to the cliff while Forster fell alone to his death.

But if the anchors held? If the rope didn't break?

No, that didn't seem possible. Something had to give.

What if it didn't? The rope, of Rixtir origin, was the strongest I'd ever seen. The anchors, too, came from the Founders' Gear, and they seemed unlikely to fail. Where did that leave me, then, other than straining against the weight of someone who detested me, had used me strictly for his own purposes, and repeatedly had tried to kill me?

During Forster's fall and the first moments afterwards, Aeslu had been stunned into near-immobility. She followed his descent but seemed incapable of speech, much less of action. Even at the time I knew that her lack of response showed something far more complex than helplessness. She was a strong, forthright woman. Several times already during our ascent she had saved my life. Why, then, did she falter? Why did she do little more than watch me struggle?

She was waiting for me. Waiting for the word, the nod, the signal. Ice-hatchet in hand—first merely held, then raised—Aeslu waited for me to let her go ahead and do what Forster Beckwith had done to his companion in the Hindu Kush.

For a moment I almost told her to go ahead. "Do it!" I'd shout. "Just do it!" The hatchet would descend; the fibers of the rope would part; the severed end would shoot over the edge, trailing Forster.

I said, *"Don't."*

Aeslu gazed at me as if the word made no sense.

"Don't. Put it down."

She hesitated briefly, then set the hatchet to one side.

"Help me get him up."

At once she set to work with a clarity of mind far exceeding what I would have managed under the circumstances. She anchored two Rixtir hooks into the ledge we were roosting on. She tied a length of rope onto each hook. She secured the resulting loops onto Forster's rope in a way that eased some of the pressure on my hands. Although I wasn't quite sure what she was doing, the procedure sufficiently resembled certain Western techniques—what mountaineers call "tying off the rope"—that I watched her with confidence and great relief. Soon I could let up, cease fighting with the rope, and soothe my screaming muscles.

14

It took all our strength to get Forster up to the ledge again. Even so, we barely made it. Aeslu lost her grip at the last moment; the jolt came close to yanking him over the edge. He fell sideways instead of head-first, though, and this probably saved him, for the friction of his body against stone helped me check his descent. Then Aeslu managed to tug hard enough that we could pull Forster up once more.

When he was back with us, I was appalled to see his condition. His body slumped hideously to one side—arms flaccid, neck limp, head jolting with each of our tugs.

"There!" Aeslu cried. "Right there!"

I reached forward to grab Forster. I got hold without losing my balance and pulled as hard as possible.

When the rope slackened for a second, I nearly slipped. Then Aeslu reached out, took hold of Forster's right arm herself, and pulled hard enough that we managed to get him up again.

I'd seen the blood but hadn't registered the quantity. Suddenly Forster seemed virtually drenched. His face and chest were slick with blood. I was astonished by how bright it looked.

Aeslu muttered a curse or prayer in her own language.

"Don't let go!" I shouted, though she showed no signs of relenting. "Let's get him all the way up."

We rolled Forster away from the edge and onto his back. This was awkward: we now had no place to stand. The ledge sloped enough that we could easily have stumbled or toppled off. But Aeslu was already anchoring some sort of hardware into the wall; before I knew what she'd done, I found myself clipped into the rope again. We could crouch beside Forster—I at his head, Aeslu at his feet—without much danger of slipping.

Forster started moaning just then: a horrible gurgling sound. He moved slightly.

"Forster! Forster, wake up!" I shouted. I began probing his scalp with my fingers. He was clearly hurt, but I couldn't tell how badly. Scalp wounds bleed so profusely it's hard to tell the difference between a minor cut and a mortal wound. My big fear was that Forster had smashed his skull.

"What has happened to him?" Aeslu asked.

"He'll be all right," I told her. "I'm sure he'll be all right."

Then I turned my attention back to Forster. "Look at me. Look up here."

He moaned, glancing around. He tightened his face when he started coughing. His teeth were red; his whole mouth was full of blood. The sight made me gag. Blood was everywhere. Forster's face streamed with it; his chest was now soaked.

Aeslu asked, "How badly hurt—?"

"I don't know. Maybe it's just a scalp wound. Maybe something worse."

Forster tried speaking but the words didn't make sense. I could see why: some of his teeth had been knocked out.

"You'll be all right," I told him.

He glanced at me, then toward Aeslu. The look of desperation in his eyes couldn't have been more obvious. Somehow that desperate gaze frightened me more than all the blood. The gravity of our situation struck me then—struck me hard.

Aeslu had begun rummaging through her pack; a few moments later she pulled out a leather bag. When she removed its contents, I saw small clay jars, copper tubes, bundles of dessicated leaves. Rixtir medicines?

I didn't know what these things were or what good they'd do, but I couldn't object when Aeslu set to work ministering to Forster. I had nothing better to offer him.

15

Aeslu and I soon decided that Forster wasn't so badly
hurt as I'd first thought. However shocking his
wounds—they looked especially bad on someone as
big and robust as he—none of them was grave. The
bleeding stopped. He perked up. He showed no signs
of shock. The situation soon improved to the point
that Aeslu and I no longer feared for his life.

Of course his improvement presented its own difficulties: he couldn't get comfortable on the ledge,
couldn't even speak with us clearly, and grew irritable
under the weight of his frustrations. It was hard to
watch him. Forster kept touching his puffy lips and
bloody teeth. He looked at his sticky hands, hair, and
clothes with an expression of bewilderment and sadness. His efforts at speech baffled him at least as much
as they baffled us, for the words didn't come out right
and sometimes made no sense at all. "—get me dorse—"
he said. "Harssa. No: out of hearse." Trying to get
across to us, he gestured helplessly, stabbing at the air.

Aeslu crouched beside him. "You will be all right,"
she said. "I promise."

Forster shook his head. He raised his right hand to
his face and kept touching his lips, nose, and forehead.

Looking after him was painful—not in the ways that
Forster felt pain, of course, but painful in its own way.
We couldn't do much for him. We had little food, and
what we had was too difficult for him to chew with
an injured jaw. We had water, but only what we
melted from snow, which must have felt intolerably
cold. We had only a few blankets and some Rixtir folk

medicines. These we offered, and he accepted them. But from the look in his eyes—a mixture of confusion and fear—we could see how small a difference we made.

Forster dozed off somewhat later, giving Aeslu and me our first chance to speak together in private.

"Why did you spare him?" she asked at once. The words in Rixtir sounded less accusatory than my English translation does now; even so, her question was whetted to a fine edge.

"I do not know," I told her, "but I had to."

"You don't *know*?" There was no mockery, just bafflement.

"I'm not saying there wasn't a reason—I just don't know how to explain it."

"He is the Man of Ignorance, the Man of Darkness—"

"I know that."

"—the Cutter of Wounds—"

"I know he is."

"—and yet you spared him when you had a chance—"

"Aeslu, listen to me."

"—and not just spared him, but hauled him back up—"

"*Listen.*"

Raising my voice like that roused Forster. He stirred, muttering, while both Aeslu and I stared at him. Then he settled down again: spoke words neither of us could understand, struggled briefly to find a comfortable position, and at last fell silent and still.

Aeslu turned to me again. Before she could speak, I said, "I almost gave you the signal to cut him loose. I wanted to. I wanted more than anything to be rid of him. Don't you understand how much I loathe the man? But I didn't say go ahead. Not because I couldn't, but because I wouldn't."

She waited, watching, confused by my words.

"Do you recall his story about the other mountain climb? How he cut his friend loose?"

She nodded once.

"I kept thinking about what he'd told us. How easy it would have been to cut the rope. How little Forster could have done about it. How much he had it coming. And I wanted nothing more than to be rid of him."

"We should have done it."

"Aeslu, we could have. I could have done it myself, too, if I'd had my hands free. I could have cut the rope with a hatchet, an axe, a knife. I could have gnawed through it with my own teeth for lack of any other way. But I wouldn't. Not because it would have been wrong. Just because—"

She stared, waiting.

"Listen to me. This isn't the first time I've faced this sort of thing. Late in the last war—the war down in the Lowland—something happened, something I've never told you."

Aeslu's expression didn't change, but I could sense her attention focus on me further.

By October of the year we call 1918, I explained, our side was winning. We had our enemy on the run. Their retreat wasn't a full-scale rout, though—the Germans were still fighting hard. But we'd already chased them out of France back into their own country. It was only a matter of time before their resistance collapsed altogether.

One afternoon—a cold, rainy afternoon—my company entered a German village just the other side of the border. The place was deserted. No enemy soldiers in sight. No villagers. Even the farm animals were gone. We couldn't trust the appearance of the place, though: snipers had caught us off guard in the past, and in fact just one day earlier one of them had shot my best friend through the eye. The bullet took the whole back of his head off. We weren't taking any chances now. We scoured the whole place, checked every smashed-up house, barn, shed, pigsty, and chicken coop. Even so we didn't find a soul.

On the way out, though—everyone else had gone ahead a few dozen paces—I heard an odd sound from a stone storage shed we'd already checked. Sort of a cry. At first I thought it might have been just an animal's cry, maybe a stuck pig's. I went back anyway and looked around. I couldn't see anything at first. Just an empty shed with the roof knocked in. Then, looking down into the wreckage, I saw someone hiding there. A German. A wounded German soldier.

He was much younger than I, probably seventeen or so, little more than a boy. He was clearly hurt, struck by some roofing boards and beams that had crashed down on him when an arilltery shell or mortar round hit the shed. Blood streaked down over his face. He looked scared—terrified. I've never seen anyone shake so hard in my life. Yet I think he wasn't out of his senses. The look in his eyes showed someone who understood his predicament. Staring at me, he held up his hands, palm outward, as well as the splintered lumber lying above him would allow. *"Kamerade!"* he shouted. That's what German soldiers said when they wanted to surrender.

But I didn't let him surrender. I didn't take him prisoner. I could have spared him, and I should have, but I didn't. Not because I was angry, though I was. Not even because this might have been the guy who'd shot my friend two days earlier. Who knows how many of our men he'd killed by now? Ultimately anger wasn't really what made me do what I did. More like fatigue. I was too tired to spare him. Sparing him was just too much trouble.

Waiting for me to finish, Aeslu watched me closely, well aware that she didn't need to ask the next question.

"I reached into the pile of broken lumber," I told her. "Not with my hands—with my rifle. There was a kind of knife on the end, what we call a bayonet. The boy tried backing away, but he couldn't, for the wreckage pinned him like a rat in a trap. He had nowhere to go."

Just as I prepared to stab him, though, he grabbed the bayonet—grabbed the blade itself, and took hold of it hard enough to yank me forward. My moment of hesitation combined with the thrust to throw me off balance. I toppled into that heap of broken lumber. The boy and I then fought over the rifle. Tug-of-war, literally. He was much stronger than I. He had the advantage of mortal dread, too, from the very start—though soon enough I was fearing for my own life as well.

He shoved me with the rifle butt. I fell sideways into a fallen beam. When I slashed at him with the bayonet, he used the motion to knock me over. I ended up on my back. He would have overwhelmed me just then if my fall hadn't dislodged some of the lumber, which clattered onto him. He fell right beside me. Then I regained the advantage: scrambled up, took hold of the rifle, swung it around, and brought the butt down on his skull.

When I'd fallen silent Aeslu said, "He was your enemy—"

"Maybe so."

"—not your companion."

"Maybe so."

"And Forssa, too, is your enemy."

"Maybe so. But I still didn't want to cut him loose. Not just to spare *him,* though—to spare myself. I wouldn't do it because I would have become him. Would have become Forster. The Man of Ignorance. The Man of Darkness. Lord knows I've come too close already." I gestured away from the Mountain, toward the glacier below. "Far too close."

"But to pull him back up!" she exclaimed, her voice suddenly much louder.

"What should I have done? I couldn't just sit there."

"We *rescued* him."

"He'd have pulled me down, too."

"We rescued the Man of Ignorance!"

"Aeslu, I couldn't wait there till he died, rotted, and fell apart."

When she looked at me again, I could tell that her anger was gone but the bafflement remained.

"So what do we do now?" she asked.

"I don't know."

"He's hurt."

"I know he's hurt."

"Shall we try to take him up with us?"

"I don't see how we could."

"Take him down?"

"That's impossible, too."

Aeslu leaned back against the rock wall in a way that made her fatigue more obvious than the loudest complaint. "We have two alternatives," she said. "Either we abandon him and proceed upward alone. Or else we stay here with him."

Neither of us spoke for a long time. Forster, unconscious just a few feet away, muttered in his sleep.

16

For the rest of that day, Aeslu and I sat with Forster Beckwith on the ledge. He slept most of that time—slept so deeply that we sometimes wondered if he might simply have died. Now and then, however, he roused. He stirred, shifted his position, called out. And each time he came to the surface, he stayed there longer, he moved more energetically, and he spoke with increasing urgency.

I watched with two minds as Forster returned to our midst.

On the one hand, he seemed to be recovering—or if not quite recovering, then at least emerging from the stupor that had overtaken him right after his fall. This boded well for all of us. If Aeslu and I didn't plan to abandon him, then we could only benefit from any degree to which Forster improved. Was it possible that he might even recover from his wounds? I didn't know. I couldn't guess. I didn't even want to speculate. But of course Aeslu's and my own survival depended either on Forster's recovery or else on his relatively rapid decline and death.

Which brings me to the other hand. Both Forster's recovery—and, if it came to that, his death—would have left us in a terrible position. Suppose he recovered. Aeslu and I would have faced our previous dilemma: proceeding upward with our worst enemy. Suppose instead that he died. Aeslu and I would then have faced the prospect of heading up alone. Forster was at once the least desirable companion and the one most likely help us reach our destination. Either way we were in a bind.

It was hard for me to decide which of these three alternatives—Forster's recovery, his languishing, or his death—appealed to me least. Small wonder that both Aeslu and I wavered when we tried deciding what to do.

Or did our bleak prospects simplify the situation? I, for one, felt more and more doomed regardless of whatever actions we took. What chance remained that we would ever reach the Summit? We weren't far below the top—perhaps a thousand feet below, if the Mountain Stone were accurate—but the cliff that Forster had fallen from remained a major obstacle. If he had failed so miserably to surmount it, how could Aeslu and I ever think we'd succeed? And if we couldn't, then how could we see our prospects in a favorable light? Yet in some ways this bleak outlook was itself what prompted me to sit tight, wait, and do what I should have done more willingly.

Something else about Forster's periodic return to consciousness left me uneasy. Every time Forster roused, he grew more and more frantic. He struggled to sit up. He groped about like someone struggling to shake off a nightmare. He yelled, stammered, cried out, pleaded half-intelligibly for help. And each time he roused, Forster came closer to falling off the ledge—and to knocking Aeslu and me off, too.

"Let me go! Let me go!" he shouted. "Let me go, God damn it!" He started tugging at the rope that Aeslu and I had used to secure him to the cliff. Aeslu reached over to pull his hands away. Forster shoved back hard enough that she lost her balance. Although she started grappling to catch herself, she almost went over the edge; only my catching her by the wrist kept her from falling. With great effort I succeeded in pulling her back from the precipice.

She reached a safer spot on the ledge.

By then Forster had nearly untied the rope. I

yanked it hard enough to get it away from him, but he said, "No, enough! This was the whole point."

"Leave it alone."

"You don't understand."

"Forster, stop it. We're trying to help you."

"Help me? What makes *you* think you can help *me*?"

"Listen to me. I want you to stay right where you are. Don't move. I can't help you if you keep fighting with us."

Forster started unbuttoning his coat. When I reached over again and pulled his hands back, he tugged off one glove with his teeth. "As if you could make a difference! Ha!"

"What do you mean, difference?"

"Against *them.*"

"I don't know what you're talking about."

"Of course you don't," said Forster. "You'd be a leaf in the wind by comparison. Even *I* am."

These words so bewildered me that I made no effort to argue with him. "I don't understand."

"Of course you don't. It's not in your blood. It's not blue enough."

Rather than explain, though, he faded out on us. He calmed down, he settled back into place on the ledge, and almost at once he fell asleep.

One opportunity that Forster's state of mind presented, however, was access to his pack. While he slept, I managed to pull open the straps securing it; I tugged out a sweater, a jaunty touring cap, a pair of long johns, and some Swiss-made wool mittens; I worked my way toward whatever awaited me among the pack's deep strata. Some of the Lowland gear—iron pitons, carabiners, and so forth—clanked about when I touched them. Damn racket! I couldn't proceed without making too much noise.

Apparently I'd made quite enough already. Forster roused. He sat bolt upright. He glanced about, then turned to me. And he went into an instantaneous rage.

"Damn you—bastard!" he shouted. "Always poking about where you don't belong!"

"Forster, I was just checking—"

"As if the powers-that-be aren't meddlesome enough already!"

"It's not what you imagine—"

"Making sure I don't comport myself in a manner unbecoming to my heritage!"

"Forster—"

"Or that I don't go around the bend at least one time too many!" He set to work frantically stuffing his possessions back into the pack.

To my surprise, he seemed less antagonized by my genuine trespass than by an imaginary one. What, exactly, did he think I was up to? I couldn't even speculate. All I knew was that he'd caught me.

And I knew I couldn't persist. I had the advantage—he was weaker now, badly hurt, and literally tied to the cliff. I could have ransacked Forster's belongings right before his very eyes. Yet I held off.

Why? Because I feared his confusion. Not because I feared he'd hurt me; rather, because I feared he might hurt himself. My actions might have agitated him to the point that he'd go wild, injure himself further, even wriggle out of his restraints and fall off the ledge. We had enough trouble as it was without Forster running amok.

And so I felt at least partly pleased when Forster calmed down, finished packing his clothes, and, curling up against his pack, used it as a pillow.

"What is he saying?" Aeslu asked me when it seemed safe to talk. "I do not understand the words."

"Neither do I."

"Yet he is speaking your language."

"He's speaking English, but I don't know what he means."

Aeslu waited for me to clarify.

I told her, "Maybe he's badly hurt after all. Maybe the fall cracked his skull. He's talking the way someone does when he's hurt his brain. I saw that happen a lot during the war."

Her lips thickened with fear. "What will happen to him?"

"I don't know any more than before."

"Will we leave him here?"

"No one said anything about leaving him."

"We will stay with him, then?"

"Just let me think," I told her. "I don't understand this any better than you do."

She gazed at Forster briefly, then back at me. Then she said, "I am afraid."

"I am, too. But we can't do anything now anyway. It'll be dark in just an hour."

Even before nightfall, Forster was at it again. "I wanted to see if—to see if there might be a way," he told us. "You see, what I'm trying to get at— Wait. Let me start over. I wanted to see if there might be a different way of—of—of getting to where I ought to be. I just wanted to see what might be done to solve the problem."

"What problem?" I asked.

He glanced at me just then with an expression that startled me: the dazed look, at once meek and wild-eyed, of a schoolboy who has forgotten his lines while reciting before the class. The reply came a moment later: "What to do. What to amount to. *That*."

"Meaning—?"

"What to, you know, *be*."

"Forster, I still don't understand."

"Of course you don't. That's because you think you're something. But I know I'm nothing. That's the problem."

17

He went on half the night, alternately ranting, pleading, and rambling. If Forster had acted as hostile as he sounded, I'd have feared for Aeslu's and my own safety; as it turned out, though, he stayed put and did nothing to harm us. He just sat there beside us on the ledge. Where, exactly, I couldn't tell—I couldn't even see him clearly in the dark. He could have been pacing back and forth, for all I knew, having sprung himself from the ropes I'd used to restrain him. Not likely. All I mean is that our only awareness of Forster came from the incessant babble a few feet to one side. Lord knows, that was enough.

"That's why the mountain makes sense," he went on. "You can't sell it. You can't trade it. Not that some people wouldn't try. Bonds issued, stocks offered. The Mountain Made of Tickertape, eh? Fat chance! No, the Mountain means only what it means."

"Forster—"

"The Mountain is only what it is."

"Forster, listen to me—"

"That's why Dad hates the Mountain."

All the while, Aeslu and I kept to ourselves on the opposite side of the ledge where, huddling together, we shared what little warmth we could rouse from our bodies. We could have talked but didn't. It wasn't just that we were too cold, though the night was frigid. We were too scared, too confused. We had no idea what to do.

Then, around what must have been midnight, Forster stopped. It happened all at once. No tapering off—babble fading to silence. No shift from lunacy to lucidity. One moment he was raving, the next he was altogether quiet.

I listened to the stillness for a long time. What a relief. Yet it was frightening, too. Surely Forster had died. One of our three appalling alternatives had given way to another. Aeslu and I were now alone on the Mountain. It didn't take much imagination to grasp that we, too, would succumb before much longer.

Before I could think further about the situation—whether to rejoice in my enemy's death, to reflect on the calamities preceding it, to dread what might happen next—another sound jolted me.

A snore.

What I heard was an ordinary snore coming right from where the ranting had come just a few minutes earlier.

I can't say that I felt relief any more than disappointment. On some level it didn't matter to me what happened now. Simply having Forster fall silent was enough. I was too tired to care.

18

"Where's my breakfast?"

I heard the words, but they didn't register. The words themselves weren't what baffled me. It wasn't even the realization of who had spoken. I knew it was Forster. But the *tone:* matter-of-fact, calm, even a bit self-amused. Not quite what I expected from a raving lunatic.

Forcing my way out of the bedroll, I emerged from dimness into the morning's dazzle. Needles of light stabbed at me. Shielding my eyes, I hunched over in pain. Then, adjusting, I glanced about to take in my surroundings.

Aeslu lay asleep beside me on the left.

The precipice fell away to my right, with glaciers below and the Mountain Land beyond.

And behind me, when I wrenched around to look, sat Forster Beckwith. Propped against the cliff with his covers pulled up and tucked around his torso, he looked like a comfortable but somewhat irritable convalescent.

I asked him, "What did you say?"

He smiled a smile of great self-amusement. "Breakfast. Is that so difficult a notion to grasp?"

I was stunned. As if a whole night's blather counted for nothing! On the other hand, his nonchalance itself might well have been a further sign of how far his mind had deteriorated. Forster had calmed down but still hadn't regained his senses.

Yet he seemed capable of reading my thoughts. "Don't look so bewildered," he told me. "I was going through a bad patch for a while. Now things are looking up."

"Forster, do you have any notion of how sick you've been?"

He shrugged. "Just because I've been off my rocker doesn't mean I don't know it."

I couldn't believe how much he'd improved overnight. He looked awful—the whole left side of his face remained swollen, and his left cheek was still a mass of clots and abrasions—but something about him appeared to be less damaged. More to the point, he seemed to be with us there on the ledge, not off in another realm.

"Are you in pain?"

"Of course." He gestured at his face, both hands palm up, to note the absurdly obvious answer to my question.

"But you're able to move?"

"To the degree I've attempted so far."

When I asked all sorts of other questions, though—nothing more than an honest attempt to size up the man's injuries—he just brushed me off.

"Look, old man, I'd rather you didn't play Florence Nightingale. There's really no great surprise in what's happening. I took a bad fall. I got hurt. I rattled my brain a bit. No more, no less."

"You damn near lost it, Forster. You were raving like a madman."

He made a shooing motion with his right hand. "Par for the course. Cerebral contusion. A touch of swelling inside the old cranium. Nothing I haven't witnessed a dozen times myself."

"Forster—"

"I'll shake the whole business in no time."

"Forster, listen to me."

Even as we spoke he pushed off his blankets, leaned to one side, and tried forcing himself up. His size and strength allowed him to get farther than a smaller man would have in such a debilitated state. But even Forster could tell something was wrong: his right leg and

right hand didn't work quite right; his efforts didn't
accomplish what he wanted; he teetered a moment,
struggling, before he tipped backward and sat clumsily
on the same spot he'd tried to abandon.

Later, when Aeslu had emerged from her limbolike
sleep, I explained about Forster in her own language.
"He's better but not well yet. He makes sense now
but has trouble moving."

"Can he climb?"

"I doubt it. He can scarcely stand."

"Does he know he is not well?"

"It would seem so, but I can't really tell. I don't
think he's telling us the whole truth. Whether he's
hiding it from us or from himself, though, I just
don't know."

She looked as I felt: at once relieved and troubled
by Forster's improvement. On some level—some basic,
human level—it was impossible not to feel pleased
that Forster had started recovering. I suspect that both
Aeslu and I, despite our shared loathing of the man,
felt a deep fear of what awaited us if Forster died. Yet
what would happen if he regained enough strength to
join us again? What would we be in for then?

Before this conversation could arouse Forster's unease, however, we cut it short. We switched from Rixtir to English. We discussed the cold, our food
supplies, the state of our equipment—nothing that
wasn't crucial, yet nothing that lay at the very heart
of what worried us.

This: that Forster seemed at once too badly injured
to proceed, yet not sufficiently injured to justify our
proceeding without him.

19

By that stage of the climb I had grown accustomed to never seeing the sun rise. The Mountain blocked all our views to the east and most to the north and south; we saw the sun no earlier than midday even in clear weather. Dawn and noon were the same, and we spent half of each day trapped in the Mountain's shadow.

But growing accustomed to the sun's late arrival didn't mean that I tolerated its absence well. Sitting on a shadowy ledge felt altogether different from sitting on the same ledge in the sunlight. It wasn't just a question of mood—of merry sunbeams boosting our spirits—but of survival itself. Frostbite was never distant in the Mountain's shadow. When we sat in the sunlight, however, we could feel the blood pushing through our veins and our flesh warding off the ice a little longer.

Maybe the Mountain-Drawn were right: the Sun is a god, the Moon is goddess, and their light is ultimately all we need. That's certainly how it felt just then. I sat in the sunlight that morning and felt it suffusing my flesh in the most tangible way—as if the warmth were a presence that filled my depleted body, made me new, revived me. I couldn't imagine anything more pleasurable than just sitting there in the sun.

20

And the moon? That night the sky cleared enough to reveal it, though a layer of cirrus clouds above us filtered out the stars. I was delighted to see the moon when it emerged from beyond the Mountain's summit. Not that it offered any warmth, for it didn't. If anything, the moon seemed to draw warmth out of us, to chill our flesh all the more. But it had been such a long time since I'd seen anything above me except the cliffs and glaciers, day after day, that I welcomed even the icy moon. It was more than I'd expected. It was brilliant. It was white, round, perfect.

Yet the moon, too, is an avalanche, a circular avalanche, an avalanche of a single stone.

21

Forster did not improve. Or perhaps I should say that he improved, relapsed, improved once more, and relapsed yet again. He alternated periods of complete lucidity with periods of total incoherence. One moment he was busy with his ordinary activities—eating, drinking, adjusting his gear, and so forth—and the next he seemed scarcely capable of sitting unassisted. The transformations were unpredictable and terrifying. I never knew if I'd be dealing with a rational human being or a wild beast.

"Get away from me!" he shouted when I tried adjusting the ropes—the ropes that served as the only lifeline securing him to the cliff during his periods of lunacy. "Just get the hell away, Stuart!"

"I'm not Stuart, I'm Jesse."

"Like *hell* you are."

"Jesse O'Keefe."

"Tell Dad to go fuck himself."

"Just let me make sure the ropes—"

"Tell him I've done something he can't even *imagine*!"

"Forster, all I want is to tighten the ropes—"

At these words he grew even more agitated: tugged at the lifeline, tried skittering away from me, now and then even lashed out his fist. "You can't stop me now! Damn you all—you think you can stop me. Well, you can't. It's mine! I'll get there no matter what you do. The mountain is mine!"

I had no idea what was happening. I don't mean the words he shouted; the bee in Forster's bonnet was the same whether he sounded crazy or sane. I mean what was happening physiologically. Years later, during the Second World War, I worked as an administrator at Fitzsimmons Army Hospital, east of Denver, and I picked up some knowledge about this sort of thing: concussions, cerebral trauma, organic dementia. During the climb, though, I knew almost nothing. The elementary first aid I'd learned during the earlier war didn't exactly pass for medical training. I could only guess what Forster was going through. Some sort of head injury. What kind, though? I could only guess. Fragments of bone pressing somewhere? Hemorrhage? Lord knows. All I could figure out was that Forster waxed and waned, he came and went, he lost his mind and regained it so unpredictably that both Aeslu and I dreaded every interaction with him.

"Tell Dad the whole thing's his fault. The whole fucking thing! Sanderson knew that, and so do I. If it weren't for Dad, I'd have bagged the mountain by now. And I will. I swear I will. The mountain is mine!"

This much was obvious: Forster wasn't dying right then and there, but he wasn't improving, either.

22

During one of his clearheaded spells, Forster said, "I want you to head up without me."

I wasn't sure if I'd heard him right.

Before I could respond, though, he went on. "I want you to leave me here while you continue the climb. I want you to give it your best try."

What Forster said startled me into silence. Aeslu as well. Both of us sat staring at him like simpletons.

"Don't look so shocked. All I'm saying is what makes sense."

What should I have told him? "Forster! *You,* of all people! You—the most selfish person I've ever met— want to sacrifice yourself for someone else? I'm speechless."

"Listen to me," said Forster. "I'm a dead duck. I can't even get up without falling over. I'd never make it five feet up the mountain."

"We can't just leave you here," I told him.

"That's precisely what I'm asking you to do."

"Forster, you'd be dead in a matter of hours."

"I will be anyway."

"It's out of the question."

At this point he just erupted. "Come to your fucking senses, old boy! I'm dead. You hear me? Dead, dead, dead! I'm dead as the rocks here—I just haven't cooled off yet. You will be, too, both of you, before much longer. There's not a one of us who'll get out of here alive."

Impulsively I said, "But I don't see how we could simply abandon you—"

"Then you're wasting your one chance. If you leave me here, you can at least make a push for the top. I can't say you'll make it without my help, but right now I have no help to offer. Except this one thing. I can help by not dragging you down. Who knows? You might even get lucky."

We sat there together for a while. I have no idea how Aeslu felt, but I found myself so astonished that I could scarcely think. If Forster had stepped off the ledge, walked around in midair, and alighted once again before us, I couldn't have been more taken aback by what he was saying. No one I'd ever met seemed less likely to suggest the plan he'd put forth. I couldn't even start to imagine how this had come about.

Just then a possible explanation came to me. The cause of the quandary facing us—I refer to Forster's fall—might also explain Forster's response to it. He had suffered a concussion. He was out of his mind. For almost a full day, Forster had ranted, babbled, screeched, panted, all but bayed at the moon. Somehow he'd improved overnight. Now—at least during the past few hours—he had regained his normal powers of articulation. Was he any less of a lunatic, though? Did his words now make any more sense than his ravings?

The truth was, they did. Forster was right. If we remained on that ledge, we'd all be doomed. Forster would almost certainly die first—if not from his injuries, then from the cold and hunger to which the injuries left him vulnerable. But Aeslu and I would follow soon enough. Thus the question was, what alternatives did Aeslu and I really have?

Should we stay with Forster, provide him with a little consolation, and face death together on the ledge?

Or should we do as he suggested, abandon him, and proceed to make one last attempt to reach the Summit?

Even at the time, in our weakened state, I could

see that only Forster's suggestion made sense. Not because it gave us a chance to be rid of him, though it did. Not just because it allowed Aeslu to do what she had waited so long to do, though it did that, too. Simply because it salvaged the climb.

There was one other consideration. By leaving Forster behind, we not only had a chance to save ourselves, we also had a chance to save Forster. This may sound like pure rationalization. In fact, only by abandoning him did we have a chance to reach the Summit, and thus to find whomever might be waiting for us there. The Founders' descendents? I couldn't quite believe we'd find them. It wasn't out of the question, though. Twice now we'd found evidence suggesting that others had preceded us. If the Summit were inhabited, then Aeslu and I might squeak through this ordeal alive. We might even send some of the Mountain-Drawn to rescue Forster.

If we held off and stayed on the ledge, however . . .

A twinge of remorse hit me then. Forster's reasoning, no matter how articulate, was probably as deranged as his earlier bafflings; his invitation to proceed was the invitation of someone still out of his mind. He didn't know what he was saying. He didn't grasp what he was offering. He couldn't foresee the consequences.

"Are you sure this is what you want?" I asked him.

"Just *go,* God damn you!" he shouted, sputtering. "Can't you read the writing on the fucking wall? This is your last chance! The odds are slim enough that you'll ever make it—don't make them any slimmer!"

23

"I can't do it," I told her.

"This is our only chance." Despite the lack of anger, Aeslu's words seemed an accusation.

"I still can't do it. I *won't* do it."

"He is the Man of Ignorance."

"Maybe so. Maybe so." I faltered a moment. "Aeslu, I don't even know what that means anymore."

Her voice now cut with a sharper edge. "If you are the Man of Knowledge, then perhaps you should."

"No doubt. But I don't know that, either." I looked at her closely. This was the woman I loved. Was she wrong to accuse me like this? Was I wrong to counter the accusations?

"You chose to help me," said Aeslu. "You swore to help me. 'Upward to the Summit!'—I have heard those words from you time after time. Why do you hold back now? Why do you refuse to seek the Summit when Forssa himself urges you to do so?"

I could have told her that I didn't see the point. I could have told her that I questioned the likelihood that we'd find anything—or anyone—up there. I didn't voice these doubts, though; it would have been hopeless to try. Instead, I told her what my doubts gave rise to. "I won't seek the Summit at any cost."

"Cost?"

I hesitated a moment, then went ahead. "Remember the tale Forster told about the other mountain climb? How the other man dangled from the rope? How Forster cut him loose?"

She nodded.

"That's what he's asking us to do. Not quite in the same way—not actually cutting the rope—but certainly with the same result. In a sense, Forster is asking us to be rid of him. And it's tempting—I'll admit it's tempting."

"He will die anyway."

"Aeslu, I won't do it. Never mind that Forster himself is asking us to do it. He shouldn't have cut Sanderson loose, and we shouldn't cut Forster loose, either."

"Then we will never reach the Summit."

"So it seems."

She gazed at me now in bewilderment—not just that I'd do what I inisted on doing, but that in so doing I'd betray Aeslu herself. "You would rather stay here with Forssa—even though he will die anyway—than reach the Summit?"

"Let me put it this way. If reaching the Summit means that I abandon Forster and thus become what he is, then I'd rather stay with Forster and be what I ought to be."

Something changed in her gaze just then. "This is what you meant about cost."

"I want to reach the Summit," I said, "but not at any cost."

24

"You *idiots*," said Forster when I told him what Aeslu and I had decided. "You fucking idiots."

"Maybe so."

"You're a pair of—"

"Forster, save yourself the trouble. We're simply not leaving without you."

My words outraged him all the more. "Then you're wasting all we've done for nothing. Come to your senses, God damn it! Can't you see—"

"I see the whole thing—"

"—you two could make it."

"—quite well, thank you."

He stared at me with an expression of total contempt. I'd never seen him look so bad—the left side of his head swollen, the brow a mottled purple-black, the left cheek scraped raw, the beard caked with blood—yet he seemed to have his wits about him just then, which made his contempt all the more intense and burdensome. Then, turning to Aeslu, he asked, "And you? What about you?"

Aeslu kept her gaze fixed on Forster as she spoke. "My fate is the same as Jassikki's."

He chuckled at the words. "Fate indeed! And what of the Founders, then?"

I blurted, "Keep them out of this—"

"But they're in it, aren't they, if I'm not mistaken? So what about them—and their illustrious descendents?"

"What do you care about their descendents?"

He shrugged. "Obviously I don't. But *she* does, right? Isn't that the point?"

Before I could argue with him further, Aeslu intervened. "The Founders would have me do what is right," she told him. "And that is not to abandon you."

He started raving again, louder than before, and went on for a long time. We were fools! We were traitors to the Rixtir cause! We were doing even Forster a disservice—Forster, who had risked so much in getting us this far up the Mountain.

Listening, I tried to make sense of what he was saying. Not the words themselves: they were plain enough. Forster had been lucid all morning, and in some respects the lucidity held firm. Something else baffled me, though, something beyond the words.

Why was he doing this at all? Why was he offering to spare Aeslu and me at his own expense? Never in my life had I met someone as self-centered as Forster Beckwith. Every interaction I'd had with the man had been a fight, whether subtle or gross, verbal or physical, with his selfishness. Time after time I'd felt he'd used me as a stepping-stone to get wherever he was going, above all in his relentless drive toward the Mountain and the Summit. Yet here, now, was the same man offering himself as a stepping-stone to *us*.

He must have been out of his mind. A fragment of stone must have penetrated his skull. Splinters of bone must have been pressing hard against his brain. Blood must have been pooling, swelling, compressing his cerebral cortex. How else could I have accounted for the transformation in his character?

It occurred to me that night, as we all settled down for yet another night pinned to the ledge, that even Forster Beckwith had turned out capable of selflessness.

He would have been a good man if he'd fallen off a cliff every day.

25

Sounds wakened me. Or *a* sound—a single sound varying enough to seem like several. A slapping, flapping, clapping sound like a flag on a flagpole, clothes on the line, a scarecrow in a peasant's field. Almost a pleasant sound—one that fleshed out the wind, made it seem less hollow. Only cloth could make that sound. Remarkable, I decided, how many things can be made with cloth: sails, parachutes, tents, tarpaulins, lifeboats and dirigibles, clothes for the living, shrouds for the dead—

I forced myself upright. Aeslu was beside me: I could see the contours of her back and rump through the bedroll covering her. Forster's blanket lay before me, too. But that one had no contour. Rumpled, it rested half on the ledge, half off it. The half that hung over the edge was what made the slapping sounds I'd heard on wakening. The ropes, too—the ones we'd used to restrain Forster—dangled several feet down the cliff, severed, flapping free.

PART FIVE

Late morning. The shed was hot. Somewhere outside came the cry of a mountain jay: Tck tck—tchee!

Jesse O'Keefe looked toward me, yet I felt sure that he never saw my face before him. The man's eyes seemed to gaze through me, through the wall at my back, through the campus, the Rockies, and the entire world to the sights his vision found far more persuasive.

1

"Did he cut himself loose so we could continue?" she asked.

"I don't know."

"It almost seems he chose to die so we could live."

"Aeslu, I just don't know."

Sitting close together, we gazed out over the ridges and slopes we'd climbed, the glaciers below, the valleys and ranges visible now and then through the shifting clouds. I wasn't trying to refute her; I genuinely had no idea how to answer. Both of us were too stunned to grasp the full implications of what had happened.

Yet the evidence was clear enough. Forster had cut not one rope but two: the rope running across his expanse of the ledge like a railing or bannister, and the rope serving as a lifeline in case he slipped off the ledge. By all appearances he'd cut them in that order, too, since cutting the railing first might have dropped him six or eight feet, only to let the lifeline yank him short. Cutting the lifeline first, however, would have left him constrained by nothing but the railing itself. The moment he sliced through the railing, Forster could have slid forward like a sailor's corpse dumped into the sea. Everything we saw before us suggested premeditated acts and careful execution.

Where exactly had he fallen? I couldn't tell. The cliff bulged slightly about three hundred feet below where Aeslu and I were hanging, and this bulge blocked our view of its lower reaches. But I imagined Forster dropping almost straight down for most of that distance, glancing against the rock face hard enough to make him tumble, then striking the bulge, bouncing outward, and falling free till he struck the snowfield below. After that he probably cartwheeled—already unconscious, I hoped—till he sailed off the edge into oblivion. He would have gained so much momentum by then that he might easily have fallen clear down to the Mountain's glacier.

I caught sight of something just then: a flash of color out of place on the cliff below. Something green. Dark green. A patch of moss? Lichens? No—we were far too high for any such thing. That hue could only have belonged to something of human origin in a place where all else was black, white, or gray. I stared a long time trying to determine what this object could have been. Then with a jolt I realized that I was looking at a garment. Long johns. A pair of men's woolen long johns. That explained the absence of his pack. In his derangement, Forster must have dumped out his big rucksack—that, or else he'd shoved it down, letting it rupture on the cliff and strew its contents, before he jumped.

What a pathetic memorial to the man's grandiosity: Forster's underclothes, caught on protruding rocks and flapping in the wind!

But imagining Forster's descent itself was what appalled me most. In fact, grasping the reality of what had happened, I felt such deep dread that I drew back abruptly from the precipice. Had he understood the kind of death he faced? Or had he so feared the consequence of his injuries that he preferred even being dashed to bits on the rocks?

"He didn't know what he was doing," I told Aeslu. "He must have been out of his mind."

She said, "He tried to help us—to help us reach the Summit."

I gave up arguing with her. Perhaps Forster truly intended to ease our way upward to the Summit; perhaps not. Either way, however, the task wouldn't be quite so simple as Aeslu imagined. "We're still in big trouble," I went on. "We don't even have the Mountain Stone."

With these words Aeslu turned from me and started rummaging about in her pack. She pulled out something almost effortlessly.

I saw what it was at once: the same quartz pyramid that Forster had been hoarding for weeks. The sight of it virtually silenced me. "But how—?"

Aeslu smiled as she held the Stone out to me. "I took it from his pack."

"While he slept?"

She nodded.

"But how did you get past me to reach him?" I asked.

"You, too, were asleep."

"Why didn't you tell me?" I felt astonished by her subterfuge.

"I *have* told you," said Aeslu, smiling once more. Then she gestured toward the cliff with the Mountain Stone. "Upward to the Summit."

2

We dismantled our precarious camp; checked and re-distributed our equipment; packed our backpacks, put them on, and took up the tools we needed to continue; ventured uneasily onto the cliff; and headed up again.

Step by step and hold by hold we made our way higher. I went first, and she followed. Then she took a turn going first, and I followed. Neither of us felt confident of what we were doing. Both Aeslu and I climbed far better on ice and snow than on rock, yet to date we hadn't dealt with anything as steep as what faced us just then. Still, somehow we managed. Each of us slipped a time or two but avoided serious falls. The ice-screws we twisted into the slick wall before us held tight. The ropes sustained our weight. Despite all the mishaps and small accidents, despite the surfaces we cracked, the chunks we pulled loose, and the foot-holds we misjudged, somehow we kept going.

I didn't really expect to survive this stretch of the climb. It seemed just a matter of time before one of us made a mistake bad enough to pull us off the cliff. Its angle and surface had defeated even Forster; how likely was it, then, that Aeslu and I could bluff our way up? No doubt we'd end up just like Forster. If not right away, then soon enough.

Yet whatever pessimism I felt, we kept going anyway. Not because of a fundamental trust in our abilities: that was long gone. Not because of a belief that we deserved to succeed: that no longer seemed part of the picture. It was something else altogether. This, and nothing more: a willingness to take the task apart, to ignore the goal and concentrate solely on getting there, to focus on the details of what each moment demanded of us. This handhold. That foothold. This tug on the rope. That effort to twist an ice-screw into place. Only what these individual tasks required of us seemed to matter. Only these tasks seemed even to exist.

What happened—what we did and how we did it—became less a choice than a consequence. In this state of mind, what would happen to us? I was too tired, hungry, and cold to understand the question, much less to answer it.

Perhaps that in itself suggested our likely fate.

3

Something else.

For weeks now, Aeslu and I had spent most of each day tied to each other by a length of rope. Sometimes the rope was fairly long, sometimes short. Either way, we had no recourse but to stay together. More than that: we were literally bound together.

Yet we didn't chafe at this restriction on our mobility. We may have been each other's prison warden in some sense, but we were each other's freedom as well. Without Aeslu I would have died; without me, she, too, would have perished. I can't tell you how many times during our ascent of that cliff the most trivial slip could have become a fatal fall. We saved each other so many times—abruptly tightening the belay rope and stopping it short as it played out—that we didn't even bother keeping count.

That rope was more than just a safety belt, though. It was something else as well, something more basic, something primordial. I can't quite explain it.

As if Aeslu were my mother and I her child, and the rope between us was the umbilical cord....

Or as if we were twins and somehow linked to the Mountain by the same cord....

Neither of these images does full justice to what I felt. Nor to what *she* felt, either—I have reason to believe that the feeling was one we shared. For if we were mother and child linked by the cord, then each of us was the mother and each the child. Simultaneously. And if we were twins, then we were twins capable of nurturing each other.

Do you understand what I'm telling you? The images are deficient. Yet I don't know what other means I have for explaining.

4

Tied together like that, we began what we knew would be one of the most dangerous tasks of our climb. This task was to climb a groove that was part of an almost vertical snowfield extending from the last cliff—the cliff Forster had fallen from—all the way upward to the summit ridge.

Calling it a groove is both accurate and deceptive. "Groove" suggests something narrow. In fact, this groove was ten to twenty feet wide: more of a trench than a groove. Yet it was narrow in relation to its length, which was somewhere between eight hundred and a thousand feet, and in relation to the whole Mountain, which eons of avalanches had serrated with hundreds of these grooves. The Mountain's bladelike appearance was a result of precisely this process of serration. What we now undertook was to head straight up the channel confining us.

We faced two big risks. One risk was that we might fail to climb such a steep slope. This groove—what climbers call a fluting—had a cross-section like that of a bobsled run: a low center rising outward to form two steep walls. We had almost no leeway for zigzagging. All we could do was to climb straight up the groove. Western gear of that era might or might not have been up to the task. At best, it would have required far greater strength than we possessed just then; at worst, it would have doomed us to an early impasse or a quick death. The Founders' Gear gave us a fighting chance, though: the subtle hatchets, hammers, picks, and footclaws allowed much more flexibility as we climbed. Even so, that sort of equipment provided no guarantee of success. The snow was dense. It took our blows without much resistance yet held the pick-points well. At any moment, however, the surface could have given way. We could have slipped. A whole mass of snow forming the groove could have come loose underfoot. And if one of us had fallen, the slope was so steeply angled that the other would have been yanked down, too.

The other risk was that something might strike us from above. Those grooves had been etched into the mountainside by masses of snow, chunks of ice, and perhaps entire cornices that had cracked free from the Mountain, shot down the trench, and dug it a little deeper each time. These minor avalanches weren't a frequent occurrence, but neither were they what I'd call rare. I'd witnessed scores of them over the past several weeks. Even as Aeslu and I worked our way up the groove's lower reaches, clumps of snow and ice rained down upon us, none as deadly as the rockfall we'd survived earlier, some big enough to sting on impact, but all of them warning us that more substantial stuff might come down at any moment.

Yet despite these risks and the fear they inspired, we did well. We swung our axes; we kicked our foot-claws; we worked our way up. The exertion felt more difficult than anything before yet it was more productive, too. No more groping for almost imperceptible handholds. No more zigzagging up laborious routes. We made our own path. We went straight up the slope. Even the weakness plaguing our muscles and lungs seemed of no consequence, little more than a discomfort to tolerate. We didn't even bother to belay one another. The process of setting up an anchor in the snow, then having one of us proceed while the other played out the rope, would have been too laborious to tolerate. Belays seemed a waste of time. Better to move separately and simultaneously. Better to move fast and without hesitation.

Why didn't we disconnect the rope between us,

then? I suppose we kept it there because of what it represented. It gave us the illusion that we could help each other. If nothing else, it proved that we were together.

We must have continued like that for a long time, yet I wasn't really aware of time's passing. I wasn't even aware of where I was. That is, I knew I must have been somewhere on the groove, but not precisely at what point along its length. All I knew—all that interested me—was each swing of my hatchets, each kick of my footclaws, each flex of my arms and legs, each gasp of my lungs. The hatchet blades sank into the snow. The snow chips flew outward. We worked our way upward. And as we climbed, the groove around us narrowed. Its surface grew denser, steeper, and more finely polished. Each hand- or foothold felt more precarious than the one preceding. The only attention I could spare went to clinging to the mountain with all my might.

With one exception. Now and then I turned to check up on Aeslu. Sometimes she was climbing above me, sometimes below. Either way she seemed at once powerful, a strong woman fully capable of the task we had undertaken, and yet delicate, vulnerable, a wisp of warmth in a cold place. And watching her as she picked her way up the slope, I felt a desire to help her in any manner possible and a simultaneous recognition—not an insight I welcomed, but nothing I could deny—that each of us was beyond the other's help.

Then, abruptly, we reached the cornice.

Imagine climbing the angled wall of a house only to find your head pressing up against the soffit—that place where the roof juts out over the wall. This is precisely what we encountered. Except that under the circumstances, what jutted out wasn't part of a roof, but rather the underside of a great bulge of accumulated snow. The situation couldn't have been much worse. Even an overhang made of rock would have seemed an easier obstacle to surmount: we might have figured out a way to anchor slings from cracks in the stone, as climbers do routinely nowadays, and thus work our way up and over. But snow? It was an obstruction, yet one so delicate that we'd never succeed in climbing it.

Pausing, clinging to the cliff, Aeslu and I stared upward at the cornice. I could tell from her expression that she felt as downcast as I did. This seemingly insubstantial barricade threatened to block our progress just when we'd come to think nothing could stop us.

"What should we do?" she asked.

"I don't know."

"Is there any way around it?"

"None at all." Then something occurred to me. "But if we can't get around it—"

"We could go *through* it," she said, finishing my sentence for me.

I found it hard to believe we'd pull off this gambit. The conditions that might make it possible seemed at best unlikely. If the snow proved dense enough to support our weight, then it might also be too dense to let us tunnel through. If, on the other hand, the snow were soft enough to allow for easy tunneling, then it might also be too soft to support our weight. We'd be stuck either way.

What choice did we have, though, but to attempt it? If we held off, we'd almost certainly die anyway. Either we'd die clinging pathetically to the cliff, or else we'd die attempting to get off the Mountain in our starved, spent, half-frozen state. Dying in a doomed effort to tunnel upward through a cornice didn't seem any worse than the alternatives. On the contrary, it seemed much better.

That's why we did what we did. Aeslu eased her way five or six feet to the left, then anchored herself to the cliff as solidly as the Founders' hooks would hold her on such a precarious surface. Once she was secure, I then worked my way upward the last few feets to the bulging underside of the cornice; I dug my footclaws and left ice-hatchet hard into the ice supporting me; and, reaching upward with my right hatchet, I started carving away at the ceiling overhead.

The cornice snow had a texture much different from what I'd expected. Not hard—dense. At the time I couldn't think of any similar substance. Since then, with the development of various synthetic materials, I've encountered any number of things that would have seemed just like it. The closest is probably Styrofoam: light, resistant to pressure, yet capable of being cut. And that's just what I did to it. I cut the snow. First with the ice-hatchet, then with a Rixtir climbing tool that seemed like a cross between a file and an ice-pick, I hacked out squares of snow. Most of them weren't much bigger than a book. Some were the size of a standard brick. All of them came out easily, pried free with a brittle crunch. At once they fell on me, often right on my face, but without pain or damage, for they weighed so little. Then, having advanced a bit higher, I'd hack out another few squares, remove them, and proceed.

It surprised me to see how far I'd gotten. An hour's work let me tunnel in head-first up to my waist. I could have worked faster but didn't want to push my luck. My footclaws and ice-hatchet couldn't hold as firmly inside the cornice as on the cliff. I worried about cracking the whole structure, breaking loose with it, and toppling to my death in a rain of snowy fragments.

Soon my whole body was entombed in this vertical coffin. The light dimmed with every inch I advanced. The sounds I heard soon faded, too. More than once, thinking I'd heard Aeslu speak, I called out but received no answer.

"What is it?"

All I heard was the staticky noise in my own ears.

"Aeslu—are you all right?"

No response.

So this is the grave's silence, I thought. And at once I felt so panicky that I shifted my weight, lost my footing, and let the left footclaws slip free. The right ones slipped, too, but didn't come loose altogether. I struggled to keep a grip on my left ice-hatchet. I jabbed hard at the snow with the tool clutched in the other hand. Somehow I kept from falling.

"Aeslu—"

Still no response.

Even once I'd regained my hold, though, a new fear plagued me. Perhaps she'd fallen.

Then, faintly, her voice reached me: "Jassikki—"

"Are you all right?"

"What are the four kinds of sun-stone?" she asked.

I wasn't sure I'd heard right. The question came straight out of the lessons she'd taught me long ago. "Aeslu—"

"What are the six kinds of moon-stone?"

"Rise, full, pear," I answered obediently. "Almond, fennelseed, new." Perhaps she intended this catechism as a way of calming me.

"And what are the twelve kinds of snow?"

"Snow?"

"The twelve kinds of snow."

"Aeslu—"

"What are the eighteen kinds of ice?"

"Listen to me—"

"And the nine kinds of death?"

"Aeslu, stop it."

"Tell me, what are the nine kinds of death?"

"Stop it! Just stop!" I shouted, then fell silent.

That hiss again. Nothing but the hiss within my own ears.

I huddled a long time in my sarcophagus. I could barely control the impulse to descend, to crawl out, to see what was happening. Had she spoken to me or not? Was I imagining more than the staticky hiss? I wanted to know if she were all right. Yet I didn't crawl out; there was no point. If Aeslu had fallen, I couldn't possibly have made a difference to her now. If she hadn't fallen, my descent would risk the only chance she had for getting out of there alive. It was better to continue. Better to keep carving away at this tunnel.

Less than a half hour later, without the least warning, my right ice-hatchet jolted upward so abruptly that I nearly lost my grip on it. I realized at once that I'd poked through the cornice. Luckily my left hatchet held steady. That allowed me to anchor the right one again—this time outside the tunnel I'd dug—and I pulled myself partway out. Like a prairie dog emerging from his burrow, I stuck my head up and peered around. A relatively gentle snowfield slanted upward to my right.

Then I tugged on the rope to signal Aeslu, she followed me up through the tunnel, and we were out.

5

There was no time to rest. As soon as we caught our breath, Aeslu and I set to work deciding on our next move.

We had the Mountain Stone in our possession now, and what it revealed couldn't have delighted us more: We had reached the summit snowfield. Nothing lay between us and the top.

"Does this mean what I think it means?" Aeslu asked, not quite willing to believe what she saw.

I tried to restrain my own surging confidence but failed. I was delighted. "If the route marked here is accurate, we're almost there."

She stared, smiling, at the quartz pyramid she held.

I said, "Better yet, I don't see any sign of obstacles between here and the Summit. All that's left is this final slope."

Then a twinge of doubt coursed through me. The Stone showed the Mountain as it had been nearly four hundred years earlier. What if the Summit, like some of the Mountain's lower reaches, had changed during those centuries? What if obstacles had cropped up that hadn't even existed earlier? Summit ridges are notoriously unstable. Cornices might have accumulated or fallen; stone buttresses might have crumbled; entire snowfields might have slid away.

I said nothing of my doubts. We had no alternative but to push upward to the Summit. If someone were up there to meet us, we had every reason to hurry. And if no one awaited us, then we'd soon be dead anyway. Faltering now wouldn't save us.

6

That slope was both the easiest climbing we'd done so far, and the hardest. It was the easiest because the snowfield, though steep, proved to be solid—just the right consistency for the hatchets and claws we used to work our way upward. Both Aeslu and I felt fairly secure as we climbed. Yet it was the hardest climbing, too, because we had no energy. The altitude intensified our fatigue and left us weak, almost feeble, at times scarcely capable of anchoring the tools in the snow, much less of boosting ourselves up yet another step. The whole effort was an ordeal. Every move left us gasping. We had to rest after just five or six steps, and the rests lasted far longer than the stints of work between them. I felt like an old man—in fact, I felt far older at that time than I do now, at almost eighty— and I wondered moment by moment how I'd find the stamina to continue.

Aeslu looked weary, too. Sometimes she rested so long I wasn't sure if she'd manage to set off again. Her motions were awkward, even desperate: hacking frantically, Aeslu would plant her ice-hatchets in the slope, then would struggle a long time to kick her way higher. More than once she seemed on the verge of losing her grip on the tools. It wouldn't have been difficult for her to topple backward and skid down the slope. I feared for her safety as well as for my own.

Of course we could have proceeded more cautiously. We could have belayed each other and taken turns climbing. But that course of action would have involved its own risk, too, chiefly in costing us precious time. We didn't have time to spare. We had to move fast at almost any expense.

This is why we gambled as we did. We flailed about. We struck at the snowfield, kicked at it, groped our way up. Never mind that we could barely talk, so winded were we both. Never mind that we couldn't feel our toes and fingers, so deeply had the cold seeped into our flesh. Never mind that every effort we made might be in some sense doomed. We just went ahead. We clawed our way up the Mountain.

7

"There!"

Aeslu's shout made me swing around. She'd stopped about five yards away but was pointing straight ahead. At once I gazed up the slope.

"There! Can you see?"

I couldn't see a thing—nothing, at least, but the slope's vast white parabola narrowing above. I squinted, peering this way and that. Still nothing.

Snow had begun to fall. That was half the problem: what had been the simple glare of an overcast sky now transformed itself into something more complex but just as dazzling. Snowflakes shot toward us diagonally from ahead and to the left. The snowfall wasn't heavy, just bad enough to thicken the air and sting our eyes.

"People!" she yelled, louder now. "People up ahead!"

These words jolted me out of my daze. Not that I took them seriously—but three times now Aeslu had caught sight of things on the Mountain that I'd initially dismissed and soon realized were really there, and once before she'd spotted what she claimed to be a person and what turned out to be just that. I couldn't dismiss her outright.

At that moment I saw what she'd motioned for me to see: two shapes high above us on the ridge. Dark, narrow, vertical. I didn't feel positive they were people, but neither could I dismiss the notion altogether. What else could they have been? Rocks? That was it—an outcropping of rocks.

Then I saw one of them move. The motion was unmistakable. The shape turned, bent, straightened.

Aeslu began shouting again, this time in Rixtir. I couldn't follow everything she said, but I heard the words *afa'atira,* "Founders," and *serix,* "Summit." She waved furiously with one of her ice-hatchets.

No response. At least none we could hear.

She faltered briefly, then cried out again, this time a cry louder than I'd ever heard from Aeslu's voice, a cry that intermingled longing, astonishment, and desperation. She swung her hatchet back and forth, too, in a frantic effort to catch their attention.

Still no response. I could see the figures up there moving—one of them, anyway—which halted Aeslu's motions as well as my own. A long moment passed. Both Aeslu and I waited, straining to hear any words coming our way on the wind.

Nothing. No sound but the snow's hiss against us. No sight but those two dark shapes half-visible through the haze of flakes.

Then, abruptly, they withdrew. First they were there; then they were gone.

Aeslu stared upward before turning to me. Her face didn't show bewilderment so much as dismay. No, not dismay: hurt.

I expected her to say something, to ask me something, to cry out for explanation, solace, reassurance. She didn't say another word. She just set off again, straight up, now faster and even more desperately than before.

8

Within just a minute Aeslu got far ahead of me. She was a good climber on steep snow—lithe, agile, sure-footed—and her skill served her well. But her zeal did, too: the intensity of her belief that people awaited her, people who would understand why she sought them if they simply gave her a chance. Against the power of this zeal and the stamina it allowed her, I found myself helpless to keep up with her.

Then, precisely as Aeslu started disappearing into the swirls of snow, an event took place that changed the whole situation. I wasn't sure what was happening at first. What I heard preceded what I saw. A hiss that soon grew into a rush. *Whush-whush-whush!* I glanced around. An avalanche? Not loud enough. But the noise tensed me up; I knew it meant trouble.

What I saw first was Aeslu spinning about, picked off the snowfield as if yanked by an invisible hand, and tumbling toward me. At the same instant a white mass of some sort—snow or ice the size of a big pumpkin—bounded past her, slammed into the slope, gashed a big groove where it landed, then bounded upward again. Each impact made that *whush* noise, each louder than the previous. Just two impacts against the Mountain sent it past us. Another two and it was gone.

By then Aeslu had slid down almost to where I stood watching. She'd kept a grip on her ice-hatchet but had lost control of it; she couldn't seem to brake her descent. In a few moments she would gain so much speed that nothing would stop her from following that block of ice over the edge.

Without thinking I lunged at her. I landed on her crosswise, landed hard enough to hear Aeslu grunt from the blow, and at once rolled off as her body's velocity overcame my own. I flipped several times, landed facedown on the slope, and started sliding, too. Digging into the snow with both feet and clawing at it with my hatchet, I struggled to stop my own fall. Almost at once I succeeded.

I lay there a while, panting for breath. Then, suddenly aware that I could hear no sound but the hissing snowfall, I wrenched myself around to find Aeslu.

Before me lay nothing but the snowfield's lower edge. White everywhere. Not a glimpse of color.

"Aeslu?"

All I heard was the wind and the snow.

"Aeslu?"

The hiss and sputter of the storm swelled to a roar.

"Aeslu!"

Then, quietly at first, I heard a moan. Then another, this time louder.

I grabbed my ice-hatchet and stumbled down the slope.

On the other side of a bulge in the slope—a big hummock of dense snow—I found Aeslu lying facedown. One of her hands still clutched her ice-hatchet; the other groped about. She was conscious but dazed. Muttering to herself in Rixtir, she spoke words I could only start to understand: *afa'atira,* "Founders"; *ftona,* "coming"; *serix,* "Summit."

I had no idea at the time how Aeslu had saved herself. Perhaps the impact of my body against hers had slowed her enough that friction between her clothes and the snow was sufficient to do the rest. Perhaps she had managed to regain control of her ice-hatchet. I don't know. But there she was—alive and, except for some bad scrapes on her face, relatively unhurt.

I helped her up.

Still dizzy from her tumble, she needed help just to stay upright. Yet she motioned upward. *"Afa'atira."*

"They tried to kill you."

"They want me to come with them—"

"Aeslu, they tried to kill you."

"—to the Summit."

"Aeslu, listen to me," I shouted, grabbing her by both shoulders. "They shoved a block of ice down on you. They tried to knock you off the Mountain."

There was no need to press the point. Even before I finished speaking, we heard that *whush-whush-whush* again, first nearly inaudible, soon louder. Almost at once it sounded like a huge piece of cloth being ripped. Just then a second chunk of ice, this one doubly big as the first, bashed into the slope not ten feet away, splashed us with the snow it sent flying, and tumbled off.

This, if nothing else, snapped Aeslu out of her daze. She gazed at me now with total, sudden alertness. She didn't even need to ask the question she wanted me to answer.

"I don't know why," I told her.

"We are the Sun's Stead, the Moon's Stead—"

"They don't know that."

"—and we are fated to make this climb."

"Aeslu, maybe they just assume the worst. They're defending themselves."

Without responding further, she kicked her way past the hummock that was protecting us, staggered onto the open slope, and, facing upward, started to shout again. I couldn't follow the words but didn't need to.

The squall had eased. Great clouds still massed all around us. The air flickered with snow. I could see better than before, though; in fact, I could see clear to the ridge where we'd seen the two figures earlier. And there I saw them yet again: one of them taller, one shorter. By all appearances the shorter one was crouching to observe us while the taller moved about, sometimes disappearing and reappearing, right behind him.

Once again Aeslu began to shout. "I am Aeslu of Vmatta," she bellowed, her voice cracking as she struggled to shove the words past the wind. "I am the Moon's Stead—"

"Aeslu, get back."

"—and with me is the Sun's Stead—"

"Aeslu—"

"—Jassikki the Lowlander!"

Even as we watched, the taller of the two figures pushed something to the edge, then toppled it toward us. Irregular in shape, longer than wide, this object rolled briefly like a barrel, then hit something hard enough to lose its equilibrium; now tumbling end over end, it lurched this way and that as unpredictably as a football. I saw it coming straight toward us at one moment before it changed course without warning, veered away, and disappeared to our right.

Aeslu gazed in bewilderment toward the ridge.

Just as she started to call out again, I interrupted her. "Listen—we can't just wait here till they pick us off. Soon enough they'll send for others. Maybe they have already."

"The Founders' descendents will welcome us."

"Aeslu, they don't even know who we are."

"Then we should tell them—"

"That's what I'm getting at. Let's tell them. But to do that we have to survive this welcoming committee—"

At that moment a smaller chunk skidded into the hummock we were hiding behind. It bounded upward and arched toward the precipice.

"—and let them know," I went on.

Aeslu gazed at me then, and I pitied her. Not because she looked haggard, bruised, and bloody from her slide halfway down the summit snowfield. Simply because she looked so confused. I pitied her—pitied her in a way I never had before—because she couldn't grasp what was happening. To have come so far only to receive this insult! To have the people she longed for try picking her off the Mountain like a tin duck in a shooting gallery!

I decided something right then. "This is what we'll do," I told her. "You stay here. Step out now and then—just enough to draw their fire. Let them try to get you. Shout, wave, do anything you like. Just don't get hit. And while you keep them occupied, I'll sneak up and around."

She looked appalled. "They will kill you!"

"I don't think so."

"No, Jassi, they *will*. You are a Lowlander."

"But isn't the Man of Knowledge supposed to be a Lowlander?"

Shaking her head, Aeslu said, "I cannot believe—"

"Even if they kill me," I went on, "they'll find the Mountain Stone. I'll offer it to them."

"They won't let you get close enough."

"Then they'll find it on me. They'll find it, see it, and know who we are—"

"Jassi—"

"—and then they'll let you up to the Summit."

Nothing about her expression showed that she accepted my plan. Sadness overwhelmed the confusion I'd already seen. Yet I was intent on what I'd suggested. It seemed the only hope. I wasn't eager to do it—I've never been one for self-sacrifice—but I couldn't see an alternative. Besides, I knew things might take a course I never described to her, a course that might or might not lead to the welcome I hoped Aeslu would receive.

As I took the Mountain Stone from Aeslu and put it in my pack, all I felt sure of was that I had to take the chance.

9

What I hadn't told her was that I thought I could surprise our assailants. I'd ambush the ambushers. Of course if I found more than two people up there, it would be a very short fight. If I found just those two, however, I might have a chance.

What I did was to wait for the next squall—the great billows of snow that obscured our view of the people up there and, I assumed, their view of us—and then I scrambled diagonally to the left. The trick was to get as far as possible before the squall started easing; then I'd drop and flatten myself against the snowfield. The problem was not knowing exactly when the squalls would ease. More than once I got overconfident and ended up plodding along, right in the middle of nowhere, as the billows dissipated abruptly and blew my cover. I'm still not sure how I never got spotted. My hope at the time was that Aeslu's shouts distracted the people up there, and that they were too busy shoving down blocks of ice to notice me. Yet even this hope intensified my dread: what if she made herself too vulnerable? What if they finally hit her? Maybe *I* should have been the one to draw fire while Aeslu tried getting up there to reason with them.

At least the slope itself wasn't difficult. It was the least steep of any I'd encountered since Aeslu and I had left the Mountain's glacier weeks earlier. The surface, too, felt good underfoot: firm enough to give good support but not so firm that I had to hack away at it. I could kick my way up using the ice-hatchet simply to help me balance.

The altitude was another matter. I have no idea how high we were. I'd guess twenty-one thousand feet, perhaps twenty-two. All I know is that I'd never been higher. Even under better circumstances I would have found the altitude a challenge. Hungry, exhausted, and badly chilled, I was scarcely fit for the task before me. I staggered, I stumbled, I bumbled my way up that slope. Every few paces I stopped to gasp for breath. Now and then I rested, my forehead braced against my hand where it grasped the ice-hatchet's head, and I wondered if I'd ever find the energy to take another step. Sometimes I looked around, gazed at my surroundings, and no longer felt sure where I was. Snow swept toward me as I struggled up the snowfield, snow thick enough that it took furious shapes: squadrons, platoons, companies, whole battalions of snow. The noises, too, scared me: shrieks, screams, explosions, gunfire. The intervals when I had to stop, resting face-down on the slope, frightened me almost more than the struggle to meet our attackers.

Yet after a while the slope eased so much that I knew I'd made my way onto the ridge. Where, exactly, I couldn't tell. I'd navigated blind the whole way up—in fact, I'd climbed *only* when I couldn't see where I was going. But the hard part was surely over. Somewhere nearby I'd find whomever had been barraging us.

I eased ahead. The snow hit harder up there, blown almost sideways by the wind. Half the time I could scarcely see. It occurred to me at some point that I had so little idea where I was, I might end up walking right into the prey I stalked. So much for ambushing the ambushers!

Without warning the squall eased. The snow thinned to the merest flurries.

There, right ahead, were the two men.

I couldn't have done better if I'd planned every move. I'd come up right behind them. The shorter one, the one that had been on the left when viewed from below, was now on my right. Although I couldn't see him well—in fact, I couldn't see much about him—I could tell he was still lying or crouching. The bigger one went about his same business as before, hacking out a mass of glaciated snow that he now prepared to shove down the slope. The very sight outraged me. All her life Aeslu had longed to reach this summit; for almost a full year now, reaching that goal had been her duty; for weeks she had risked her life to arrive here. And with what response? Icy boulders rolled down at her!

I would have charged these two at once, but their appearance constrained me. Or at least the taller one's appearance did, for the shorter one's prone posture still made it hard for me to see who he was or anything else about him. But the other: I couldn't take my eyes off him.

He wore a robe of sorts, a garment long enough to reach past his knees, one that resembled what I'd seen the Masters wearing throughout the Mountain Land. Leather leggings—deerskin, perhaps—protected his calves and ankles. I couldn't see his feet for all the snow, but he appeared to be wearing heavy boots. Great mittens covered his hands—hands at that moment busy shoving the next projectile down toward Aeslu. And as he pushed, I saw more of his head than just the back I'd seen up till then. He wore a helmetlike mask that obscured all his features. I'd seen masks like that before, too—not just in Hyoffissorih, where I endured my first trials in the Mountain Land, but later, at other times of conflict—and the recollections brought forth by this sight intensified rather than diminished my fears. The face resembled that of a puma, though the mouth had sprouted boar's tusks. Never mind that it was merely a mask. Every time I'd crossed paths with masked Rixtirra, I'd had to fight for my life.

I stared half-paralytic for a few moments. I saw this man shove the ice boulder off the edge, saw him step back and watch the results of his handiwork, saw him set to work again preparing yet another missile.

I could have called out. I could have hailed him, made my case in Rixtir, hoped for the best. Or I could have taken out the Mountain Stone, flaunted it, and waited for the astonishment and obeisance that Aeslu felt sure would be forthcoming.

I didn't.

I raised my ice-hatchet with both hands and, shouting suddenly, I charged.

10

He turned just as I reached him. The mask he wore hid his expression, but even a glimpse of his eyes showed I'd caught him by surprise. Yet he moved fast: swung his ice-hatchet to fend me off. The two staves hit hard. I managed to keep hold of mine, but the impact threw me to the right. I lost my balance, fell, and skidded in the snow.

Even while falling I knew how close I was to the brink. I'd seen the ridge from below. Maybe a cornice had cracked off earlier that year, forming an icy precipice; in any case there was a sheer drop of ten or fifteen feet before the snowfield's more gradual incline took over. If I went over that edge, I'd pick up so much speed that slowing my descent would be impossible. I had to pull back at any cost. So when I scrambled toward my assailant, I knew I'd left myself vulnerable to his counterattack.

He swung again. The hatchet's blade plunged into the snow right next to my face. I grabbed it with my free hand, tugging hard. My tug didn't seem to affect him, but his own did: he yanked so abruptly that he threw himself off balance, toppled, and landed right on top of me. We flailed and skittered about, kicking and clawing at each other, till we got free. Then we both scrambled to our feet.

Facing him again, I felt more and more alarmed. This wasn't working out as I'd planned. The man before me was far stronger than I and not half as winded by our struggle. I could scarcely catch my breath; my whole body ached from lack of oxygen. Yet his appearance also left me breathless: not just his size and strength but his mask, too, the puma face and the boar's tusks, everything crusty with snow. It didn't matter that I knew a man—just a man—watched me from behind that mask. The sight left me shaking.

We circled each other slowly. By then the snowfall had picked up again, shoving gritty ice at our faces; we shifted this way and that, each trying to use the wind to our advantage.

And the other man? Surely my opponent's ally would attack from the rear at any moment. I didn't dare look around, though, leaving myself open to another strike.

"I am the Sun's Stead," I shouted suddenly in Rixtir. "I come in homage to the Founders and their descendents!"

The only answer was a laugh.

"With me is the Moon's Stead, who will honor you as well."

Yet more laughter.

"Let us join you at the Summit."

My efforts to pacify him got nowhere; if anything, they outraged him further. For right then he struck out at me, this time with a sideways blow.

I ducked. I heard the ice-hatchet whir past my head, but it missed me altogether. At once I swung about, bringing my own hatchet full circle. I missed him in turn.

By then he must have regained his balance: he struck out again. I scarcely had time to raise my hatchet in self-defense. His pick struck mine with a loud clank. The head glanced to the left, sparing me a direct hit, but the blow knocked my own stave into me, the point jabbing me hard in the chest. The heavy garments I wore saved me from a wound; the impact, though, knocked me off my feet. I stumbled, fell, and landed hard on my back.

I can't claim to have followed everything that happened next. The fall had stunned me; I couldn't get enough air in my lungs. Just staying conscious took all my effort. Yet when I saw a great bulk loom over me, then bring down an ice-hatchet toward my face, I knew I was about to die.

Then at once another bulk slammed into the first from behind; and, with a weight heavier than I thought possible, both came crashing down onto me.

11

"Jassikki."

I recognized the name but couldn't remember what it meant. The resemblance of my own name caught my attention. Jassikki. Jesse O'Keefe. For a long time I lay there, well aware of the sensations I felt—simultaneous pain and cold—without knowing what they, too, meant. Then, with great effort, I managed to open my eyes.

A face stared down at me. Welts and abrasions marred the forehead and nose; the lips had split in two or three places; patches of skin had peeled, leaving its hue a mottle of pink and brown. Yet I didn't start at the sight. I stirred in longing. "Aeslu—"

"You must get up," she said. "Quickly."

"Where is he? That man ... ?" I fumbled to explain myself.

"Quickly."

Maybe it was pain that brought me to my senses. My back, head, and shoulders pounded as if repeatedly struck with hammers. I could barely move. But the pain itself told me what had happened. My attacker ... How he raised his hatchet for the death-blow ... How the attacker himself then fell aside ...

I forced myself up. The pain didn't relent, but I managed to push past it and get up anyway. Aeslu supported me on one side while I fought the waves of dizziness washing over me. Then, still clutching her, I looked around.

The man I'd fought with lay a few paces distant. Half on his back, half on his left side, he still wore the boots, leggings, robe, and mask that he'd been wearing earlier. Blood had started seeping through the exposed side of his mask, and snow was already accumulating on his clothes.

"Dead?" I asked.

"Dying."

Even as we spoke, I heard him start to moan. And with the moans came a few motions, too: the twitch of a hand, the stirring of a foot.

I forced myself up. I looked around, saw an ice-hatchet lying nearby half-covered with snow, grabbed it, and raised it.

Aeslu stepped over to the man even as he struggled and managed to sit. Without hesitation she grabbed his mask by its lower edge and, in a single motion, ripped it upward and off his face.

Both of us stared for a long moment. Then she broke the silence: *"Forssa."*

Neither of us could grasp the truth of what she'd said; both of us just kept staring. Never mind that the body's massiveness could only have been Forster Beckwith's. Never mind that the scalp wound and caked blood were precisely what we'd seen on his head just a day earlier. Never mind that the features—the ruddy face, the ice-blue eyes, the blond hair and the beard—argued persuasively against any lingering doubts. It simply didn't seem possible. Forster lay dashed on the rocks far below, not here at our feet. Forster had cut himself free to save us, not to sneak upward and thwart our ascent. This couldn't possibly have been Forster. Yet it couldn't have been anyone else.

"Why?" she asked him, her voice betraying bewilderment more than anger. *"Why?"*

Dazed, he sat there glancing about, wincing repeatedly, as if close to losing consciousness once again. He didn't avoid our gaze but didn't meet it, either. Then, in a nearly matter-of-fact tone, he said, "The mountain is mine."

Aeslu spoke firmly, loudly: "You have no right to the Mountain."

"It's mine."

Before either of us could speak again, Forster leaned forward and, shifting his weight, forced himself up. The effort looked so painful that both Aeslu and I hesitated to respond; it didn't seem within his powers to succeed. Yet he managed to crouch. With a grunt he got upright from all fours. Aeslu and I backed off at once.

"You don't even know what to do with it," he said, now yelling, his speech slurred, "or what to let it do to you. Do you hear me? *The mountain is mine!*" He lunged at Aeslu.

She dodged him, but he caught hold of her anyway. With a single yank he threw her down so hard that she skidded toward the precipice. I'd jumped toward him by then—slammed hard into his right side. Yet despite his injuries Forster was still so strong that he just shoved me back.

Aeslu rolled away from the edge. She managed to stand, then staggered two or three steps toward me. Bellowing, Forster caught up with her almost at once. "You don't deserve it! It's wasted on you! You can't understand it! Just get off, God damn you! Let me have what's already mine!"

We had no weapons to fight him with. The ice-hatchets must have been somewhere close by, but I couldn't spot them. I swung at him with my hands, struck him time after time, without the least effect. It wasn't just that Forster was so big, nor even that he was stronger than anyone I'd ever known. Something else left him invulnerable to the blows that Aeslu and I delivered against him. No, not invulnerable: oblivious. He must have been almost unaware of us by then, too badly injured or too thoroughly dazed, to notice what we did. Yet he seemed as dangerous as before, maybe more so. He caught hold of my coat and flung me down hard enough to knock me breathless.

Lying there, I saw Forster move toward Aeslu. She

didn't back off or resist him. She just rummaged through my pack. Her actions baffled me at first— made me nearly panic. What was she up to, wasting precious seconds for nothing? Then I saw what she had in mind. She pulled out the Mountain Stone. To distract Forster? I couldn't even guess. But she must have had some kind of strategy; she always did. And all the while Forster looked cagey but not fully conscious, an automaton built to fight but unaware of its own strategies, even of its own motions. He was simply fighting. He approached warily, backing her toward the edge, intent on cornering her. Another few steps and he'd have her at his mercy.

Aeslu's expression showed her alarm and desperation: now she glanced my way without any hope that I could extricate her. I forced myself up, of course, but couldn't attack without sending all of us over the edge. Her only hope was the Mountain Stone. Clutched in her right hand, she wielded that chunk of quartz so that the angle of its base jutted outward like a hatchet. If she could land even a single blow against him . . .

"The mountain is mine!"

With those words he rushed her. He staggered forth, arms extended. He groped at Aeslu. He grabbed what he was after.

Did she understand what Forster had wanted? Did *he* understand, even?

All I know is what I saw.

Aeslu's right hand swung back as if to strike Forster with the Mountain Stone. Forster reached out just then—not to block Aeslu but to grab at the Stone itself. He caught hold of what he sought. The momentum of his leap tore the Stone from Aeslu's grasp but then carried Forster well beyond, so that he lost his balance, stumbled past the precipice, and went over the edge. Aeslu fell, too, but skidded and stopped just short of the brink.

In the few moments that these events took to happen, I'd dashed forward, then pulled myself back in time to see Forster's descent. Side by side Aeslu and

I watched him skitter down the summit snowfield. He must have been conscious at least partway down: during the first few seconds, I saw him trying to dig the Mountain Stone into the slope to brake his descent. It didn't work. He gathered speed. He lost control. His body started to cartwheel. By the time he shot off the cliff, Forster was tumbling end over end.

12

Aeslu and I embraced. We held each other for a long time in relief, bewilderment, and joy.

"It was Forssa."

"Aeslu, he's gone."

"Forssa."

"He's gone forever."

"But it was *only* Forssa."

And the other man? Even as I glanced around I understood our mistake. There was no other man— just Forster's huge Lowland pack, the pack I thought he'd tossed down the cliff the day before, the pack he'd used to haul up some Rixtir clothes to fool us with, the same pack he'd set up as a dummy to trick us still further.

At some point I realized what I should have known all along: that my reassurances gave Aeslu only half of what she craved. True, Forster Beckwith was dead. Even our victory against him, though, left her half-defeated. Where were the people—the Founders' descendents—that Aeslu had expected to come down and meet her?

We wept for a long time—Aeslu, in her complex grief; I, in my helplessness to console her. Then we made each other stop: the wind was so harsh that the tears stung our faces. Yet we found it hard to move, to take action, to do anything but stand there clinging to one another.

"Aeslu, we have to keep going."

She struck my chest once, feebly. "But why?"

"Forster Beckwith is dead. No one's stopping us."

"No one is coming for us, either," she said wearily.

"Maybe they still don't know we're heading up."

"There is no one up there to know."

"Aeslu, we can't be sure."

"No, there is no one."

"Maybe so," I told her. "Maybe there's no one at all. But the least we can do is find out."

It felt odd to be making the case that should have been Aeslu's; it felt odder still to find her making mine. Yet I shared the bewilderment and despair permeating each word she spoke. Perhaps our reasons differed. Mine was revulsion at realizing how Forster had faked the whole situation—not just his pretending to die a noble death that spared his companions, but also climbing ahead of us to make his own bid for the Summit. He had even masqueraded as a Rixtir intent on bowling us off the Mountain. Aeslu's reason for bewilderment was being cheated of proof that we now approached the goal. Yet no matter which of us argued for and which against, what advantage did we gain by faltering this close to the Summit? And what choice did we have but to continue?

Here's how I saw it. We'd lost almost all of our equipment—we had only our cold-weather garb and a couple of ice-hatchets between us. We had virtually no food left. We were so tired that we could scarcely walk. Both of us were suffering from multiple injuries, malnutrition, altitude sickness, and impending frostbite. To make a bad situation still worse, we had discovered that someone who might have been one of the Founders' descendents was in fact our worst enemy. We'd vanquished him once and for all, yet we now had even less reason than before to believe that anything awaited us at the top but an icy death. Why, then, should we proceed?

Because there was one small chance. There was the slimmest possibility that even Forster's final reappearance didn't altogether prove the pointlessness of our quest. Perhaps we would still find what we sought after all. If not, then wouldn't it be better to die at the Summit knowing what we'd gone there to discover rather than to die wondering?

13

The storm spared us in one respect: there was little wind. Now and then gusts came, but no blast. Simply the usual up- and downdrafts. Thus the snow didn't fall so much as it billowed. The flakes came from everywhere at once and headed off everywhere—rising, falling, drifting, hovering. What I saw all around reminded me of nothing so much as a drop of water viewed under a microscope: tiny creatures swarming in all directions at once. There was something vital and vibrant, almost exhilarating, about the sight.

Yet the situation was fully as dangerous as what we would have faced with the wind shoving at us harder. We couldn't see what surrounded us. The Mountain had long since disappeared. Without depth or breadth, the landscape around us was nothing. The view was nothing. We could have been anywhere or nowhere. The immensity of the Andes shrank to something smaller than a broomcloset. Smaller than that: if I stuck my arm straight out, I could scarcely see my hand. My feet had long since vanished. I could hear Aeslu right beside me but couldn't see her. The snow felt so gentle that it beguiled us, soothed us, caressed us, yet in some respects it was devouring us alive. Not as a shark or a tiger devours its prey—intead, as microbes devour a larger organism: swarming, clinging, overwhelming.

For this reason I fastened a rope around Aeslu's waist, then tied the other end around my own, not so that either of us could rescue the other from a fall, but simply so that we could keep track of one another.

If we fell, we'd at least fall together. The rope gave us nothing more than a sense that neither of us was alone. Perhaps by then that was all we hoped for.

14

We groped our way up. We plunged our hatchets into a snowfield we couldn't see. We pulled ourselves up a slope we could only imagine.

At times I found it hard to believe we were moving at all. Not only could we not see what we were doing; we couldn't feel anything, either. With each passing moment my hands and feet grew more profoundly numb. The aches I'd felt—first a tingle, then a deep throb in each finger and toe—had worried me so much that I grew reassured when the pains diminished. Then I realized that the diminishment of pain, not the pain itself, should have been what worried me. Joint by joint my whole body was fading out on me. Before long I couldn't tell if I were still connected to the Mountain at all.

I swung the hatchet. I struck out straight ahead. Nothing. To my horror, I discovered that even the hardest blow met with no resistance. I may as well have been lashing out at a cloud. Yet I didn't seem to be falling. I must have been sustained by some means or other; if nothing else, I should at least have heard my left hatchet grinding against the snow that anchored it. The right, though: it struck nothing more substantial than air.

I hooked the right hatchet in the crook of my left arm. Then I reached forth with the right hand, jabbed forward, probed the space ahead of me.

Nothing there.

I thrust the whole arm forward, brought it down slowly, waited for it to touch something. As before, I couldn't feel anything, but I heard an abrasive sound as my glove made contact. Contact with what? I didn't know.

A sharp tug on the rope nearly pulled me loose.

"Aeslu," I called out. "Come up here fast."

I could heard the crunch of her hatchets as she approached.

Now I returned to whatever lay before me. Some sort of shelf. If only I could have caught a better glimpse of it!

Just then the wind shifted, the snowfall eased, and I found myself staring straight ahead at something dark. Blue, gray, blue-gray. At once the storm intensified and the snow came down again so hard that whatever had appeared before me now vanished.

Yet I'd seen it; I knew it was there. And knowing that, I could reach forth, stab my hatchets into an almost horizontal surface, and pull myself off the slope onto something so nearly level that it supported my weight without much effort.

15

It was a cave. Unlike what we'd found earlier, though, this one was almost entirely unobstructed. No massive icicles barred the way in. No builtup drifts barricaded it. A cornice overhung the entrance, it's true, and in fact that great awninglike mass of snow was big enough that Aeslu and I would never have seen the cave if our route had taken us on either side by more than a few yards. But the entrance itself was wide open. Once I'd reached it and realized what I'd found, I could crawl right in.

Of course this discovery wasn't altogether reassuring. After what had taken place earlier inside the Mountain, the thought of entering it again filled me with dread. I pulled myself partway into the cave; I peered in. I couldn't see much at first—just a blue-glowing passage through the ice toward darkness within—but what I saw left me weak with fear. The loud silence I'd come to loathe inside the Mountain swelled louder and louder within my ears; my whole body ached in recollection of the blows I'd taken; my throat tightened as if still gripped by an unseen hand. In many ways all I wanted was to back out, descend a few yards, and find another route upward, a route that would take me around the cave. Never mind the cold, the wind, the snow. Freezing to death seemed better than seeking refuge inside the Mountain.

I went inside anyway. I anchored my ice-hatchets one by one in the cave's sloping floor, I pulled my way up, I reached a level surface. Even then I was astonished by how weak and numb I felt; I couldn't feel my hands well enough to know what they were doing without watching them. For a while—I'm not sure how long—I lay there on the ice heaving for breath.

"—let—"

Bits of sound reached me, though I couldn't tell from where. I listened. Did they have something to do with me?

"—sik—"

At some point I realized that Aeslu was calling to me. I forced myself up. I turned carefully, lost my grip, almost slid out of the cave, then dug into the ice with one of my hatchets and caught myself. I called back hoarsely. Once, twice, three times.

She didn't respond at first, so I set up a belay, anchoring myself with a couple of ice-screws from the Founders' Gear, then tugged twice on the rope. Aeslu tugged back. A few moments later, I could feel the rope slacken as she started climbing.

She reached the cave's mouth quickly. I saw the head of one hatchet first, then the other, as she dug them into the ice. Almost at once Aeslu pulled herself up. Gasping and grunting, she struggled on the slippery patch right before the first level stretch. I would have helped her up but couldn't—I didn't want to risk losing my grip on the rope. For the minute or so of her most precarious effort, both of us were so busy that we caught little more than a glance at each other.

Then she was up. Aeslu scrambled over to where I sat. She took my hand, pulled herself around, crouched beside me. She did a double-take and stared into the ice cave.

I could tell by her expression that she felt as startled and alarmed by this sight as I did. Yet I could also tell that she understood exactly why I'd gone ahead and climbed up here. By then her whole body was shaking from the cold.

All I said was, "Let's get out of the wind."

Together, crawling, we headed in deeper. Of course

everything around us was ice, so the place was cold, yet the stillness of the cave felt almost luxurious.

The light diminished quickly, dazzling glare fading to a deep blue glow.

Abruptly, Aeslu stopped. She had been right beside me but looking ahead while I was looking down; now she motioned at something right before us.

I couldn't see what it was at first. I thought it must have been nothing more than irregularities in the ice—ridges, folds, bumps. Then, as my eyes adjusted to the dim light, I saw more clearly.

Two bodies lay before us near the cave's far end. I might have felt horrified by this sight if astonishment hadn't overwhelmed all other emotions. Not just because there were these two bodies: something else about them shocked me. I could see at once that they were a man and a woman. How, exactly, I can't altogether explain, for they were both heavily clothed. Perhaps their contours, their differing shapes even under bulky garments, told me what I saw. What also jolted me was noticing their positions, for they lay together in a tight embrace. For reasons I find difficult to explain, I struggled to deny the obvious. This is a sculpture, I told myself. Someone carved these two figures out of ice. Yet I could tell that despite their color, which was gray-white, and their texture, which was bristly with frost, these shapes were human. They had once been alive. And however long they had been lying here, they were perfectly preserved, solid as the ice all around them yet still clutching each other as if their bodies provided the world's only warmth.

Aeslu stared at this sight for a long time. Even while I kept staring, though, she crawled closer to get a better look. She reached out at one point: touched the man's forehead. At once she pulled back, uttering a faint cry. Then, kneeling, she bowed before them.

I watched her but said nothing. The more I observed the scene before me, the better I understood. The two bodies' intricately embroidered robes didn't clarify the whole situation. The gear lying nearby—

packs, coils of rope, and two ornate, scepterlike ice-axes—made it easier to understand. Yet ultimately it was the facial features of these two people that convinced me of what I saw: both were elderly; both were grand, even regal in appearance; both simply *looked* like who I thought they were. The woman's hawklike nose, high cheekbones, and elaborately braided hair revealed her to be of pure Indian lineage, yet she was uncommonly tall, five eight or ten, the biggest Andean woman I'd ever seen. The man was bigger still, but his bald head and thick beard made his Western origins unmistakable. No wonder Aeslu found this sight upsetting.

For a while she muttered to herself in her own language, though whether in lamentation or prayer I have no idea. Then in English she said, "They never reached the Summit."

What should I have told her? "I'm sorry, you're right. The Founders never reached it. They never built the holy city your people have striven to reach for centuries. Your whole culture has pursued an illusion from the start." Of course not.

Yet nothing else I might have said—gentle, consoling words—would have reassured her. "Maybe you're wrong. Maybe these aren't Ossonnal and Lissallo at all, but some other couple instead." Or: "Never mind, it doesn't matter. So what if they never made it to the top?"

In fact, I couldn't really say anything at all. And I didn't.

I just sat there and watched, listened, waited.

16

Aeslu wasn't the only one shocked by our discovery. In finding what we'd found, she had the most to lose: what she believed in, what she hoped for. But certainly the two bodies lying frozen near us inside the snow cave said something about my own situation, too. For months I'd been wading deeper and deeper into the Rixtir scheme of things; now I found myself submerged even farther over my head than I'd expected. I was sitting just then on a mountain that had already come close to killing me several times. I had no idea where I was or how close its summit lay, much less how to get there. Having come to hope that a city might await us at the top, I'd staked my life on finding what we sought. Yet it was now clear that even the progenitors of the Mountain-Drawn had never reached their destination. Discovering their failure wasn't simply a point of historical interest, though; nor did the implications affect Aeslu alone. It certainly boded ill for my own situation. What chance was there, really, that Aeslu and I would survive to tell of what we'd found?

We lingered in that cave for a long time. I suppose in some respects we had no choice but to stay there; the storm outside would have killed us in a matter of a few hours. A snow cave isn't what I'd call cozy, but coziness is relative. The snow couldn't reach us, the air was still, the temperature was steady. Never mind that for all practical purposes our surroundings were a tomb. Staying there may seem morbid, but leaving would have been suicide. Under the circumstances we had no choice but to stay put.

We had another reason to stay, however: Aeslu wouldn't leave. She wouldn't even move. She sat beside the frozen Founders as if mourning her own parents. She watched them for hours. At no point did I see her weep. It's not just that the Mountain-Drawn are disinclined to display their emotions; it's that Aeslu herself seemed far beyond tears. At times gazing toward the Founders, at times simply sitting there with her eyes closed, she wasn't so much watching them as keeping watch—bearing witness. Yet I suspect that something else was in progress, too. Something deep, physical, even physiological. She was in shock.

"There's nothing you can do," I told her. "You couldn't possibly have known."

She stayed there motionless, not even blinking. The cave's gray-blue light imparted an icy color to her face; I found it easy to imagine how Aeslu herself would end up just as cold and solid as the two bodies lying before her.

I didn't know what else to do, so I kept offering whatever consolation I could find. "Don't be sad. Your people were right all along: Ossonnal and Lissallo really did set off for the Summit."

No response.

"They almost made it, too."

Still no response.

"There's no way anyone could have known they fell short."

Dead silence.

"What matters is that they tried—and that you did, too."

At some point the fatuity of my words finally penetrated my brain and, like the cold seeping continually deeper into our flesh, struck me silent as well.

How long did we sit there? I have no idea. We couldn't follow the passage of time by any ordinary means. I had no watch, and the light inside the cave would have made midday seem like dusk. I suspect that we lingered at least a couple of hours. All I know is that after a while, aching from our immobility, I grew restless. The blizzard raging outside ceased to alarm me; the certainty of death on the mountainside no longer left me cowering. We'd die no matter what. Keeping the company of corpses weighed on me more heavily than hastening the sequence of events that would make me one myself.

"We can't stay here," I told Aeslu.

She remained as silent as before.

"Before much longer we have to make our move."

Lacking any response, I started wondering if she'd died even while we sat there together. I reached out and touched her.

She gazed up at me for an instant, then away.

I said, "We ought to go."

Nothing persuaded her. At least nothing prodded her into action. She didn't argue with me or rebuff my words; she simply didn't respond. It's possible that she never even heard me.

At some point I grasped the irony of my supplications. Why did I bother? We were almost out of food. Even if we somehow reached the Summit, which seemed doubtful, we'd starve long before we ever made our way back down again. And food was in some respects the least of our problems. At our altitude just then, we were growing weaker with each passing day, and our fatigue left us more and more susceptible to the cold. Soon enough we would end up like Ossonnal and Lissallo.

Was this sense of doom partly what affected Aeslu? Was the vigil she kept as much for herself as for the progenitors of her race? I couldn't tell, and she wouldn't have answered me if I'd asked. In some ways I suspect that the answer was no. She had always struck me as almost unwaveringly devoted to her people; even her sense of commitment to me—her love for me—was more a matter of what fate required of her than of what any personal desire prompted her to do. I'm not saying that she didn't love me. I believed then, and I still believe, that she did. But she loved me because it seemed the right thing for her people. For this reason it's hard for me to imagine that the prospect of her own individual death worried her. If the Founders—the Masters, even—had ordained that Aeslu should jump off the Mountain, she would have done so. And so I couldn't perceive her state of mourning as self-concerned. She mourned the Founders. She mourned what their bodies, lost somewhere short of the Summit, meant for the Mountain-Drawn.

No, I was the one who worried about my own skin. I was the one trembling at the thought of my own death. Simply my physical death? Maybe, maybe not. It's hard for me to take full stock right now of my mental state back then. Certainly the prospects of corporeal extinction weighed heavily at the time. But something else did, too. Though I'd not been subject to the Rixtir beliefs and assumptions to the degree that Aeslu herself had been, I hadn't been immune to them, either. I hadn't come to the Mountain Land just to bag a few peaks and go home. I'd been casting about in more ways than one. And so I'd have to admit that finding these two icy corpses here chilled me in more ways than what I attributed to viewing this memento mori. The bad outcome of Aeslu's quest guaranteed a bad outcome for mine as well.

So in some respects what Aeslu and I felt put each of us in a similar position. Both of us had reached the end of the line. Yet I sensed even then that we responded differently to the situation. Aeslu seemed to feel that she'd lost everything. In contrast, I felt somehow that I now had nothing more to lose. I can't say that this realization put me at ease, but I suppose it freed me in at least one respect. Maybe Forster Beckwith had been right about transcendence. The Mountain didn't offer it in the sense I had imagined earlier. On the other hand, he was wrong in an important way. Giving up on a particular quest didn't mean there was no quest.

"Aeslu, listen to me," I told her. "You can see as well as I what's going to happen to us. In a short while we'll both be dead—dead no matter what we do. Don't you understand? Why are we cowering with two corpses in this gloomy cave?"

No response. I may as well not even have existed.

I went on: "What's to be gained if two more people die without reaching the Summit?"

Again no response.

"Did Ossonnal and Lissallo want to fail? Would they have wanted their descendants to fail as well?"

Although she said nothing, Aeslu turned slightly in my direction just then.

But having seen at least some evidence that she'd heard me, I couldn't hold back any longer. "Let's continue the climb—let's try to reach the Summit. Maybe we'll die before we get there. Maybe we'll freeze to death just a few hours after leaving this cave. But maybe we won't. Maybe we'll make it to the top. We'll reach what Ossonnal and Lissallo tried but failed to reach."

She listened while I spoke—listened closely. I knew I'd convinced her; I could see that old fire smouldering somewhere in her eyes.

I wasn't prepared for the words that followed.

"You would go where even the Founders have failed to go? You would desecrate the memory of what they tried to do?"

"Aeslu, it's not desecration—"

"I would rather die!" she blurted. "I would gladly die to hold back from taking what belongs to them alone."

"But don't you see—?"

"I see all too clearly. We Mountain-Drawn have long craved the Founders' company as our spiritual parents—"

"They're dead. Aeslu—*dead.*"

She shook her head. "That changes nothing. If they have failed to reach the Summit, then we must hold off from reaching it, too."

"Is that what they would have wanted?"

"I can never do what you are suggesting."

I sat there a while longer. After hesitating a moment, I took a coil of rope from what lay near the Founders. Then, my whole body aching, I forced myself onto all fours; I grabbed my pack and my own ice-hatchets; and I eased down the cave's passageway to where it opened out onto the mountainside. With each step, the way drew lighter—far lighter than before. I could scarcely keep my eyes open by the time I reached the entrance.

The storm had begun to ease. Snow continued falling, but sparsely now, in fact so sparsely that the sunlight filling the sky illuminated the flakes from behind and left them radiant. The air teemed with sparks.

But it wasn't really the weather that convinced me to head up again. I believed what I'd told Aeslu. I believed that we owed it to her people to finish the task. If she wanted to come along, so much the better. Even if she didn't, though, I was intent on reaching the Summit.

17

This is why I decided to go ahead. I never told Aeslu that she, not I, was ultimately the apostate, but all in all I believe that to be true. It made no difference that I was a Westerner, not a member of the Mountain-Drawn. It made no difference that I hadn't grown up steeped in the Rixtir ways, myths, and lore. What did make a difference, though, was the real heart of the matter. The Mountain itself. The climb. The Summit. Nothing seemed farther from the Founders' legacy than to consider their frozen bodies more significant than reaching the Summit.

And I told her so. "If you want to stay, then stay," I called back to where she sat inside the cave, "but I'm heading up."

Somehow I kept expecting her to follow me. She didn't. And so, after hesitating briefly at the cave's mouth, I soon headed upward again.

A new layer of snow covered the mountainside. This made climbing more difficult than earlier, but it was less difficult than I'd feared. The snowfall had been so wet, and the storm had pelted it so violently, that the new layer had formed a dense coating over what lay beneath. Now, with the temperature dropping as the sky cleared, this coating was on its way to becoming a crust. It might well turn to ice. For the moment, though, it helped more than it hindered. The ice-hatchets cut into it easily; their points dug deep into the old snow beneath. My footclaws cut in just as well. I worked my way up faster and with far less effort than I'd expected.

Only my hesitance to abandon Aeslu held me back. With almost every step, I faltered, glanced down toward the cave, and looked to see if she were following. All I saw was the cave's bulging cornice.

Then, as I made my first move without looking for her, a single word reached me from below. "Wait!"

18

We climbed in unexpectedly fine weather—the sky clear, the sun bright, the air still—and made good progress. The ridge seemed to lead straight toward the Summit. The snow was soft enough to tolerate our kicks and hatchet blows yet firm enough to sustain our weight. Nothing went wrong. The Mountain no longer resisted us; in fact, it took us into its embrace. At least that's how it felt at the time. For despite the effects of altitude, hunger, and exhaustion, Aeslu and I climbed better than we ever had before. Every move we made brought the desired result. Each of us understood what the other was doing—even anticipated what the other was about to do—so that our actions meshed perfectly. Even the most difficult pitches felt less like a struggle than like a dance, a pas de deux on a desolate, vertical stage.

Or did it only seem that way? Were we too intoxicated by fatigue to perceive our true circumstances? Far from being precise and masterful in our actions, were we perhaps so drunk that we couldn't grasp our own ineptitude? In short, were we suffering from the rapture of the heights?

I don't think so. It's not that we weren't in some sense intoxicated. You can't get that high up and not feel the effects. The same holds true for fatigue and hunger. But I don't believe that we had reason to doubt what we were doing. It's hard to kid yourself when the merest slip is a mortal error. Even if our brains had lied to us, adrenaline would have told the truth. So I suspect that our confidence was well-founded. Why we climbed so well, I have no idea. We just did. Maybe we had no choice. Maybe, with all else lost, we simply had nothing else to do. We were incapable of *not* climbing. All we could do was climb. We were aware only of each other and of the Mountain.

The day faded; the sun sank. Then night fell and stars erupted overhead. No moon yet—the Mountain itself blocked our view to the east. Incapable of seeing well enough to continue, Aeslu and I hunkered down, dug a foxhole in the snow, and huddled close. Neither of us could stop shaking. All we could do was cling to each other and share what little warmth we had between us.

But the cold intensified. I have no idea how long a time passed; all I know is that it seemed forever, not least because our only unit of time was the shiver. I know as well that the peril of our situation grew more and more obvious. How long could we ward off the cold that with every passing moment soaked deeper and deeper into our flesh? How long could we keep from freezing to death?

Soon all I wanted was to sleep. To curl up here, to embrace Aeslu in my tingling arms, to doze off and never wake up.

"Hold me," she said, the words blurring. "Just hold me."

She was fading, too, her flesh growing heavy, her blood slowing in her veins.

I hugged her, letting Aeslu's head nuzzle against my neck. Then, not quite willingly at first, I eased back, jostled her, shook her by the shoulders till her head bobbed. "Aeslu—Aeslu, we can't do this."

"I want you to hold me."

I kept thinking about Ossonnal and Lissallo. Within half an hour we'd fall into a stupor. Even a brief rest would inevitably lead to sleep, to a deep chill, and thus to death. It's not that I cared much about my own fate; I could feel the cold calling to me, beckoning with its song of oblivion, and I wanted to heed the call. But Aeslu? I wouldn't let that happen. I wouldn't let her end up like Lissallo, gray as marble—at least not without fulfilling what we'd set out to do.

So it wasn't fear of death itself that frightened me. It was the fear of cold, of all our heat draining away like blood. Nothing I could do would stop it. No effort, no restraint would help me. That helplessness scared me more than dying; a sense that we were lost, we were beyond human grasp, we were growing more and more like the ice all around us.

I knew I couldn't save us—I had no illusions about that—but maybe I could delay the inevitable. I could prod us on to the Summit before we succumbed. We could at least try. And in trying, we could stir a little warmth into our blood long enough to keep us alive till we accomplished what we'd set out to do.

Better to climb. Better to die climbing.

"Let's go," I told her. "Come with me." I disengaged from her embrace, took her hand, tugged at her.

Her only response: "I want to sleep."

"So do I."

"Sleep."

"No—not yet."

"Leave me alone." The words were soft, but it wasn't just sleep that softened them.

"Come with me."

Somehow I pulled her upright. Shaking her, prodding her, I managed to get the pack on her back and an ice-hatchet in each hand. She could barely stand.

"Aeslu, we have to go now."

"Go?"

"Upward to the Summit."

She nodded, wavered, nearly lost her balance, then reached out with her right ice-hatchet and dug it into the slope hard enough for it to hold. "Upward to the Summit."

Then the moon rose over the Mountain, and we climbed by its light. By moonlight the rocks were black and devoid of detail, the ice glowing with a cold phosphorescence. The light, for all its gentleness, made everything it touched more extreme. The rocks looked even harder than they were already, the snow softer than it could have been. Never mind. We didn't care one way or the other. All we wanted was to keep going, to climb, to reach the Summit.

19

We were no longer climbing, we were falling, never mind the effort, we were falling, falling upward, falling upward as helplessly as if we'd been plummeting to our deaths, for the Mountain had us altogether in its thrall, the Summit drew us forth powerfully, irresistibly, totally. The Summit rose before us and above us, a vast gray-white dome filling half the sky. It no longer seemed part of the land. It sparkled. It glowed. It picked up so much light from the moon and stars in the sky's other half that I found it hard to tell the heavens from the earth.

Aeslu and I climbed together, not quite side by side, but close, without speaking. We couldn't have spoken if we'd wanted to. At least *I* couldn't have. The effort of climbing took all my breath. I felt as if I were drowning. I panted hard, I inhaled fast and deeply. My throat and windpipe ached with every breath, my lungs burned from the dry cold air, yet I couldn't shake the faintness and the fear of passing out at any moment. My muscles raged against me, too—every sinew searing against the bones. Each step I took required a long rest afterward. I stepped, rested. Stepped, rested. Stepped, rested. Sometimes I stepped, then rested so long I couldn't remember how much time had gone by since the last step. That's when I started counting—a step, then a count of ten—just to keep track. Even so I gasped for breath, and the steps I took still winded me far beyond what a count of ten could remedy. A count of twelve, then. Fifteen. Twenty. Soon I was resting till I couldn't remember what I was doing there at all. I'd been standing there forever. I'd been partway up the Mountain for eternity. I'd always been climbing the Mountain; I'd always be climbing it. Then, nudged by the wind, I'd jolt myself and, if only to avoid toppling over, I'd take another step.

Bits of snow came loose up ahead, tiny bits of new snow broken loose by the wind, bits no bigger than marshmallows and far softer, and these bits came bouncing down, hissing and skittering, sweeping past and disappearing below. Some struck me—face, shoulders, chest, hands—disintegrating at once and blowing away. I felt no pain; they were too soft. But the rush of them, their sudden approach from ahead and their disappearance behind, intensified the sensation I felt, no matter how laborious my effort, of rushing headlong toward the Summit.

"We'll soon be there," I told Aeslu.

"The Summit," she answered from my left, the words barely audible over the wind.

"You will reach what your people have longed for."

"Ossonnal and Lissallo await us there."

"And what will you tell them," I asked, "once we arrive?"

"That you made this possible. That I love you."

"And what will they tell you?"

"That we have reached the refuge. That the Mountain-Drawn must follow. That we shall live with them at the Summit."

Then I turned, glancing to my left, and saw that Aeslu wasn't there at all, but rather to my right, at least ten paces off, staring straight ahead as she fought to keep going.

I had no strength to call out and ask if we had really spoken. I just kept climbing. I just kept jabbing the ice-hatchet's stave into the slope, kicking one foot into place, then the other, and resting my forehead long enough against the hand that grasped the hatchet's head to jab the stave in yet again.

I was trudging up a trail somewhere in Peru, my

pack on my back and my walking stick in one hand.
I was on my way to do fieldwork in the Andes. . . .
Then I turned and saw where I was: somewhere high
on the Mountain Made of Light.

I was slogging through the mud somewhere in east-
ern France. A wounded soldier lay on the litter I
helped to carry, and I took care not to stumble as I
wallowed on. Then I turned and saw where I was:
somewhere high on the Mountain Made of Light.

I was pulling my sweetheart on a toboggan near
Northampton, Massachusetts. She was singing to me
as I pulled, singing in a light, breathy soprano. Then
I turned and saw where I was—

After a while the wash of recollections ceased to be
mine. It wasn't that the recollections ceased, simply
that I felt no connection to them. Neither did I feel a
connection to the efforts I made. My body performed
the task. My lungs gasped for breath, my hands grappled with the hatchet, my feet kicked their way into
place. But something other than my body—the soul,
the mind, call it what you wish—waited, neither in
repose nor in distress, all the while just watching the
ordeal that the bones, muscles, sense organs, skin,
brain, and viscera seemed nearly incapable of endur-
ing. Would I make it to the Summit? Perhaps. Would
I falter, stop in my tracks, freeze to death? No doubt.
That something-other watched, wondering. I perceived
no indifference there. Quite the contrary: great antici-
pation. Yet the something-other rode my flesh as
calmly and attentively as voyagers to the moon ride
their lunar capsule. The something-other wanted the
flesh-and-bone vehicle to reach our destination, to accomplish our task. Yet there was no anxiety. Instead,
there was nothing more and nothing less than an
awareness that the outcome of everything I'd been,
done, and striven for—whether as Jesse O'Keefe, as
Jassikki, or as anyone else—would soon be evident.

At some point I wondered what we'd see from the
Summit. Would the clouds nestling around the Mountain relent enough to give us a view? If so, how far

would I be able to see? All the way down to the Mountain's glaciers? To the avalanche whose tides of ice and snow had decimated the Mountain-Drawn? To the pass that the Heirs and the Umbrage had taken into the Inner Realm? To the valleys and villages whose people had allied themselves with me or with Forster Beckwith? To the cities where the Masters had judged us the source both of great hope and great dread? To the paths I'd traveled with Aeslu and Norroi the Tirno? To the lands beyond—to Peru, America, Europe, Asia, Africa?

And if clouds welled up from the world below, what then would we see? In dense cloud cover, would Aeslu and I even manage to find the Summit at all?

Snow.

Snow had begun to fall again. I saw nothing I could identify as clouds; nothing billowed or massed around us. Yet there was snow.

20

"Aeslu?"

I looked around—left, right, above, below. I couldn't see her anywhere. All I saw was snow.

"Aeslu?"

The storm wasn't harsh or dense; under easier conditions I would have called it nothing more than flurries. But in a white place at night, with moonlight the sole illumination, even a light snowfall left me uncertain as to what, if anything, I was seeing. All I knew was that I couldn't find Aeslu.

I stopped, turned this way and that, listened closely. The snowfall's hiss and the shriek of my own inhalations made it hard to hear anything like the swish of Aselu's boots on the slope. Surely I could have heard her shout, though. . . .

I cursed myself for the daze I'd gone into, then bellowed her name two or three times.

No answer—unless it was the falling snow.

Then I staggered sideways to the right, hoping to cross the path Aeslu might have taken upward, but I found no footprints. I backtracked, this time overshooting where I'd stopped on first noticing that I was alone, and continued as far to the left as I'd already gone to the right. Once again, no footprints.

So she still must have been below me. I turned about, tried to figure out which way was down, and bellowed several times more.

Again no answer.

By this time I was close to panic. Mostly I felt worried about Aeslu. I couldn't believe she'd slid away:

this slope was too gentle and the snow too soft for a fall to get out of control. Even so, I had no idea where she was. Had she collapsed? Simply passed out from fatigue? More likely. Yet I doubted it. No matter how exhausted, Aeslu had been holding up better than I; surely she wouldn't have just faded out on me like that. I didn't have any idea what had happened, though, and I didn't know how to find her. And beyond my concerns for Aeslu, I felt a deep chill at the thought of wandering about on the Mountain alone.

I stayed right there a long time. Long enough, in fact, that I quickly grew chilled. The wind nuzzled at me, wound around me, slithered up my cuffs and down my collar.

Come, said the wind.

Join us, said the cold.

We'll keep you company, said the snow.

Once again I headed up. Leaving Aeslu frightened me, but staying put and freezing to death frightened me still more. I couldn't believe that Aeslu had faltered, stopped, weakened. I felt confident I'd find her somewhere above. Already the slope seemed to be flattening out. More than once I raised my boot to kick in a step only to find nothing there. I wasn't climbing now—I was walking.

21

Yet even as the slope eased, the snow deepened. The task of fighting gravity grew easier precisely as the task of slogging through the drifts grew much more difficult. Within the next few hundred paces, I found myself almost overwhelmed.

I stopped now and then, called out to Aeslu, then continued. I would have been frantic if I'd had the energy. All I could do was stop, shout, and continue.

Then I forced myself into motion again, now less a motion of walking than of wading, slogging, floundering. I felt like someone waist-deep in surf. The snow swirled around me, hissing. But at least in surf I could have known when to brace myself for another wave, when to struggle, when to rest, when to hold my breath; here I was drowning almost without knowing it. I couldn't even see where the falling snow left off and the fallen snow began.

I was sinking. Snow welled up to my thighs, at times clear to my waist. I fought to keep on the surface, I kicked and clawed, I twisted, I grappled about—yet only managed to dig myself deeper into the snow. Then my boots struck something solid—some ice, some old snow, anything, I didn't care—and I got my footing back. I pushed myself to the surface and made a little headway. Maybe I should have stopped then and rested. Right now I can't even remember if the thought crossed my mind. All I wanted was to keep moving, to keep heading upward. I barely caught my breath before heading off again.

There's an exhilaration that comes with such a clear

sense of purpose. Nothing mattered but getting to the Summit. So simple. I recall starting to cry from the intensity of my desire. Only the fear of my tears freezing held me back. I didn't want anything to make matters worse. So I pushed ahead, stumbled around, without any thought of what direction to take. All I cared about was the Summit.

Then my efforts got the best of me. What I thought might have been progress—the big strides, the sense of lightness, the rush of snow all around—was something else. I was sliding. I'd probably gone too far, I'd worked my way over the ridge. Within seconds I'd start gaining speed and start to fall.

Before I could even cry out, though, I struck something. Struck so hard I stopped short. The jolt stunned me. I gave up for a moment—just sat there heaving for breath.

All for the best. I'd gotten carried away. I needed to get my bearings again. Needed to get my breath back. Needed, as I'd just found out, simply to decide what I was doing. But this was all impossible: the wind took away what little air the altitude had left me, and I couldn't see anything around me but snow.

Just then something bashed into me and knocked me down. The blow left me stinging all over. My face ended up pushed into the snow and snow got shoved into my mouth, eyes, and nose. Yet if nothing else, that revived me. I flailed about, sputtering, as I struggled with the weight pinning me down.

I don't know how long I took to realize that it was Aeslu. My body wasn't the only part of me close to becoming ice; my mind was also half frozen. Yet at some point I felt her warmth, felt it even through all those layers of alpaca wool and deerskin, and I felt her softness, too. Was Aeslu as addle-brained as I? As dazed from our collision? Even once we'd quit struggling, neither of us spoke. She forced herself off me, then slumped into my arms again. We clung to each other for a long time.

Then at last she said, "I thought you were gone."

"I thought *you* were."

"Don't leave me."

"I am right here."

We could have said more, but we didn't. There was no point. Neither of us needed to declare anything to the other—to vow we'd never part or anything of the kind. We both knew we were doomed. The snow had started to let up again—we could see individual flakes coming down now, countless yet individual, no longer an opaque mass—but the wind had already intensified.

Aeslu settled in, her arms around my waist, her head against my chest, so that she gazed off to my right. In turn I hugged her about the shoulders and rested my left cheek against the top of her head.

I have no idea how long we clung to each other. Maybe five minutes, maybe an hour, maybe longer. All I know is that in that interval, the sky started to lighten; moonlight shifted to dawn. And I know that Aeslu, moving slowly at first, began to stir. I felt her weight shift against me. Then, before I could ask what was the matter, I heard her voice.

"Look."

It took me a while even to get my eyes back open— the blown snow had crusted them shut. I looked around without seeing what she might have meant.

Then I turned far to the right. Abruptly I saw it.

Some distance away—eighty feet, maybe a hundred—the snowfall had eased enough to reveal a horizontal row of large stones. I thought initially that they might be tombstones, for they had a funerary look to them. When I got a better notion of the distance, though, I realized that they weren't of human origin but natural instead: an outcropping of some sort. They rose in height from left to right. The highest—what had caught Aeslu's attention in the first place—in fact protruded above anything else in sight.

Struggling to her feet, Aeslu forced herself up the low incline between where we'd been resting and the stone formation now just half-visible in another squall.

I struggled up, too, and followed.

22

For a long time we stared at the view before us. Neither of us spoke. The only sound came from the snow that the wind whipped up and flung hissing at our backs.

Then Aeslu said, "The Summit."

She was right. This *was* the Summit. Yet what concerned us wasn't ultimately the outcropping of rocks we'd found—rather, the focus of our attention was what the outcropping led to. For those rocks were in fact the edge of a crater right at our feet, the rim dropping fifty or sixty feet straight down, the bowl below then losing another two or three hundred feet of altitude as it declined toward its center, the other side rising to another rim about half a mile from where we crouched. Snow filled most of this bowl. Covering the middle third, however, was a lake. And in the middle of the lake, an island. And on the island—half-veiled by the steam rising from the thermal waters surrounding it—a city.

I kept telling myself that this wasn't possible. Ossonnal and Lissallo had never reached the Summit; they had succumbed on the way; they were long dead, their bodies gray-blue and hoary with frost in a cave far below where Aeslu and I now stood. There was no refuge for the Mountain-Drawn. The Summit was simply a summit. I was imagining this sight. Yet no matter how hard I refuted what my own eyes told me, no matter how many times I turned away to shake this image from my vision, no matter how urgently I told myself that I'd suffered delusions time after time throughout this climb, I always saw the same sight when I peered yet again into that crater.

A city.

A city that could only be what Aeslu and I had ceased to believe we'd ever find.

When vapors rose thickly from the lake, or when the wind blew hard enough that the air between us and the sights below thickened with spindrift, I could see only that the city existed. All details vanished. When the wind relented, though, I could tell more about it. The lake filled the crater's middle third. The island rose from the lake to form an irregular dome. Four stone causeways extended from the city, each of them stopping just short of the lake's shore. The city itself covered the whole island with small structures built between a series of concentric lanes. Four streets, extensions of the causeways, ran from the lower reaches of the island to the upper, crossed the lanes, and met at the center. That center was also the island's summit, and a low conical edifice marked the spot. All this I saw when nothing obstructed my view. How large the place was, however, I couldn't say. At least a full city block long, maybe longer. I'll tell you this much, though: what surprised me more than the size of the place was its shape and complexity. And, of course, simply finding it there at all.

Transfixed by the sight, we looked at the city below for a long time. Snow and steam thwarted us. We'd get an especially good look; then suddenly the spindrift would intensify, the vapor would thicken, the city would disappear. At such times Aeslu emerged as if from a trance and grew agitated. She'd peer ahead to penetrate the veil. She'd move this way and that, pacing along the crater's rim, to find a better view. More than once she got too close to the edge and might easily have toppled over. Yet anything I said to warn her had no effect; she was oblivious to my voice.

"The refuge," she said out loud. "The Founders reached the Summit. They reached it and built a refuge for the Mountain-Drawn." She went on like this for a while, speaking more to herself than to me, no matter what I said.

Then, abruptly, Aeslu started to shout. Speaking in some odd dialect of Rixtir, she bellowed into the crater while motioning frantically with both arms. The only word I caught was *s'sathara,* "people," but she went on for a long time. Then she stopped waving; she felt silent. She waited for the wind to ease. She tilted her head slightly to hear better. Almost at once she started shouting and waving yet again.

"The wind is too loud," I told her. "They'll never hear."

Between shouts she said, "They will! They *will* hear me!"

"Aeslu, we'll have to go down there."

My words seemed to snap her out of the trance. She turned to me, looked my way, and noticed me as if for the first time since our arrival at the rim. She pulled off her pack without answering and began to pull out the necessary gear.

Under ordinary circumstances our descent would not have required great skill. The crater's walls were almost vertical but not very high—I guessed sixty feet at the time, certainly no more than eighty. All we needed to do was find a solid anchor-point, secure a doubled rope, throw both ends over the precipice, assume the standard rappel position, and slide down the rope to where the more gradual slope began. Yet the circumstances at the time were anything but ordinary. Aeslu and I were exhausted from the climb. We were close to collapsing from hunger. We had both been hurt in our fight with Forster Beckwith. Worst of all, we were in imminent danger of freezing to death. Just pulling the equipment from our packs took all the strength and attention we could muster.

Then there was the question of the equipment itself. In fighting with Forster we'd lost a full pack of gear. We had our hatchets left, plus one small pack containing a few bits of food and a rope. Other than that, nothing remained except literally the clothes on our backs. Would these meager supplies be enough to see us the short distance of our goal? I don't know what Aeslu was thinking just then, but I was doubtful. Yet we had no alternative to using what we had and hoping for the best.

Almost at once I wondered about another risk: the rope might be too short. It was of a standard Rixtir length equivalent to about a hundred and twenty feet. A safe rappel requires a doubled rope. We planned to descend a doubled length to the crater's floor. If the wall we descended were no more than sixty feet tall, we'd be fine. If it were longer, though, we'd end up dangling some distance from the bottom. How long a distance? We didn't know. Five or six feet wouldn't be too far to jump. Longer than that might require down-climbing—assuming, of course, that the wall didn't slant in such a way as left us dangling free. We considered using a single rope, of course, which would have given us well over a hundred feet, but both Aeslu and I thought better of that possibility. Who knows what this rope had been through? How much abuse could it tolerate before breaking?

If only we'd known more about the distance we had to descend. . . . But we didn't.

We decided to risk the doubled rope. Better to dangle ten or fifteen feet and take our chances from there than to plummet forty feet when the rope broke.

Aeslu went first. I offered to take the lead, but she refused. She was intent on going first. I made no effort to dissuade her—not because I wanted Aeslu to take the greater risk, but because it seemed fitting for her to go ahead in this last stretch of the journey. Once we'd found the right anchor in a jutting boulder, Aeslu slipped the rope around her body, backed off the edge, and headed down.

"Upward to the Summit," she told me just before easing herself backwards.

I noted the irony of Aeslu's words but said nothing. I just crouched, eased closer to the precipice, and peered over to watch. Her form diminished quickly as she let herself slide down the rope. She proceeded without difficulty. Shoving herself outward from the cliff, she descended smoothly.

Then she encountered a gradual bulge in the wall which, once passed, almost entirely blocked my view of her. I could see Aeslu only when she pushed herself away from the rock. During the intervals between I saw only the rope twitching against the cliff. Soon I couldn't see her at all.

I called out: "Aeslu!"

No answer. The rope ceased twitching, too, which worried me.

"Aeslu!"

When I still heard no response, I gazed off toward the lake, the island, the city: people there would have spotted her by now. People would see her coming down. People would come to meet us.

"Aeslu!"

At once a shout reached me from below: "Jass—"

My whole body tensed up. I heard the sounds but couldn't tell if they were a cry of panic or exaltation.

Suddenly I saw her backing off from the cliff. Half-walking, half-sliding on the snow, Aeslu had worked her way free of the wall. She waved, danced, motioned to me. "I am down!" she shouted. "All the way down!" Before I could ask anything about what she'd encountered, she went on: "The rope goes almost all the way to the bottom! Jump the rest!"

I didn't even ask anything more. All I wanted was to be down there with her. And so, nearing total exhaustion, I took hold of the rope; I looped it around my shoulder, down my back, and under my right thigh; I took up the upper end in my left hand, the loose end in my right; I stepped back off the cliff; and I, too, descended.

23

It was easy, it was nothing, it was just gravity taking me down. At least that's how it felt right then, my hands half-frozen and my brain not much warmer. And somehow, sliding downward, I truly believed that my grip on the rope was strong, my footing on the rock was sure, though time after time I tilted too far back or not far enough, and more than once I skittered about, bumping into the wall. Yet I felt no pain, I didn't care how hard I hit, all I wanted was to follow Aeslu down, down, down, I wanted it so badly that I slid clear past the rope's end, fell free for a moment, landed with a crunch, and skidded down a snowy slope till something yanked me short.

Pain brought me to my senses. Having skidded across some protruding rocks, I felt my back and right shoulder rage against the blow. I rolled onto my left side. Writhed. Then forced myself up. Glanced around.

Aeslu had already left: I caught sight of her halfway down the slope. Without hesitating I took off after her, following the curve of the packed snow that formed the crater's bowl, but I couldn't keep up with her, she was too fast, too desperate to reach the goal, and my feet weren't working right anyway. I kept stumbling. Every fall turned into a slide—the snow underfoot was steep and icy.

I skidded right into her.

Aeslu had fallen, too, and for a while we just lay there, both of us panting hard. Then, pushing and pulling, we managed to sit.

Neither of us could speak. We were both winded; every inhalation caused us to shriek. All we could do was clutch at each other for support and struggle for breath. The air had a sharp smell—acidic, sulfurous—that didn't make the task any easier. My head pounded. At one point I thought I'd pass out.

Yet even before the effort grew less laborious, I couldn't help but notice where we were.

We'd reached the lake. The ice tapered off unevenly, at times extending all the way to the water, which had eroded the sheet to form ragged miniature grottoes and bays, at times sloping more precipitously to reveal the bedrock beneath. Beyond lay the water: black, white, and blue from the reflections of stone, ice, and sky on its surface, with palls of steam rising everywhere. Beyond the water—maybe ten yards away, though the steam made it look farther—was the near end of one of those causeways.

Aeslu struggled to her feet. Before I could say anything, she skidded downward to the shore—one of those stretches where the ice had deteriorated to expose the underlying rock—and at once she stooped, dipped her hand into the water, and splashed two or three times.

"Aeslu—"

She never even glanced back at me. Instead, without hesitating, she waded in. She was knee-deep in two or three steps, waist-deep in ten. Steam swirled around her body as she pushed her way forward.

"Aeslu, listen to me—"

I heard her speak then, but not to me. As she approached the causeway, Aeslu called out in one of her languages, words she chanted more than spoke, words I couldn't understand.

Then I, too, went down to the water. I couldn't believe how she'd waded in—plunged, really, without the least gasp—but at once I understood why. The water wasn't cold. I can't tell you *what* it was; my hands were too frigid even to guess at the temperature. I suspect that the lake was only lukewarm, though it felt much hotter to my disoriented nerves. All I knew was that it wasn't cold. And since Aeslu had made it clear to the other side by then, I waded in, too.

It wasn't deep. The bottom sloped downward fast, but I reached the causeway before the water reached higher than my waist. Getting up was easy: a flight of rough stone stairs emerged from the water. What purpose the moat served, I couldn't tell—it hadn't been much of a barrier to cross—but that sort of speculation didn't interest me just then. I had enough to concern me in just keeping up with Aeslu. She was nowhere in sight. Scrambling up the stairs, though, I saw her right ahead on the causeway, the mass of the island looming beyond.

I didn't even bother calling out. Anything that took my breath would have slowed me. All I did was run.

No doubt I felt as desperate as Aeslu, but my desperation differed from what she must have been feeling. Aeslu was desperate to reach the city. I was desperate to keep her from reaching it alone. It wasn't just that plunging headlong into a strange fortified city seemed less than—what shall we say?—*wise*. A short while before that time I'd been a soldier, though not a good one, but able to know we weren't handling this situation well. What concerned me was something else.

Despite our literally breathless arrival in this city, I hadn't failed to notice the absence of the welcoming throngs that Aeslu had expected. Did this suggest that the denizens of the place awaited us so stealthily that we'd missed them altogether? That they lurked somewhere beyond the parapets we now approached? That we'd suffer the onslaught of their sling-stones at any moment?

Maybe so.

Or maybe not.

Maybe I was a fool not to back off, at least to proceed more carefully, given what we would soon encounter. But I didn't. I chased after Aeslu as fast as

I could. I closed the distance between us. I pursued her not to protect her from the inhabitants who awaited us but from those who didn't.

24

The place was deserted. By all appearances it had been deserted for a long, long time. The gate into the city had rotted, fallen, and disappeared, leaving just the hinges on the gateway once supporting the gate itself and a brown stain on the paving stones below. The roofs on the dwellings within the city walls had vanished, too—not just whatever shingles or thatch had formed the roofs, but the roofbeams as well. The copper kettles I saw here and there inside the houses had collapsed like rotten pumpkins. Earthenware pots had fared somewhat better, with some still entirely intact, but others were smashed to shards. Blocks of wood that might once have been chairs or benches had crumbled into loam. Ice caked everything on the north side of every room. A thick layer of yellow-gray dust coated everything. I wandered from room to room, peered in at every stop, and saw the same desolation no matter where I went.

Not just things. People, too. Fifteen, twenty, perhaps twenty-five in all—a number that somehow made them striking both for seeming abundant and for seeming scarce. That crater-city wasn't a big place, yet it had apparently been built to house a dense population. If people had come forth to greet us, I would have expected at least a few hundred of them. But the number alone wasn't what struck me when I first started noticing bodies. Rather, it was the situations I'd found them in, their circumstances. *In medias res.* In the middle of things.

I saw a family—a man, two women, and some children—slumped over at a table set for a meal. Pottery bowls and flasks sat right before them. One of the women, resting with her forehead on the table, looked as if she had dozed off at breakfast.

I saw three men lying around the remnants of a hearth. One of them clutched the tatters of a cloth scroll in his left hand.

I saw a man and a woman clothed only in yellowish powder and entwined in an amorous embrace.

I saw a mother huddling with her children against a wall. With both arms outstretched, she protected them from a blow far more diffuse than the one she must have been anticipating.

I saw a man prostrate before the Rixtir's mountain symbol carved on a wall.

Not long ago—in fact, when I was about seventy-five—I visited Pompeii and Herculaneum, in Italy. What I saw there reminded me at once of what I'd witnessed as a young man gazing about at the Mountain's Summit. The sense of a place hastily abandoned. Of the procrastinators' lives snuffed out almost in mid-breath. Of a once-thriving city frozen in time. Or perhaps I shouldn't say frozen but preserved, for the sulfurous dust that coated everything here seemed to have forestalled any corruption of the flesh and left the dead merely dessicated instead. The bodies were dry, husklike to the touch but vague in appearance, devoid of facial features, texture, and expression. As grotesque as my description may sound, the sights I'm describing, like those I saw later at Pompeii, inspired far less fear than pity.

One difference between Pompeii and the Summit, however, was striking. The Summit wasn't just the ruin of a city. It was both the ruin and the source of its ruination. It was simultaneously Pompeii and Mt. Aetna. Something had driven the people away. An eruption? I doubt it. The city up there showed few signs of the damage a volcano can unleash. The masonry was intact; only the soft structures—wood, thatch, leather, flesh—had deteriorated. Why had so many people fled, then? The altitude alone might have driven them down. Or was it something else? The venting of poisonous fumes, perhaps? That seemed more likely, given the yellow dust and the apparent suddenness of whatever had taken place there. Still, I didn't know. All I knew was that the great refuge of the Mountain-Drawn had been all but totally deserted. We'd arrived a few centuries too late to find the demigods whom Aeslu expected here. We saw no sign of anything alive.

With one exception: the wet footprints I kept spotting now and then. Footprints that I soon found far more compelling than all the yellowish huddled simulacra. Aeslu's footprints, which I followed as fast as possible.

Aeslu may have been ahead of me, but she wasn't difficult to track. And so I followed those footprints into the city, through its alleyways, up its staircases, around its circular corridors, and up still more staircases until, in a place that was both the city's highest point and its center, I found her.

The place itself was a kind of turret, a truncated cone, which I climbed by means of a stone stairway spiraling around its exterior. The summit was a platform about ten or twenty feet across. From there I could see the entire city below, the lake surrounding the city, the crater sloping upward from the lake, and the crater's walls rising vertically from there to the rim. Great palls of steam rose around us to meet the snow sifting from above.

But this view, no matter how much they caught my attention, wasn't what concerned me at the time.

Aeslu lay in the turret's center. With both knees drawn up and both arms pulled close to protect herself, she huddled on her left side, squeezed her eyes shut tight, stammered fast and low, and trembled hard. If only the snow and the wind had been what chilled her!

I went over to Aeslu at once. I crouched. I hugged

her, caressed her, stroked her hair. "They reached the Summit," I told her. "Ossonnal and Lissallo got here after all. They built the refuge."

If she made any response to my words, I never detected it.

"I don't know why they went down again," I continued, "or what happened to the other people. But the Mountain-Drawn were right all along."

No response.

"Aeslu—the Founders reached the Summit."

At some point I realized that she wasn't even hearing me; she was somewhere else altogether.

25

For a long time I held her. I felt convinced that Aeslu was dying—overcome at last by the rigors of exhaustion, hunger, and cold. Soon I, too, would succumb. I felt no ability to struggle any longer. And so for a long time she lay curled up, motionless in my arms.

She did not die. I realized at some point that no matter how deeply Aeslu lay in shock, the insults to her body were by no means the worst she'd suffered. I just kept holding her. I sang to her. I spoke to her.

"I can't make things different from what they are," I said. "I can't take away the hurt and disappointment. But I love you. I love you. I'll stand by you and help you do what needs to be done. Shall we go down and tell the people what we've seen? Maybe we should. They need to hear. Perhaps they'll understand. Then you can guide the Mountain-Drawn toward what they need to do next."

She said nothing, did nothing.

Steam rose all around; snow swirled about us.

I told her, "Aeslu, we can't stay here. There's no point in lingering. I don't know if we can save ourselves, but we have to try. Let's do what we can. Let's help each other, all right? Let's try to get down from the Mountain."

She gazed off to my left. Her eyes looked as vacant as those of someone in a coma.

"Listen to me: I love you. Let's find someplace to be together. Peru, America, I don't care which. Anywhere you want. I'll look after you—"

At some point I perceived the emptiness of my

words. Aeslu had just seen the sun, the moon, and the stars snuffed out; now here I was, hands outstretched, offering the guttering candle of my love. Small wonder she said nothing in return.

I eased her down. I got up, ventured off briefly to make sure she wouldn't panic, then left long enough to scrounge for some materials. I found timber, bits of dried fiber, and some flints. After repeated tries— so many that I almost gave up—I managed to start a fire. Nothing much at first: smoky and reeking of sulfur. Still, it was a start. Soon it gave off a little heat.

If nothing else, I could offer that.

Aeslu kept her back to it for a long time. Then, forcing herself up and around, she turned, swiveled slowly, and raised her hands to warm them before the fire.

PART SIX

"And so we went down," said Jesse O'Keefe.

I hesitated to push him further—he looked so weary—yet I knew he hadn't told the tale to its conclusion. I said, "Yes, but how?"

Jesse looked up at me with an expression that combined perplexity and amusement. "Look. I could tell you how I left the Mountain Land, but I won't. That's another story. The one I've told is the one you asked to hear. I am an old man. The day is almost over, I'm tired, and I have a few more tasks to finish before I go home."

"I've taken too much of your time," I told him.

"Not at all. You've taken what you needed."

"I should go."

He made no objection. On the contrary, Jesse O'Keefe eased his chair back, stood, and stretched, then crossed the room to his rack of lawn sprinklers. He pulled two of them down. Instead of heading out, though, he carried them back to the table we'd been sitting around the whole afternoon. He hoisted them up onto the tabletop and sat before me once again.

"Let me say this: leaving was simply what had to happen. Leaving was less of an adventure but just as much of a necessity as going in, making the climb, and reaching the Summit. It's no accident that the Rixtirra's symbol was what it was." With these words, Jesse picked up a pencil and scribbled the sacred peak on his notepad.

"What do you mean?" I asked.

"From the first time I saw this symbol," he said, "I was struck by how those two lines hint at a sense of motion. One of them seems to be moving upward, the other downward. This was especially obvious whenever the Mountain-Drawn painted the lines with their brush-like pens, as they often did, but I could detect the same motions even when the symbol had been carved in stone."

He fell silent briefly. I almost spoke, but he cut me short.

"The motions show what must happen. It should have been obvious to me from the start. It wasn't." Jesse O'Keefe stared at the lines he'd sketched, then ripped the top sheet off the pad, crumpled it, and tossed the wad into his wastebasket. "Draw your own conclusions."

"But how did you do it?" I asked. "How did you get down from the Mountain?"

He smiled at me. "So earnest," he said. "So earnest." Before I could object to his gentle condescension, though, he continued. "We got down the same way we'd gotten up—with a bit of skill, some force of will, and lots of blind luck."

"You had no food. You were exhausted and half-frozen."

Now he laughed. "Half? If only we'd been so lucky!"

"But surely you can imagine why I'm curious."

"All right, then," said Jesse O'Keefe. "Let's indulge your curiosity." He tilted his chair back again.

*   *   *

To put it tersely, we waited out the storm. This gave us a chance both to avoid the bad weather and to warm ourselves inside the crater. I should stress that I still assumed we'd be dead within a few hours, maybe a day at most. Even so, I now felt as strong an urge to get off the Mountain as the urge to climb it had felt just a short while earlier. What had seemed an impossibility now became an obsession.

Aeslu gradually emerged from whatever daze had overtaken her. We rested all day and slept overnight in those relatively warm surroundings. We ate what little remained of our food supplies. Then, setting off mid-morning, we worked our way out of the deserted city, across the causeway, through the lake, and up the crater's slope. From there we scaled the rope we'd left in place and reached the rim without much difficulty. We then tried to retrace our route off the summit dome.

Before descending, though, we made our way back to the top. The real summit. And there, resting briefly, Aeslu and I looked out over what lay below.

It's hard to describe this sort of view to someone who's never seen it. The only thing comparable is what you've no doubt seen from the window of an airliner—that sense of looking out over the world, of being literally above it all. Thick clouds covered the land, yet the cloud cover lay so far below us that it seemed a feature of the land rather than of the sky. The sky itself was clear, pale blue, and painfully bright. Yet my airplane imagery doesn't go far enough. The view from an airplane doesn't do justice to what we saw. Gazing out a little plastic window does nothing to convey the breadth and depth of the view from the Mountain's summit.

We stood on something that was part of the earth—rock and ice—yet we gazed out over what seemed like the whole planet. We turned in every direction and saw as far as the eye could see: the lesser peaks surrounding the Mountain; the land dropping away east and west to the Amazon Basin and the Pacific; the jungle and the ocean stretching outward till the earth's surface curved and each view swung around to become every other. In fact, we seemed to be at the center of a great circle whose circumference was the entire world.

The effect of all this was both exhilarating and terrifying. I couldn't look out on that view without feeling a great sense of power. We were the hub that the world spun around! At the same time, I felt insignificant. We were lost, doomed, drowning in a vast sea of mountains. I couldn't imagine any better than before how we'd ever get out of there alive.

Why, then, did we linger at the summit? And why, being doomed, did we bother to try getting down?

Maybe it was nothing but instinctual self-preservation. Or maybe it was merely self-delusion. I didn't know then; I'm not sure now. My own impulses were well beyond my grasp, and I couldn't even guess at Aeslu's. What I can say, though, seemed clear at the time. It wasn't just survival. It wasn't a delusion. I couldn't have explained at the time, but all the same I understood something at the summit.

Gazing out over that view, I might have found it hard to imagine that anything beneath us even existed, much less mattered. Everything persuasive, everything powerful, resided in this lofty realm. The mountains glinting in the midday sun. The glaciers spread among them. The great wheel of the earth, the dome of the sky, the sun overhead. From the summit I saw the breadth and depth of the world. Yet what struck me then was simply that the world went far beyond my grasp. Beyond my sight. Beyond my ken. And I realized then what I should always have known: the world is incomprehensible. I'll never grasp it, much less understand it. Oddly, what I understood was that I'll never understand. The point of the quest turned out to be perceiving the hopelessness of having undertaken it at all.

And so what I wanted was to climb down. If not to reach the ordinary world below, then at least to seek it. It's not that I ceased fearing the world, the people in it, or their potential for destructiveness and cruelty. Yet somehow I saw my need to belong down there among people, not in the lofty realm around me at the summit. I reached a truce with the world.

How could we make it down, though, given our lack of food and equipment? The situation turned out far different from what I'd imagined.

Retracing our path out of the crater, over the summit, and down the summit snowfield, Aeslu and I managed to find the cave in which we'd discovered the frozen Founders. Not an easy task, but we did it. We *had* to do it. For it occurred to us at some point that if we could locate that cave again, we had at least a slim chance of survival. The two bodies weren't the only things inside that cave. Ossonnal and Lissallo hadn't died for lack of provisions, that much we knew. Their packs lay stuffed with equipment and supplies. Ropes. Hooks. Ice-hatchets. Clothes. Paper and writing tools, even. Yet none of these things interested us at all compared to something far more mundane: food.

At first we weren't even sure it was food. My initial thought was that we'd found some sort of fuel—blocks of a tarlike substance to burn. It resembled pitch: black and shiny. But before long Aeslu and I had each succumbed to the temptation of a taste. It was sweet. And so we proceeded first to nibble, then to gnaw on these blocks with an urgency that surprised us even at the time.

Perhaps it surprises you as well. How could we eat something so questionable in appearance—something almost unidentifiable? Unless you've been that hungry, you probably won't understand. I'm talking about hunger beyond pain in the belly. Hunger so intense that the whole body aches. Hunger so severe that one ceases to think of "food" as a category meaning things appropriate to eat. In 1957, when an Italian climber named Claudio Corti got stuck on the north face of the Eiger, in Switzerland, he became so famished that he ate the leather straps off his climbing boots. We weren't quite that badly off, but we were close. Neither Aeslu nor I were inclined to be choosy.

How had the stuff lasted, though? Those blocks of whatever it was—pemmican, for lack of a better term—were almost four hundred years old. All I can say is that whatever else, the Founders' food had a long shelf life. The Rixtirra had made it to be durable. No doubt it would have kept well under any conditions. Sitting up there frozen for a few centuries wasn't any threat to its freshness. What the Founders had inadvertently left behind was a little freezer-burned at the edges, as we'd say nowadays, but not bad otherwise.

So what we found there helped us revive ourselves. I can't even fathom how debilitated we must have been. It took me years to regain the weight I'd lost during the climb. Yet what we ate there by sucking on ice-cold tarry stuff somehow made a difference—in fact, more of a difference than I would have thought possible. Did the Founders' provisions have some sort of special properties? I have no idea. Perhaps we were so run-down that almost anything would have seemed a miraculous elixir. In any case, the food then allowed us enough strength to take advantage of the other supplies we found there. Supplies that replaced our own depleted stocks. Supplies that restored not just our strength, but our hope as well. Supplies that provided us a means for working our way down.

PART SEVEN

At this point Jesse gazed at me intently. "As for what happened after," he said, "I've already told you that's another story. I ask your forbearance."

"You can't really expect me not to ask."

"I'm asking precisely that."

"But surely—"

"Please don't."

I felt no recourse but to consent to his request. Then at once curiosity of another kind got the best of me. Before I could hold myself back I asked, "And the Rixtirra—?"

Jesse averted his gaze. "Ah, yes—the Rixtirra."

I waited for him to continue.

"You saw for yourself," he went on. "You met some of them in Lima."

"Just a few—three or four. But even they claimed they were no longer the Mountain-Drawn."

He nodded almost imperceptibly. "So there's your answer."

I still wasn't satisfied. This may have been my answer, but it wasn't his. "The avalanche at the Mountain's base may have killed several thousand people, but many thousands more remained elsewhere in the High Realm. Tens of thousands, even. No matter what might have happened in the years following, some of them survived. Most of them, even. Many of them had children, and their children had children. Yet no one *speaks of the Rixtirra anymore. There are no more Mountain-Drawn."*

"So it would appear."

"Then tell me this: what did them in?"

Jesse O'Keefe waited a long time before answering. He sat with both hands resting on the table before him. A trapezoid of late-afternoon sunlight lay slanting across the wood. The sun's angle at that hour, the stillness of the room, and my own sense of expectation made it possible to see not just the quiver of the light lying there but even its delicate progress over the table-top. "Nothing," *he said at last.*

"What do you mean, nothing?"

"That's just it. What the Rixtirra had based their life on was nothing. It turned out to be nothing."

"But the Mountain—"

"I don't mean the Mountain. I mean how they perceived the Mountain. What they conceived of it to mean."

"But you climbed the Mountain—"

"Look at it this way," *said Jesse O'Keefe, leaning back abruptly.* "What would the Israelites have felt if Moses had gone up Mount Sinai, found the Burning Bush all burned out, and come down to his people empty-handed?"

I gestured uncertainly.

"What would the ancient Greeks have felt if Homer had climbed Mount Olympus and found its summit uninhabited?"

I did not answer.

"It's not that the Mountain was nothing, or that the Summit was nothing. I mean simply that when Aeslu went up, she found nothing of what she expected, nothing of what she hoped for. Perhaps it would have been better if she'd never made it down again. Perhaps she should have snuggled up against Ossonnal and Lissallo—frozen to death just like them. She didn't. Why, I don't know. But she might have been happier to have finished her life like that."

"Perhaps she owed it to her people," *I ventured.*

Jesse stared at his gloved hands where they rested on the tabletop, the light slinking over them. "Perhaps she did. But something else took over. The impulse to survive? A desire to state the truth? I have no idea. But she didn't stay up there. She came down with me."

"And told the Mountain-Drawn?"

"And told the Mountain-Drawn."

I hesitated to ask my next questions but did so anyway. "Did they believe her?"

"Yes. No. Yes and no."

"Some did, some didn't?"

"Predictably."

"Did they stop fighting one another?"

"Of course not. At least not for a while."

"The legacy of Forster Beckwith," I said.

He glanced up at me then, abruptly, with a hint of a smile on his face. "If only that were so."

"But surely Forster—"

"I'm not saying Forster wasn't to blame. But he alone wasn't to blame. I was, too—though in some respects my blame was equal to Forster's. But ultimately the key issue isn't really blame at all. Or not just blame. Maybe it's change. Change in the sense that Forster himself described to me—the particles that transform water into ice. Or at least that transform one substance into another."

"So are you saying," I interrupted, "that the Rixtirra simply underwent a transformation—?"

"What I'm saying is that some of the Rixtirra survived but their culture died, though not because anyone intentionally killed it. I suppose it died of grief."

We sat there a few minutes. From outside the shed came a scattering of campus sounds: laughter, a dog's bark, a snippet of music on the radio.

Once we were down, our troubles weren't over yet. You know the old adage about killing the messenger who bears bad news. . . . Well, the Mountain-Drawn didn't kill us, but it wasn't for lack of trying.

The official response to Aeslu's tidings was subdued.

Both the Heirs and the Umbrage listened to her intently—so intently, in fact, that they ceased bickering with one another long enough to hear her out. Aeslu told her story in a series of audiences with the Masters as we worked our way out of the Inner Realm and into the more populated areas. At each step not just the Masters but their Umbrage nemeses as well listened to Aeslu as if everything in their lives depended on what she was telling them. Which of course it did. And perhaps this ultimately explains their response: stunned silence. For Aeslu's report about what we found on the Mountain left everyone in the lurch. It's as if the Mountain-Drawn caught themselves playing a game of charades they'd been taking too seriously, and at just that moment what they had all been pretending was true actually made no sense. Small wonder they were dumbstruck.

Why did they believe her? As I mentioned earlier, some of them didn't. Many did, however. It wasn't just that Aeslu herself tended to be persuasive. She also brought evidence to show her people. We had carried down Ossonnal and Lissallo's climbing tools—the elaborately engraved ice-hatchets we'd discovered with the Founders' bodies—and these tools lent further weight to what Aeslu claimed. We had brought other evidence, too: a document from the summit cave further implicating the Founders. Implicating—and in some senses damning them. Not quite what the Heirs and the Umbrage found convenient or even acceptable. Thus the authorities listened to us, thanked us, and dismissed us.

The unofficial response, though—that was something altogether different. Let me say simply that I never imagined having to run such an arduous and protracted gantlet. And in our condition, yet. Oddly, part of what saved us was our wretched physical state at the time. We were both so badly scabbed and scarred that we ended up almost unrecognizable. I suppose we looked like any of countless haggard refugees among the Mountain-Drawn. What made the most difference, however, wasn't our own state so much as that of the Mountain Land itself. Whole towns went up in flames. Umbrage attacked Heirs. Heirs battled Umbrage. The common folk fled for their lives. In the midst of all this upheaval, Aeslu and I could sneak by almost unnoticed.

And so we left the Mountain Land and went all the way to Huaraz. Even in those days that was a sizable town, the capital of Ancash Province and certainly the biggest city in that part of Peru. It had been my starting point a year earlier; I felt a strong pull to go back there. I wasn't entirely sure why. At the time I suppose I felt concerned about Aeslu's health. We'd both suffered a lot during the climb. Exhaustion and malnutrition were the least of it. Frostbite was our biggest problem—hands, feet, face. Even a single gangrenous finger can end up fatal. Whatever spell I'd fallen under during my ten months among the Rixtirra, I now felt great urgency to seek the solace of chloroform, hydrogen peroxide, and iodine. If not for my own sake, then for Aeslu's. Five or six of her toes had turned black. My hands were in bad shape, too. I wasn't about to survive the believers' wrath and let us succumb to sepsis. In short, I revealed my true colors.

She recovered. I recovered. We rested for several weeks in Huaraz. We stayed in a run-down hotel and ate in dumpy cafés. It was quite a change for both of us. What I once would have considered a backwater town I now found a metropolis rife with huge hoofed beasts and strange wheeled boxes that transported people at ludicrous speeds. Still, we adjusted. I did, anyway. I hoped somehow that Aeslu did as well.

Did she? All I could do was hope for the best. Aeslu's relative youth and her facility with languages gave her a better chance to cope than most people would have had. Out of sheer necessity, if nothing else, she would make do. Surely she understood that given what had happened in the Mountain Land, we could never go back. Even so, Aeslu spent most of her time sitting on the patio of our hotel, from which she gazed up at

the peaks of the Cordillera Blanca rising west of the
city. Something else troubled me: she fell silent. It's
not that she couldn't talk—we chatted now and then—
but she had almost nothing to say. Nothing interested
her. The articulate, curious, eloquent Wordpathguide
I loved to hear speak about so many things now ran
out of words.

Then, leaving Huaraz with intent to reach Lima, I
found out where we stood.

Even in those days there was considerable traffic
between the Andes and the coast. Crude buses traveled the road from Huaraz up the Callejón de Huaylas
to the valley's high end, then over the pass at Conaco-
cha, then downward by means of an unpaved road
to the coast. Aeslu, though terrified of motor cars,
consented to come along. I figured this was all for the
best. What were the odds of her eking out an existence
in a provincial city? And of course I couldn't remain
in the backwoods. If nothing else, I needed to make
sure all my papers were in order.

At the pass we stopped. The bus, a jitney improvised from a Ford Model A, needed a rest. The passengers did, too. Most were *mestizos* on their way to
visit relatives in Lima. We stood around stretching our
legs and eating whatever food we'd brought along.
The *puna*—the Andean high plain—rolled away from
us in every direction but one. We were literally at the
edge of the *sierra*. To the west, though, the land fell
away—great bulging ridges, the haunches of incalculably vast sleeping beasts. I'd hoped that the weather
might be clear. And it was—at our altitude. This was
late June: the dry season in the Andes but winter
along the coast. Heavy overcast lay below. We could
see it even from there. The world seemed to be
swamped in a dark gray tide.

"What is that?" Aeslu asked me, gesturing to the
west.

"The coast," I answered. "The way to Lima." I
wanted to say anything but the only words that would
make sense to her in identifying this view.

"The Lowland?" she asked.

"Well—it's where the water meets the shore."

"The Lowland."

I gave in. "I suppose you could call it the Lowland."

She gazed outward for a long time.

Not long after that another jitney, coming up the road from below, pulled alongside ours and stopped. This vehicle, like our own, was full of passengers and loaded high with their belongings—baskets, burlap bags, suitcases, even two crates of chickens strapped to the roof rack. A man got out to speak with our driver. During this interval, most of my fellow passengers returned to the jitney and boarded it. The other vehicle set off.

"Time to go," I said.

When I turned, though, Aeslu wasn't beside me.

I glanced around, couldn't find her, forced my way onto the bus, couldn't find her among the passengers waiting there, forced my way off again, and still couldn't find her anywhere around the road. The tundra landscape all around was empty except for the Huaraz-bound jitney now receding fast.

It's not that I didn't understand what had happened, nor that I didn't respond. I wasn't sure when she'd stepped away, but I knew at once she'd given me the slip. For a moment I felt the impulse to run after the other bus. I could have done so. I could have told our driver—could have bribed him on the spot, even, if that's what he required—to swing about and give chase. I could have cried out, cursing fate, the sun, the moon, or Aeslu herself.

There was no point.

She knew what she wanted.

I only wish I could have helped her find it.

PART EIGHT

"Before you go . . ." said Jesse O'Keefe, and he let the words linger in midair.

I waited.

"I believe you promised me something," he added.

"Promised?"

"The photograph."

I was stunned by my thoughtlessness. "Of course—I'm so sorry. I've intended to give it to you all along."

He could have chided me but didn't. Jesse O'Keefe simply waited while I rummaged about in my leather case, located the envelope, and removed it. I took out the photo and set it down before him on the table.

He stared at the photo for a long time without picking it up. All the while I watched his eyes: how the lids narrowed, how the pupils widened, how the gaze shifted this way and that—almost imperceptibly small motions—as he took in the image caught on the paper. I expected his eyes to well up, as they had when I'd first showed him this photo, but they didn't. Yet Jesse's whole demeanor changed, most noticeably in his posture, which sagged little by little and left him hunched over the dog-eared photograph. Then, removing the work gloves that he'd been wearing throughout each of our conversations, he reached out and picked it up.

What he did shocked me. It wasn't that he picked up the photo; it was what he picked it up with. Each of Jesse's hands was missing a couple of fingers. Two or three of the remaining fingers lacked one or more joints. His hands looked like clumps of badly pruned twigs. I'd seen other mountain climbers maimed like *that; given his story, I knew that the damage couldn't have had any source but frostbite. Despite my shock, though, I did whatever I could to avoid staring. All the more reason to watch his eyes.*

"Where did you get this?" he asked without glancing up.

"From a friend of hers."

"One of the Mountain-Drawn?"

"Formerly."

"Anyone I knew?"

"Esperanza Martinez—the one who used to be Issa-palasai of Mtoffli."

"The Keeper of Records, if I recall."

"That's the one."

"Who took it?"

"I don't know. Maybe Esperanza herself."

He seemed unable to do anything but stare at the picture. "Any idea how long ago this was taken?"

I could sense what he was driving at. "Esperanza never said. From the type of photographic paper, I'd say maybe ten years ago." I hesitated before continuing. "I'd guess it dates from right before Aeslu's death."

After a long pause he said, "I see."

We sat there in silence for what must have been just a minute or two; without either of us moving, though, the time felt uncertain and much longer. Jesse said nothing and did nothing except to gaze at what lay before him. More than once I considered leaving: I'd switch off my tape recorder, thank him for his time, push back my chair, stand, and leave as quietly as possible. Something kept me there anyway. "I want you to have it," I told him.

Only then did he look up. His response was a single nod. But he set the photograph between us—sideways, yet—as if to show me one last time what I was relinquishing.

An old woman stood in a doorway. She wore clothes typical of elderly Latin American women during the mid- or late 1960s: a cotton print dress of indeterminate shape and color, practical shoes, a dark cardigan sweater buttoned all the way up. Yet if this attire suggested a background of mixed blood, the woman's features looked altogether Indian. Her skin was dark, though lightened somehow by its web of wrinkles. Her face retained the high cheekbones and hawkish nose that Jesse had noted in his earliest journal entries. And Aeslu's hair . . . Once pure black, it had turned pure white—a soft glacier of hair descending from the summit of her head, down her shoulders, clear to the ground.

The doorway surrounding her revealed nothing beyond. The walls on either side, though, gave at least a few hints about the woman posed there. To the right, painted on the whitewash, were the words

BODE
"El Cumb

truncated by the photograph's right-hand edge.

"What's this?" asked Jesse, pointing to the words.

"I assume it says bodega. Esperanza Martinez told me that for some years Aeslu ran a little store."

Jesse glanced up at me. "A store?"

"This was after she retired. For a long time before that she taught school. Elementary school."

"I don't suppose Esperanza told you what subjects."

"Languages."

This word prompted a smile. "Of course. It would have been languages."

"Spanish, mostly to Indian children just arrived from the sierra, but some English, too."

"What, no Rixtir dialects?" asked Jesse with another smile, broader now. "No T'taspa? No Vmatta? No Qallitti?"

"The Peruvian government wouldn't have been too supportive if she'd tried."

By then Jesse had started examining the photo again. "This, though," he said, nudging the letters beneath BODE.

"It's probably what it appears to be," I answered. "El Cumbre."

"The Summit."

I waited for him to go on. Jesse continued gazing at the picture, but what he saw lay somewhere else altogether.

I glanced at my watch. Seven-twenty. Great shafts of summer light came in through the shed's window and door, angled across the room, and left trapezoids of glare on the wall opposite. "I should go," I told him, scooting my chair back. "I've taken up far too much of your time."

"No—not yet."

I just sat there.

"Tell me—" Jesse faltered before finishing.

After giving him a chance to continue—a chance he ignored—I said, "I'll be glad to tell you whatever I can."

"Did she marry?"

"Esperanza Martinez said no."

"And she never had any children?"

"No children."

"I see."

"And she died some years ago?"

"Nineteen-sixty-six or sixty-seven. Esperanza couldn't remember which. She wasn't sure about the cause, either. What she said made it sound like some kind of intestinal parasite. Amoebic dysentery, that sort of thing."

I expected him to say "I see" yet again, but he didn't.

He stood. I did, too. He kept the photograph of Aeslu in his maimed left hand. Now and then he glanced at it, glanced almost compulsively, as if worried that the image caught there might somehow fade unless he kept a close eye on it. We remained there by the table for longer than I found comfortable.

Unsure what else to do, I thanked him and made my way to the open doorway.

"I suppose you'll publish all this," he said just then.

"I have your permission?"

He gestured with one hand to show me out. "Lack of my permission has never stopped you in the past."

And so I left his garden shed, left the campus, left Boulder, and left Colorado. Since then I'd spent a long time transcribing the tapes and preparing them for the purpose that Jesse O'Keefe both resented and, I think, anticipated. He made no further effort to amplify or modify what he told me during those summer days in 1975.

With one exception.

Some months later, I received a small package in the mail. In it I found a handwritten note and the photocopy of a brief document.

Boulder, Colorado
16 October 1975
Dear Mr. Myers,

If you intend to publish our interview (as I assume you do) then I suppose you should be privy to the enclosed document—one I mentioned having discovered among the Founders' possessions in the cave. I would have offered this to you last summer but hesitated for reasons that I imagine you will surmise without assistance. Nevertheless, I now feel obliged to provide all the pieces of the puzzle you seem intent on assembling. Do with these pages what you will.

One last consideration. You will ask, of course—as well you might—why the original has been in my possession rather than in some other party's. In Aeslu's, for instance. In the Masters'. In someone else's among the Rixtirra.

All I can say is that I tried turning this document over to its proper owners. I offered it to the Mountain-Drawn long ago. Once they understood its implications, however, they refused to have anything to do with it.

Here again, draw your own conclusions.

Sincerely yours,
J. O.

PART NINE

With Jesse's note there was a second document, an almost indecipherable scrawl I recognized as archaic Spanish but required several days' work to translate.

I am Ossonnal, once called Diego Alvarado Osorio y Nalgún, born of a Castilian father and a [word uncertain] mother, in the city of Rimac [Lima], in the year my father would have called anno Domini 1535. My chosen wife, Lissallo, and I were the first to call ourselves the Mountain-Drawn.

In the time required by the Moon to swell and fade twenty-seven times, we set off to find the [word uncertain] mountain of our domain; sought to climb it; attained its Summit with a band of our people; founded the city we intended as our refuge; and settled in for the trials awaiting us.

The trials have not been those we expected. The dangers have not been those we feared. Storms, cold, and invading [word uncertain] have threatened us far less than what we ourselves did. For in fact the people, formerly our equals, began to worship us; tried to gain favor with us; argued endlessly, claiming this or that point to their own advantage; grew dissatisfied; squabbled with one another; and risked the common good. We tried to stop the spreading damage but without success. The people, though claiming to serve us, soon paid us no mind.

We are not gods, merely a man and a woman. We are not immortals who would leap from peak to peak, merely two humans who would climb mountains in pursuit of what the Climb can teach us. We are not saviors who would rescue our people for eternity, merely the father and mother of our race, thus intent like any other parents on protecting our children for the brief span of our lives.

They would not listen. The disagreements grew, and what we saw all around us revealed our fate.

We [word uncertain] the malcontents.

The people paid us no mind.

We threatened to expel them.

The people paid us no mind.

We prepared to abandon our refuge.

Still the people paid us no mind.

Thus, not five dawns past, we left the last city we have founded and tried to make our way down the Mountain. We expected that this, if nothing else, would make the people come to their senses.

Some followed; some did not.

Then a storm struck, hammered at us, [word uncertain] us. Many perished. Now we two, Ossonnal and Lissallo, founders of the Mountain Land, have ended up alone once more. We have taken refuge in a cave in hopes of waiting out the storm. The storm has not eased. For long we have huddled here, together, not sure what to do.

The cold worsens. We are weak. Our limbs grow numb. We can scarcely write. We have only one another to give us warmth.

You who find these words: do not pity us.

We were not mistaken to seek the Mountain, nor to find it, nor to climb it—only to think we could remain forever at the Summit.